MW00564607

THE GAP

FORT INDIANTOWN

The Gunner's Dream

Words and Music by Roger Waters
Copyright © 1983 Roger Waters Music Overseas Ltd
All Rights Administered by BMG Rights Management (US) LLC
All Rights Reserved. Used by Permission.
Reprinted by Permission of Hal Leonard LLC

First Edition: 2019
THE GAP
JOHN WITHEROW

Published by:
PENTIAN
info@pentian.com

Plaza Magdalena, 9, 3rd floor
Seville 41001
Spain

Printed in Spain
ISBN: 9788417102265
ISBN e-book: 9781524301385

Layout, design and production of this edition:
© 2019 Pentian

All rights reserved. No part of this publication may be reproduced, distributed, or transmitted in any form or by any means, including photocopying, recording, or other electronic or mechanical methods, without the prior written permission of the Publisher.

THE GAP

FORT INDIANTOWN

JOHN WITHEROW

PENTIAN

Backers who have made the edition of this book possible through Pentian.com

Thank you for participating in the Publishing Revolution

Alayna Witherow
Brian Ashe
Cait McAllister
Cari Witherow
Cathy Smyth
Christina Suran
Dean Phillips
Dustin Perrin
Ella McAllister
Frederick Faett
Frederick Ulrich
Geoff Moulton
Jairo Marino
Jeffrey Helm
John Hare
Leonard Gordon
Michael Fisher
Michael Bramnick
Nicole Gruber
Peter Stein
Robert Bein
Sandra C Boylan
Seth Witherow
Wendi Witherow
Wendy Vlahos
William Anderson

The greatest dangers to liberty lurk in insidious encroachment by men of zeal, well meaning, but without understanding.

Justice Louis Brandeis
Dissent, Olmstead v. U.S.

A place to stay
Enough to eat
Somewhere old heroes shuffle safely down the street
Where you can speak out loud
About your doubts and fears
And what's more no-one ever disappears
You never hear their standard issue kicking in your door
You can relax on both sides of the tracks
And maniacs don't blow holes in bandsmen by remote control
And everyone has recourse to the law
And no one kills the children anymore
And no one kills the children anymore

Roger Waters, The Gunner's Dream
from *Pink Floyd, The Final Cut*

Prologue

On March 31, 1972, Kim-ly died in a nameless sub-hamlet of Ba Long, South Vietnam.

She was small for her age of three. She had long black hair and curious brown eyes, and her prominent cheekbones were pink and rounded. In the rising heat of the mid-morning sun, she rolled naked on a stream's bank abutting the little village, while dipping her head in the passing water, mimicking the way her mother doused soiled clothes. With each submergence, the thicket of huts encircling her plunged into the earth, and the energy released in that wonderful violence transported her deep into a green ocean, aloft into the blue heavens, and back again. She was far from the grasp of strange bad things that she couldn't comprehend.

Underwater a cool quiet blanketed her ears, and she held her breath for a long time, so as not to surrender the moment. The forced silence lent a mystical quality to the day, making it almost possible to forget the heat. The quiet was a pure thing, a magical thing.

In a moment her lungs cried for fresh air. She lifted her head and breathed, and the water slipped from her face in streams and rivulets, sealing the corridor to her dream world. After another instant of blinking and transition, she fully emerged into the world she could touch, and in that world's imperfect sky, she heard a disquieting rumble gathering strength—a harbinger of something terrible to come.

The noise swelled into an explosive hammering layered over rhythmic throbbing. A dark blotch sprouted from the sun, growing so quickly it threatened to swallow the day, and the air boiled frantically as if fleeing from the fearful, descending presence. As it approached, the spot took the shape and color of a green sphere; through rising panic she saw the fast-moving ball as a kind of airborne platform on which men knelt cradling sticks that spit fire in staccato bursts.

Thick-boughed trees shielded the village from above, but the flying balls had come before, and with their arrival the sky had rained horrible stinging drops that melted leaves and wilted limbs. This time the drops rode on thunder, tearing through the naked branches and hurtling into the earth, punching holes in the ground and gnashing at huts, and people were falling, and her mother was lunging for her, telling her to hurry but to stay calm and everything would be all right.

Suddenly the water shrouded her ears and gave her quiet again.

She heard nothing, but she could still see the ball, turning on its axis, shifting shape and becoming oblong. It seemed as if it saw her too and that the sight of her gave it pause, the pure but broken skin of an innocent floating in bright water upon a burgeoning red pad. The ball slowed and circled, wobbling as if dazed by the consequence of its own aggression and shocked by some sudden realization of a dreadful mistake.

As the ball faltered, another crested the trees, cutting a linear swath through the air, powerfully, confidently, and darkly. Misshapen implements jutted from every crease of its green skin, leveled to its murderous sibling as if poised to spear it from the sky. This *one loosened its own needles of fire sent straight into the other's path, turning it away sharply.*

The second ball gave no chase, but it arced abruptly, as if its heart stuttered or perhaps broke. From powerful flight, it transitioned smoothly to a descending semicircular glide, its shadow slipping across the water and passing over the little girl, while for an instant, absorbing her. In her last moments, she felt the twisting currents of air tugging at her limbs as if to lift her to the blue sky again, and with a strange serenity, Kim-ly let her head dip beneath the water's surface, just as she had before, to quietly reenter the gentler world of her dreams.

•━•━━━•━••━•━━━•━•

After turning the attacker away, the defending helicopter gunship hovered briefly and then lit on the ground in a halo of red dust, and a young Vietnamese man dropped from the craft once earthbound. He went to the girl's dead mother. The woman's thin arm was extending into the water, and her frozen eyes were still begging her small one to return. With emerging grief, he saw the others in the village, the dead, the wounded, and the rest clambering to one another and to the fallen in shock.

The pilot had no breath to shout. He only managed to shake his fist at the echo trailing the retreating Huey helicopter that, as quickly as it had arrived to devastate the village, disappeared over the treetops. The pilot struggled against his own emotions to remain standing, finally succumbing, crumbling. He pulled the stricken woman's limp form into his arms, and there, at the edge of the little nameless village at the outskirts of Ba Long, he rocked on his knees, and he wept.

PART I
WEEKEND DRILL

Chapter one

To fly.

A childhood fantasy fulfilled, a lifelong goal accomplished.

June 20, 1990: Anxious and full of vigor, Second Lieutenant Mark Ashford stepped onto the macadam flight deck at Muir Army Airfield in Fort Indiantown Gap, Pennsylvania, reporting for his first assignment as a helicopter pilot and platoon leader in the Pennsylvania Army National Guard. The lean twenty-two-year-old swept his gaze over dozens of perfectly aligned helicopters arrayed on the flat black surface before him as if on the veneer of a staid pond, all seeming to float at virtual attention, primed to respond to his guiding touch at their controls.

Ashford blinked his washed-out blue eyes and ran his fingers through his freshly cut, sandy hair. His vision fixed upon a Blackhawk helicopter, and his lips curled into a savoring smile. The Sikorsky Model UH-60 Blackhawk was a long, sleek, low-slung helicopter with a cabin area that resembled the interior of a small bus. It had twin, cigar-shaped engines positioned over the cargo doors, four blades perched sixteen feet above the ground, and three wheels set subtly beneath its eleven thousand-pound girth. The outstretched tail boom bore black painted letters proclaiming the machine's allegiance to the United States Army; beneath the tail rotor, a horizontal stabilizer protruded, like the tail fin of a dolphin.

In the helicopter's vicinity, Ashford had the humbling sensation of being dangerously close to a mammoth beast at rest. Though its energy was only potential, in stasis, he sensed its great power nevertheless. Ashford knew every inch of the Blackhawk helicopter, having spent the last several months learning to fly them at the Army's rotary wing flight school at Fort Rucker, Alabama. He understood the aircraft's aerodynamics, the mechanics that made it tick, its capabilities and limitations. He knew how to bring its powerful engines to life, to make them hum and then commence their high-pitched, penetrating moan, until the blades began to spin and slip across the windscreen in a frenzied blur. Ashford appreciated the delicate feel of the controls, and he hungered to take them once again, like the reins of a stallion, to guide a Blackhawk into flight.

Ashford counted only three Blackhawks on the flight deck. Several two-man observation helicopters and shark-shaped Cobra gunships spotted the perimeter, but the main tarmac was populated mostly by Huey helicopters, the predecessors to the Blackhawks. The Bell UH-1H Hueys were smaller than the Blackhawks and modest by comparison. They were two-bladed crafts, rounded and snub-nosed in appearance, in the manner of Chevrolets from long-gone model years. Each had a single engine housed in an oblong cowling behind the rotor assembly. The design and technology originated in the 1950s, and there had been no significant upgrades to the airframe since that era.

Hueys had been the Army's workhorses in Vietnam, and Ashford respected them as reliable and time-tested machines, powerful in their simplicity but still used and useful. He had piloted them as trainer aircraft in flight school and had enjoyed the experience. But they were of another generation, not his, and he had lost interest in them during his Blackhawk training. Ashford thought that he was finished with the Huey.

The young lieutenant turned to face an enormous ribbed-metal structure, an aircraft hangar, appearing to frame the base of a seventy-foot control tower rising out of the edifice like a castle spire. Adjacent to the hangar stood a brick administration building that housed the pilot facilities. The entire complex was nestled against a line of the Appalachian Mountains, a tree-covered ridge stretching endlessly into the southwest. From the foot of the highlands, the valley spilled southward into the horizon and was cluttered with whitewashed barracks, commissaries, mess halls, supply rooms, and other structures characteristic of an aged military reservation. The uplands were notched with clefts, the closest of which was called Indiantown Gap to acknowledge a settlement of peaceful Native Americans whose legacy was the land they had minded for a century while barely leaving a mark.

Inside the hangar's colossal bay doors, dozens of other helicopters were in various stages of disassembly, with open cowlings, engines hoisted on hydraulic lifts, and scattered rotor blades lined up against the wall like giant canoe paddles on a boat launch. The sprawling, glossy cement floor was marked in trails with painted lines. Yellow and orange lifts and trucks glided along these linear routes like trains on a track. A generator blared, and rough-looking men poked about the machines with the sort of measured care administered by seasoned zookeepers tending a wild herd.

As he entered the hangar, Ashford yielded to permit a line truck to pass from the tarmac into the building. The tractor-like contraption was equipped with a tow bar used to ferry helicopters. Ashford nodded at the operator and then scanned the place for pilots; for his initial appearance, he wished to make an impression—one of assurance and of competence. He was distracted by a great shadow and lifted his eyes to view the light-green under-belly of a CH-54 Skycrane. Shaped like a monstrous dragonfly, the five-bladed helicopter dominated the west entrance bay; the tail rotor alone was taller than Ashford's own six-foot frame.

A voice drifted above the generator's drone. "Who's the new guy?"

Ashford lowered his chin and turned to face a plump warrant officer with a square head and low hairline. The man's bulging, flaccid stomach stretched the vertical seam of his one-piece flight suit, exposing the zipper running from his neckline to his crotch. Another warrant stood beside him, hooded in the shadow of the giant sky craft. Both men seemed to be in their late forties to early fifties, and both wore patches signifying service in the Vietnam War.

"He's not a new guy; he's a lieutenant," the thinner warrant replied. He wore an outdated two-piece flight suit so faded that it seemed to have no color of its own—the material appeared to only reflect the dull green hue of the surrounding helicopters. Peeking from between the parted zipper at his neckline was a triangle of white, a considerable departure from the regulation brown T-shirt. The warrant officer's hair was tousled and in des-perate need of a trim, and his mustache overgrew the corners of his mouth in a purposefully unkempt fashion. Ashford recog-nized these classic badges of a poor military attitude.

The warrant officers extended no hands and offered no intro-ductions—as a substitute, Ashford silently read their names from black leather tags velcroed to their suits. The fat man's name was Gene Winston; the other was Nick Trent. They seemed to be sizing Ashford up, like old bulls engaging a youthful rival.

"Mmm," Winston said, intoning the words that followed with an exaggerated lisp. "He sure is cute." Winston batted his eyes and cupped his generous chin in his fingers. "What say we join the mile high club handsome?"

Ashford's eyebrows slipped high above their natural resting place, wrinkling his forehead and widening his eyes. Members of the "mile high club," he knew, were marked by the usually fictional distinction of having had consummated some form of sexual act in an airborne helicopter. Ashford suddenly felt tiny beneath the struts of the Skycrane. He felt his face flush.

"And he's shy too," added Winston. "Just how I like 'em."

Ashford stammered out some words of greeting, fumbling to gain sync with the warrant's banter. Winston, Ashford thought, seemed abrasive but harmless enough. Trent, however, even in this brief encounter, appeared to be an imposing force. The deep lines in his face sketched an absolute confidence, but the dark eyes that peered from that stoical platform, although motionless, seemed utterly prepossessed.

After a moment, Trent spoke while taking in Ashford's own name tag with an air of aloofness. "We saw you eyeing up the Blackhawks."

"Great machine," Ashford said.

"Yeah," said Winston, "ten thousand moving parts all made by the lowest bidder."

Ashford chuckled reservedly. "Still, I like the way they move."

"Bet you say that to all the boys."

Ashford thought Winston's feigned promiscuity to be incongruous; something about his pear-shaped physique appeared distinctly asexual.

As Winston engaged Ashford in conversation, Trent locked Ashford in a gaze that seemed truer than any rifle sight. "I suppose you can fly them," he said.

Ashford cocked his head and offered a modest half-smile in response. "The Blackhawks?" he asked, his voice measured with a tone of respect for both Trent and the aircraft.

Trent answered with an impatience that bordered on bitterness. "Helicopters, helicopters. Can you pilot a helicopter, Lieutenant Ashford?"

Ashford paused, once again caught off guard. He wished to remain open and friendly, but he felt cornered. By rank, he was Trent's superior, but at the moment, he felt desperately inferior.

"There's a new girl in the unit who can fly," said Winston. "W-Zero-One Morrow, and she's gorgeous to boot."

Trent ignored his effusive companion. "Can you fly, Lieutenant?" he repeated, as if he had not been heard.

"Well it'd be an absolute first for a lieutenant," Winston chided.

Trent appeared pleased with Winston's witticism, but his eyes glowed dully, almost maliciously, as if savoring some unwholesome secret.

The growling noise of a diesel engine filled Ashford's ears, suddenly overpowering the din of the generator. Ashford's eyes deflected to the pavement, and he felt his face drain, paling with the realization that his feet rested upon a painted traffic line.

"Look out, kid!" a startled voice cried from Ashford's rear.

Ashford jerked his chin over his shoulder. An approaching yellow blur snagged in his peripheral vision. He instinctively lunged sideways. A line truck rolled along the painted path, directly over the location he had just cleared. A Huey, lumbering in tow behind the truck, brushed against Ashford's retreating backside, flicking him off balance. His arms and legs flailed.

As Ashford stumbled, the truck angled through the entrance bay, dragging the impotent helicopter outside onto the flight deck. The operator shrugged his shoulders, the apologetic gesture suggesting he hadn't seen Ashford until the last moment, as he had been watching his cargo. Winston would not have seen either, since his vantage point was from ninety degrees. But the oncoming vehicle had been directly in Trent's line of sight, and he must have seen it coming. He could not have missed it, yet he had said nothing.

The eyes of Trent and Winston met, and then the warrant officers turned to depart without expression of concern or offer of assistance. Ashford stared at their backs, straining to compose himself. His face was crunched in an expression of disbelief. He struggled to find his voice. When he did, he let it ring out with as much certitude as he could muster.

"I can fly," Ashford called after the warrants.

Trent looked over his shoulder. "Huh?"

Ashford soberly met his gaze. "Helicopters, helicopters," he mimicked, unable to contain the sarcasm spilling into his voice. "I can fly a helicopter."

Trent hesitated for a long second, holding an imprecise stare, as if gauging the height of a mountain in a distance. Then he waved his hand in a dismissive gesture while leaning his head and eyes to follow the Huey in tow.

"Well that one sure got the better of you," he said. Then he was gone.

———————

Ashford stood on the hangar floor for a long time, feeling dwarfed in the wide space. He had a good deal of experience with warrant officers from flight school—most of his instructors were warrants. They were an intermediate brand of soldier, superior in rank to the enlisted but outranked by commissioned officers, even fledgling ones such as he was. Warrants were technicians, trained to perform specific and often sophisticated tasks—in the case of aviation warrants, to pilot aircraft. Most were highly proficient pilots and prided themselves as such. Some were fiercely independent-minded, often manifesting a disregard of military conventions. Those warrants, Ashford knew, frequently directed their distastes in subtle ways toward younger, inexperienced commissioned officers.

In the final phase of his flight training, Ashford drew Warrant Officer Ike Donavon as his instructor. He was a man younger than Ashford's twenty-two years, yet in his own mind and compared to Ashford, he was a seasoned veteran. Donavon had logged fifteen hundred hours in the helicopter, which true veterans joked was just enough experience to make a pilot dangerous. But his comparative mastery was undeniable to Ashford, who himself had manifested several obvious and persistent weaknesses, principally in night flight and in instrument flight. Time and time again, Donavon guided Ashford through maneuvers by working his own set of the dual flight controls, a teaching tactic that few of the veteran instructor pilots employed unless the aircraft was in physical danger. The drawback, understood by other instructors, was that students were slow to gain their own feel for the helicopter.

Donavon seemed to enjoy Ashford's frustration when the young warrant handled the controls to guide him. "Not like that, LT," the Texan would say with a lingering inflection that irritated as much by delivery as by content. "Oh, now you're doing it wrong again, LT. Feel my lead, follow me through with the cyclic."

Others among Donavon's students requested transfers to different instructors, a practice that was sparsely employed because of its potential negative reflection on the student. Through his determination, however, Ashford had largely overcome his weaknesses and graduated near the top of his class. In the end, he overcame Donavon as well. The once insufferable warrant officer seemed to grow proud of his top student, even attending Ashford's graduation ceremony—a rare undertaking for a warrant officer instructor pilot and a first for Donavon. After the proceedings, they met at a local tavern. "I think you'll actually make it, Mark," Donavon had said in a diminutive toast, for once dropping his interminable shorthand for Ashford's rank. Ashford, the older of the two, had taken this as a high compliment.

Ashford's experiences with Donavon, he thought, were nothing compared to his brief encounter with Nick Trent. For one thing, Donavon was a kid, highly skilled, but still just a kid. Trent was perhaps fifty and a war veteran. Several of Ashford's instructor pilots had been Vietnam vets. His teacher in the primary phase of his training had flown in the Battle of Ap Bac in 1964, the first engagement in which American advisors had participated. His tactics instructor was a wizened, stone-deaf vet who had extracted troops from the Ia Drang Valley during one of the most intense battles of the war. His instructors were solemn men, tried and tested and proven, and Ashford held each one in awe. Their life experiences made them men of remarkable confidence, of deep knowledge, and of strange power.

But there was something different about Trent, a presence about him, an aura of sorts, an energy that seemed negative, perhaps menacing, even dangerous. Donavon and other instructors had antagonized the young lieutenant, but their actions were more in the nature of unwarranted and condescending pampering; Ashford had always felt physically secure in their presence, reassured by it more precisely. Trent, on the other hand, had stood directly in front of him and watched, just watched, as he was nearly flattened.

Ashford couldn't relieve his mind of the memory of Trent's unwavering gaze before, during, and after the near miss. The warrant officer's cold eyes had never moved, and he hadn't lifted a finger.

Chapter two

Without a word, Trent and Winston crossed through double doors into the administration building. They traded nods with another man in the corridor, and when they were alone again, Winston clapped a flabby hand on Trent's elbow, his voice assuming an uncharacteristic earnestness. "Uh, Nick, that was pretty close, huh?"

"What?"

"With the lieutenant back there."

"Oh. Yeah."

"I mean, we almost had to peel the kid up off the deck."

"Pretty near."

"You were getting ready to say something, weren't you? You know, sound the alarm, ehm, hoist up the red flag. You know what I mean, don't you?"

"Sure, Gene," Trent said, although his voice resonated with uncertainty.

"That's what I thought. Hey, sure was close though." Winston patted Trent on the shoulder blade and released a disquieted laugh.

Trent parted with Winston in the hallway and turned into the crew lounge, a bland expanse noticeable only for its sameness with the rest of the place. He nodded at a pair of enlisted men seated at a table and dropped thirty cents into an outdated vending machine to retrieve a steaming hot cup of coffee. He sat alone at a small corner table and watched the black liquid quivering in the paper cup in his hand. He steadied a cigarette in his fingertips and, after two unsuccessful attempts, lit a match.

Pale fluorescent light filtered through the wooden blades of a ceiling fan rotating slowly above, casting translucent shadows about the room that were barely noticeable yet which captured the edges of Trent's attention. He blinked his eyes, trying vainly to blot out the disturbance. He blew on the coffee and was discomfited by the unsteadiness of his breath. Even Trent had been surprised by the inertia that had claimed him a few moments earlier and by how far he had allowed things to go before intervening, that is, if he could still have done anything at all. It had seemed so unreal, so desperately funny, the joke being played on the butter-bar lieutenant, standing there with his day-old haircut and his wrinkled flight suit straight out of the plastic bag, casting about for some common ground where there was none ever to be found, attempting to plant the seeds of friendship in a barren field, trying so hard at everything, just as the line truck bore down on him from behind.

Actually, his own timing had been perfect, Trent assured himself. No one had been hurt, and the lieutenant had learned a valuable lesson—the lesson of distance. But as Trent reflected, he couldn't shake the haunting sensation that his inaction was born of impotence and not intention, that he had nearly caused serious injury to the young and earnest man, that something in his very nature had prevented him from acting, and that the same something might foreclose him from ever again making another sane or decent contribution to the world around him.

The fan, Trent thought. The cigarettes, the coffee, the guilt. The fan. It was all familiar, circular. Trent lifted his eyes to the swirling blades, watching the cigarette smoke mingle with the steam from his coffee and disburse in the light wind buffeting his face. With the breeze and the heat and the smells, it all came back as if in a dream, the place where it all had started, the beginning of his undoing. But it was not the wooden fan above him that he saw, and it wasn't that fan which he cursed.

Under dark canvas, in the dank interior of an Army GP Medium tent, the little circular fan rested on a wooden crate beside Trent's bunk. The atmosphere was thick with stale cigarette smoke. It was April, 1972, Trent recalled, some twenty years earlier and half a world away, in a place called Vigilance Base Camp, which was situated just south of Quảng Trị, the northernmost province of South Vietnam.

Trent sat on his bunk, sipping coffee and toying with the toggle switch on the fan. Its stubbly steel blades began a slow turn. As they gained momentum, the hollow base began to vibrate and then wobble, until the fan, as if with a mind of its own, clattered across the tabletop as if out for a stroll.

Trent switched off the current and lifted the circular steel cage from the housing. He picked up a steel file and rubbed it against the exposed blade tips, shaving away tiny metal fragments a millimeter at a time. Then he restored the power. The fan ticked arhythmically, and each successive turn of the blades made matters worse, until the unsteady amble resumed again and again. For the past several weeks, every day and every night, Trent tinkered with the fan. He was frustrated with it, absorbed with it. While other men wrote letters to their girlfriends, swapped stories, played cards, and slept, Trent carved away at those blades like some artist on a single-minded mission, steadfastly determined to restore the fan to a semblance of its original form. The wobbling blades slashed into his nerves at first and then yielded a dull sensation of omnipresent soreness. This tiny appliance presented an obstacle to him as formidable as the most difficult landing zones in Vietnam.

Trent sighed and put the fan aside, trying to forget it, failing. He stooped by his cot, rubbing his eyes. He was an energetic twenty-three-year-old who in his native Pennsylvania had moved with the agility and grace of a tennis player. But his liveliness had been drained by the War, and his shoulders sagged under its weight, the accumulated burden of three combat tours and a thousand combat air assault missions.

Trent rubbed his cheeks and then pulled his clipboard from his flight bag to review the afternoon's mission, which was the same as the one before it and the ones on the previous day and the day before that. The pilots of the 162nd Aviation Company, a venerated combat helicopter lift unit, were finishing their part in a hasty extraction of four hundred troops from Vigilance Base Camp. They were Raven flight, a flight of three Hueys. Two South Vietnamese Air Force pilots, VNAFs, were assigned to support them in snub-nosed Charlie Model Huey helicopter gunships that the pilots called Gunnies. The VNAFs were Watch flight—Watch One and Watch Two. Same call signs, but the radio frequencies would be different; he would have to pick those up at the briefing.

Trent unfolded his tactical map. Relief seemed to leap from the page in three dimensions, in the way musical notes dance in brilliant hues before the eyes of an orchestra conductor. Trent saw pointed blue mountain peaks, green rolling hills, and expansive terraced paddies. He didn't need the map to summon the vision, since it was burned into the pathways of his subconscious. But the map was part of his routine. And routine was important. Routine was sanity.

Start with Red Route, Vigilance to Vũng Tàu. Refuel at Landing Zone Wellspring, the halfway point. Trent's fingers slid gently along the three hundred-mile trek toward Vũng Tàu, a peninsular seaport jutting from the Mekong Delta into the South China Sea. His hand drifted in varying angles and planes, following the rough contour of the land. Drop the troops at Vũng Tàu. Return via Blue Route...

Trent's hand froze. No. Do not return. There was to be no return. Land at Vũng Tàu. Get on a plane. Don't look back. Can't look back.

Trent stood abruptly. He emerged from his tent and lifted his eyes to the surrounding landscape to forestall an inevitable interior monologue about returning home. Jungle-covered foothills surrounded Vigilance Base Camp, and behind them the blue peaks of the Annamite Mountain Range rose strikingly in the distance. The relief acted as a cauldron for the moist atmosphere that hung over the base camp. Hot, heavy air pressed down upon shirtless men hurrying about the partially disassembled camp. Some were swinging hammers to loosen wooden stakes, and others were rigging equipment into cargo nets and truck trailers. Like bloated gargoyles peering over the encampment, dull green Huey helicopters crouched on the western fringe.

From across the airstrip, a young Vietnamese man approached. He held his body erect and moved with an efficiency that seemed a quiet compensation for the oppressive heat. His thick black bangs flopped over his forehead, and his flight suit hung loosely from his angular frame. His name was Le Song; he was nineteen years old and the pilot of Watch One, the lead gunship. He and his wingman had orders to assist in the evacuation of United States soldiers from Vigilance due to the growing shortage of American pilots in Vietnam. The VNAF gunships protected the troop-carrying Huey helicopters by laying down suppressive fire when needed to engage attacking enemy soldiers. Trent knew Song to be a skilled and capable pilot, mirroring his own abilities. On the missions they had flown together, Song had demonstrated bravery and good judgment, commodities that seemed scarce among the general ranks of the VNAF. Over the course of time, Trent had developed an abiding respect for the young man.

Song's usual manner was one of confidence and ease, but he approached with an unfamiliar reticence in his gait. He stood a few yards from Trent and dipped his head in a modest bow.

"Please, may I ask a question?" Song's English was slow but clear, and his voice resonated with same quiet dignity as his deportment.

Trent closed the distance between them with an easy step. "Sure, Song, ask away."

Le Song's breath came more quickly than usual, and his chest moved in shallow expansions. "It is about Ba Long," he said slowly, as if testing the waters.

Trent straightened, squinting with interest. With no apparent justification, a sub-hamlet of Ba Long had suffered a brutal air attack three days earlier. Although a handful of senior officers had been assigned to investigate the killings, the investigators seemed preoccupied with other matters: the evacuation of Vigilance Base Camp, the conduct of their extra duties, and the poker game in the officers' mess. There was so much else going on in the War, and they seemed to have little time for an embarrassingly awkward situation, with little-known circumstances, regarding a tiny village nestled in the jungle far to the north, just to the far side of obscurity. On his own, Trent had led a handful of the warrant officers to the village the day after the massacre to take in the facts and draw their own conclusions.

"Do you know what happened at Ba Long?" Song asked. His voice ordinarily contained an excited, rhythmic quality, like the wings of a hummingbird, but of late, Trent had noticed, it engendered a subdued timbre.

"I looked the place over," Trent said. "The attack was definitely aerial, most likely a Huey; it looks like it was a single ship. She came out of the free-fire zone from north to south. I'm guessing the pilot gave his gunners the go-ahead right over the village, probably just as he saw warm bodies through the trees. Then he landed on the bank. I counted eleven dead: ten in the village and a little girl washed up on the bank a quarter mile downstream."

Song closed his eyes against these facts and nodded slowly. "Yes, only the aggressor did not land."

"Well, there were fresh skid marks in the dirt on the stream's bank."

"Not the aggressor's."

Trent stepped closer and lowered his voice. "There were two birds?"

Song nodded again, this time with his brown eyes open. "The second was a witness."

Trent considered this. The explanation made sense—the strafing marks suggested that all of the bullets had been fired from the air. And the imprint from the helicopter skids indicated that the chopper had circled to the south and landed with the tail rotor pointed at the sub-hamlet, not an optimal position to defend against angry villagers whose brothers and wives and daughters and sons you've just murdered. "Are you this witness?" Trent asked, selecting a lower key.

Song seemed to prefer a narrative over directness in his response. "I am patrolling the DMZ. I leave my flight for a bad vibration. On the way back to the base camp, I see a Huey a klick north of Ba Long. It gives me comfort to follow with distance, in case I go down. But the pilot seems lost. I prepare to signal, to let them know I am there, when—"

"When the Huey opened up," Trent said.

Song's eyes dropped to the soil. He lifted a stick from the ground and lofted it into the air like a paper airplane, though possessing no aerodynamic quality, it dropped lifelessly to the ground. "I could not believe," he said, "and when I realized, I almost brought them out of the sky. I came at them, I had my finger on the guns but only shot across the nose. Then I circled and landed beside the water."

The air around Trent seemed charged. "You get the Huey's tail number?" Trent asked, at once sensing he was asking too much, too fast. Still, he could not restrain himself from probing again. "Who was it?"

Song's silence contained a refusal that seemed less obstinate than reluctant. When he spoke again, he did not lift his head. "My wingman, Duong, says our country has failed us. He says you are leaving; all Americans will leave in the end. He says it is the beginning of our own end. I told him to speak of such things is unwise. But he tells me I am blind. And I know the Northerners; they are just over that ridge." Song tipped his head at a not-so-distant mountain.

"They're close all right. And we're definitely pulling out. But what does your friend think that has to do with Ba Long?"

"He wants to use my knowledge to our advantage. He says it is a valuable thing, what I know. Duong says this information is like gold, and for holding it to myself, he could arrange our passage to America."

An odd excitement was growing within Trent, and he strained to hold his features level. "Sounds like you're playing with fire. What do you think?"

Song's responsive nod was laced with understanding. "I think I am afraid," he said.

Trent gazed at Song, considering his emaciated appearance, his youth, and his latent and misguided hopefulness. Then his eyes strayed to the helicopter gunship Song flew. Trent silently examined the battered war machine: the Gatling gun comprised of a mass of corpse-gray metal tubes arranged in the shape of a perfect cylinder; the seventeen-pod rocket launcher suspended horizontally alongside the fuselage like a coffin over an open grave; and the skull-shaped grenade launcher poised on the helicopter's nose for optimal performance of its own grisly function. Even Dante couldn't envision a more loathsome hell for a boy of Song's mold, Trent thought, than to christen him master of a machine capable of such devastation.

From their conversations, Trent had learned of Song's background. He had been raised in Dak Ranh, a small hamlet in the north-central Mekong region on the flight route between Vigilance Base Camp and Vũng Tàu. Over the past two decades, the Saigon government had repeatedly provoked the villagers into a tense alliance with the Viet Cong and their allies, the North Vietnamese. Saigon, empowered by American aid and equipment, wielded its might with abandon, employing random bombing, artillery shelling, and napalm attacks in its own hinterlands in a dubious effort to drive away its enemies.

In the early summer of 1962, South Vietnamese soldiers had torn the villagers of Dak Ranh from their homes and ancestral grounds and herded them through fifty-seven miles of jungle into a restricted area near Biên Hòa as part of Prime Minister Diem's Strategic Hamlet Program. Diem, in consultation with advisors from the United States government, believed that his army could better protect the peasants from the political influence of the Viet Cong by relocating them into centralized, guarded villages. The misguided initiative was abandoned several years later but not before it had dispirited and embittered scores of the populace.

Song had escaped after he was injured when his school bus traversed a Claymore mine acquired by the Viet Cong from the American arsenal. He was transported to Saigon for medical attention, and there an elderly military physician, tending to his recovery, recognized the abundant promise in the solemn youth. The doctor arranged for Song to attend a Catholic institution operated in the manner of a military preparatory school. While Song was in school, a president was lost to Washington and a dictator to Saigon. In the summer of 1964, Song hitched a ride to the strategic hamlet, only to find that the villagers had liberated themselves from the place and in their anger, virtually destroyed it. He learned from the few villagers that remained that his family had returned to the land of their ancestors at Dak Ranh.

Unlike his family, Song had not connected the multiple deaths he had witnessed to politics, perhaps because Saigon and Hanoi bore responsibility for events that were equally as horrible. Song's eventual induction into the South Vietnamese Air Force was for much the same reason as many young men are swept into war—he had been in the wrong place at the wrong time. Bright students at his school were singled out for leadership positions in the military. After flight school in America, Song returned home to a raging and confused war, in which his leaders measured victory by the quantity of human carnage. Though reticence was common among the ranks of the VNAFs, Song earned a dozen air medals and a Silver Star, top honors for a Vietnamese soldier, on missions that carried him into Cambodia, Laos, and North Vietnam. In his mind, Trent sifted through what he knew of Song's life, and he marveled that even some fragment of youth had survived.

"There is more," Song said, breaking Trent away from his internal vision. "Duong said we are to be blamed for the massacre at Ba Long."

Trent's brow stiffened, and he clicked his teeth. "Where did he get that?"

Song's shoulders rotated in an arc. "He said these things can be heard everywhere, in harsh whispers and sharp glances. He said I would hear too, if I pulled my head out of my ass and listened."

Trent fell silent. He had also heard some of the pilots musing that the VNAFs might be responsible for the killing at Ba Long. But the possibility was inconsistent with the physical evidence he himself had observed, and he had dismissed the talk as idle gossip. With hindsight though, it also seemed to him that the rumors had been something more than random, as if fueled to generate the kind of misdirected certainty that could dampen more reflective thought.

Trent let his eyes settle on Song's anguished face. Just a boy, Trent thought, whose best years had been dedicated to defending one corrupt Saigon regime after another. Now, with the gradual withdrawal of American troops, a painfully protracted exercise in which the 162nd was finally taking its turn, death or imprisonment almost certainly awaited South Vietnamese officers such as Song. It was only a matter of time.

"Can you help us?" Song asked, his puzzled gaze suggesting that he might have repeated his plea, while Trent's mind drifted.

•—•—————•—••—•—————•——•

Can I help? Trent thought, returning to the present with a shudder. No, he couldn't help then and can't help now. Nothing for Song, or for Ashford, not even for himself. Almost a quarter century had gone by, and it was just like yesterday—it often bewildered Trent to reflect upon how much of the past he carried with him day to day. In Vietnam, he had returned to his little table fan after speaking with Le Song, just for a few moments, to whittle away a few more shards of steel, to take one last pathetic stab at mutilating it back into sync, and again he had failed, just as he had failed Song, just as he would have failed the young lieutenant had good fortune not intervened.

Trent's troubled eyes traveled from the blades of the ceiling fan above him, to his coffee that had become lukewarm, and then to the cigarette burned to half its length in his fingers.

Chapter three

For Mark Ashford, the remaining introductions could fare little worse than his initial encounter with Trent and Winston, and he resolved to begin again.

Starting again was nothing new for Ashford, since he was in that stage of youth when one always seems to be a freshman. When he graduated from high school, he began his scholastic education anew at the Pennsylvania State University. When Ashford surmounted college, he moved to an entry-level position as a draftsman at a small architectural firm in Gettysburg, Pennsylvania. When his father died, he opened a new and more solitary phase of life, and he still regarded himself as a neophyte in that venture. Ashford joined the National Guard and was christened a lieutenant, a novice among commissioned officers; he further interrupted his career as a draftsman to become a fledgling trainee in rotary-wing flight school. Now, he was a beginner again at the unit level.

Mingled with his pure love of flight, Ashford had a burning desire to shed this pattern of perpetual infancy, to move at last from amateur to expert, and to grasp the all of something. And as Ashford had structured his internal rite of passage, indeed arranged his life, the culmination was to conquer the art of flight. Ashford had irreversibly set his heart on mastering the Blackhawk, on invulnerably taking the machine to the skies.

Yet, at the moment, Ashford felt far from invulnerable as he followed the path of the warrant officers from the hangar into the administration building. Away from the blue skies he yearned to conquer, he found himself in a maze of narrow corridors, with walls made of cinder blocks and painted a dingy yellow. The atmosphere seemed vaguely at odds with itself, brightly lit yet conveying some trace impression of an intricate web of shadows.

"Five thousand one hundred sixty-three."

In the wide space of a hall junction stood a balding, wiry man, with brown eyes that, even in profile, seemed to glow with warmth. His fringe of graying hair was arranged in a horizontal stripe cupped around his head and unconnected to a floating widow's peak. Parallel silver bars topped his shoulders displaying his rank of captain, his name tag bore a pair of senior pilot wings, and like Trent and Winston, he also wore a green-and-black arm patch identifying him as a combat veteran. The captain was arranging foot-long, white plastic numbers on a tall, green signboard. Ashford approached him with more trepidation than he would have liked, still smarting from the incomprehensible warrants.

"Now it's five thousand one hundred sixty-four," said the captain, pulling the numeral three from a hook on the plywood board, dropping it into a tool box, and carefully replacing it with a four. The number swayed on the nail pegged in the single digit position like the undulating arm on a metronome.

"Pardon?" Ashford said.

"Five thousand one hundred sixty-four days without a Class A accident," the captain said, gliding his fingers beneath the giant numerals for emphasis.

"That's quite an impressive record."

The captain closed the box and stepped back to survey his work. "We call this the Board. The regulation model is about a third this size, so I put together this homemade jobby. Think it's tacky?"

"It gets your attention."

"It should. We've had no fatalities or major equipment damage from an aircraft crash in fifteen years. That's for all of the units that utilize our flight facility, covering the entire National Guard Eastern Area Training Division. Our record is one of the best in the country, and we're very proud."

Ashford appreciated that the record was truly impressive for those who live in a culture of loosely controlled risks. "But how many lieutenants get run down by line trucks?" he said softly, his forefinger set against his lips.

The captain's features narrowed, and Ashford merely smiled in response, his ears focusing upon something in the intonation that he had not yet encountered at Fort Indiantown Gap. The hint of concern in the captain's manner sparked a glimmer of hope; perhaps this was the introduction he was searching for— someone who might be more his mentor than tormentor.

The young lieutenant had not thought to offer his hand, but the captain grasped it from Ashford's side nonetheless and introduced himself as Kevin Crawford, Operations Officer for Company B, 28th Aviation Battalion, as well as a full-time instructor pilot. For his part, Ashford was silently grateful that Crawford had not led the introductions with his own rank. When the captain asked him if he were just back from flight school, Ashford's eyes dropped self-consciously to his wrinkled green flight suit. He had put it through the washing machine twice and ironed it repeatedly, but it still would not conform. And even worse, it produced an acrimonious odor characteristic of Nomex, the flame-resistant material used to make the cover-all-style suits. He silently compared his to Crawford's flight suit that was smartly aged and fit like a glove. Shrugging off this distraction, he told Crawford that he had just completed training at Fort Rucker that month, and Crawford explained that Battalion staff was assigning all new aviators to Company B. "It's the best unit for cutting teeth, since you're freshly qualified in the Huey."

Ashford did his best to conceal the rush of disappointment. He had worked hard to gain his Blackhawk qualification, and confinement to a Huey, even temporarily, seemed a hard setback. "I might be a little rusty in the Huey."

"Ah yes. You got your Blackhawk transition. I checked over your records. Second in your class, and the guy that beat you didn't reach for the transition."

"I saw a couple of new Hawks on the flight deck."

"I'm sure you did, but they're not ours. They belong to Company F."

"Does Company B ever get to use them?"

"Unfortunately, no. Right now we don't qualify for that kind of training priority. Nope, we can't touch 'em as of yet. For now, you'll get some basic line experience in some good old 1950's technology." Crawford tipped his head in the direction of the Hueys on the hangar floor.

"Line experience?" Ashford asked, doing the utmost to continue inching forward against the turns.

Crawford explained that Company B was a general-purpose lift unit, focusing on troop transportation, particularly air assaults. He expressed his own partiality toward these missions but acknowledged that because the Huey was so versatile, the unit was frequently burdened with missions he described as ash and trash, or VIP and supply missions. Crawford promised, however, that he would try to arrange for air assault training for Ashford from the outset. "Indeed, you're very lucky. You'll learn from very experienced pilots in Company B. Lot of vets."

Ashford again contemplated the two other veterans he had encountered, but he said nothing. He fixated momentarily upon the signboard behind Crawford, the numeral four still swinging gently, and then he asked how long Crawford had been with the unit, silently performing the math to convert five thousand one hundred sixty-four days and confirm the captain's own translation.

Crawford looked over his shoulder and sighed. "I've been here long enough to see day zero. A Skycrane went down in a training area west of Carlisle."

Ashford shuddered slightly as his imagination projected the image of the huge body of a CH-54 Skycrane disintegrating, thousands of bits of metal spraying from the spontaneous eruption. "Mechanical failure?" he asked, before he thought better of it.

"It's a great aircraft too." Obviously, Crawford had evaded the question but had left Ashford with the impression that this might be something worth probing another time. The captain gestured for Ashford to follow him into a meeting room.

* * *

A thicket of bright orange plastic chairs, constructed without ergonomic design, faced a rickety wooden podium and a blackboard. Fifteen or so men were scattered about the room, all dressed in flight suits. Ashford laid his cap on a chair and stood a few paces behind Crawford.

The introductions seemed peculiarly uncomfortable to Ashford. Though the handshakes seemed friendly enough, the voices and expressions all seemed to contain a degree of reservation, as if there were a collective effort to demonstrate that some form of judgment was being withheld. Ashford knew that he was as much of an unknown to these men as they were to him, but their experience and solidarity afforded them the decided advantage. And despite everything that Ashford had read to try to understand, Vietnam remained a virtual mystery to him, yet before him stood many men wearing indicia displaying that they were privy to its imposing secrets.

Another set of introductions was underway across the room. Several warrant officers flocked around a young woman, also clothed in a flight suit. She stood smiling, with her back arched and her arms folded comfortably across her stomach. Velcro straps held the coverall snug to her flat middle, and her shiny, chestnut-brown colored hair was pulled tightly away from her face and tucked neatly under the rim of her canted hat. Ashford realized that she was the one the warrants called W-Zero-One Morrow, for her entry-level rank of Warrant Officer One. Looking around, he was taken aback by the many faces surrounding Morrow, faces which appeared quite open, with tongues moving freely— wings seemed to be lifting around the young woman, taking her under. By virtue of her sex, Ashford thought, Morrow could be at considerable disadvantage in a military unit; the acceptance of her could be disingenuous and condescending. Yet he couldn't discern a bit of reticence or falsity on the part of these warrants.

The difference, Ashford knew, was of rank—he was a superior; whereas, Morrow was one of the warrant officers' own. At that moment, Ashford felt the weight of his commission bear down upon him like an anvil. He stared at the warrants, veterans of the Vietnam War, heroes all around, and him, a veteran of nothing, a hero to no one. Some comfort could be taken in his introduction to Crawford, although Ashford knew that the captain's own administrative duties would constrain his ability to spend time with Ashford in the helicopter.

Ashford, who normally managed to be upbeat, recognized that his thoughts were beginning to slip toward an unwanted pattern of self-doubt. While he prodded himself to consider how far he had come, he could not escape the realization that there would be no Blackhawks and perhaps no mentor; indeed, it seemed as if there might even be men in critical functions who would focus their energies against him. As he took a seat and faded gratefully into anonymity, Ashford glanced across the room at Trent, who, after paying his own respects to W-Zero-One Morrow, had seated himself, propped a badly scuffed boot upon a chair, and buried his wind-burnt face in a paperback novel.

Momentarily, Crawford called to Trent, not seeming to notice his apparent unwillingness to be reintroduced, and Ashford once again confronted the uncompromising eyes of the warrant.

"Nick," Crawford said. "This is Lieutenant Ashford. He'll be your platoon leader, and I'm assigning him as your copilot today. I'd appreciate it if you'd spend some quality time with him in the orientation."

Trent's mouth widened, the corners slightly depressed. "Sorry, Kevin, I heard he's Blackhawk qualified."

"So?"

"He's way too good for me. Besides, I have a date with W-Zero-One Morrow. I already cleared it with my acting platoon leader."

Crawford stared into Trent's eyes a moment longer than would have seemed polite or, from Ashford's vantage, safe. "All right, I'll go up with the lieutenant then."

"But who'll fly your desk?" Trent said. Drawing no reaction, he tried again. "Your life insurance premiums paid current, Kevin?"

Crawford edged forward, far into what Ashford could see that Trent regarded as the limits of his own personal space. "Since you're making crew assignments, would you like to conduct the morning briefing too?" The captain spoke with a degree of menace that Ashford would not have expected from the man.

Trent did not parry, but rather, changed tact. "What is that smell?" he said, drawing a theatrical breath through his nose. Ashford instinctively knew that Trent was referring to the aroma of his new flight suit.

Crawford's expression didn't waver, and Trent finally seemed to realize his audience.

"Here's hoping the LT doesn't screw up your numbers, huh Kevin?" Trent gestured toward the Board in the hallway and interposed his book as a barrier to further conversation.

Crawford took Ashford aside. "Like I said, you'll learn a lot from these guys, but don't let them take advantage of your inexperience. Guys like Trent follow their own rules. They'll pull out all the stops to try to rearrange the whole world to their own liking. Nick has apparently picked his own copilot for today's flight—a new female pilot who just transferred from the D.C. Guard. Trouble is, he has no business selecting his own crew. Platoon leaders make crew assignments using their judgment based on mission requirements.

"Remember, the warrants may be older than you, but you hold rank. They're technicians—their job is to pilot the aircraft. Commissioned officers function as the leaders, on and off the ground. And that includes young lieutenants. Now come on. Not everyone here's a tough guy like Trent."

<hr />

"Good morning and all come to order please," Captain Crawford said, having stepped to the podium. He tapped on the wooden surface, causing the pilots who remained standing to grudgingly sit down. Ashford, for the moment, took comfort in the formality of a structured briefing.

"First order of business," said Crawford. "Anyone happen to notice the Board today?"

"Five thousand one hundred sixty-four," a small chorus of voices intoned, most belonging to the few younger warrant officers. From this response and Crawford's cheerful expression, Ashford inferred the exchange was a ritual exercise.

"I trust you're ready to be all you can be this weekend," Crawford said. "As you know, we're preparing for our annual jaunt to scenic AP Hill, Virginia next month for two weeks of fun in the sun."

"Kevin always did think he was Johnny Carson," a voice said, not bothering to whisper.

"This year," Crawford continued, "in its infinite wisdom the Army has assigned a team of four evaluators from the 101st Airborne Division to follow us through our paces at annual training and decide whether you guys can still cut the mustard or have to be mothballed. From Battalion's perspective, the jury's still out on that question. It's been subtly suggested that, if we want to get our twenty-year letters and ride off into the sunset, we should take this inspection very seriously. Seriously, that is, no joke.

"Today's training is air assault operations, which is the main focus of the evaluation. But before we get to that, we'll have a classroom briefing on threat operations. As you know, Captain Zuckerman is the new intelligence officer for Battalion."

A large, round-faced man with a thick mustache hopped from his chair and pivoted on his heel in a dramatic about-face maneuver, yielding a penetrating squeak. He smiled at the pilots, white teeth showing through wide lips.

In the rear corner of the room, Nick Trent dropped a boot to the floor, his still-outstretched leg displaying red stripes circling his civilian-style white socks. Reading glasses set low on his nose, he peered over the paperback as he spoke. "Army intelligence. That's an oxymoron."

"Pardon me?" Zuckerman said.

"A contradiction in terms," replied Trent, reclining on his chair's rear legs. As Zuckerman angled his jaw in puzzlement, Trent lifted his palm to his forehead.

Crawford cleared his throat. "So now without further ado," he said, "heeere's Captain Zuckerman." Crawford walked briskly to the rear of the room and sat beside Trent as if to serve as ballast.

Zuckerman gathered himself, with his face and manner exuding solemnity. "Gentlemen, in today's military theater of operations, we have two options. We can be supremely prepared or be crushed by the lethal machinery of the mother of red death—"

"Whoa, boy," a voice cracked. The man's pupils made tiny arcs underneath his eyelids.

"Anyone tell this idiot that the Cold War's over?" another voice whispered, less timidly.

Zuckerman continued to speak mechanically while thumbing through a stack of index cards. Abruptly, Trent spun in his chair to face the windows, and then he rose and strode rigidly to the doorway like a patron turning away from a distasteful performance. "There goes one," he said, still peering out the window as he passed into the corridor.

Winston was next to rise, and he offered a diminutive curtsy to Zuckerman before following Trent's course from the room. He mimed 'bathroom' and pointed to his crotch, winking at Ashford as he passed.

Zuckerman seemed dumbstruck. Several other warrants followed behind Trent and Winston, and finally Crawford did the same. "You might as well come along," he told Ashford. "We won't get anything done for a couple of minutes anyway."

They followed the warrant officers to the flight deck. The warrants stood in a cluster behind Trent, who faced the runway, transfixed. Across the open expanse, a white two-story building was engulfed in flames, surrounded by firefighting equipment and firemen standing idle. Flames poured from the windows, and black smoke billowed from exposed segments of the frame.

To Ashford's surprise, a soft voice spoke into his ear. "They burn the buildings to clear out the old stuff," said W-Zero-One Morrow.

Ashford's eyes were focused on the warrant officers. "They look like they're . . ."

"Yes, I heard it does something to the guys who've been around the block."

Ashford broke from the absorption, smiled modestly, and introduced himself. Jesse Morrow's saucer-shaped eyes were slightly lopsided, but her relaxed smile pulled them into harmony with her features in a delicate and wholesome way. As he conversed with Morrow, it seemed as if he were speaking with a friend since grade school. Warmth and openness were in her expression, and she moved with a gracefulness that Ashford knew would easily translate into pilotage. He thought Morrow to be unmilitary but in ways far different than Trent—she was appropriately groomed, and she wore the uniform correctly. The military trappings seemed to disappear, however, as they shared tales from flight school and talked about their hopes of blending in with the unit. Ashford was beginning to formulate an internal ledger, with Trent and Winston on one side versus Crawford, and now Morrow, on the other, although he quickly found himself readjusting this calculus to place Morrow in a class of her own.

In the meantime, Crawford had mixed success as he was shepherding warrant officers back into the briefing room. Returning to the flight deck, he took Ashford and Morrow by the elbows.

"Ahem," he said purposefully. "You two aren't going to miss much if you skip this particular briefing and go pick up your flight gear. Go check in with Master Sergeant Spencer. All the way down the main hall, to the left. Don't get lost along the way."

Morrow shrugged, smiled at Ashford, and led the way. Ashford noticed that Morrow was similarly focused on accomplishing everything essential to flight.

◦━━━◦━◦━◦━━━◦━◦

After the two departed, Crawford turned to Trent and Winston, who were still facing the flames, and asked, "Shouldn't you two be in the classroom? You know, the threat briefing?"

"The only threat," Winston said, "is that Zuckerman will pop an artery preaching, what was it Nick?"

"The mother of red death."

"Yeah, red death, that's right. So, the newbie sure kisses ass like a lieutenant, huh?"

"Born commissioned officer for sure," Trent said.

Crawford scowled. "Why don't you lighten up on the guy?"

"Take it easy, Kevin," replied Winston. "He's the one who took the commission. He's supposed to be able to handle us."

"Maybe that's the way the manual reads," Crawford said. "But they don't arrive as pre-packaged, seasoned commanders. Old saws like you and me have to help them get there. It takes time. And maybe it takes just a little longer when you aren't dropped right down in the middle of a God damn war."

Trent turned away from Crawford, pulled his paperback from his pocket, leaned against the side of the hangar, and stared down as if reading. His eyes were focused, however, on the silver wings embossed on his name tag. He looked at the worn graphic as if it were an old unhealed wound, sore and festering, and his face burned as if overtaken by the still-unquenched flames across the tarmac.

• ━ • ━━━ • ━ •• ━ • ━━━ • ━ •

The ALSE room, an acronym for aviation life support equipment, was on the far side of the break room. Anxious to collect their gear and move closer to flight, Ashford and Morrow entered through yet another orange door. They observed a sea of equipment: dozens of mesh flight vests hanging from hooks, rows of helmets, piles of flight bags, towers of boxes, and drab green items strewn across shelves and stands, giving the impression of a movie prop room. From behind a row of flight helmets, a stout black man emerged, naked from the navel up, with the arms of his flight suit tied around his waist. Blotches of raised skin covered his torso.

"I know what you're thinking," said Master Sergeant Reggie Spencer.

"You do?" Ashford replied.

"I'm out of uniform."

Ashford chuckled nervously. "Only half."

"Believe it or not, I have a waiver signed by the flight surgeon. In my little kingdom here, I'm authorized to run around stark naked. I was just getting dressed, so you missed the full show."

"Just my luck," Morrow said lightly.

Spencer offered the pair an engaging look. "Keep up that sense of humor, maybe you got a chance around here."

Ashford felt himself relaxing. "As long as you keep your pants up."

"We'll be all right, LT, you and me," Spencer said dryly, "so long as you let her do the jokes." He turned to the equipment and began assembling two piles on the floor: flight suits and bags, mesh vests, gas masks, and survival radios.

Morrow broke the silence. "What's the waiver?"

"I got this stuff when I got back from Vietnam." Spencer brushed his fingers against a patch of raised skin on his shoulder. "No connection to my service, of course, at least according to the military docs. Nothing to do with mission after mission of dumping Agent Orange all over the jungle, with the rotors spewing the stuff all over the place." Spencer paused. "The only time it all lets up, believe it or not, is when I fly through the Gap."

"The Gap?" Morrow asked.

"Sure, our Northern Training Area is to the north side of Indiantown Gap. That's the big break in the ridge just to the west of the control tower." Spencer pointed to the window. "Up there it's cool and free and different. Sometimes I feel like I'm flying over the ridges in Vietnam, on the good days, before I had these sores all over me." Spencer clawed at his arm. "For me, there's something mystical, maybe spiritual, about it."

Spencer dropped a large duffle bag on each pile, and Ashford and Morrow knelt and anxiously gathered their gear. Standing above them, Spencer asked, "So what do you think of the guys?"

Ashford raised his eyes and hesitated. "They have a lot of experience."

"You could say that. Who did you meet?"

"Uh, Captain Crawford. And... Warrant Officer Trent."

"Ah now, what did you think of him? Mister Trent, I mean."

"He's... he's a little gruff."

"Gruff? Is that all you got to say? I was privileged to fly with the Chief in Vietnam."

Ashford made no reply. The subject of Vietnam was one he knew he would have to approach cautiously. Morrow followed suit, staying close-lipped. They thanked Spencer, finished packing their gear, and left for the remnants of the briefing.

When the room was quiet again, Nick Trent stepped from behind a rack of helmets. He struck a match and touched it to a cigarette.

"Come on, Chief," Spencer said, "you know you're not supposed to light up in here."

Trent spoke through a cloud of white smoke. "Reggie, would you knock off the privilege nonsense. And you know I don't like being called Chief anymore. And what are you filling the kid's head with that other nonsense for?"

"It ain't nonsense, Nick. Okay, so my lesions never got any better, not in twenty years. Good of you to point that out."

"You know I didn't mean—"

"—but I like to feel there's somewhere different, so that's my business. Sometimes I think you could use a place like that yourself."

"More like I could use a drink."

Spencer squeezed white cream from a tube and rubbed it onto his rash. "I can't get the spot on my back, right in the middle. You mind?" Trent took the cream without hesitation and administered it in the places where Spencer directed. "Oooh, that feels good. That was the spot. And that was it there too."

"If you say so." Trent moved to the sink and rinsed his hands as Spencer pulled his flight suit over his shoulders and resumed his work. Trent stood looking in the mirror and blotting his hands with a paper towel for several minutes, long after his fingers were dry.

Ashford had parted with Morrow and paused for a moment to reflect before reentering the briefing room, and Trent caught up with him in the hallway. The surly warrant officer's mood seemed to have lifted.

"So, LT," Trent said, "you staying overnight at the Officers' Quarters?"

Ashford was surprised the man was speaking to him after their introduction and what had followed. He answered warily, telling Trent that he lived in Gettysburg. "Kind of far to go home."

"Why don't you meet us at Club Zimbabwe tonight for a drink?"

"Club Zimbabwe?"

"It's the avant-garde name they've given to the former NCO club. Everyone goes there. On Fisher Avenue, right next to the gas station."

"I thought I'd go for a run this evening."

"Afterwards then. Join us at the Zimbabwe after."

"I might just do that. Thanks."

"Just don't forget the name. You don't want to get lost."

"Club Zimbabwe," Ashford said. He considered Trent's invitation, and his sense of unease lingered long after he had returned to the briefing room.

Chapter four

Over the years spent in Vietnam, Nick Trent's skin had developed a tolerance for even the most direct sunlight, so he knew that the burning sensation at his temples originated from within. Le Song's words had intrigued him, and as he toyed again with his hopelessly crippled fan, Trent speculated about the identity of those responsible for the killings at Ba Long. At the same time, he realized that the imminent departure of the 162nd would likely prevent their discovery and thwart the rendering of a just account.

Through all of his preoccupations, Trent always maintained an uncanny sense of time, and he emerged from his tent moments before the appointed time for the preflight briefing. As the canvas flaps drifted closed behind him, Trent noticed Le Song's wingman, Duong, exit the rear of a supply tent and hurry across the cantonment area to the runway, where Song was performing a preflight inspection. Trent watched as Duong gestured excitedly to Song, as if conveying information of great importance, although Song remained stoical and seemed to be having difficulty understanding, or accepting, whatever his friend was trying to impart. When Trent resumed his course, he glimpsed another figure departing the supply tent and moving behind the mess tent; as the flaps were rolled from the bottom and tied several feet above the ground, the quick movements of the man's boots were visible to Trent for the entire length of the tent. Curious, Trent started to follow.

"There you are, Chief," said a voice from behind Trent, breaking his chain of thought and causing him to abandon his course. It was Paul Olofson, Trent's copilot, who had called out Trent's nickname. The Army's honorific for warrant officers was Mister, but enlisted men often called the senior warrants Chief as shorthand for the advanced grade of Chief Warrant Officer. In the 162nd, though, Trent was the only pilot whose peers permanently branded him with the title in place of his surname.

Trent looked over his copilot, a skinny college-kid-turned-warrant officer. One of very few replacement troops, Olofson was ten weeks in country. Trent was trying hard to make certain he lived through his eleventh.

"You check over the aircraft?" Trent asked.

"Bird's fine. Hey, they figure out what happened at Ba Long the other day?"

Trent lifted his eyebrows. "I'd call it a massacre. Some idiot flew over a sub-hamlet and shot it up. Killed twelve civilians."

"But who? And why?"

Trent shrugged. "I don't know the who, but the why seems simple." He toed a straight line in the red dust, indicating the left side. "Free-fire zone is here. That's Indian country. You can shoot any living thing with impunity." Trent dug his heel into the dirt on the other side of the line. "Ba Long is here. That's a restricted area. You better not shoot unless you're getting shot down or have got clearance from Vigilance. Nobody reported getting shot at and no one had clearance."

Trent lifted his face slowly to Olofson and fixed his gaze hard upon him in mock accusation. "Looks to me like it was someone who couldn't read a map."

Olofson squirmed. "Come on, Chief," he said, fingering the tactical map protruding from his breast pocket. "I was flying lifts with Braverman all day. Ask him. We were nowhere near Ba Long. They'll figure it out though, won't they? Get 'em just like they got Rusty Calley?"

"Nope. They're rushing the investigation on account of the bug out. They'll blame it on the VNAF Gunnies."

Olofson brightened, like a child who solved a puzzle. "Makes perfect sense. They're probably right."

"Nope."

"What do you mean?"

Trent considered his response and selected his words carefully, withholding the rest of what he had learned from Le Song. "I flew over Ba Long the day after the Massacre. I saw the strafing marks. Bullet holes were sprayed all over the place. The ground wasn't chewed up in lines like a Gunnie would make with its Gatling. No, the guns were M-60s, and the airplane was a Huey."

"Well if it's dead, it's VC." Olofson's voice betrayed the pretense with which he repeated words he had heard from hardened veterans. "They were at least VC sympathizers for sure; they got what they deserved."

Trent sighed. "And I thought I could make a combat pilot out of you."

"What?"

"It's all about judgment, Paul. What I've been trying to teach you. It's not how well you handle the flight controls or talk on the radio. It's knowing when to go up and when not to, when to land and when to fly on by, and when to shoot and when to hold your fire. When to stand your ground and when to pull up stakes and move on. The rest is nothing in comparison—a monkey could do the rest."

Trent's tone changed, turning inward, as if he were suddenly muttering only to himself in muted consolation. "A little girl washed up on the bank a quarter mile downstream of the village. If you'd only seen her. Then you'd know."

Olofson gazed down at the rough sketch in the dirt.

•—•—————•—•••—•—————•—•

Trent and Olofson joined a group of men gathered beside a large tent that functioned as the Tactical Operations Center. Suddenly the flaps parted and from a tunnel of darkness emerged Captain Harrison Harker, first platoon leader for the 162nd and air mission commander for Raven flight. His black regulation-cut hair formed an inevitably true line across the top of his head, as if he ran a straight razor along his forehead. He stood tall and superior, a spit-shined boot propped upon a sandbag revetment, and a closed and manicured hand resting upon his waist. If he had had a pipe, Trent would have sworn the captain was masquerading as a young Douglas MacArthur.

"Listen up," said Harker, his voice deep and gravelly. "We're on a short leash, so I'll make this quick. Everything's the same as this morning except the internal Fox Mike and chalk order. Frequency is thirty-nine point four five. Trent, you take the lead, I'll fly trail. We're flying the inland route again.

"We're to rendezvous with the Company Commander on a long final for Vũng Tàu. Major Tarsavage is forty minutes ahead of us with Falcon Flight following Green Route along the coast. They'll lager at LZ Stray Wolf during refuel. If our timing's right, we should have them in sight when we hit III Corps. Major wants both flights coming into Vũng Tàu joined in a single V formation; we'll form the right side. And he wants it to look sharp."

"Screw the Savage," Trent muttered.

Harker bristled. "You have something to say, Chief?"

"We can make the Savage's formation nice and pretty. But aren't you going to brief us on getting there in one piece first?"

"Come again?"

"Are you going to give us the tactical report or inspect our undershorts for skid marks?"

Harker paused, the left corner of his mouth depressed to anchor a sneer. "All right, Chief, here's a safety tip. Might just save your life. Let the VNAFs take point for the landings. Nobody here needs to have his ass flapping out in front on his last mission. Am I right?"

Trent stared vacantly, the thousand-mile gaze of a combat veteran. Harker's shoulders seemed to swell, his chest ballooning, as if he had achieved some small victory in a long-fought match. "Gentlemen," he said, "there's no other way to say it but that this is it. Let's make Major Tarsavage proud by nailing this last one."

Trent turned to Olofson for an internal crew briefing. Olofson stared over Trent's shoulder at the two Vietnamese pilots standing by the gunships, across the airstrip, on the runway of loose red dirt. Trent barely heard Olofson muttering as he nodded to himself.

"Dinks could too have done it. I bet they did anyway."

•—•—————•—••—•—————•—•

From a distance, Trent watched Song climb into the left seat of the gunship. He could see Song's movements in the cockpit, fluid and methodical, like those of a dancer. In seconds, seemingly without conscious effort, the helmet was on his head and thick straps stretched over his shoulders and buckled into the lap belt. With grace, his fingers twisted and clicked switches on the overhead and center consoles.

Trent looked over his own aircraft, checking that the crew, passengers, and cargo were secure. Then he climbed into the cockpit beside Olofson, donned his own helmet, and pulled the trigger on the collective lever, firing the engine. Through slowly turning rotor blades, he watched choking clouds of red dust swirl in great hoops around the two helicopters positioned to his sides.

In a moment, Song's gunship lifted nimbly from the earth and drew closer to the three climbing Hueys, paralleling his wingman in the companion gunship. Seconds later, shining green hills twisted dizzily as the flight snaked through a narrow valley beaming with hues of luminescent green. But the breathtaking view was lost to Trent. Every bit of his concentration was devoted to contemplation of the massacre at Ba Long, the volatile knowledge borne by Le Song and his wingman, and the personal decision that Song was to make before they reached Vũng Tàu.

Ninety minutes passed as if they were a single instant. Abruptly, the rolling sea of lush jungle disappeared beneath the Huey's belly, giving way to a sprawling paddy that unfolded before its windscreen. They were skimming alongside the western foothills of the Central Highlands, plunging southward toward the vast sweep of rice lands nourished by the Mekong, the great river of Indochina. Trent surveyed the open plain with military precision. First he searched for danger directly below, propelling his vigil outward to the southernmost boundary of the field. Only then did he allow his eyes to linger momentarily upon a frail human figure perched upon an irrigation dike, a conical straw hat shielding the stooped woman's wrinkled face.

Trent straightened as the terrain transformed beneath him. "A little lower," he said into the narrow boom-mounted microphone resting on his lower lip. Since the Viet Cong had acquired larger numbers of surface-to-air missiles, Trent was uneasy unless the helicopter skids skimmed the treetops. From the cockpit's right seat, Olofson lowered the collective lever abruptly, and the Huey sank into the paddy below the tree line. As Trent checked the engine gauges, red tracer rounds flashed above the treetops off the left wing, like sparks sailing from hot coals.

"Geez, they're everywhere," said Olofson. "For all we know, they could even be in the Gunnies. Who ever thought of the concept of joint operations? Hell, there's no way to tell these slopes apart. Friend or foe? VNAF, Cong, ARVN, sapper... can't tell the difference. Why do they let the sons of bitches fly cover anyway?"

The kid should be happy to have gun cover, Trent thought. He turned his head to check on the infantrymen strewn across the gray-metal cargo floor behind him, those closest to the sides clutching a thin wire spanning the open doorway spaces. The two helmeted crew chiefs cradled their weapons as if they were made of precious metal. "Everything okay back there, Reggie?" Trent asked.

Three weeks earlier, the barrel-chested Marine corporal had been separated from his infantry unit and rescued from the jungle by Trent. Thereafter, Reggie Spencer steadfastly flew as Trent's gunner. Spencer stepped on a floor-mounted mike switch located beneath his perch in the rear of the Huey. "Locked and loaded, Chief," he said, maintaining steady eye contact with the ground. "Wait a minute. I got movement in the western fringe."

"Can you hit 'em?" Olofson said.

"Hold your fire," Trent directed. All faces weathervaned to the west. The foliage along the edge of the paddy trembled, as if someone were running parallel to the helicopter just inside the tree line. The Huey drifted off course with Olofson's set gaze, crabbing toward a grove of almond-shaped trees jutting from the paddy surface. Trent locked the trees in his peripheral vision and shifted the bulk of his attention to the suspected enemy movement.

"Got 'em in my sights," Spencer said, training the machine gun on the quivering branches.

"Hold," Trent said.

"Target moving to the north."

"Hold."

Suddenly two children sprang from the jungle. A clay water jug dangled from a pole straddled between them, carried on limber shoulders, and they smiled and pointed tiny fingers at the helicopters. Spencer swung the machine gun wide and to the rear.

"Jesus," Olofson said. "We could've—"

"See how easy it is?" said Trent. "It can happen so quickly. Probably that's what happened at Ba Long. Except the pilots didn't wait to verify their targets."

Olofson continued to stare, oblivious to the approaching clump of trees, and the nose of the helicopter advanced within a few feet of a collision. Trent popped the collective lightly with his gloved forefinger. The Huey skirted skyward, the skids sliding over the treetops as if they were glazed with smooth ice. Olofson jerked the cyclic left, but Trent cupped the controls in his hands, neutralizing the control input. "Just hold your course. We've got plenty of clearance now. And you don't want to overcorrect, because the Gunnie is just out our left door. You've got to be more careful."

Olofson's eyebrows vanished up underneath his helmet. "I saw him."

Trent's manner was soft and conciliatory. "Sure, Paul."

"Do the Gunnies have to fly that close?"

Both pilots glanced over the black armor plating straddling the open doorway space and, as if at Olofson's suggestion, the gunship banked left. Olofson continued to stare. "Paul, you're fixating again," Trent said. "You need to devote a little bit of your attention to everything. You have to scan—horizon, terrain, and instruments. Try concentrating on the navigation. That'll get you looking around. Next landmark is the streambed. See it?"

Olofson's helmet pitched as if it were swaying on a fulcrum, and he searched the far tree line for navigation cues.

"Imagine the treetops are a continuous horizon," Trent said. "Look for the notch in that line. It's subtle, but it's there."

Olofson pointed his chin at a shallow dip in the contour of the trees. "Cuts into the jungle twenty degrees off the nose."

Trent's voice became reassuring, like a grade-school teacher praising a student who had a small success. It was the tone he had employed with countless young men he had mentored over the course of the War. "Good. We'd make a combat pilot out of you yet. If there was time."

"Yeah, I got it."

Trent shifted his focus inside the Huey to the fuel gauge.

"Ten minutes into fuel reserve," said Olofson. "How far to LZ Wellspring?"

"Fifteen klicks," Trent said.

"Cutting it close, huh?"

Trent nodded, unzipped the breast pocket of his flight suit, and pulled out a cigarette. While reaching for his matches, he spotted several helicopters at a distance, the apparent targets of the sporadic gunfire. Tracking their course, he momentarily neglected the yellowed roll of tobacco balanced between his lips. For an instant, the Huey floated, and silence seemed to supplant the dull whine of the engine. Trent gazed at a cluster of youth that encircled a pair of yoked water buffaloes towing a primitive plow.

He watched Song's gunship come parallel to the irrigation dike and trail a pair of hollow-log sampans as they skimmed across the water, and Trent imagined the young Vietnamese pilot softening his touch on the controls to emulate the fluidity of their movement. In that moment, Trent remembered that the village was Song's childhood home. His eyes followed as Song angled his gunship toward the western edge of the paddy, but his vision hastily retreated from the blinding glare and lingered on the battered remains of a downed Huey, the main fuselage and its fragmented tail section rising strikingly from the shallow water like a solemn monument to its former crew. That relic of recent times recalled Trent's drifting thoughts. He looked for Song's gunship, but its form was obscured by the sunlight. Probably saying goodbye, Trent thought, as he glanced again at the fuel gauge.

"What happened to the Gunnie?" asked Olofson, as the lead Huey crossed the boundary between the paddy and the jungle.

Trent leaned out the window, and the stiff wind tore the unlit cigarette from his mouth, and he groped for another. "He's lagging a little behind."

"I like to keep 'em in my sight. I've heard stories about South Vietnamese troops de-assing Hueys in LZs and turning to fire at the departing bird. Buddy of mine from the Eighty-Second Airborne got cut down that way. Just think what the dinks could do with a Gunnie."

"Don't let your imagination run away with you, Paul. I've flown with these guys before. They're okay. Slow up around this bend. Wellspring is a couple klicks ahead."

"Harker didn't say anything about Wellspring in the briefing. Guess the tac report was the same as this morning."

"Or maybe he didn't get a current report. Either way, we should've insisted on hearing one at the briefing. We'll both have to keep that in mind for the next brief... well, when we get to the States."

Olofson squinted at Trent. "We're really pulling out, huh?"

"Sure looks that way."

"I've been here less than three months, and it isn't any too soon for me. These little people sure bear us ill will."

Trent blinked into the orange sun. Each time he approached the end of a tour, his emotions swirled, out of sync and discordant, like the wavering blades of the little table fan that haunted him. The first time, he felt pure craving to escape the grim visage of the War and the attendant fear, gloom, and despair. But when he had reached the United States, inexplicably the hunger reversed itself. Self-confident and self-reliant, Trent could ignore the mixed reactions of civilians who were his former peers, but inside he harbored a hollow feeling of incompleteness that propelled him to monitor and scrutinize the War day by day. For him Vietnam represented the end of familiar rhythms; the unrecognizable blur of the War had become the familiar. Terrified faces. *Tic, tic*, bullets tearing through metal. Shouts. Blood. Anguish.

Yet in spite of his dreadful remembrances, he had an inexplicable yearning to be there, to finish what he had begun. Finally, to Trent's relief, and to his horror, in the wake of a shortage of combat pilots, the Army sent him orders to report for a second tour. At the tour's end, Trent's nerves were frayed to the point of snapping, and the craving to escape infected him again, but he was less certain of its nature, knowing the mixed blessing of being sent home, unfulfilled and unwelcome. This third time, he was leaving with little possibility of returning. Ever.

The fan raged in Trent's mind, unbalanced and unchecked.

"Am I doing okay here, Chief?" Olofson said nervously.

Trent snapped against the taut mesh seat and inhaled deeply. "Just stay in this streambed. There's one more S-turn. When you get to the second bend of the serpentine, roll out level. That's a short final for Wellspring." Trent fidgeted with the FM radio. "Goddammit, the crew at Wellspring isn't answering. Stay low and slow until we make radio contact."

"I can't get any lower." Olofson allowed the skids to brush the treetops in further protestation.

Trent ignored the foolish gesture and flipped the radio dial to the flight's internal frequency. "*Watch One, Raven One. Unable Wellspring. Will you try?*"

"*Affirmative,*" Song's voice responded. "*Wellspring, Raven flight. Copy?*" Song repeated the inquiry twice. "*Raven One, Watch One. Negative Wellspring.*"

"*Roger. Say fuel status.*"

"*Bingo,*" Song said, signifying low fuel.

"*Roger Wellspring. Raven Flight in the blind. Pop smoke for clearance.*"

A thin specter-like stream of yellow smoke rose from the thick jungle canopy a mile off the right front of the Huey.

"*Wellspring. Confirm yellow smoke if able,*" said Trent. No response. "*Watch, Raven One. Hang back until we get some kind of authentication.*"

Grainy static crackled in Trent's earphones, as a familiar gruff voice filled the common radio frequency reproachfully. "*You got the smoke, Trent,*" said Harker. "*It's obvious their transmitter is down. Just send the Gunnies in first, and then get your butt on the ground. We're low on fuel.*"

"Yeah, old Harker uses A-number-one radio procedures," Olofson said, seeming to take his cue from Trent's scowl.

Trent imagined Harker's stern visage peering over the console in the trail Huey. Harker was too chickenshit to fly this mission in the lead Huey where the air mission commander belonged, Trent thought. Must be because we're all so close to the endgame.

"Watch, Raven Leader," Harker said. *"You have your orders. Get on final approach now."*

"Aye aye, G.I.," came Song's mocking response. *"I land now."*

Spencer keyed the intercom. "Hey, Chief, sounds like the VNAFs are right in tune to the universal signal broadcast by an asshole."

"Sure does, Reggie," said Trent. "Better make sure your big stick is ready back there. I got a bad feeling about this."

As the flight rounded a bend in the streambed, Trent put pressure on the cyclic with his index finger, signaling Olofson to further slow his airspeed. Song's gunship nudged forward, pushing to the forefront of the three Hueys and then decelerated almost immediately. Two clearings appeared before Trent; the gunship floated almost directly above the first, a diamond-shaped hole in the jungle. Trent recognized the furthermost clearing as Wellspring. It was an almost perfect circle, large enough to accommodate four Hueys. Fuel lines stretched from black rubber bladders nestled against the tree line.

"Coming down," Olofson said.

"Easy, easy," said Trent. He continued to scan the second clearing. Abruptly, he took hold of his set of the dual controls. "I got it."

Olofson released the controls. "What's up?"

Song had halted his descent and was hovering nose-high off the western edge of the Wellspring landing site. Trent could feel the Vietnamese pilot's uneasiness. Everything seemed in order below, but something was amiss. The gunship resumed its slow descent, and Trent crept closer to the edge of Wellspring. As the floor of the fuel site came fully into his field of view, Trent judged its appearance normal, although no helicopters were present. A solitary Vietnamese man stood centered in the opening, signaling in the manner of a ground guide.

But something was wrong. The signals were not clear. They seemed erratic, almost nonsensical.

Song's radio transmission came sharp and unexpected. "*Go around!*"

Trent snatched at the collective. "Open up, Reggie!"

Red tracer rounds streaked past the Huey from the rear. Trent recoiled. The machine guns retched a thunderous volley of explosions. The Huey bucked.

"Huh?" Olofson stammered. "What the hell's going on?"

Trent did not respond. The whole of his concentration was spent piloting the Huey. Reverberating with the machine gun fire, Spencer's charged voice gave Olofson his answer.

"Are you blind? It's an ambush!"

Chapter five

In the twilight air, the Blue Mountain ridge loomed black against the sky over Fort Indiantown Gap. Dark gray clouds blew and gathered against the mountaintops. Ashford was finishing an hour-long run along a narrow road carved into the base of the mountain, fairly certain his unfamiliar course would return him to the flight facility. He raced shaft-like shadows cast from black tree-bodies, vaulted wooden tables in a picnic ground, and jogged under a water tower with red-and-white legs painted like candy canes. Ashford's long, confident stride made him an ideal distance runner; he never ran less than six miles, he ran hard, and he almost always ran alone.

Thin veins of lightning flashed like luminous scratches against the darkened sky, highlighting an approaching thundercloud, and a low peal of thunder gave further warning of the oncoming storm. The air suddenly cooled, and Ashford quickened his pace, not because he was frightened by the storm but because it struck a chord deep inside him, exhilarating him. He was in his element, alone, testing his strength against only himself.

He considered the central focus of his life to be an individual effort too. He was fiercely determined to become the best pilot possible. But his duties as a commissioned officer burdened him with authority over others, and the resistance he felt from some of the warrants, particularly Trent, seemed to be a visceral threat to his life's ambition.

After he reached the flight facility, Ashford showered in the locker room. He dressed and followed Trent's directions to the club. He parted louvered bat-wing doors and scanned the unfamiliar barroom.

Clusters of tables littered the wooden floor sloping to a horseshoe-shaped bar on the far side of the room, and blue-and-red bar lights hung over stools dotted its perimeter. Ashford didn't recognize any of the men seated at the near counter, and his view of the far side was obstructed by shelves stocked with bottles. A pair of young black sergeants dressed in worn camouflage uniforms leaned on a jukebox near the door. Ashford removed his cap and said hello.

"This is Club Zimbabwe, isn't it?" he asked.

The sergeants stared at him severely. "Look here, Lieutenant," one said. "You may hold rank, but you can't come in here and talk trash like that. This is the NCO Club, that's Non-Commissioned Officers, emphasis on the Non."

"Got no caviar or crumpets here," said the other sergeant scornfully.

Ashford reflected on the name of the club he had been given. He remembered how Trent had stressed it to ensure that Ashford would speak the name. With a cold suddenness, Ashford realized he had been duped into uttering a racial slur. He stammered a heartfelt apology that sounded awkward and lame, as the bartender waved him over.

Ashford acted quickly on the invitation. "I guess this isn't Club Zimbabwe."

"No and there is no Zimbabwe club, son." The bartender offered only a glimmer of compassion for Ashford's plight. "It's a country in Africa."

Ashford's ears burned and his eyes stung. Across the bar he saw Trent's brooding visage glow in malevolent victory beneath a blaring red light positioned as if to spotlight the warrant's triumph. Trent hoisted a glass in an apparent toast to Ashford's discomfort.

"It's okay, kid," the bartender said, chuckling. "The old farts prank the newbies with that Zimbabwe routine all the time. It's just that they don't usually make quite such damn fools of themselves."

Ashford circled the bar to the far side of Trent. He joined Kevin Crawford and Reggie Spencer, who were at his side. Trent leaned forward and winked at Spencer. "Meet everybody's straight man," he said of Ashford.

Ashford smiled wanly and struggled to ignore the comment. He was beginning to think he would have to make this his habit with Trent.

Crawford asked Ashford what brought him, and Mark replied that Trent had invited him. Crawford said he meant what brought him to Company B, and Ashford paused self-consciously, his eyes pointed to the polished bar surface. "All my life I wanted to fly," he said. "When I was a kid, I'd go to Gettysburg Airport and watch the single engine planes glide from the runway. A few times one of the owners took me up, and I loved it. I wanted to get lessons, but my parents were scrimping to send me to college, so I put my savings towards that too. It wasn't until after college that my boss let me take time off to go to flight school. The Army gave me the free ticket. So, well, how did you come to Company B?"

Trent scowled and spoke before Crawford could answer. "He had a great travel agent. Name was Uncle Sam. Told us we'd get to go to a foreign land, meet lots of interesting people, and kill them."

"Don't pay any attention to him," said Crawford.

"Pay no attention to me whatsoever." Trent stood and stretched and then lifted his glass and sauntered to a table occupied by two women. Both were clothed in mussed waitress uniforms; the one facing Ashford wore heavy pancake makeup on rounded cheeks. Trent engaged them in conversation. In a moment he sat close to the larger woman, wrapped his arm around her, and smiled, though in truth he did not appear to be happy at all.

"Isn't he married?" Ashford whispered.

Spencer shrugged. "Some go looking for solace in funny ways. I say that's their prerogative. The guys have a saying. Whatever's done on drill weekends stays here. That's the rule I follow."

"I read you loud and clear," Ashford said.

"You should save the radio talk for the helicopter and the Battalion Commander," said Crawford, tilting a bottle to his lips.

Ashford asked the bartender for a beer and listened to the crew members chat about the upcoming summer camp and detail bits and pieces from their home lives. He was content to sip his drink and listen. After a few moments, a young private approached Spencer, quizzing him about how he became a crew chief. Spencer told him his military career began in the Marine Corps.

"You're a former Marine?" the private asked.

"There are no former Marines, son," Spencer said. "Once a Marine, always a Marine. I wore the uniform in Vietnam and am proud of it."

"Wow. You were in Vietnam."

"Nothing to wow over. Messed up a lot of guys' lives. Almost messed up mine."

The private's eyes were like saucers. "What happened?"

"It's not something I talk about. But see that pilot over there at that table with those ladies? Name's Mister Trent. He saved my life over there and taught me how to stay sane and did the same for dozens of other guys. You're looking for a real-life hero, there he is. Last three weeks in Vietnam, I stayed just as close to him as I could, because I knew if I did, I'd make it. Every minute with him I felt absolutely safe."

Ashford lifted his eyes to Trent, who was chugging a beer, with a cigarette still hanging from the side of his mouth. "He doesn't seem like that now," he said to himself.

"What?" Spencer asked flatly.

"Nothing."

"What do you know? To really know a man, you got to know where he's been, what he's been through."

Ashford mulled over Spencer's words. His own experiences with Trent contradicted Spencer's every syllable; Trent didn't seem to be a hero or even a good man—he seemed baleful and self-centered, irreverent, and unfaithful. Ashford longed to explore Spencer's tale, to question every detail, to learn what the sour warrant could possibly have done to enlighten so many lives, and to learn why he seemed bent on making Ashford's own existence miserable. But he couldn't find the words; he had no right to ask, not now. He would have to build a foundation. He would need to earn trust.

Lost in self-reflection, Ashford was startled when a coarse hand clapped hard upon his own shoulder. An oversized infantry sergeant stood behind him in a mud-covered camouflage uniform, appearing like an old sailor straight from the brine. His face was wrinkled and mottled. Small beads of liquid dripped from the corners of a wispy mustache, and his foul breath bore the heavy stench of hard alcohol. "There you are, Chief," the sergeant said, mistakenly employing the honorific associated with a chief warrant officer. "You guys are the greatest. Hey, Corporal. Yeah you, Stevens. Get over here. Bring the private first class over too. Come over here and meet the Chief."

Ashford nodded and tried to return to his drink; he wished he hadn't worn his flight suit. Young infantrymen suddenly encircled him. The other flight crew members disappeared behind the crowd.

"You pilots were the best in Vietnam," the old sergeant continued. "Didn't matter what kinda shit we were in. Right through the rockets and the smoke and the bullets and the hell, there you'd come like some angel of mercy swooshing down from God Almighty on high in heaven above. You guys would save our asses. What-ya-say, Chief?"

The sergeant's young companions stared intently at the young lieutenant, the whites of their eyes shining in curious ignorance. "I wasn't there," Ashford said.

"What-ya-say, Chief?"

"I wasn't in Vietnam."

The sergeant squinted his watery red eyes, and the dark circles beneath intensified into deep gullies. He held his face close to Ashford's, examining the young pilot closely. "Little young, I guess." He leaned against Ashford's chair and breathed deeply. "No matter. You got all the makings. You'd come get us outta calm or storm. Bullets and blood and madness. You fly boys always come through."

"Well certain things you have to take into account." Ashford instantly regretted his reply.

"Account you say?"

"Like the weather—"

The sergeant pounded both fists on the bar. "The weather, damnation! Not when our lives are on the line. He'd come in hail and thunder, boys." The sergeant turned to his audience as if trying to enlist their support. The lingering odor of his breath made Ashford peek through the corner of one eye.

"The aircrews' lives have to be considered too," Ashford said, although he couldn't comprehend why he was resisting; his arguments seemed automatic, as if calculated by his subconscious to reveal his every hidden insecurity. "You have to consider—"

"You have to consider?" The sergeant's eyes narrowed and played around the room. But suddenly he went pale and silent. He stared into the shadowy smoke-haze lingering in the recesses of the room as if recollecting, as if he saw a platoon of ghost-soldiers emerging from the darkness and gliding about to surround him. When he shook away the affliction, the sergeant stammered an apology. "Lemme buy you a beer, Chief."

"I already have one. And I'm not a chief warrant officer. I'm a lieutenant."

"Bartender, set us up. Me and the Chief and the corporal and the private."

Ashford only took a few swallows from his glass. His throat burned, his head swam, and his face felt flush with heat. He excused himself, pushing his way through the soldiers and down a corridor to the lavatory. There, he stood under a fluorescent light, staring at all the little imperfections in his face, invisible to others but to himself, intimate. He bent over the sink and splashed cold water on his face. He looked up in the mirror and splashed again, but he found no relief in the water's chilly bite. Ashford was engulfed in doubt, truly unsure how he would react in combat. He had never had a desire to participate in war. His only wish was to fly—the Army was merely an expedient. But the device had taken on a life of its own, thrusting him into close proximity with men of raw experience and generating troubling questions about how he would perform in their stead.

Of course he would act heroically, he told himself. Wouldn't he? How would he balance the lives of his crewmembers against the lives of those he was tasked to assist? How would he face the test, the trial by fire? How had Winston and Trent done it? The warrant officers had confronted mayhem and death and had survived. It seemed ludicrous to put him in charge of such men, him fresh from flight school, uninitiated, with bare minimum flight experience.

How could he ever command them?

Chapter six

"Raven One. You got the bad guys?"

Trent did not respond. His crooked arm held the collective high, pumping power from the engines and priming the rotors with untoward force to speed them to safety. He flung the Huey into a ninety-degree bank. The craft spun on its side as if tethered to a pivot point. The pilots sat mutely as the sideways jungle careened surrealistically across the windscreen.

Over the crazed jack hammering of the machine guns, Trent heard a sickening rumble in the rear. The tail boom quivered, and this soon amplified to a terrible vibration that spread quickly through the airframe. The nose yawed severely. The Huey shook with tremors that made it difficult for Trent to hold the controls steady. The helicopter sank, its nose angled in a dangerous tuck.

Olofson grasped the sides of his seat with both hands, unconsciously lifting his torso. "Tail rotor's gone!"

With a damaged tail rotor, airspeed was critical to streamline the Huey and retain control. But Trent couldn't manage to coax the craft to accelerate; although he lowered the nose, it continued to lurch and spin and sink. With the marginal control he was able to exert, Trent threaded the Huey through the treetops. Branches and leaves lashed the underside.

In the low ground to his forefront, Trent seized upon a tiny clearing. As he struggled to manage a semblance of an approach, he caught a glimpse of a VNAF gunship, Watch Two he guessed, hovering on their left flank, spitting chunks of metal into the tree line in defense of the stricken Huey. Suddenly a searing streak of red light shot from the ground like a lightning bolt, punching a black hole in the sky where Watch Two had hovered a second before. A concentric circle of rubble spread through the air. The debris settled into the jungle canopy, like residue from an exploded shell.

"Oh God," said Olofson, staring awestruck into the gray smoke, streaming from the jungle as if carrying the soul of the dead pilot to the heavens.

"Heat seeker," Trent mouthed.

Olofson's eyes widened as he seemed to be taking in the ground rising and swelling. "*Mayday!*" he transmitted. "*We're going in, we're going in!*"

The Huey slithered across the treetops. The remainder of Raven flight, which had halted several hundred yards short of the ambush, gained airspeed and pulled away safely.

"*Hang in there, Raven One,*" a voice said. "*We'll send someone back to pick you up.*" The voice belonged to Harker.

"*You can't leave us,*" Olofson pleaded.

"*We're shot up, over gross, and out of gas. Hang on I said. That's an order. I said we'd get help. Major Tarsavage should still be at LZ Stray Wolf. That's twenty minutes down the Dung River. We'll be back in the hour.*"

"I don't believe this," Olofson said. "I do not believe." Trent spotted a tree break in the clearing and the Huey sluiced through it. "Slow down, Nick. Please, slow down!"

Olofson clutched at the flight controls. The helicopter lurched against his rough touch. Trent wiggled the controls to allow Olofson to sense the steadiness of his own hand; he methodically rolled the cylindrical throttle between his fingers to minimize the torque of the rotor system. Olofson held the controls frozen, appearing to be locked in some internal conflict between his panicked attempt at pilotage and an outright surrender to Trent's skill and rationality. Twenty feet from the ground Trent asked Olofson if he wanted to live or die, and Olofson finally submitted.

Freed from Olofson's death grip, Trent lifted the nose of the Huey. The tail bounced against the ground, leveling the still-airborne craft. Trent pulled in collective, increasing blade pitch, to avoid a crash. The helicopter floated momentarily. He put the nose high in the air again.

A foot from the ground, Trent yanked what remained from the collective's range, trading the remaining rotor speed to slow the rate of descent. The Huey hit the ground with the left skid low, flinging the pilots' arms and legs wildly into the air as if stuffed with straw. The skids bore into the earth. The helicopter pitched forward. Finally the Huey halted, shuddering like a mastodon downed by predators. The slow-turning blades continued to flop against the rotor stops, jarring the airframe, as if teasing the occupants, until finally exhausting the inertia of their spin.

"Christ," Olofson breathed.

Trent scanned the terrain; all was still except for a gunship, Watch One, making a slow zigzag over the clearing. "*Watch, Raven One,*" Trent said, keying his mike.

"*Watch,*" Song said.

"*Say status of unfriendlies.*"

"*Approaching.*"

Trent evaded Olofson's frightened stare. "*Any thoughts?*"

"*Pick up*," Song said. His gunship sliced through the tree break on a fast approach. Trent and Olofson unstrapped quickly and motioned for the footsoldiers to exit the helicopter. Several had been hurt in the crash, and their comrades were wrapping the wounds with bandanas.

Trent jogged around the Huey and touched the bullet holes in the tail rotor driveshaft. He paused to watch the gunship land, and then he pulled his flight gear from behind his seat and slung his chicken-plate body armor over his shoulder. Trent pointed toward the gunship, and the ground soldiers hustled forward carrying two of the wounded. Olofson followed, as if he found safety in numbers, while Trent muttered in disgust. He yanked Olofson's flight gear from the cockpit, recalling the words of his instructor at Fort Wolters, Texas—a combat pilot's flight gear is as sacred to him as a rifle is to an infantryman. Never to be left behind.

When Trent reached Song's gunship, Spencer had most of the soldiers on board. The Charlie model gunship was smaller than its larger brother, the H model Huey, which was designed for lifting troops, and it was a far tighter fit. Two soldiers sat with their feet straddling the rocket pods, held from under their armpits by others. Olofson squatted sandwiched between two infantrymen, appearing tiny and earnest. Trent pitched his gear at him.

Trent hurried alongside the gunship. He grabbed packs and gear from the soldiers and threw it all into the field. He tried to explain to the soldiers that they would need to lighten the load, but his words were lost in the rotor and engine noise. When he was satisfied he had done all he could do, Trent seated Spencer in a small space he had cleared on the far side of the gunship and returned to the crash-landed Huey.

Trent knew he didn't have much time. He stroked the Huey as a cowboy would an old horse with a broken leg, and then he pulled the pin on a fragmentation grenade and pitched it into the cockpit. Trent scrambled for the tree line but decided there was no time. He dropped to his knees and hunched forward.

The blast crashed in his eardrums before he touched the ground, and the shock of the explosion pitched over him like a wave. He rolled, stumbling to his feet.

Already under attack from a hidden enemy, the overloaded gunship lumbered forward with the skids burrowing into the earth. Trent grasped the airframe, and a pair of arms helped him to a tenuous seat on a ground soldier's lap. He clung there watching helplessly, as Song vainly tried to coerce the helicopter into the air. Trent knew that the weight of the soldiers was preventing the helicopter from taking flight; the craft was like a soaring eagle tethered to a cinder block.

Trent shouted to the soldiers to throw everything out. A pack he had missed flew across his shoulder and a flak jacket followed, and then a string of ammunition sailed by. None of the weapons were abandoned, however, since the soldiers' creed prevented it, and Trent, clinging to his own flight gear, had little choice but to reluctantly honor their similar tenet.

The seat of Olofson's pants abruptly exploded into a mass of red and purple gore. Blood spattered in thick droplets against the gray bulkhead. "I'm hit!" Olofson shrieked. "Oh God, I'm hit!"

"Push him off," a voice cried in panic. "He'll bleed to death anyway."

Hanging in the doorway, Trent bent his arm awkwardly to allow his fingers to slip into his breast pocket, from which he pulled a silver-sheathed bullet. With calm precision, he slid the revolver from its holster in his flight vest and chambered the single bullet into one of the six empty holes in the cylinder. A flick of his wrist brought the bullet even with the barrel. He pointed the gun toward the voice. "I'll shoot the first man who touches him."

Trent would never be sure what took place in the next instant. He felt the arm wrapped around his chest relax and his own grip on the bulkhead loosen. He twisted his hand, to improve his grip or to pull free, he would never quite be certain, and the other arms which had held him slipped away. He tumbled to the ground, rolling.

With the lessened load, the skids of Song's gunship no longer dug as deeply into the ground. The chopper accelerated slowly. Finally, it rose to a laborious hover, circling the perimeter of the tiny clearing, generating airspeed to outrun the swirling vortices that prevented the rotor system from biting into clean air. Trent saw Spencer pushing through bodies, working his way to the near side of the gunship. Their eyes locked. Trent pointed a finger at Spencer and gave a look that contained a terrible command to stay put. Spencer froze in place with mute horror.

On the third circle, the gunship soared from the clearing as if hoisted by an invisible hand. Trent stared at the departing helicopter, and for an instant his eyes held Olofson's shock-filled stare. The wounded man's expression was contorted by pain, but there was something else there, a weak beam of gratitude, or perhaps pity.

After the gunship crested the trees, Trent began to rise, but he ducked into the weeds as tracer rounds sailed across the field, sinking into the remains of the smoldering Huey. Apparently the enemy hadn't seen him yet. Still twenty feet from the tree line, Trent lowered his head below long blades of elephant grass and prayed.

From the corner of his eye, Trent caught the outline of Song's gunship skidding across the treetops and sinking low into the field. Even from a distance, the throbbing rotor seemed a surrogate heartbeat. A volley of machine gun fire spat from the Gatling into the tree line. Trent saw the fire was being returned; as quickly as it had dropped into the field, the gunship disappeared. The trees were still and silent.

* ━ ━ ━ ━ ━ ━ ━ *

Trent lay motionless for what seemed to be an eternity. The only sound was the flapping noise from the gunship's rotor system drifting in the distance; Trent wasn't sure when it became an echo and then a memory. He peeked through the weed tips and glimpsed the images of a dozen black-clad forms creeping into the field. Hunched at the waist like crouching tigers, the figures moved fluidly, like apparitions in a dream. The focus of Trent's vision shortened involuntarily to blades of grass, and the crouching forms seemed to melt into the blurred jungle.

The revolver remained in Trent's hand, but he kept his vision from it. On missions, he refused to carry a loaded gun, as he believed a thirty-eight would be of little use in the jungle. But he kept the revolver and the single bullet separately for a dreadful and solitary purpose—so he would never be taken alive by the enemy.

Trent lifted the revolver, resting the barrel beside his temple. Myriad thoughts passed through his mind, but mostly he remembered how he had taught many young pilots to continue piloting the helicopter no matter what the situation and never to surrender to fate, regardless how catastrophic the emergency or how imminent the crash. It was the same for him in his circumstance—he was unready to surrender control over the unfolding events.

Trent pushed his thoughts outward and the revolver away. The black-clad figures didn't seem to be moving, only growing. Their shadowy silhouettes widened until they appeared to fill the field. Mesmerized by the danger, Trent fought to steady the pace of his breath. In quick spurts he felt cold terror blanketing his body, and then calmness suddenly overtook him like a wave.

He forced his mind to focus on the repose. His heart rate slowed, and he became oddly fascinated by the notion that he may have sacrificed self-protection in favor of something nobler. He felt strangely purified, as if bathed in a cold crystal mountain stream, and for an instant, the fan-like churning of his emotions suspended.

In that moment of abandonment, Trent held a fleeting clarity of thought that, if lost, might take a lifetime to recapture. For the first time he felt the weight of the sins of war lifted from him; he embraced a restored innocence as if it were a child held to his breast. He clearly saw that he had fought the War in as good conscience as was manageable, doing nothing to shame himself—the shame laid with others who were half-a-world away. In free-fire zones he had refused to allow his gunners to fire when his instincts told him the intended targets included civilians. From villages under attack, he had evacuated innocent children. In raging battles, he had swooped into danger to pluck out the wounded. And in the forefront of his mind he had always held the lives of the crewmembers and soldiers that were entrusted to his care. He had never betrayed their trust.

In that instant Trent felt no guilt or sorrow or shame. Perhaps this realization was an awakening, Trent thought, and the culmination of his life. Maybe he had found peace at last, he considered, as his fingers tightened around the revolver.

Chapter seven

Through the Gap, north, and into the foothills of the Appalachian Mountains, sixteen-year-old Brandon Christy kicked a soccer ball with his instep, sending the sphere skidding across the roadway surface. The macadam scuffed hard against the smooth leather, and the resultant sound was dissonant, matching the boy's mood, which was as dark as his complexion. He trotted unsteadily, dragging the soles of his sneakers. His shirt fluttered open and untucked, and his head hung low.

With each arrival, Bran approached his home with increasing dread. The altercations between his mother and her longtime boyfriend Rayful Bigelow had become more frequent and increasingly violent. From an eighth of a mile away, Bran heard muffled and distorted sounds resonating from the small dreary trailer, like voices beckoning from a nightmare.

"Don't threaten me." Bigelow's voice had a distinctive nasal quality that provoked a visceral response in the pit of Bran's stomach. Bran could picture Bigelow's thin frame gliding, the way he did, as if surfing on a wave of slime.

Peg Christy's voice met Bigelow's with firmness and defiance. "It's not a threat. I'm telling you. If you don't stop involving the boy with your drugs, I'll call the cops."

"You'll get him busted too."

"Better now while he's sixteen than after he reaches eighteen. It won't go on his permanent record."

"You won't get your own kid busted."

"Then I'll find a way to get you without involving him. For God's sake, Rayful. Leave him out of it. Since the kid was fourteen, you've had him out in the middle of the night doing God knows what. He has no idea of right from wrong. How could he?"

"He just helps me grow a little weed in my Garden. That's not so bad. Just illegal. There's a difference."

Brandon knew Bigelow as part scavenger, part con man, part card shark, part entrepreneur, and part mad scientist—a little of everything, a lot of nothing. On the street, Bigelow's unheralded nickname was the Scrounger. For several summers, Bigelow enlisted Bran to help in his attempts to grow various strains of cannabis in a place he called his Garden, a well-hidden venue tucked deep in the mountain crevices. Together they hauled burlap bags filled with rich topsoil, fertilizer, bone meal, and various other nutrients to the Garden. The Scrounger's one successful harvest became his conceit, as the crop had been featured in extravagant photo layouts in various counterculture magazines. The work was backbreaking, and Bran fervently hated it, though it was not the physical labor he despised as much as the illegal fruit of the undertaking. In downtown Harrisburg, he had seen the impact of drug abuse upon the community, and it saddened him to contribute to the scourge. But the Scrounger chided that he had to help pay the bills, and tending toward a serious disposition, Bran reluctantly submitted.

The Scrounger had two new projects. In the first, he was soaking hundreds of Benzedrine inhalers in a vat of solvent stored in a metal shed behind the trailer. The product, Bigelow had explained to Brandon, would be a layer of methamphetamine he could skim from the mixture. He would sell this as speed or christen it with a new popularized name, Madonna perhaps, had it not been used already.

The Scrounger was also cultivating a reputation as a "cooker" of specialized drugs. At immense personal risk, he accepted one kilo of cocaine hydrochloride and a quarter-kilo of heroin to combine into a saleable potpourri-style product for a Harrisburg kingpin whose street name was Cruise. Bran knew the Scrounger didn't actually cook the drugs; the likelihood of a successful product from his efforts would have been slim. Instead, Bigelow took the bulk of the contraband on what he described as a business trip to Mount Cobb, situated in the Pocono Mountains mid-way between Harrisburg and New York, and returned with a different, rock-like product packaged in small plastic bags. The Scrounger claimed to have transformed the product from the cocaine and heroin.

Bran had seen crack, and these rocks bore a resemblance. But there were marked dissimilarities. The Scrounger explained away the differences, professing they were an incident to an improved production process. He dubbed the product Rocket Pack, and many from Harrisburg who had consumed the drug had raved about it. To date, it was his most successful pursuit.

As Brandon approached the trailer, the voices grated on his eardrums.

"And what did you do for his sixteenth birthday?" Peg scolded. "Tried to give him a quarter pound of dope to peddle to his friends. What kind of role model is that? Look at you. You never made it past the sixties."

"We don't live in the world as it should be according to Peg Christy," Bigelow said. "I tell you, the fact it's illegal don't mean it's wrong."

"It does mean it *will* ruin his life. Let him have his chance, Rayful. Please."

"I gotta get down to Whatta Deal. Meet a customer."

"Thank God I never married you, you has-been, no, you never-was."

"If you remember, I never asked."

Bran was midway down the tree-lined lane leading to the trailer. Through the screen door, he could see Bigelow's silhouetted hands sweep across his lanky body, waving off his mother's reproach.

Listen to her, Bran thought. Always trying to improve everything. With heavy thread, she futilely stitched daily at the furniture's gaping holes that reappeared overnight, and she hammered nails into things that were old and worn and useless. It was the same with the Scrounger. With hopefulness defying reason, she steadily tried to improve him, to fabricate a human being from what Bran regarded as nothing more than a wasted pile of flesh.

Two years earlier, at Peg's insistence, she and Brandon had moved from Hill Manor, a low-income housing project outside center city Harrisburg, to live in Bigelow's dilapidated trailer in the run-down country setting on the outskirts of Lykens, a small town due north of the Fort Indiantown Gap military reservation. At least here, Peg Christy had said, her son would not be surrounded by the utter hopelessness of others. But on that score, she had failed to take the Scrounger into account.

Bigelow did have one pursuit that appeared to be legitimate. On the outskirts of Harrisburg, he managed a used automobile dealership called Whatta Deal, where the owner only cared about the profits and allowed Bigelow to oversee the manner in which they were reaped. The Scrounger had boasted he would one day use the dealership for money laundering. At present, all he lacked was the money.

Stepping closer to the door, the Scrounger's form took on clarity and color. Brandon stared at the unkempt forty-five-year-old, his thinning, greasy hair drooping in a ponytail on his slender curved neck and his sunken eyes set in a hard gaze over rough stubble. When Bigelow turned toward him, Bran averted his eyes in disgust. At least with his own father, the mental image was blurred, fragmentary, and capable of being fleshed out with comforting details, not soaked in tangible baseness. Bran pushed through the lithe branches of an umbrella-shaped weeping willow. He flopped against the trunk, hunched his shoulders, and pulled his fists to his ears.

"Tell the kid to get down to the lot by six," Bigelow said, brushing crumbs from his T-shirt. He straightened the unbuttoned Hawaiian shirt overtop and puffed futilely on a crushed cigarette.

Peg's voice seeped suspicion. "What's he doing on the lot?"

"You know. Sweeping up. Washing cars. Taking care of business. Helping pay the bills."

Peg hesitated. "Well, I don't care for your hobbies or your business."

The Scrounger released a cackle that sent chills up Bran's spine. Through the screen door, Bran saw the shadow of Peg's figure over the stove, touching something to a flaming gas burner.

"Go ahead and laugh, bastard," Peg said. "Laugh while Rome burns. Burn, baby, burn."

"My High Times magazines!"

Heavy sounds of a struggle filled the air, and Bran jumped quickly to his feet. Peg burst through the screen door, followed closely by Bigelow. She waved a handful of magazines, their edges touched with fire, and she scurried around the side of the trailer. The breeze fanned the dancing flames. The Scrounger continued close behind.

"Last November's issue is in there. You're a dead bitch," he whined. "Has the picture of my award-winning sativas."

Peg rushed for the metal shed. She held the flaming magazines high above her head like some medieval torch-bearer carrying purifying flames.

Words of warning rose in Bran's rigid throat. He remembered the Scrounger's attempts to conjure methamphetamine. The chemicals, the solvent... probably flammable. Maybe explosive.

Peg threw aside the metal sliding door. She tossed the burning magazines into the shed and slammed the door closed. She spun to face Bigelow. "You can take your sativas and shove—"

Frozen in mid-step, Bran heard no more words. His hands stretched forward, and his scream of alarm was drowned in a crushing instant of exploding sound and blinding light. Heat roared past his body. Bran's eyes involuntarily closed, but a vision burned through the darkness of closed eyelids.

The shed splintering instantaneously. Its four walls collapsing outward, slamming against the ground and recoiling high into the air, only to fall again amidst dancing flames that sprang from the ground. His mother's form disappearing in convulsing waves of light, sound, and motion. The Scrounger's body appearing to take flight, spinning as it fell.

The remnants of light imploded into blackness.

⁜

On the south side of the Gap, Mark Ashford stood eight feet above the macadam hardstand atop the roof of a Huey, his back silhouetted against a clear, awaiting sky. He leaned on the mast and inspected the rotor system's collage of interconnected swash-plates, control tubes, rings, bolts, and wire safeties. He silently named each part of the assembly as he examined it. Crawford stood on the macadam beside the Huey, scanning notations in the logbook.

In anger, Ashford had told Nick Trent he could fly—now it was time to prove it. But to realize the dream, to achieve mastery over the helicopter, he would first have to conquer each of a hundred details: aerodynamic studies, meteorological analysis, mechanical processes, pre-mission planning, preflight, radio procedures, and control technique. It seemed he would also have to surmount an invisible barrier separating him from the men he would have as mentors.

One of these men strolled along a row of diagonally parked Hueys. Nick Trent was accompanied by Jesse Morrow, and he beamed as he conversed with her.

Crawford called the pilots' names in greeting, and Trent and Morrow approached the open Huey. Listening to conversations among the warrants, Ashford had learned more about Morrow. She had been a homemaker married to a helicopter pilot stationed at Fort Eustis, Virginia. Three years ago, her husband was killed in a horrible helicopter crash, the kind resulting in a sealed coffin. The official report cited pilot error as the cause. For reasons the warrants debated, after a short period of grieving, Morrow undertook warrant officer training and became a U.S. Army aviator. For six months she flew with the D.C. National Guard, but two months ago, she transferred to the Pennsylvania Guard and had become a coveted addition to Company B. Ashford marveled at how little she displayed the wounds of her past.

Morrow gazed up at Ashford and winked. "Going out with the new LT, Kevin?" she said to Crawford.

"The basic orientation," Crawford said.

"In that case, we'll make sure to stay clear of Central Pennsylvania," said Trent, his tone more abrasive than his words.

Morrow smiled disarmingly, ignoring Trent's antagonism. She said she had heard that flying in the Northern Training Area would be interesting, but she didn't mention the conversation with Spencer. Trent quickly shepherded his copilot down the row of parked Hueys, as if trying to keep her to himself. A current of air from behind pressed Morrow's flight suit to her body, and Ashford could not help but notice that her seat was filled nicely.

Crawford guided Ashford through a flight safety briefing, pointing out the locations of safety equipment, including the emergency beacon, which was housed in a rectangular box the size of a slim telephone and attached to the helicopter bulkhead behind the pilot seat. Crawford noted that the beacon was triggered by the force of a crash, automatically transmitting a homing signal. The two pilots climbed into the cockpit, and Crawford read from a laminated checklist as Ashford checked the circuit breakers, switches, and gauges and readied the helicopter for engine start.

"I'll be your fireguard," said Crawford, dropping from the Huey and setting his helmet on his head, smoked visor down. "Watch the EGT closely for a hot start. This time of year, it can come up on you pretty suddenly." Crawford pulled a fire extinguisher from beside Ashford's seat and stood forty-five degrees off the nose of the Huey.

Ashford felt sweat trickle from beneath his helmet. He had become familiar with the Huey start-up procedure in flight school but had flown Blackhawks for the past few months and was somewhat unsure of himself. He reviewed the procedure in his mind—pull the trigger, watch the exhaust gas temperature, and bring her slowly up to flight idle. Only one engine, not two like the Blackhawk. Should be easy, like riding a bike. Crawford is waiting. Well, here goes.

Ashford eased the trigger to the rear. His eyes skimmed the instrument panel and the consoles, their presentation of switches, knobs, and gauges elegantly simple to the experienced pilot but endlessly complex to the unlearned. The high-pitched sound of the straining battery resonated through his earphones and obliterated the steady pounding of his heart. The igniters clicked, the engine let out a low moan, and the needles bounced to life. The rotor blades started a laborious turn, straining to overcome their own inertia; they made a sweeping sound that swelled as they gained speed. The blades slid by the windscreen rhythmically, until they blended into a translucent disk. When the torque meter reached forty percent, Ashford released the trigger and let out a sigh of relief.

Crawford climbed in beside Ashford and plugged his mike plug into its receptacle, simultaneously scanning the engine gauges. "Good job. Just don't forget to yell clear before you pull the trigger."

Ashford winced. Rookie mistake, he thought.

They completed the engine run up, and Crawford called out the pre-takeoff check.

"RPM?"

"Sixty-six hundred."

"Systems?"

"In the green."

"Avionics?"

Ashford paused.

"It's okay," said Crawford. "I've got them set. Crew, passenger, and mission equipment?"

"Everything's all strapped in."

"Let's take her out." Crawford flipped his radio selector switch from intercom to the UHF frequency. "*Muir ground, Bandit Two-Three, Alpha Four, VFR Northern Training Area, with the numbers. Request clearance to hover.*"

"*Bandit Two-Three. Altimeter two niner niner eight, winds two-four-zero at seven. Clear to hover taxi short of west pad.*"

Crawford folded his hands across his chest. It was common for instructor pilots to feign impassivity to demonstrate confidence in a student. Ashford knew Crawford was watching over the helicopter like a hawk but was grateful for the gesture.

As Ashford lifted the collective lever, the rotor blades increased pitch, no longer feathering through the atmosphere but biting hard into it, straining to create lift to prompt the bulky heap of metal to defy gravity. The blades coned skyward under the stress. Finally, almost magically, the Huey creaked to life. Slowly the aircraft rose from the ground, right skid first, teetering for a second. Then the nose slid right, scraping the left skid hard across the cement pad. Ashford struggled with the pedals to adjust the thrust of the tail rotor to compensate for the increased torque generated by the rotor system. His nervousness translated through the controls into the movement of the helicopter; he felt as if he were juggling ten balls at once.

"Relax, Mark," Crawford said. "I have the same trouble sometimes. Everyone does. Often it takes a conscious effort to make yourself relax. Try to make your wrist feel light and direct the cyclic with slow, smooth movements. Nick likes to tell his copilots to handle the cyclic as if they were squeezing a woman's breast."

I wonder what he's telling W-Zero-One Morrow to squeeze, Ashford thought. The shift in focus of his attention quelled his jitters. The Huey steadied, and Ashford furtively dipped his head toward his shoulder in a futile effort to clear the dampness from his cheek.

With permission from the tower, Ashford maneuvered to the West Pad and landed facing west. The pilots ran through another pre-takeoff check and called the tower for takeoff clearance. On takeoff, the Huey lumbered forward. Grass clippings swirled like confetti, the nose dipped, and the skids skimmed a few feet off the ground. As the Huey gained airspeed, it shuddered.

"I'm going into instructor pilot mode," Crawford said. "Explain what's happening to the helicopter aerodynamically."

"We just passed through translational lift. The rotor blades outran their own turbulence and gained efficiency, hence the shudder followed by increased lift."

"Good. We'll review the traffic pattern, and I'll show you some ground references. This is your orientation flight, so relax. You're not being graded."

No, just checked out, Ashford thought. He knew how important initial impressions were, and he wanted to make a good one.

Ashford lifted the collective to climb faster, and the helicopter swelled into the wind. Piloting a Huey was easier than flying a Blackhawk, and for his level of experience, Ashford excelled at both. But there were so many things to remember, everything requiring concentration and focus, nothing easy yet, nothing completely second nature.

Their takeoff path paralleled a forested mountain ridge out the right door that bounded the Appalachian Mountains. Telephone poles appeared in the windscreen and then slid beneath the instrument panel. Dingy white buildings appeared and then disappeared too, and a trailer court replaced them, buttressed by a wide-open grassy field and an azure lake.

Crawford introduced Ashford to the airfield's traffic pattern: pass the trailer court that skirted the Fort Indiantown National Cemetery, a manicured field populated with tombstones arranged in geometrically perfect patterns; bisect several clusters of the white-shoebox structures; and arc around the water tower onto final approach to return to the airstrip. As they flew, the captain mentioned some of the area's history: the Susquehannock Indians, the earliest known inhabitants; the use of the Fort to train replacement troops for assignments in Korea in the 1950s; its service as a holding area for Vietnamese refugees in the early 1970s; and a similar housing of Cuban refugees later that decade.

"Most of the buildings were built in the late thirties," Crawford said. "My Dad got his final training here before his deployment to Europe in World War II. He calls that the Good War."

"I don't think there are any good wars," Ashford said.

"Maybe not, but there are necessary wars."

Does he think Vietnam was a necessary war, Ashford thought. Despite his curiosity, he didn't allow the question to pass through his lips. He reminded himself that Vietnam would be a sensitive subject with these men. Although he was intensely curious, it seemed best to let the veterans speak about the subject if and when they wished.

"*Muir Tower, Bandit Two-Three. Turning final,*" Crawford transmitted.

"*Roger Bandit Two-Three. Cleared to land.*"

"Okay, Mark, the two white concrete pads north of the runway are East and West Pads. Line your approach up for the farthest, which is West Pad."

The two cement squares were aligned between the long macadam runway and the hard ramp that served as the resting place for dormant aircraft. The hangar and the administration building flanked the ramp. The tiny, still helicopters below seemed like tadpoles aligned and evenly spaced beneath the brick tower. Three Blackhawks stood along the western fringe of the hardstand. Ashford stared wistfully at the sleek, modern helicopters and sighed; it seemed he would not be flying them again for an eternity.

"Pre-landing check," Crawford said. "RPM sixty-six hundred, instruments in the green."

"Thanks." Having forgotten to call for the check, Ashford chided himself to concentrate.

Crawford complimented Ashford on the landing as the Huey touched down on the pad, bouncing only slightly. He suggested they head out through the Gap and into the Northern Training Area, and he called for clearance. Ashford lifted the Huey confidently from the pad and climbed and turned into the deep saddle cut into the mountain ridge.

The Huey pitched in the wind shunting through the Gap. The mountainside plummeted away into a broad river valley on the north side of the Gap. A sea of living green appeared, brimming with a thousand nooks and crannies and switchbacks and hidden draws longing to be explored. Forested mountain ridges stood up in lines, folded like carpet, seeming to rise and fall with an audible rhythm. Foothills were blown against the mountain-bases like snowdrifts, forming a rim for rolling meadowlands and populated valleys. Ashford knew that to the experienced pilots, the training area seemed small, but to him it was a vast adventure awaiting.

"I have the controls," Crawford said, gently taking them into his hands like a virtuoso would his instrument. "You were doing fine, but right now it's more important for you to take a look at the map and get a sense of the lay of the land out here."

As Crawford took the flight controls, Ashford felt the Huey suddenly tamed. The slackness he had fought disappeared into the silky, deliberate movements of Crawford's wrist, and the helicopter responded gracefully, man and machine seemingly in harmony. With his left hand, Crawford spread a topographical map over the center console.

"We have about twenty-three square miles up here. We're authorized to train at low-level, contour, and nap-of-the-earth altitudes. But we must pay close attention to heed all the No-Fly Areas circled in red on the map."

"There's one at twelve o'clock, about two miles."

"Good. Most of the areas have concentrated populations. A few are only one or two houses where someone called in about the noise."

"We had a similar set-up at flight school. Every once in a while we flew over a house by accident. The instructors used to just shrug and say 'sound of freedom.'"

Crawford smiled. "That happens sometimes up here too. But down at Rucker, the local economy depends on the base more and people here aren't quite as accommodating. We try to be good neighbors. I'm going to contour level now, about sixty knots, and I'll stay about fifty feet above the trees. Navigate me to LZ Lois by the route marked in blue on the map."

Ashford watched the needle on the airspeed indicator slide from ninety to sixty knots. The Huey dropped, the ground grew and spread beneath them, and the trees sped by in a blur.

Crawford crossed the parallel ridgelines, following the terrain. He dropped steeply into a valley on the north side of the first ridge and then rose suddenly in a draw up the adjacent ridge. He banked and dipped into a wide, flat-bottomed trough carved into the top of the ridge and fell away into the next valley, untouched by marks of civilization. Ashford lowered his head to glance at the map. Brown contour lines swirled across the green paper, depicting the varying elevations of the landscape. Open fields were designated by first names, mostly women's, as landing zones, LZs, available for practice approaches. Colored lines connected the landing zones, signifying designated flight routes. When Ashford lifted his gaze outside the Huey, he had lost his orientation.

"You need to find a known point," Crawford said. "First rule of navigating and the rule when you get lost: Always go back to a known point."

"Uh, can you take me back to the saddle in Stony Mountain?"

"You got it."

"*Hey, Kevin.*" Ashford recognized the wry inflection in Trent's tone.

"*Bandit Two-Three here. Go ahead,*" Crawford transmitted.

"*We're a flight of four and Gene out your left window.*"

Five Hueys were rippling over a tree-topped ridgeline to Ashford's right rear, four grouped in a close formation, the fifth lagging behind almost as if it were a separate flight.

"*Roger,*" said Crawford, when he spotted the Hueys.

"*I noticed you're still right-side up,*" Trent said. "*Guess you haven't let the LT touch the stick yet.*"

"*Your checkride is due the fourth quarter, eh Nick?*" Crawford replied. "*Your current demonstration of radio procedures doesn't bode well.*" Crawford turned to Ashford. "Even though we have common frequencies separate from air traffic control, we practice tactical radio procedures, namely radio silence, except when necessary for position reports and flight safety. But we have a few smartasses who just won't play."

"Why did he say a flight of four and Gene?"

"In Vietnam, a Huey piloted by a young lieutenant flared too steeply on an approach to a hot LZ. Gene Winston was close in formation behind, and he flew right into the lieutenant's tail rotor. Both helicopters crashed, and Gene spent a week in the jungle with the ground unit until he could be flown out. Since then, he always flies trail and maintains a healthy distance. It's a running joke that, even when he flies in formation, his helicopter qualifies as a separate flight."

"*Army aircraft operating in the vicinity of Indiantown Gap,*" said a new unfamiliar voice. "*This is Life Lion on guard frequency, Manada Gap, fifteen hundred feet. I have an emergency pickup approximately a klick southeast of Lykens. Appreciate it if you boys would give me some room. It's a little hard to see down there with your green machines.*"

"Aircraft at twelve o'clock high," Ashford said.

"Good call," said Crawford. "That's a helicopter ambulance out of Hershey Medical Center. Mike Daniels is the pilot. He used to be a member of Company H."

Crawford flipped his selector switch to UHF guard frequency, a special band reserved for emergencies. "*Life Lion. This is Bandit Two-Three. Operating single ship in the vicinity of the Ranger Pad. There's a flight of five Hueys seven or eight klicks to our southwest. Will clear the area to the west and be operating out of LZs Lois and Priscilla. You listening second platoon?*"

"*Roger. Clearing to the west. Hey, Mike.*"

"*Hey, Nick. Thanks much, Kevin.*"

"*Just say so if there's anything we can do,*" Crawford said.

"*Pray on this one, I guess. There's been an explosion of some kind at a trailer site with a couple of people nearby. Dispatch said it looks pretty bad, at least for one of them.*"

"My dad used to say they never send Life Lion up unless someone has one foot in the grave and the other on a banana peel," Ashford said.

Crawford remained silent. He dropped the Huey onto the treetops and flew to the V-shaped end of Broad Mountain, bringing the helicopter to a high hover where the terrain dropped off steeply into the valley below. The leaves beneath them fluttered and rippled outward in broadening concentric circles.

"The long flat town is Lykens," Crawford said.

"Look there," Ashford said. "Life Lion is going in just past the wooded area south of the town. You have the smoke?"

"You've got sharp eyes," Crawford squinted at the tiny blur that was the helicopter landing in the distance. "That's one of our No-Fly Areas."

"Guess they can bend the rules just this once."

Crawford sat silently, hovering, watching for a minute until the Life Lion helicopter landed in a swirl of brown dust. Then he banked the Huey and accelerated. "Okay, I'll show you a few LZs, and we'll go back and practice ground maneuvers at the base."

Taking turns at the controls, the pilots twisted their way up and down the river valleys and in and out of tight fields. Ashford sensed his confidence growing. Crawford gave him the controls coming out of a tight landing zone situated on the western edge of the Northern Training Area, and Ashford brought the Huey to contour altitude about fifty feet above the treetops. Peering west into the valley before him, in the distance below, he spotted a Huey hovering low over the skeletal frame of a house under construction. "Who's that?" he asked.

Crawford's smoked visor covered his eyes, but Ashford recognized the disgust in his scowl. "If I'm not mistaken, that's your Battalion Commander checking the progress on the home he's building. All I can say is the Northern Training Area ends right about here, and low-level flight is prohibited outside the Northern Training Area."

"So he's illegal?"

"No, he's a colonel." Crawford crossed his arms over his chest. "Come on. Let's head back to Indiantown Gap."

Ten minutes later, on the parking pad, Ashford lowered the collective steadily and the Huey settled smoothly to the ground. Crawford patted Ashford on the shoulder and told him to tie the rotor blade down and that they would debrief in his office. He departed the Huey. Ashford held the controls until the main rotor blade wound to a stop. Then he stepped from the helicopter, threw his head back, and breathed deeply. He had not made a single major mistake, and he knew that at least Crawford didn't consider him a danger. With any luck, the captain might think he had potential.

·•·————·•••·————·•·

Brandon Christy regained consciousness slowly, his senses awakening one by one. First he felt a steady vibration coursing through his body, and then he smelled kerosene. A whining sound crescendoed like the tone in a hearing test, transforming to a continuous hum that seemed to envelope him.

Bran tried to move his arms, but they were pinned in place, and he couldn't raise his torso. He willed his eyes open, blinking away sweat and grime and blood; through the sticky mixture he saw silver metal glimmering all around him. Bran turned his head into a gushing wind. The dream-like aerial view made little sense at first. He saw drifting green cornfields, ambling country roads, and clusters of houses the size of matchboxes. His gaze settled upon a modern cement building to his forefront, rectangular in appearance, with bands of square, black windows ringing the structure. Comprehension began to take shape—the building was the Hershey Medical Center. His memory reawakened in the same fashion as his hearing.

The ground rushed up to meet him as the Life Lion helicopter landed on a cement pad on a flower-lined flat about fifteen yards from the hospital's auxiliary emergency entrance. White-suited attendants rushed to the opposite side of the helicopter, their uniforms billowing like marshmallows. Momentarily, Bran glimpsed a silver gurney speeding away from the helicopter, flanked by jogging attendants.

He struggled in his berth. The engine noise waned and the swirling air subsided. Unexpectedly, a large hand squeezed his shoulder. It was the pilot. He was tall and wore a thick mustache; his hair was gray-brown and curly with silver streaks spiraling wildly throughout. He wore a blue, coverall-style flight suit and spoke with a deep and calming voice, but his face seemed wooden.

"Easy, kid," Mike Daniels said. "You've been beat up pretty good."

"My Ma?" Bran asked with wide eyes.

"They just took her inside. She's getting the medical help she needs. Just relax."

Bran strained hard against the straps. "I need to see her."

"I'm supposed to wait for the attendants."

"Please."

Daniels seemed to connect with Bran's resolution; it appeared to be something he respected. "All right." Daniels unhooked the heavy nylon straps from around Bran's chest. "I'm not supposed to do this, but—"

Before Daniels could finish his sentence, Bran sat upright. He flung his legs off the stretcher.

"Easy, easy," Daniels said. "One step at a time."

Bran dropped to his feet. He put one foot forward and then sagged. Daniels was there behind him, steadying him with big strong hands. Daniels didn't carry him but merely prevented him from falling, giving Bran the time he needed to regain balance. This gentle but firm support was more than the Scrounger had rendered in five years.

"Thanks." Bran looked at the big pilot, silhouetted against the sleek blue-and-white chopper, with the admiration of a child staring into the eyes of a soot-covered fireman.

"I want you to see your mom, kid, but I got my job to think about. You're supposed to go in flat on your back, but I'm willing to walk you. You have to stay with me though, and we can't go busting in on the doctors. We won't be helping if we get in the way. I can check on your mom first and then get you in to see a doctor. But we do this my way. Deal?"

"Deal." Bran accepted the pilot's extended hand.

Glass doors slipped aside, and Daniels hurried through with the boy leaning on his side. Two attendants appeared in a corridor, rolling an empty gurney. Bran glanced at Daniels, and the pilot nodded. Obligingly, Bran straightened his tattered shirt, sat on the padded table, pivoted, and lay down. An attendant draped a red fabric strap across Bran's waist, but Daniels waved him away. The pilot told Bran to wait while he went to learn of his mother's condition, and he had been gone for several minutes when Rayful Bigelow rounded the corner. The Scrounger appeared filthier than usual, older, and frightened.

"How's Ma?"

Bigelow's neck snapped to each side and then centered itself. "Haven't heard nothing yet. Can't do anything for her now anyway. Look, coupla cops have been asking about me, and I think I'm gonna split. I have to ask you to do some things—"

A young police officer in a black-and-gray uniform overtook Bigelow from his rear. "I'd like to have a few words with you. Just came from your place."

Bigelow backed away from the officer. "Lost everything in the shed, huh?"

"Not quite everything." The officer pulled an envelope from his shirt pocket and flopped it onto the gurney. The contents spilled: charred white powder in melted plastic.

"What's that?" Bigelow set his eyes wide.

"Cocaine, I'm guessing. I'll need to take you to the sta—"

"Not mine—"

"You have the right to remain—"

"You're not listening. Must belong to the kid. Huh, Bran? Fess up here. What the hell's going on?"

"—anything you say can and will be used—"

"All right, take it easy. Just give me a minute with the kid. My girl's in bad shape."

The officer's expression remained implacable. "Two minutes," he said. The policeman walked to the end of the corridor where he was joined by another officer; both stood poised within eyesight.

The Scrounger's head snapped again, though this time not from wariness but apparently from anxiety or exasperation. "Listen good, kid. This may be the last time I can talk for a while. Get up to the Garden every three days it doesn't rain and open the irrigation channels for a half-hour. Make sure you're not followed. There are some nitrogen supplements in the storeroom at Whatta Deal. In a week, put 'em in the soil, not too many. And pinch back the female plants to keep them from flowering so the resin builds up in the leaves. After that, get some bone meal up there. And if Cruise calls from the Burg, tell him I'll be a little late fixing up the next batch of Rocket Pack."

"You don't give a damn about Ma."

"Sure I do. You'll take care of her too."

Bran averted his eyes, and Bigelow grabbed him by his shirt. "Look here, runt. I was close to a real score, real close—" Bigelow glanced at the policemen starting toward him. He released the boy and raised his hands in an *everything's-okay* gesture.

"You got to be a man and do these things so we can get some bucks rolling in," Bigelow said. "Know how much this will cost? To take care of her? Get her the right doctors, the right medicine?"

"No."

"I tell you it'll cost plenty. And you have to help find a way to pay, you understand?"

"I understand."

"Know how important my Garden is to me?"

"I know."

"This business with Cruise is ten times the deal. Talk real nice to him. Tell him it'll be soon. Buy me some time. Get him to rest easy. Got it?"

"I got it." Bran wanted nothing to do with the Scrounger's pursuits, legal or illegal, but Bigelow touched a chord with his reference to the hospital bills. Bran considered the equipment, the space, and the staff. It would be expensive.

The officer stepped down the corridor, clearing his throat. "Let's go, Bigelow."

"Do a good job?" said Bigelow.

"Sure, Rayful," Bran whispered.

The officers grasped each of the Scrounger's arms, and he limped down the corridor with an unsteady gait that seemed more a matter of intention than injury. Midway down the hall he halted. He twisted his waist to face Brandon and gave a thumbs-up signal.

Bran turned away. Daniels was standing beside the gurney. Bran's eyes met the pilot's, and he saw concern penetrating the solemnity. Daniels was close enough to have overheard at least the latter part of the conversation, and he must have seen Bigelow with the police escort. But Bran was too preoccupied to be embarrassed by the Scrounger. "How is she?"

"She has a concussion and was burned pretty badly, son, but the doctor has a lot of hope. I've seen him work before, and I trust him. He's one of the best."

"Can I see her?"

"Maybe soon. Right now we have to let the doc do his job. Let's you and me go over some paperwork for the nurses. Could be useful to your mom." Daniels asked a number of standard questions: biographical information, medical history, and insurance. Then he asked if any relatives should be notified.

"She just has her boyfriend," Bran said.

"Guy that was here?"

Bran turned his eyes to the floor.

Daniels nodded sympathetically. "Any other kin?"

"She has a brother."

"Know his name?"

Bran shrugged. "Last name is Christy."

"How about his address?"

"No."

"What about a phone?"

Bran shook his head.

Daniels laid the metal clipboard on the gurney at Bran's feet and rested his hand on the boy's shoulder. An attendant gestured. Daniels cleared his throat. "They'll have a doctor look at you now," he said. "I'm on call, so I have to go. But I want you to have my card. I'd like to talk to you again. Maybe there's something I can do. Give me a call in a day or two?"

Bran offered no reply, but Daniels gave him his card. The attendant wheeled the boy into the corridor, leaving Daniels standing in the hallway, with his brow furrowed.

"Soldier Man," Brandon called, and Daniels cocked his head.

"Her brother. He called once and kidded with me that he's the Soldier Man. His name is Deric. Deric Christy."

Chapter eight

Alone in the jungle, Trent continued to toy with the idea of death as the enemy was overtaking him. Suddenly though, his breath quickened, and the clamminess overtook him again. The fragile trance was broken. He was no philosopher or guru or saint, he thought. He was just a pilot, and one presently without means to practice his craft. If he had finally found peace, it was a consolation for which he had no time.

Charlie was close, and he had to move. He had to get into the trees.

Without warning, a gunship knifed through a downwind break in the trees, banking hard to the south and spitting fiery sparks into the southern tree line. The creeping tigers turned into scattering ants in the wake of its fury. The diversion was all Trent needed. He ignited and rolled into the western tree line. Trent ran fifty feet into the jungle and halted, resting with his back against a tree.

Sweat poured from his face. He heard the gunship engaging the Viet Cong again. Then the helicopter crossed directly over his head; he could feel the breeze from its rotor and the heat from its engine. The flapping noise steadied, as if the gunship were hovering over the trees. Trent couldn't see through the jungle cover, but he knew it was impossible for Song to hover with the weight of the troops he had taken on, without the benefit of the cushion of air provided by a close proximity to the ground. Trent hadn't seen any clearings to the west. Yet, he heard the steady throbbing.

Trent didn't take the time to debate with himself the impossibility of a rescue. He broke into a run, charging through choking walls of vines and underbrush, pushing on toward the blaring engine. In another forty yards, it came into sight.

The gunship was hovering sideways and descending into an area where the trees were thin. The whirling rotor blades were sawing through the treetops, violently pitching sticks down; the impact sounded like the chopping of a dull axe. Trent admired Song's vertical technique. He knew the rotor blades would be ripped apart if Song tried to horizontally lower the gunship into the break.

When the gunship reached the center of the tree break, its skids were five feet from the ground. The brush was too thick for Song to descend any further. Trent reached up to grab a skid, and a hand extended down to meet his and hoisted him onto the cargo floor. There, Trent's eyes met those of Reggie Spencer; as Trent skidded on the smooth metal surface of the deck, he held Spencer's hand a moment longer than necessary. Trent smiled grimly, but only for Song, Spencer, and himself, since the gunship was empty. Song had unloaded the infantrymen to return light.

The gunship sailed straight up and accelerated quickly. As Song banked to the south, Trent climbed over the center console into the empty seat in the cockpit. His flight helmet hung from a hook, and his flight bag was on the floor beside the console; his steadfast crew chief had prepared for his arrival. Breathless and almost speechless, Trent plugged his microphone cord into the receptacle. "Thanks," he said, grinning like a child.

Song nodded and blinked through steam pouring from his skin. Trent recognized the pallor. "You hit?" he said.

"On the second run." Song leaned over the console, turning to expose his left side. Blood streamed from a fresh wound just above his collarbone, and deep gouges marked the chicken-plate armor. Although the well-placed rounds hadn't penetrated the armor, each had inflicted a crushing blow to Song's chest, and shrapnel from the ceramic armor had punctured his neck.

Trent reached across to remove the chicken-plate. He pulled Song's left hand from the collective, placed it over the wound, and grasped the helicopter controls. Without a word, Song released his grip as if in relief. The gunship glided over the treetops at 120 knots.

"The grunts?" Trent asked.

"Two kilometers south by southwest," Song said weakly.

They picked up the soldiers in a rectangular clearing, plainly selected by Song for use as a runway. The men carried Olofson's limp form on board.

As the gunship cleared the treetops, Trent banked hard to the east. His eyes flicked nervously to the fuel gauge. One hundred pounds of fuel remained, leaving him less than ten minutes in the air before the engine would starve. Trent accelerated to 118 knots, an airspeed that he calculated would allow the helicopter to travel a maximum range, given the heat and humidity. He quickly found the Dung River and dropped below the tree line into its bed.

<hr />

The Stray Wolf landing site first appeared to Trent as a lime-colored oval slat cut into the deeper shades of green of the surrounding jungle foliage. With closeness the ellipse widened and helicopters, fuel bladders, and equipment appeared, first as dots and blurs and then with the clarity of their own colors and shapes. Trent ignored the ground guide's frenzied hand signals and set up his approach straight to the ground on the first available inch of soil beneath him. The engine starved of fuel seconds before the gunship landed. Trent performed a smooth autorotation to the ground, bouncing his rump as if coaxing a slowing bumper car forward, until the gunship safely skidded to a stop. He leapt from the helicopter and crossed his arms over his chest in a signal to summon medics.

From beneath a camouflage canvas tent that was partially concealed in the tree line, a stretcher crew jogged forward, bending at the waist as they approached the slow turning rotors. The newly arrived infantrymen attended to their own wounded, but their injuries were minor compared to Olofson's. The group lifted the young warrant officer's unconscious body onto the stretcher, and the medics applied a pressure bandage to his buttocks and strapped heavy gauze in place with a belt. Then they disappeared into the medical tent.

Trent hurried across the front of the helicopter and carefully pulled Song from the pilot's seat. Cradling the youth in his arms, Trent gently laid him on the ground and lifted the helmet from his head. Song's straight black hair was wet and matted.

A second stretcher crew approached the two men. Trent told them that Song's ribs were likely broken. "Go easy putting him onto the stretcher," he said.

"It's a dink," said one of the medics. He was a thin man with striking blood-red hair and matching freckles that starkly contrasted with his fair skin. A green cloth tag identified him as Sergeant Bender.

From his knees Trent glowered at Bender. "No, he's a lieu-tenant, *Sergeant,*" Trent said. "You'll want to take good care of the lieutenant, don't you think *Sergeant?*"

"Okay, take it easy, Chief. We got hit pretty hard here this af-ternoon, and we think the bad guys are still out there. So we're all a little jumpy. We're getting the hell out of here as soon as we gas up two more flights out of Camp Kreider."

Trent eased his tone. "Alright, Bender, I'm a little jumpy too. But the fact is, this young fellow just pulled me from an early grave, and I'm looking to return the favor."

"Don't worry. He's lost some blood and looks like he's had the shit beat out of him, but I seen worse that made it. Besides these little guys can take just about anything."

Trent's eyes bored rivets into the sergeant's skull, and Bender recoiled. "Like I said, we'll treat him right, Chief."

The medics lifted Song onto the stretcher. Bender worked carefully: washing, cutting, and bandaging. With his glances, however, he revealed greater concern for Trent's reactions than for the care of his patient. After the medics carried the stretcher away, Trent stood for a few moments counting the fresh holes in the bullet-pocked gunship, in the windscreen, the underbelly, the blades, and the tail section. When he finished, he squatted like a watchdog at the foot of the gunship.

"Christ, Trent," a voice said, "decided not to wait for us to come back, eh?"

Trent stood slowly and turned to face Captain Harker. "Might've been a long wait."

"Fair enough, Trent. Fair enough. How's your copilot? What's his name?"

"Paul."

"Heard he got shot right in the ass. Hell of a thing, eh?"

"I was just going to check on him."

"You do that. From here on in, you, your crew, and me are in the Huey over by the medevac bird. Major Tarsavage says there's a battalion of VC on our western flank. Jet jockeys dumped a shitload of napalm on their location. They were only half dug in, and we think we hit 'em pretty hard. Little shits are still coming though, and we aren't standing to fight. We're hauling the ground crews out with us and taking as much gear as possible. Major Tarsavage is calling Roving Thunder to drop napalm on the equipment we have to leave behind. Aircraft's already preflighted. Just hold your finger on the trigger. I'll be in Operations. You see me coming, fire her up."

Trent nodded. "Look, one of the VNAFs pulled us out of the ambush. He took a couple of rounds and needs looking after. I want to make sure he's evac'd with us."

Harker turned and strode to the medic station. He stood over Song. His eyes ignored the startling wounds, and he stared into Song's face. Finally, wearing a self-satisfied grin, he turned to Trent. "The other VNAF bought it, eh?"

"You hear me, Captain? He needs to come with us."

Harker turned and started for the operations tent. The roar of an incoming flight of Hueys left his response barely audible. "Don't worry. I'll take care of it."

Olofson lay on a cot at the far end of the medical tent. He was unconscious, but Bender said his wound was no longer life-threatening. Trent sat by him. He retrieved his revolver from his survival vest and carefully plucked the bullet from the cylinder, tucking it into his pocket. The act contained the comfort of a ritual, signaling the passage of grave peril.

Trent moved to Song's cot. He bent to pick up a long weed and put the end in his mouth. Song was stripped to the waist and the blackness of his bruised torso was startling; the concussion from the bullets must have felt like a sledge hammer crushing his chest. Song opened his eyes.

"Pretty nice flying back there," Trent said.

"Cảm ơn."

Trent felt heavy sadness in the young pilot's voice as his lips formed the Vietnamese words for thank you. "Sorry about your wingman," Trent said.

"He was an old friend."

"I've lost friends here too."

"He planned to go your country. He said the captain arranged it."

"The captain?"

"Captain Harker."

Trent rubbed his cheek. "No offense, but that's damn strange. Harker's not the kind of man who does favors."

"That is what I said."

"He tell you why?"

Song blinked his eyes and gazed at Trent as if trying to see if this were a man with whom a confidence could be shared. Then he gave a look that said the secret should not be shared with anyone. "He did not tell me."

Trent studied the lines forming crow's feet on Song's face. "You have plans for after the War?"

Song hesitated. "Long ago, I worked the good earth. I still know how."

"We'll get you the hell out of here."

Song nodded sadly. "Cảm ơn."

"It'll be a good new life."

"It is very sad to leave so much behind."

"But you have so much ahead. Things will change quickly for you back in the World, but you'll get accustomed fast."

"You call your country the World, because it is what you know. To you, my country is strange and foreign. It is the same for me. To me, the World is here. Your country is a mystery to me."

"It just takes some time."

"Here in my country, we say oxen walk slowly, but the earth is patient. I have seen in your country that the earth is not so patient."

Trent's eyes lingered sadly on Song's wounds. "Hey," Trent said, "when we were on final approach, one thing I couldn't help notice. The fuel gauge bottomed out miles before we reached Stray Wolf. You didn't even blink."

"That chopper will fly two minutes after the gauge goes to zero."

Trent stifled a smile. "And the other couple of minutes?"

"The wind spirits are friendly today." Song smiled weakly.

Trent laughed. "You'll be all right, kid. I'll see to it, I will, I will. You just need a couple belts of rice mush and a good lay." Trent lifted his eyes to the field. Crew chiefs ran to the tree line and motioned to waiting troops. Spencer waved from the Huey assigned to their crew.

"Look, I've got to go. They'll put you in the medevac helicopter. You'll be right behind us all the way."

Moments later Trent sat in the copilot seat of the Huey, readying for takeoff. He carefully watched as medics loaded Olofson into the medevac helicopter. Harker approached from the rear, but he ran his index finger horizontally under his throat, signaling Trent to refrain from starting the engine. Harker loaded his own flight gear through the cargo door and then leaned into the cockpit.

"Major Tarsavage is having trouble coordinating napalm with Roving Thunder," Harker said. "Looks like we might have to shoot the area up with rockets."

"The VNAF isn't in the medevac bird yet," Trent said.

Harker peered inquisitively at Trent. "Don't worry. I'll take care of it."

Trent watched Harker disappear into the operations tent. Twenty minutes passed. A second flight of helicopters refueled and headed south in lowlands of the Dung River. Finally Harker emerged from the tent, this time walking briskly and nodding at Trent. He made a circling motion with his finger, and Spencer, who was standing outside the helicopter, gave a thumbs-up. Trent pulled the trigger. The engine whined and the rotor blades began their turn. The engine reached flight idle, and Trent checked the gauges. He looked over his shoulder and saw Harker talking to one of the medics. Trent tried to follow the movement of Harker's lips, but suddenly Harker moved rapidly toward the Huey. The medics lifted Song from a cot to a stretcher and loaded him into the medevac helicopter. Trent breathed relief.

Harker climbed into the Huey and pulled the straps around his shoulders. "Mission brief is simple," he said. "This is Exodus flight, flight of five, we're number five. Grunts are right behind me. Spencer will strap them in. From here, we just follow along to Vũng Tàu. Major Tarsavage is in Exodus One. I'll do the flying, since I don't have to lead the flight. Take your last photos on the way, 'cause there's no coming back."

Trent answered the radio check and watched the troops load. The four Hueys before them lifted smoothly from the field. Harker followed about eighty feet behind.

Trent turned to the field for a final look, and movement caught his eye. Two soldiers carried a stretcher from the medevac bird. Song's motionless body lay on the green canvas. The medevac helicopter lifted from the ground, but the slight, prostrate body remained helpless and alone in the field below.

Trent put his hands firmly on the controls. "I got it."

"The hell you do," Harker said assuredly, though his grip on the controls loosened with the force of Trent's command. "What's wrong with you?"

"They just pitched the VNAF out of the medevac bird." Trent's voice was as tense and determined as his grip on the controls.

"No they didn't. Why would they? We can't go back. We're already over gross."

"Seems like you're always over gross when you're turning your back," said Trent. As Trent rolled level on short final for the field, thick rods of fire shot across the Huey's nose.

Trent tensed reflexively and then leaned the Huey on its side to evade the rocket fire. A shark-shaped Cobra gunship crossed their path. A fuel bladder set against the western tree line erupted into a ball of fire. Trent circled to reestablish his approach.

"*Sorry, Nick,*" the Cobra pilot transmitted. "*I didn't see you. What the hell are you doing?*"

"*I'm on short final. We left one wounded behind.*"

"*Roger. Charlie's almost to the western tree line. I'll give cover.*"

"*Negative, negative. You hear me negative,*" Major Tarsavage transmitted from the lead helicopter. "*This is Exodus leader. Snakes are to hit the second fuel bladder now and join the formation pronto. Exodus Five, get your ass in formation.*"

"I have the controls," Harker said, lightly but meaningfully shaking the oversized joystick rising vertically from between his boots.

Trent jerked the dual flight controls hard, and the Huey shuddered violently. "Ever hear of blue blades?" he said, alluding to mast separation, bane of a Huey pilot. "You know, one blew east, one blew west."

Chapter nine

A blanket of haze hung low over the flight deck at Fort Indiantown Gap. The Sunday morning sun hovered a quarter-way along its journey, burning the shape of a dull yellow globe into the opaqueness. Ashford stood on the hardstand. He had resolved to speak with Nick Trent about his attire and attitude before the end of weekend drill, and the present seemed as good a time as any.

Ashford completed a walk-around of his assigned Huey. He watched Trent sitting expressionless on the skid of an adjacent Huey, his face buried in his paperback. Jesse Morrow reclined on the bench seat above him, humming an unrecognizable tune. "Looks like we'll probably get off the ground before ten," said Ashford, his face uplifted to the sky.

Trent peered up from his novel. "In the civilian world we'd be good to go now."

"Visibility's a little low for me too, LT," Morrow said, pulling herself up. "You two hear about the explosion in Lykens yesterday?"

"Just what we heard from Life Lion yesterday," Ashford said.

"A woman is in critical condition at Hershey Med," Morrow replied. "Then get this. They say a guy was making speed. Cops found cocaine too."

"I thought nothing ever happened in quiet little Lykens," Trent said.

"My hometown," said Morrow. "I'm just as surprised as you are. The lady may die."

"Only the good die young," Trent said.

"That's why you'll be around a long, long time Nick," said Captain Crawford, stepping around the nose of the Huey.

"I have to stick up for my pilot in command," Morrow said. "Nick's a very good pilot."

"That may be," said Crawford, "but he's one hell of a rotten person."

"Saints are in heaven," said Trent.

Morrow laughed. "I'll take a good pilot any day."

Crawford gazed at Trent's uniform and seemed to lose his humor. "Nick, the two-piece uniform is no longer authorized. Why don't you check with supply and trade in for some brand new one-piecers?"

Trent raised his hand. "You suddenly the fashion police, Kevin? Two-piecers are cooler than the coveralls, and you can shed the top when the humidity reaches two hundred percent at AP Hill. I heard they're grandfathering them for the Guard."

"Funny the Battalion Commander didn't hear that."

"Screw the colonel."

"Look, Nick, I've got a sense of humor too. But I'm under pressure to pull off the best camp possible this year. We have to learn to play together if we're to get through without incident. And you know that Lieutenant Ashford will be answerable as your platoon leader."

Trent smiled, a grin of true amusement or true malice, and he turned to Ashford. "Luck, kid. They tell you what happened to your predecessor, what was his name? Witless?"

"Lieutenant Witmore," Crawford corrected.

"Yeah, Witless. He had the job of supervising me too. They grounded the dimwit after four months. Developed some sort of nervous twitch in his arm." Trent shook his left arm in a mock convulsive shudder.

"Lieutenant Witmore is on medical leave," Crawford said. "We expect him to return in a few months."

"Not to flying status," said Trent. "They don't put you back on flying status with a nervous condition. That leaves you and Dickless."

"Lieutenant Dickson." Crawford dropped his chin in surrender. "Just do us all a favor, Nick, and keep a low profile at camp."

"That's me, Kevin. Mister Woodwork."

Crawford resumed his stride toward the flight facility, and Ashford followed. "Thanks for the help," Ashford said. "I was just getting ready to say something to him about his attitude."

Crawford nodded and then flicked a questioning glance, as if assessing Ashford's determination and drawing no firm conclusion. Ashford asked if Trent was responsible for Witmore's condition.

"He put a lot of pressure on the kid," Crawford said. "Nick's an excellent pilot. Best we have. But like I've said, he'll buck you on the little stuff like the uniform and the haircut. And something runs deeper in him and a few other guys."

"A problem with authority?"

Crawford halted and turned to Ashford. "Some call it 'malicious obedience.' At times they'll follow orders literally to a point of abstraction, when it's bound to get people in trouble. They rely upon their experience to pull everyone out at the last minute."

"They'd sabotage a mission?"

"Not intentionally. But I've seen it go too far. Fifteen years ago two Cranes flew to our Carlisle training area for sling load training. The weather was bad, but the lieutenant in charge was insistent. He was also pretty shaky on his flying. Three seasoned warrants let him fly into a cloud."

"Guess he learned his lesson."

"He didn't have time to. The cloud ended in the side of a mountain."

Ashford winced. "That's the crash you mentioned yesterday."

"Company H lost a lieutenant and two good warrant officers, one warrant officer dead, another one who was in the second Crane quit the unit in shame or disgust. You heard him on the radio yesterday—the medevac pilot from Hershey Medical. Mike Daniels."

Ashford held the door to the administration building for Crawford. "I'm not one hundred percent sure I'm cut out for the leadership end of this," he said. "I signed up to learn to fly."

Crawford rolled his eyes. "You told us. Look, Mark, you're a smart guy. You've got a degree of basic common sense that's apparent from the way you handle yourself. That's something we've found lacking in some of the lieutenants we've had in the past. We have high hopes for you. But you'll need to learn to deal with the bullshit in your own way. And it won't help to whine about your flying time."

Ashford followed along, gazing at the tile floor. He knew he could excel at anything requiring only his own perseverance. Meeting general standards of the military was a matter of the utmost simplicity—he could shine his own boots to mirror finish, press his uniform, and demonstrate appropriate courtesies. He could progress in developing his individual flying skills at a rate much faster than the Army expected. But he could not dress Trent or shave him or muzzle him; Ashford had no idea how he could require Trent to comport with standards that appeared to be so foreign to his nature.

It seemed clear that to manage Trent's behavior, Ashford would have to learn more about the belligerent warrant.

———————————————————

The mid-morning briefing was bland and uninformative. Afterwards, Ashford set out for Company B Headquarters, a dilapidated white rectangle identical to the one he had witnessed in flames, as well as a hundred others Ashford had seen from the air.

Inside, the walls were incompletely sheathed in drywall and painted light green, and green metal desks crouched against the building's partially exposed, skeletal frame. The lights also seemed to glow green. Several young enlisted men roamed the office, and Ashford introduced himself to the first he encountered, asking to review Company B's personnel records. A sergeant guided Ashford behind a row of dust-covered file cabinets.

Ashford pulled a worn folder from a drawer labeled "T." He laid the folder on the table as he would antique porcelain, silently questioning his right to invade Trent's privacy. He reminded himself though that he was Trent's platoon leader and had every right to examine the man's record, particularly in light of his conduct. The young lieutenant unhooked the string clasp and lifted the cover. Glued inside the flap was a black-and-white photograph of Trent clad in a dress green uniform, a picture that must have been ten years old. Trent's failure to update the photo and his other records probably accounted for the fact that he was outranked by younger men. Even in the decade-old picture, the warrant's hair was unkempt, his mustache grew wild, and the medals pinned to his uniform didn't properly reflect citations contained in his record.

Ashford flipped through tattered papers, reading them with a fascinated reverence, like an archaeologist encountering an ancient script. Three combat tours in Vietnam. Medals including a Bronze Star. Supporting affidavits detailing multiple tales of bravery. An affidavit by an infantry colonel, whose unit Trent rescued after a failed combat assault on an enemy stronghold, as well as a glowing citation from a major, telling of Trent's flight into the heat of the battle to deliver much-needed supplies to his troops. The final affidavit was written by a man named Paul Olofson who appeared to have been Trent's last copilot in Vietnam. It said:

> I have been back from Vietnam for four months now and have been pleased to accept a direct commission to first lieutenant. As my first official duty as a commissioned officer, I wish to recommend that CW2 Nicholas Trent receive the Silver Star for selfless actions taken in our final flight. On April 2, 1972, my final mission in Vietnam, I was flying lifts as CW2 Trent's copilot. We were ambushed, and our Huey was crippled. Against the odds, CW2 Trent safely landed the helicopter, saving the lives of nine men. When it became apparent our rescue helicopter was overloaded, CW2 Trent disembarked and remained behind alone to face an advancing enemy. I was wounded on takeoff and have little recollection of what followed, but for the rest of my life I will never forget the unwavering bravery CW2 Trent displayed.

At the bottom of the affidavit, a handwritten note was stapled, saying:

Captain Harker:

Enclosed is a courtesy copy of my kudos for Nick. After I recovered from my wounds, I was transferred to Fort Rucker. I've been assigned to study helicopter-related War Crimes and have a personal interest in the Massacre at Ba Long. I would dearly love to see the reports of your investigation and get your personal insights. I'll contact you shortly.

1LT Paul Olofson

Ashford scanned Trent's military citations but saw no mention of a Silver Star. On the reverse side of the list, Ashford found an acknowledgment of Olofson's recommendation and a handwritten scrawl: *Further Consideration Refused by CW2 Trent.*

Ashford found the duty sergeant and asked him to make photocopies of the two documents. While the soldier stood over the copier, Ashford inquired if there were a way to locate people who had been in the service.

"If they're in the Guard or Reserves, we could track them down through main headquarters in Saint Louis. All the records are kept there. I could give them a call. Should be some unit drilling there this weekend."

"Great. See if you can find out where this Paul Olofson is."

The sergeant fingered the affidavit. "I can try, but this was twenty years ago."

Ashford returned to the file area and continued through the papers. A conspicuous lapse of ten years interposed between Trent's service in Vietnam and 1982, when he returned to the military in the Pennsylvania Army National Guard. Thereafter, Trent's evaluation reports were consistently mediocre, and all noted that Trent habitually tested the limits of authority. The only other common thread running through all the reports was the acknowledgment, sometimes grudging, that Trent was a pilot of the highest distinction.

The desk sergeant returned waving a yellow pad. "This Olofson's still in the system, Sir," he reported. "He's a major, the full-time instructor pilot for the 336th Medevac Detachment stationed at Stewart International Airport."

"Where's that?"

"It's a little over an hour's drive from New York City. Just north of West Point." The sergeant handed Ashford the copies of Olofson's affidavit and the accompanying note. Ashford studied them with reflection.

He had always wanted to visit West Point.

After closing Trent's file, Ashford pulled Morrow's narrow folder from the cabinet and set it open on the table. He refrained from leafing through the pages but only gazed at her picture, concentrating on the carefree expression she held for the photographer.

●—●———●—●●—●·———●—●

The afternoon's training was air assault operations. Crawford and Ashford flew the third Huey in a flight of five. They practiced all modes of flight, skimming low-level at ninety knots, slowing and banking and rolling with the contour of the land and then swooping down into wind-swept treetops to fly nap-of-the-earth. They orchestrated insertions into sprawling burnt-grass meadows and extractions from breaks in the forest in which they could barely hover vertically. When they returned to the flight facility, Ashford should have been utterly exhausted but instead was exhilarated for having spent the day in the helicopter.

Thirty minutes after they landed, Ashford stood at attention on the hangar floor in formation with the rest of the company.

Captain Jerome Zuckerman may not have been completely at home in front of the twenty-two warrant officers, thirty-five enlisted personnel, and four commissioned officers, but he showed no sign of unease. He was at once all ignorance and all confidence, a ball of unfocused bluster, destined for greatness among his peers and ridicule among his subordinates.

"Gentlemen," Zuckerman said, "I am under consideration to take the reins of Company B, Twenty-Eighth Aviation." Zuckerman paused as if expecting acknowledgment from his audience, although none was forthcoming. "As you know, we're facing a very important evaluation at camp. If I am selected for the honor, I intend to guide this company to a superior performance."

Someone farted. Intermittent chuckles followed, and voices buzzed softly. Crawford approached Zuckerman and whispered in his ear.

"Ah-hem," Zuckerman told the assemblage. "As I said, together we can defeat a mighty hoard."

"Hell's he talking about?" a voice whispered.

Zuckerman made an imprecise about-face, as if he didn't know in which direction to turn, and then he disappeared into the administration building. Crawford waited until the doors clanged. He stared at the assemblage, appearing troubled and worn.

"Our illustrious instructor pilots report we had a good day of training," Crawford said, his voice echoing off the high metal ceiling. "In four weeks, you'll need to report Friday night at six p.m. for annual training. I know some of you will have to find a way to leave your regular jobs early, but those are the Battalion Commander's orders."

"Asshole," a voice said.

Crawford continued with barely a pause. "Company B will be divided at camp this year. Sergeant Spencer will remain at the Gap with his maintenance team to conduct full Phase Maintenance on a Huey, tear her down to the bones and put her back together again with new parts. His group will set up camp on the other side of Peters Mountain. They're training here to have access to the hangar facilities. For the rest of us, if the weather cooperates, we'll embark for lovely AP Hill Friday night.

"This camp will be our toughest ever. The evaluators will be watching at every turn, and the colonel will be riding us to perform. Realistically, we may not completely live up to his expectations given our outdated equipment and the time constraints. But we'll all do our best, and that's all I can ask from any of you.

"One area where we're consistently weak is basic soldier skills. For two weeks, we'll need to think like soldiers. Some of us may think of it as a game, like passing a test. Others consider it preparation. I prefer to try to think of it that way. We are, after all, paid to be ready.

"You all know your flying. Let's try and score some bonus points on the other stuff. You know what I'm talking about. Shave, wear your hat, salute, and just generally pretend you don't have a stick up your ass. If I have to get down on my knees, I will."

"But he doesn't swallow," a voice said.

"That's it, fellas," Crawford said. "Godspeed."

The captain had barely finished his sentence before the pilots and enlisted men rushed past him, eager to catch up with their other lives.

Chapter ten

"Ever hear of blue blades?"

Ninety feet above Vietnamese soil, in the cramped cockpit of a Huey helicopter, Chief Warrant Officer Nick Trent and Captain Harrison Harker hunched side by side, each silently gripping his set of the dual flight controls, each desperately trying to override the other's movements. In the belly of the Huey, a half-dozen weary and sodden infantrymen rested against the U-shaped metal bulkhead. Two crew chiefs manned M-60 machine guns anchored to pylons ascending from the Huey's underbelly.

Trent pushed the cyclic control forward. Overhead, the blurred disk sketched by whirling rotor blades tipped forward, and the nose of the Huey canted with parallel form. The pressure Trent applied wasn't forceful, but it was steady and determined, as if he intended to press the cyclic until it fused to the instrument panel. Harker was quick to parry. He shifted his weight forward and cradled the cyclic with his right hand, hauling it aft with a force that was equally calculated and restrained. The Huey leveled.

Harker held the defensive crouch, waiting and watching. Then he furtively lifted the collective lever beside his left thigh, and the Huey swelled as if riding the curl of a whitecap. Sensing the control movement, Trent bore down hard on the collective lever beside his leg. The flattening pitch of the rotor blades caused the Huey to settle into level flight and cast off a hollow, throbbing resonance. The din sensitized Trent to the hundred delicately balanced metal parts spinning harmoniously above his head and the catastrophic result if their consonance were to be shattered by a wayward control movement. The exposed helicopter floated like a weighted balloon in a balmy breeze—an easy target for an unforgiving enemy.

Harker shook the cyclic gingerly. "Come on, Nick, give her to me."

Trent jerked the stick viciously. Above him the rotor head clanged against the mast. The Huey convulsed. Trent clenched his teeth to conceal an irrepressible shudder.

"Gawd!" Harker bellowed, bracing his shoulders against the seat back.

"One blew east, one blew west," Trent said, his brown eyes cold and belligerent.

Harker puffed, though he had not physically exerted himself. "Bastard," he said between breaths. "You're way over the edge, Trent. There are ten good men behind us. You can't risk their lives for one dead dink."

Tilting his head to the rear, Trent glimpsed the foot soldiers. Then he shifted his vision to the smoked-plastic chin bubble at his feet. Through its transparent contour he saw a motionless human figure on the ground below, centered in an abandoned open-field encampment, laying alone and helpless. "His name is Le Song. And he's not dead."

"Why else would medevac roll him out? Come on, give her to me now."

Trent felt a feather touch on his shoulder from behind. With a glance, he caught the eyes of Reggie Spencer, manning the machine gun behind him. Wordlessly, these familiar and steady orbs told Trent that he only had to say the word, and the encounter between the pilots would be ended, swiftly and finally.

Trent eagerly accepted the eyes' invitation. "Reggie, if this asshole doesn't let go in the next ten seconds, blow his head off with your thirty-eight."

A solid mass thudded against Harker's flight helmet. The captain's eyes bulged wide, windowing the shock of his imagination conjuring the details of a thirty-eight caliber revolver. Harker's muscles spasmed involuntarily. His clenched fists dragged the flight controls into the seizure. The nose of the Huey tipped skyward, and clouds sluiced across the windscreen. The fuselage bucked violently.

Trent scrambled to level the helicopter. In that moment, as he regained control and composure, he alone appreciated the irony. On what they calculated to be their last flight in Vietnam, in final retreat from a common foe, so near to sanctuary, he and Harker had turned against each other, as if consumed by some primal infatuation for a War they both truly abhorred. But the demented tone of his own voice shocked Trent. It seemed as if he watched from outside the Huey as another person clung to the controls and rocked the Huey defiantly and then ordered Spencer to shoot Harker if he didn't surrender the helicopter.

With the metal pressed hard against his flight helmet, Harker lifelessly dropped his hands from the controls.

Tarsavage's voice filled Trent's earphones. "*Trail aircraft, get back in formation now goddammit!*"

Trent fought to maintain poise and perspective. He would try to reason with the Savage. "*Exodus One, this is Exodus Five. We've left a man behind—*"

Harker cut Trent out. "*Exodus Leader, it was the VNAF. The medics rolled him out on their way up. He must've been dead. We're taking fire.*"

"*Exodus Five,*" said Tarsavage, "*you'll fall in now or I'll guaran-damn-tee you'll spend the rest of your career in Leavenworth.*"

"You heard him, Trent," Harker said. "You can't throw away your career. This is your life."

"You're going to make good on your promise," said Trent.

"What promise?"

"To the VNAFs."

Harker inspected Trent's features as if trying to discern what he knew. The delivery of his words suddenly became deliberate. "There were no promises."

"*Exodus Leader, Roving Thunder. Over.*" The voice on the radio was unfamiliar but deep and self-assured. The voice of a jet pilot.

"*Roving Thunder, Exodus Leader.*"

"*Roger. Our ETA at your location is three minutes. This one'll have to go down in a hurry. Things are a little busy right now.*"

"*Roger Roving Thunder. We'll clear the area.*" The radio background noise changed, indicating that Tarsavage had switched to the internal flight frequency. "*Hear that, Trent, you clown! You've got F-4s knocking on your door. Get those men out of there now or God damn you, I'll let the jet jockeys drop napalm right on your empty, stupid pin head!*"

Trent's eyes were wet and his mouth was dry. His tone or expression must have betrayed a trace of doubt because, although he held the controls tightly, Harker slowly moved his hands back to them, applying skyward pressure to the collective to prevent a descent and lateral pressure to the cyclic to stop the turn.

At first, Trent's surrender was imperceptible, even to himself. The Huey began to drift away from Stray Wolf in the direction of the departing flight. Trent's control movements began to lose life, and Harker's gained power with that realization. In another moment, Trent slumped over the stick, barely touching it.

The clarity Trent had discovered at the crash site just hours before was lost, the innocence forgotten. The peace he had found for an instant no longer was his; it belonged to Le Song and the hundreds of baby-faced boy-men Trent had watched leap bravely from his helicopter and disappear into countless jungle tree lines, never again to reappear. Their faces were as clear to him as his own reflection in a mirror, and he could feel the stares of a thousand others who he had not seen and didn't know.

No longer did Trent recall acts of heroism on his part; his mind was clouded by doubt. Had he truly kept his gunners from firing on innocent civilians on all occasions? An M-60 machine gun hurling hundreds of bullets per minute does not distinguish between the enemy and the innocent. Had he properly balanced the lives of his crew against the lives of soldiers on the ground? There were judgments he had made that may have been wrong. Had he pulled free of the gunship at Wellspring, or had he merely been the victim of a faulty grip? The latter seemed more likely now. His world was out of balance again, the uncontrolled fan reactivated.

Harker turned sharply to glare at Spencer, who held forward a right-angled flashlight as if pointing a gun and winked. As an enlisted man, Spencer had been issued an M-16 rifle, not a revolver. The rifle hung behind Spencer's seat, undisturbed.

At least Harker could hardly prosecute Spencer for assaulting an officer with a flashlight, Trent thought. Somberly, he took a last look at the beautiful but scarred landscape of Vietnam. He dropped his hands from the flight controls and shut his eyes.

●—●●————●—●●●●●————●—●●

Song lay motionless on the stretcher, staring at the departing flight, now little more than specks on the horizon. He felt the heat from the burning fuel bladders and breathed the thick smell of petrol.

If the Viet Cong had not yet located the field, this spectacle soon would draw them. Closing his eyes, Song touched his leather satchel and fought to let go of fear and reason. He found that it was not so difficult; having fought for so long in a War among his own people, for a cause that he did not understand, perhaps there was little reason left to slip away.

Tightening the threads of his cocoon, Song shunned awareness of his plight and conjured mental images of his beloved Vietnam. Blue Mountains. Tangled teak and mahogany forests. Deep winding valleys. Great surging rivers. Elegant white-sanded shores. The visions were unmarred and exquisite, like Asian silkscreen paintings magically brought to life. Song strained to screen out the images that he abhorred. Bomb craters. Vast stretches of barren defoliation. Desecrated temples and tombs. Ravaged bodies and agonized faces.

Finally, the young pilot focused upon the image that he found most appealing. In his mind's eye, he recreated the paddy of his childhood and tried to complete his search for his mother through the glare. As he concentrated, the light and the heat intensified, and the vision of his mother's awaiting, open arms became increasingly clear.

Song gently drifted through the air, closer and closer.

•—•————•—••—•————•—•

"*Exodus Leader, Roving Thunder. Over.*"
"*Exodus Leader here. Go ahead.*"

"*Ordinance away... Ordinance on target... objective destroyed. Sweet Mary mother of Jesus, you should have seen that one. That was spectacular!*"

"*Roger Roving Thunder. You have our undying gratitude.*"

"*Like to say we'd do it again soon for you Exodus Flight, but it looks like we'll have to settle for a drink back stateside.*"

"*Roger that, and I'm buying. Any movement on the target area?*"

"*Negative Exodus. Not in this century.*"

PART II
SOLDIER MAN

Chapter eleven

Knuckles tapped softly against the window of a gray sedan parked curbside on the corner of Route One and 25th Street in northeast Washington, D.C. Chain-smoking in the driver's seat sat a seasoned Drug Warrior of the highest credentials.

Agent Donald Sage of the Drug Enforcement Administration was a thin, pale man with a narrow, lightly pockmarked face. His most distinguishing feature was a silver-sheathed tooth, in the top front position, that he flashed like a badge of honor. The false incisor replaced one he lost to a twenty-two caliber bullet that had torn into his the face and exited the left side of his neck. The blemishes, too, were souvenirs of violence and not remnants of youthful acne; they were repositories of metal pellets spewed from the lethal point of a twelve-gauge shotgun.

Sage leaned across the front seat and pulled the door handle. Agent Gerry Ramírez slid silently onto the passenger seat. "Close the door," Sage said curtly. "Where's our Soldier Man?"

Ramírez lifted his hands. "I checked down both side streets. We might as well settle in for a while."

Sage took a long draw on his cigarette and then held the roll to the crack in the window and tapped it with his finger. "He was due at the motel at ten."

"For all I know, he could be in some alley with an ice pick in his head."

"He's the biggest break we've had with D.C. kingpins in years, and you'd let him go out with an ice pick?"

"The guy won't wear a wire, Don. What would you have me do, stand behind him in Hamilton Place and tell the Drexlers not to mind me, and that I'm just there to help?"

"Funny."

"The guy's in deep. He has to take care of himself. Best we can do is to watch and wait. Give him room to reach out to us. You know that. You didn't use to be this jittery."

"Just knock it off with the ice picks, okay?"

"Whatever you say."

"I've been waiting half a decade to get an inside line on the Drexlers. You may not believe this, but this isn't just for me. When we nail the Drexlers right here in Washington, it'll be national news. Prove once and for all that the Agency can get an arm on these arrogant sons of bitches. Every Hill rat out to slice our budget will have crow to eat for breakfast."

Ramírez sighed. "All over little old Hamilton Place," he said, flipping several black-and-white photographs onto Sage's knee. Each depicted a different angle of the mouth of a bleak avenue. The street was one-way and narrow. Dilapidated cars were tightly packed against the curbs, unpleasant heaps of rust, and worn rubber. Young men sat on hoods and trunks on both sides, their legs dangling into the street, making it impossible for a vehicle to pass should a driver dare to enter. Their faces were frozen in grim stares, as if they harbored a common hatred for the photographer, whom they may not have seen but whose presence was certainly felt.

Hamilton Place was the home of Rodney and Llamar Drexler, brothers who purchased large quantities of cocaine from Colombia and heroin from Southeast Asia. They cut the drugs, packaged them for individual sale, and oversaw a vast army of hawkers who peddled the wares throughout the nation's capital. The Drexlers captained the illicit enterprise through an extensive chain of lieutenants and underlings resembling a major corporation, insulating them from the taint of the contraband. Sage led the DEA's current efforts to discover the Drexlers' foreign connections. The campaign was called Operation Solder Man and centered the ability of a single informant to penetrate the shadows of Hamilton Place and reveal its dark secrets.

Sage pitched the pictures back onto Ramírez's lap. "Charming," he said. "Home sweet home on Hamilton Place. It's all in there. Everything we need to know about shipments and locations and names. And our boy will get it for us."

"You've got high hopes," Ramírez said. "Only thing Solder Man's been doing is running clockers out of the northeast section. He's not up close and personal with the Drexlers."

"He's getting closer. Building trust. That's the reason for the call."

"Who knows?"

"Well this better be good. I need to get ready for a meeting next week."

"With who?"

"Couple days ago, the deputy director gives me a call and tells me to contact a White House aid to set up a look-see of the Agency for some bitch professor from the University of California. Wants to see me right away when she gets in. She's part of some White House task force initiative or something."

"That's nothing new. Every time they pass a new crime bill, they set up about a hundred committees and task forces. Just give her the nickel tour and get on with business."

"This tour is supposed to last a couple of months. The professor wants to tag along on some operations. She wants to see files and interview agents—hell, I guess she'll want to talk to the perps. Personally I think the President is just looking for some way to save his gnarled political hide."

Ramírez fidgeted with a set of keys. "This isn't the first time we've been through this with an administration."

"Yeah," Sage said. "Ten years ago my old boss shipped some administration guy off to Peru. Showed him some coca leaves and burnt-up drug labs, and the guy was as happy as a clam."

"You'll send this lady to Peru?"

"Nothing so exotic. I was thinking more along the lines of North Carolina."

"Carolina? What've we got cooking down there?"

Sage flopped his wrist, laying his palm flat up. "I'll call the guys in Raleigh. I'll find something or they'll find something. Maybe we've got something small going up north. Or maybe I'll make something up. My plan is to charm the professor and send her packing."

"You're a hard man, Sage."

Sage shook his head with muted delight. "Let's set it up right now," he said. He touched a button on his car phone, and the dial tone buzzed through a speaker.

"They won't be in on a Saturday."

"They're always in," Sage said, dialing. "They've got a lot to worry about."

"White House staff," a woman's voice answered.

"Yeah, Don Sage. Returning Harry Crim's call."

A low-pitched, melodic male's voice replaced the woman's. "Thank you for calling, Agent Sage," Crim said. "Our honored guest is arriving tonight from Los Angeles, and she'll be anxiously awaiting her orientation."

"Sure Harry. But we've got to agree on some ground rules."

"We'll discuss those when we meet. You should bring several active files typifying the DEA's current field operations."

"I'll find some folders. Fact I got a few in mind that are really good."

"Very well. We'll meet at my townhouse on Wednesday then. Say four-ish?"

Four-ish, Sage thought. How about four-a-fucking clock? How about four-a-fucking thirty? How about you just tell me a time? "I'll be there at four," Sage said.

"Did I say four? Maggie, be a dear and hand me my portfolio. Ah yes, there's another meeting at four. Five-ish would be better."

"Five o'clock then."

"Probably a little after."

"Little after." Sage snapped off the speaker with a swipe of his hand. "Jesus Christ! These eggheads can't even make an appointment. No wonder they're running the country into the ground."

"Shhh," Ramírez said. "There he is."

A shadowy figure rounded a corner and walked briskly along the rectangular frontage of the motel. The man passed eerily through the red fluorescent glow of a vending machine and halted mid-building. He slid a key in a door and disappeared. Sage's eyes tracked the man's progress and remained fixed on the door after it closed. He leaned back in his seat, drifting into recollection.

●▬●▬▬▬●▬●●●▬●▬▬▬▬●▬●

Sage found Soldier Man in Mexico in 1985, in the dangerous days in the late aftermath of the killing of DEA Agent Enrique Camarena in Guadalajara. The Narcotraficantes, Mexican drug lords, exerted powerful influence at all levels of government, police, and military. The choice they offered to Mexican officials was *o plata o plomo*, silver or lead. Most chose silver. Only a handful of DEA agents were stationed in Mexico, and those few had little cooperation and less assistance from a government in which corruption and terror reigned.

It was in the town of Mazatlán in the state of Sinaloa where Sage spotted Soldier Man living quietly, perhaps too peacefully. The surroundings were chaotic. Violent and depraved men ran roughshod, carting automatic weapons, driving fast cars, and showing little concern for law or life; yet this extrinsic black American worked almost invisibly as a hand on a horse ranch. Sage was in the business of cultivating informants, and Solder Man looked like a real possibility—he had the look of a man on the run. He had that sturdy gaze that meets you square in the eye but only so as not to appear to be avoiding you. He could rarely be seen in public places and lived with few possessions, as if ready to vanish on a second's notice. On a whim, Sage lifted his fingerprints from a bar glass and sent them to Washington.

A week later Sage was investigating prevalent rumors that the Narcotraficantes had openly and arrogantly constructed a prodigious marijuana plantation in the Chihuahuan desert, an area frequently overflown by Mexican authorities. Sage felt that the existence of such a large, exposed project would conclusively establish the acquiescence of the Mexican government. He had reported the rumors to Washington but was afforded no authority to act; he felt thwarted by bureaucrats and stifled by turf wars with other agencies. Though American agents were forbidden from overflying the desert, on his own authority Sage commissioned a private pilot and discovered and photographed the farm, complete with irrigated fields, barracks for peasant workers, and barn-like drying sheds. Cannabis covered the ground as far as the eye could see in every direction, waving like Nebraska corn.

For his indiscretion, Sage was reprimanded by Mexican officials and targeted for death by the Narcotraficantes. A group of thugs sprayed his car with machine gun fire and shotgun blasts. Miraculously, Sage survived with only flesh wounds.

The Agency's response to the threats on Sage's life was not to intensify the pressure on the Narcotraficantes as Sage would have wished. Instead, DEA Washington recalled Sage to the home office.

Sage was happy in Mexico. If one wants to hunt tigers, he always said, one has to go where tigers live. The years in Mexico should not be wasted. He had spent time cultivating informants and learning the players, where they ate and breathed. He had penetrated the infrastructure of the Narcotraficantes as they reaped profits from their own marijuana and poppy fields and conspired with the Colombian Drug Lords to flood the United States with contraband. Sage had learned so much and had so much yet to discover.

Sage had grimly prepared to leave Mexico as ordered. On the day of his departure, he received a teletype message from the FBI. The fingerprints he had forwarded belonged to a convicted felon from Washington, D.C. who had escaped from the corrections facility at Lorton, Virginia in 1973, having served less than one year of a five-year term. It was suspected that he was aided by a prison guard who was also a Vietnam veteran. The escapee's crime was a distribution offense. His name was Deric Christy.

At that moment, Sage knew that he wasn't returning home empty-handed. He would bring with him a new informant, a man already on the run, ready-made for use as a confidential source in the D.C. drug market. He had discovered Soldier Man.

•—•————•—••—•—————•—•

Sage and Ramírez quietly slipped from the sedan and entered through the unlocked door of the motel room, lit by a single dim lamp. The furnishings were worn, but the bed was crisply made, and folded clothes were tidily arranged on a rickety bureau. Leaning in the corner among the shadows, with his arms folded across his stomach, stood Deric Christy.

Sage feigned a white-glove test on the bureau and then gestured toward the bed. "Nice place. Least you got a maid."

"I do it myself," said Christy. He stood tall and fit; the only mar upon his smooth, lean visage was a deep, uneven scar pointing to his glassine left eye.

"What have you got for us?"

"I wanted to talk."

"Talk? Just talk? You got nothing? You drag us out in the middle of the night—"

"I spoke to my lawyer."

"You what?"

"You heard me."

"You pulled this bullshit two years ago too. You don't have a lawyer. Any lawyer would be disbarred for not turning your ass in. Anyone gives you something to eat or a place to stay can be arrested. You always seem to forget. You're persona non f-ing grata. Got that?"

"I want some assurances."

"What kind of assurances?"

"Expungement. Of my record."

"I already guaranteed you that. Just do what you're told."

"It's been five years. We want it in writing now."

"What's this 'we' crap? You mean this ambulance-chaser? Just give me his name and I'll clear it up with him, straighten it out real fast. How's that?"

Christy stared blankly.

"That it?" Sage said, raising his open palms.

"That's it."

"You arrange a meet for nothing? You know how dangerous this is? Next time you call, you better have something, or we'll shove your ass back into Lorton where you belong. Got that?"

A cloud came over Christy's face. It seemed as if he were stoically trying to fight off some unseen force attacking him from all directions. In a few seconds, however, he appeared to overcome the moment. He turned and disappeared into the bathroom. Sage heard splashing water.

"Geez freakin' whiz," Sage said. "You get this guy, Gerry?" He flailed his hands. "Let's get out of here."

Ramírez followed Sage back into the dark shadows of the street.

Sage hung his head in disappointment. Ramírez reached for the car door, but in his peripheral vision, he sensed movement. As he turned his head, his eyes focused on a young black man on the sidewalk, nearing the corner of the motel. He was walking briskly. His head was shaved clean, and he wore a black vest draped over his bare chest. For an instant their eyes met. The young man's expression was angry and hard, and then it transformed almost imperceptibly to recognition. He darted around the corner of the motel.

"Get in quick, Don," Ramírez said.

147

"What is it?"

"We're made."

"One of the Drexlers' boys?"

"Had to be."

"Let's move."

Car doors slammed and the engine fired and revved. Sage rounded the corner feeling like he was riding on two wheels. "There he is," Ramírez said, pointing.

The man was running down a side street. He vaulted a rod-iron fence and ducked under a brick alcove. Sage pushed his heel into the brake pedal. The rear wheels of the sedan skidded into the curb. Both doors flew wide open, and the agents were on the ground, running.

They followed the alcove into a narrow courtyard. Garbage cans and smoke-blackened oil drums lined the sides, and the walkway was of broken brick; Sage could feel the sharp edges through the soles of his shoes. He reached under his arm and flicked out his nine-millimeter Browning, hiked his pant cuff, and slid a shiny thirty-two caliber pistol from an ankle holster. The stubby handle of the small revolver was wrapped in dirty adhesive tape, and the serial number was filed smooth.

The agents froze in the shadows. No footfalls, Sage thought. He's trying to wait us out.

Sage listened hard, screening out the buzzing of electric meters. Heavy breathing fell from the far side of the courtyard. Ramírez knelt beside a brick grill. Sage crept forward, holding both guns trained on the shadows, sliding his right shoulder against the brick walls.

"Hey you," Sage called. "Vest. Come out of there. We need to talk."

Silence.

"Come on, kid. You haven't done anything. Come out where we can speak."

A faint voice drifted from the darkness. It was quiet by intention, not from any weakness of its master. "You cops?"

"What do you think? Come on. I just want to talk."

"You're gonna ice me."

"No one's here to shoot you." Sage halted behind a chimney, judging this to be adequate cover. "Nice and easy," he said. "Come on out."

"Say your piece from there."

"And wake up all the nice people? Gimme a break, my friend. What we have to talk about is private. You know, man to man." Sage leaned around the chimney. His silver tooth glistened in the moonlight. He pulled back the hammer on the thirty-two caliber. It clicked loudly.

A tight series of explosions resounded in the darkness. A ricochet hit by Sage's left ear, spraying bits of brick and mortar against his cheek. He recoiled behind the chimney. Blinking his eyes, in his mind he pinpointed the location of the muzzle flashes. He dropped forward on one knee, pointing the pistols into the shadows. He saw nothing.

Suddenly a splintering noise penetrated the silence. Light pierced the darkness, and Sage saw the pencil outline of a doorway. With a crash, the image suddenly collapsed into a rectangular blotch of light. There, for an instant, Vest's form stood silhouetted. Then he disappeared into the light.

Vest had kicked in the door of a row house and was making his escape into the structure. More volleys of gunfire followed from inside, muffled by the walls of the building.

Sage leapt to his feet. He dashed for the door, with Ramírez following at his heels. Sage made a wide arc, and Ramírez pulled up short.

Sage went in low, but his right arm caught on the doorpost. The shooting pain from the impact took his breath and caused his muscles to spasm. His nine-millimeter erupted, blasting a hole in the wooden doorframe. The weapon bounced from his hand and down the wooden steps, coming to rest among a cluster of garbage cans.

Sage's upper torso was inside the row house. He discerned movement. He spun and rolled on his shoulder, thrusting the thirty-two forward.

Before him stood a young girl in pink pajamas, the kind with feet. Her features were fragile, as precise as a doily, and her dark hair was braided away from her face in ribboned pigtails. Her thumb was planted in her mouth, and her eyes were set wide in a dreamy sort of terror. She slowly looked down at the pajama feet, soaked in a dark liquid that trailed behind her. Sage lowered his remaining pistol and scrambled to his knees. As he did, he saw another blur.

Vest suddenly appeared in the interior doorway behind the little girl. He swung a MAC-10 automatic pistol from his hip.

Sage dove across the wooden floor. The floor boards clattered and jumped in sync with the explosions.

Sage low-crawled behind a couch and emerged at the far end. He fired three shots into the doorway before he realized that Vest was gone. He pulled himself to his feet and leapt over the couch. Before him lay the girl. She had fallen face down. Her elbow was angled high against her head and her hand was underneath her face, as if her thumb were still in her mouth. A single red spot swelled in the center of her back.

Ramírez appeared in the doorway. "Oh God," he gasped.

"Get an ambulance," said Sage, his pale face cast in stone. "But don't ID yourself."

Deftly, Sage navigated through the house, following the path that he believed Vest had taken. He wove down a dark narrow hall and emerged in a small kitchen. Broken dishes, food scraps, and utensils were scattered on the floor, and a side-door stood ajar. Sage kicked it and slid around the corner of the doorframe into an open alleyway.

Sage squatted, looking and listening. Two- and three-story brick buildings reached up from littered gutters. Some of the entranceways and windows were guarded by wrought iron and broken boards, others stood open on broken hinges and latches. Only a few trash cans sat upright; most had spilled their contents onto the sidewalk and street. A layer of liquid filth seemed to have flooded the scene, touching everything. Despite its chaotic appearance, the area seemed motionless. Like a photograph.

Footfalls sounded in the distance. Sage darted up the alleyway at a full sprint, running high on his toes to dampen the echo. After a hundred yards he stopped and listened again. No sound ahead. He turned quickly, sweeping the gun all around him. Nothing but darkness. Vest had lain in wait once, he thought. Maybe . . .

Sage ran fifty feet and rounded the corner of a brick wall. He halted and continued stomping his feet still for several seconds, lighter and lighter. He picked up a stone and tossed it against a row house. Then he froze and rested his back against the wall, suppressing the heaving of his chest. Sage counted to twenty. Abruptly, he stepped back into the alley, his weapon pointed down the path he had traveled.

There, in the gutter, crawling from behind a clump of refuse, was Vest.

Sage didn't look for the MAC-10. He did not shout a warning. His gun came around automatically. It seized its target and blurted his rage through its muzzle. The reports of the three rounds resounded like cannon fire in the narrow confines. Sage clicked the hammer against several empty shells before he ceased pulling the trigger.

Vest tried to stagger to his feet, but his knees failed him. He crumpled to the ground.

Sage ran to him. He kicked the MAC-10 from Vest's hand and eased him to the walkway. Blood splashed freely from the young man's throat; its sweet metallic smell was thick and sickening.

"Tole you you was gonna waste me," Vest hissed. As he spoke, part of his wind escaped through the opening in his throat, making his voice like a hoarse whisper.

"Shut up, kid," Sage said, his own breath ragged. He pulled a handkerchief from his hip pocket to try to stanch the flow of blood and then thought better of it. "Didn't have to be this way." Sage looked at Vest, up at the houses, back at the blood, over at Ramírez now standing beside him, and back at Vest. "You called all the shots here. What's your name?"

"Ain't nobody."

"Well Nobody, how about telling me about the Drexlers and clearing your conscience?"

"They gonna find out your boy."

Sage quieted his body. He looked into Vest's eyes, his expression an unsettling mix of sympathy and self-satisfaction. "Won't find him out now, will they?" he said.

Vest craned his neck, and his lips quivered. He seemed as if he were desperately searching for an external source of the lake of blood rising around him. Then paralysis overtook him, and his face took on a chalky cast. The angry, agonized expression dissipated. Finally only a taciturn sadness remained in the wide-open, still eyes.

Sage slid the dead man's eyelids closed and lifted his own chin to Ramírez. "The ambulance?"

"On the way. Won't do the little girl any good. And two adults are dead. Ma and Pa, I guess."

Sage stared at his blood-stained trousers. Years of cultivating Soldier Man were about to end fruitlessly due to an act of carelessness on his part, he thought. He never should have agreed to meet Christy at the motel. Then savage decisiveness set in upon Sage's face. His handkerchief already in his hand, he rubbed the thirty-two and pitched it into a garbage can. He glanced at the row houses. Not a single bulb was lit. "You get my other gun?" he whispered.

"I looked everywhere for it. When I got back outside, it was just gone."

"Thirty-two's a street piece, but the nine-millimeter is my service gun, Gerry. If it gets found, it puts me here for the world to see."

"We're here anyway, man. This is too big a mess to walk away from."

Sage listened to the wailing sirens as they became louder. "Couple blocks away," he said. "We stay here, the Drexlers will know their guy was killed by the DEA, and Soldier Man's dead. Five years will be wasted. No. This thing has to go down... like just another drug shoot-out, where Vest and the civilians got caught in the crossfire. Turf war or rippers, something like that. We can't have been here."

Ramírez was drenched in sweat, and his cheeks were drawn. He breathed with an air of helplessness. "I won't be involved in a cover-up."

"It won't be a cover-up. I'll clear it with the Agency. It'll get okayed, believe me. The security of a major operation is at stake. We'll give our statements. We just won't let this be twisted and distorted on Live at Five."

Ramírez gazed at the courtyard. "You can do what you want. I'm staying with this until that little girl has a proper funeral."

"You said it yourself. There's nothing we can do now. Should we drag Soldier Man down with her?"

Ramírez stumbled backwards, appearing confused. Sage took him by the elbow.

"Come on, Gerry," Sage said, guiding Ramírez toward the sedan. "Time to go home."

⁕

Deric Christy stood mutely in the shadows of an alcove, watching the agents slip into the gray sedan and disappear into the darkness. In Christy's left hand, barrel extended toward the ground, hung Sage's nine-millimeter pistol, the trigger guard loosely touching his half-extended finger.

Chapter twelve

Twenty days had passed since Ashford's first weekend drill. He sat at his workstation at the architectural firm in Gettysburg, sketching headers and footers and exterior walls. Occasionally the charcoal stick between his fingers scratched out the form of a rotor blade slicing a sharp path through the air. More unexpectedly and unconsciously, his fingers sketched a woman's cheekbone or eyelash and then a personal and inevitable smile. The delicate features never quite jelled into a complete face, but Ashford knew nonetheless that they belonged to Jesse Morrow.

One week before summer camp, Ashford arrived at Stewart International Airport in New York in the early afternoon. By telephone, he had arranged an interview with Major Paul Olofson on the pretense that he was interested in joining the 336th Medevac Detachment.

Ashford parked beside a gray military hangar set along the western expanse of the airfield. A Northwest Airlines jet crouched in takeoff position on the runway rim, cutting the air with its shrill preparatory whine. Ashford covered his ears and ducked through a door in the sheet-metal side of the hangar. In the rear of the building, past a thicket of Hueys, he found the glass-faced administrative offices and Olofson's nameplate on a door, and he knocked. The major emerged from behind a padded room divider. He was of medium height with a blunted nose turned upwards toward curious green eyes. His salt-and-pepper hair was still thick, and there was something boyish about his manner, but his stride contained a stiff and unnatural bow-leggedness contradicting the youthful impression.

"So you're Lieutenant Ashford." Olofson scanned Ashford's open-collar sports shirt and khakis; obviously he had expected a uniform. "You bring along your personnel file?"

"Uh, no Sir."

"I see. May I ask what your interest in the 336th is? Moving to the area?"

"No."

"It's a long commute from Pennsylvania."

"Yes, quite a drive."

"You own a private jet?"

Ashford smiled weakly. "I'd be very interested in your unit if I lived in this area."

"So you didn't come to join the 336th."

"No, and I apologize for the fib. I'm not in the habit of it, but I needed to talk to you and wasn't sure you'd agree to speak with me."

"Spit it out, kid. I'm dying of suspense."

From his hip pocket, Ashford lifted copies of the papers he had found in Trent's personnel file—Olofson's affidavit and the accompanying note to Harker. He handed them to the major, who examined the documents carefully, as a homeowner would a search warrant. "Where did you get these?" Olofson asked.

"Mister Trent's personnel file."

Olofson squinted and slid the tip of his tongue along the inside of his lower lip. Ashford spoke quickly and with insufficient forethought, desperate to explain himself before Olofson drew conclusions. "I'm his platoon leader, and I wanted to know about him. I mean where he's been. What he's been through."

Olofson studied Ashford's face for so long and so directly, that Ashford felt a compulsion to avert his eyes. "I planned an orientation flight for your interview," he said. "Scheduled a couple of cadet lifts down at West Point. You bring your flight suit?"

"In the car."

"Get it. We're going for a ride."

•—•—————•—••—•——•—•

Thirty minutes later, they were in a Huey high above the earth. Ashford handled the controls, and Olofson sat indifferently with his wounded rump resting on a blue egg-crate foam cushion. Olofson's eyes rested on the deep green forest sliding away beneath them, and he only spoke to offer truncated directions.

The forest fell away, and they banked south into an immense cliff-walled gorge, its sheer rock sides sliced dramatically into the landscape by the flow of the Hudson River over thousands of years. The wide, rippled face of the river was untamed and beautiful. On the south side of a tree-covered knoll lay a sweeping panoramic view of the West Point Military Academy. Set over a medieval retaining wall, majestic gray buildings rose grandly from the bleakness of a rock-faced peninsula. The structures were of all styles, from a towering Gothic column to a modern rotunda; in scale and severity all evoked the same overpowering sense of greatness and immortality.

"Like our little boy's school?" asked Olofson.

"Breathtaking," Ashford said, his breath truly taken.

"Two hundred years of tradition unhampered by progress."

Ashford felt the tension lighten if only by a degree. "That could be said of the entire Army, I guess."

"It has been. We're early for our pickup, so let's take a little tour. Take this bend." Olofson pointed to a draw leading into the mountains. "Take it hard."

Four hundred feet above the ground, Ashford maneuvered the Huey into a forty-degree bank. They sliced into a forested gorge, and two fields opened before them. The closest rested on a hill plateau; the other was set deep in the chasm, hundreds of feet below. Ashford couldn't see the floor of the more distant field that appeared only as a depression in the trees.

Abruptly, a red light flashed in the center of the console—the engine warning light. Ashford started as if he had been touched by a live wire, and the Huey juddered with his spasm. A shrill alarm filled Ashford's ears, warning of diminishing rotor speed.

The Huey dropped as if it were suddenly filled with lead. Ashford's stomach followed. His wide-searching eyes glimpsed the engine tachometer needle gliding in a semicircular arc toward oblivion. Instinctively Ashford rolled his left wrist to check the position of the throttle. When he realized that it had been displaced, he applied resistance to return to full RPM, but he felt Olofson overriding his input.

"Ah ah," Olofson said. "Simulated engine failure."

Ashford was suddenly relieved by the pretense of the emergency. Relying on his flight-school training, he reacted by immediately lowering the collective lever, the standard emergency procedure. With the flattening pitch of the rotor blades, the rotor RPM needle stabilized as the upward airflow through the blades preserved their momentum.

The Huey cut a path through the air, midway between the two potential landing zones. Ashford still couldn't see the far field, but it appeared to be fairly large. The nearer opening was quite small, and a power line bisected it at an angle perpendicular to the Huey's flight path, posing a dangerous obstacle. Ashford would have to maneuver quickly, almost instinctively, to reach the field due to its higher elevation, and the time that it took to consider the possibility had nearly foreclosed the opportunity.

"Better make a decision," Olofson warned.

Ashford pointed the nose of the Huey to the distant field, allowing the Huey to fall away into the gorge. In a few seconds the skids brushed the treetops, and the Huey crossed the tree line. Ashford finally saw the ground. The spherical cut was surrounded by a barbed-wire fence and crowded with half-buried Quonset-style huts. No space was available for a Huey to land without risking a collision with the buildings.

"Power recovery," Olofson announced. He seized the controls and rolled the throttle full open, drawing the collective up firmly. The rotor blades chomped into the air, yanking the Huey from its downward glidepath. With a graceful gesture, Olofson banked sharply away from the field.

"Congratulations," said Olofson. "You successfully crashed and burned in the ammo dump. Chances of survival were probably less than ten percent."

Ashford tried to collect himself. "I wasn't familiar with the layout."

"That wasn't the point. I gave you a Devil's alternative. You were able to recon the small field with the wires, a dangerous but entirely survivable option. But you had to act quickly, almost on instinct, to survive. You had just enough altitude and time to make a two-seventy and come in parallel to the wires from the north."

"But I gambled for better and went for an unknown." Ashford's tone was dejected. "The instructor pilots didn't make it quite so realistic at Rucker."

"It's very real out here. Try adding to that an environment where everyone you meet is trying to kill you. Then perhaps you may begin to understand Nick Trent."

Ashford swallowed hard, but no moisture was available to cool his dry throat. "What would he have done?"

Olofson laughed in an unsettling manner. He told Ashford that Nick Trent would never have climbed into the helicopter before he knew exactly where the ammo dump was located, as well as every other flight hazard within miles of his course. He explained that it harkened back to something Trent taught him in Vietnam, something he would never forget.

How it was all about judgment, not how smoothly the pilot flies the helicopter or how well he talks on the radio. It was knowing when to go up and when not to, when to land and when to fly by, and when to shoot and when to hold fire. When to stand your ground and when to pull up stakes. "The rest is nothing in comparison," Olofson said. "A monkey could do the rest."

There was something pleading in the major's tone, as if he bore sacred knowledge that he needed to pass on before it was lost or forgotten. Then his voice hardened. "Now what else did you want to ask me about Nick Trent?"

Ashford had no words to say.

•━•━━━━•━••━•━━━•━•

They landed at West Point on a rectangular field of close-cut grass that lay flat along the river at the base of the battlements. On the plain, blank-faced young men clothed in starched camouflage fatigues stood at precise attention in groups of seven. When the skids were solidly on the ground, the first group approached the helicopter in a disciplined formation.

Olofson explained he would take the first lift to demonstrate the flight route. Ashford exited the cockpit and supervised the loading. The young men held their faces rigid and did not meet his eyes. They sat rigidly in their seats, while Ashford checked that their belts were properly fastened. Though their bodies were thoroughly disciplined, Ashford detected something untamed in their eyes, some indestructible sense of wonderment, some glimmer of anticipation.

As the Huey climbed from the plain, the mood in the helicopter gradually transformed. A cadet reticently leaned forward and poked his head into the wind; his short bangs smoothed against his head, and he grinned and gulped in the magnificent aerial view of the Academy. Others apprehensively sat back but seemed to draw ease from their peer. Momentarily, another cadet hung his boots emancipated over the edge of the cargo deck and wiggled his feet, as if he were treading on the air above the military school. The mores that bound them on the ground seemed to be dissolving in the swirling, free air.

Olofson laid the Huey on its flank to reveal a stunning side-view of the cascading cliff face, the agglomerations glinting and sparkling in the sun. The cadets released whoops and hollers, as if exhaling after holding their breaths. "It's a first-year class," Olofson said. "It's their initial look at the Academy from the air and the only time they've been completely free from their cadre in months."

Ashford glanced over his shoulder again. The cadets pointed and grinned and elbowed each other so no wondrous sight would be missed by anybody. Ashford knew the precious moment of freedom was fleeting—when they landed they would tuck their chins and straighten their bodies and instantaneously respond to commands that made little sense to their young minds. But in this one instant, they were free to be boys again, just boys, and the feeling infected Ashford too. It was perhaps why he had always wanted to fly.

The pilots flew the course four times, providing orientation rides to the remainder of the cadets. When the fuel was low, they turned up the Hudson River toward Stewart International. After they landed, Olofson told Ashford to shut down the Huey and close it up, and he disappeared into the hangar. When Ashford finished, Ashford found Olofson's office dark and empty. He exited the hangar by a back door and found the major staring blankly at the green mountain tops silhouetted against a great blue sky, with the egg-crate cushion dangled from his fingertips.

Ashford cleared his throat, and Olofson turned to face the young lieutenant. Standing with his back to the mountains, the older man appeared insignificant. "Do you have a girlfriend?" Olofson said.

"Not right now, but there's someone I'd like to get to know."

"Why don't you do it and stop meddling in other people's business?"

Ashford stood quietly, feeling as if he had no right to be heard.

"You fly pretty well for a lieutenant," Olofson said, his tone appearing to search for evenness. "I don't mean to be hard on you, but Nick Trent is a man I respect wholeheartedly. And he's entitled to his privacy."

"I can understand that, but I really need some help. I joined the National Guard to learn to fly. It's all I ever wanted to do. It took me forever to get into flight school. I wasn't great friends with every instructor pilot there, but I found some common ground with every one of them.

"Then I report for duty at Fort Indiantown Gap. First guy I meet is Nick Trent. He stands right in front of me and doesn't bat an eyelash while I nearly get taken out from behind by a line truck. Then I learn that the lieutenant I replaced is on medical leave with some nervous condition Trent takes credit for. I'm just looking for a way to survive, and the only way I can see to do that is to figure him out. A crew chief he flew with in Vietnam told me I'd have to learn where he's been. That's why I came to you, because you've been there too."

"Who's the crew chief?"

"Sergeant Spencer."

"Reggie?" A smile played across Olofson's lips. "Well, that figures. He never let Nick Trent go anywhere without him." Olofson returned to his communion with the mountains. "I was only in Vietnam ten weeks. Just long enough to get shot in the ass. Chief was there a lifetime compared to that. He's forgotten more things about staying alive in a helicopter than I'll ever know."

"You call him Chief?"

"That's what everyone called him then."

"I heard he doesn't care much to be called that now."

"I don't suppose he would. Tell me something, did Reggie tell you to come see me?"

"No, I came up with that brainstorm on my own."

"All right, kid. You got a couple pieces of a puzzle. There may be a lot more pieces, but I can tell you there's no solution. I don't have any answers, you see, I only have questions."

"I don't even know the questions."

"Perhaps you shouldn't. Opening the past is a dangerous undertaking."

"I don't want to open it up. I just want to understand it."

Olofson sighed. "You're nothing if not persistent. You read my affidavit. Everything that I said is true. Nick was easily the best combat aviator in our unit, probably the best in the entire Army. But he always seemed to be on a slow burn. The only time I ever saw a peaceful expression on his face was when our rescue ship lifted from our crash site in Vietnam. Nick was there on the ground, surrounded by Viet Cong, just watching us lift away. Looked to me like he just wanted to be left there. Second to the hole in my ass, it's the scariest thing I have ever seen."

"What happened after that?"

"Hell if I know. I was all fucking shot up. Only thing I've been able to piece together is that some bad blood came between him and Harker."

"I haven't met the man, but I heard that he's our Battalion Commander."

Olofson released a low whistle. "Jesus, the Army is one small world."

"If you didn't see Mister Trent after the War, how do you know about his problems with Colonel Harker?"

"Harker tried to pin the blame on Nick for something that happened in Vietnam that he couldn't possibly have done."

"Can you tell me about it?"

Olofson shook his head. "You said you didn't want to disturb the past. Right now you're in a helicopter and the engine's quit and you're falling really fast. You see a tough LZ on a plateau and another field that might serve better, but you can't see it. What do you do?"

"I didn't know what to do. That's why I'm here."

"I'm telling you to go home."

Ashford gazed at Olofson's sagging back. He saw how the major shifted his weight to alleviate the soreness of the old wound, and he began to think he had erred in enlivening the pain of emotional injuries long since reconciled or repressed. He stammered some words of thanks and started toward the parking lot.

"He had this fan," Olofson told the mountains, as if Ashford were no longer present.

Ashford came back to him. "What?"

164

"Nick. In Vietnam. Had a little circular table fan that put out a pretty good breeze for its size. The kind that oscillates. One day it got knocked over. When Nick picked it up and turned it on, it started to vibrate and bounce across the tabletop. Nick decided to rebalance the thing. He removed the guard and started at the blades with a file, trying to shave off just the right amount to get the thing running smoothly again. Every day we'd come back from our missions, and he'd get out that file and work on the fan, and he'd turn it on and not be satisfied and start with the file again. Our last day in Vietnam, the thing sat on his table running with no blades at all. Just the spinning post in the middle."

Ashford was also looking at the mountains and considering the impotent fan. The silence grew.

"After the War," said Olofson, "I was assigned to study War Crimes."

"Like My Lai?"

"Thuan Yen actually. My Lai was the name the Army gave it on some map. Yeah, I studied that psychopath Rusty Calley. But my principal assignment was to study the behavior of aircrews. And in Vietnam I'd been right on top of something big. Three days before our evac, a Vietnamese village at Ba Long was decimated by a helicopter armed with M-60 machine guns. Officially the massacre was perpetrated by South Vietnamese pilots flying Gunnies, Charlie Model Hueys. But I remembered Nick had told me the physical evidence wasn't consistent with the official conclusion. So when I got the job at Rucker, I started following up."

"What did you do?"

"You saw my note to Harker. I interviewed him. He told me the VNAFs were responsible."

"You didn't believe him?"

"Nick saw the scene soon after the attack, and I never knew him to be wrong about something like that. So I asked Harker for the photos and reports and physical evidence. He told me every-thing was lost in our bug out."

"Did you tell Colonel Harker what Trent said?"

"He told me two things. First thing he said was that Trent was wrong. Second, he said that Vigilance Base Camp's flight logs showed Nick's helicopter was the only U.S. aircraft flying in the vicinity of Ba Long at the time of the massacre."

"Oh my God. He thinks Trent did it?"

"He implied it."

Ashford spoke quietly, almost to himself. "That would explain a whole lot about his behavior."

Olofson's voice took on the violent force of a thunderstorm. "Look, kid, I only spent ten weeks there and I'm certainly no expert on Vietnam. Only thing I do know is if Nick Trent was any-where in the vicinity of Ba Long, those people wouldn't be dead."

Ashford let the words linger before speaking. "Who else did you interview?"

"No one. I wanted to talk to Nick, but he was already out of the Army. So I let it die."

"Why?"

"My job was to study aircrew behavior in known and record-ed incidents, not to investigate unknowns. I had the same choice I gave you today. As I said, a Devil's choice. The known was to let the thing die and let history record that the VNAFs shot up Ba Long. The unknown was to follow this thing wherever it led and risk crashing and burning."

"You've given me a lot to think about," Ashford said. He thanked Olofson for his time and started again for his car. When he was a hundred feet away, Olofson called after him.

"He would never have let you get hurt."

"What?"

"The line truck. Nick would never have let it hit you."

"How do you know?"

"I know."

"What the hell was he doing then?"

"Waiting."

"For what?"

"Till it got close."

Ashford dropped his hands wide in frustration. "Why's he playing with me?"

"It's not you. The game is with himself."

"I still don't get it."

"It's a game of chicken. He's seeing how far he'll go and probably scaring the hell out of himself along the way. I've seen the same thing with other guys, and none of them has been through what Nick has."

"What can I do?"

"It doesn't help that you hold rank. He's rebelling against that too. But he'll come around. Just remember, kid. Twenty-something-odd years ago, Nick Trent was the best damn combat pilot in Vietnam."

"A lot can change in twenty years."

"I wouldn't bet on that."

On his drive from Fort Stewart back to Pennsylvania, Ashford considered what he had learned. The evidence he had uncovered was, if not damning, certainly disconcerting—Trent's own admission that the Massacre at Ba Long was committed by a U.S. helicopter; Colonel Harker's testimonial to Trent's presence in the vicinity; and Trent's invidious acts in Company B two decades later. The only contradictory evidence consisted of Olofson's and Spencer's subjective commentary.

The conclusion was one Ashford didn't want to believe yet which he found himself considering with mortification. There was yet a world of explanations, but the one that had surfaced was worse than he had ever imagined—the possibility that he had been assigned to command a mass murderer.

●—●——●—●●—●●—————●—●

After Ashford left, Olofson stood motionless, still staring at the forested hills, as if they were the Annamite Mountains looming over Vigilance Base Camp, and he was about to begin again the journey that had so changed his life. The young lieutenant had said he did not wish to pry into the past, but he lifted the lid the moment he mentioned Nick Trent. The old memories and emotions poured into the present, and the most daunting of all was the omnipresent sensation of unfinished business.

Sometime later, Olofson released himself from the mountains' grip. He returned to his office and made a long distance call to Fort Rucker, Alabama. In a whispered voice, he asked a clerk to retrieve several of his old files from long-term storage.

Chapter thirteen

In Washington, D.C., two men approached each other from opposite sides of the Mall, just as they walked from opposite sides of life. One man was black, and the other was white. One lived out of a suitcase only a few steps ahead of the law, and the other was a wealthy corporate attorney. One was a Vietnam veteran, and the other was a conscientious objector, or a draft dodger in his counterpart's parlance from decades before. One had been maimed in the War, but the other had disfigured himself.

Deric Christy was the black man, the Vietnam veteran, the man without wealth, and the man who had lost his left eye to the War. In the maelstrom that was his life, he regarded all of these qualities as being integrally interrelated.

With his one good eye, Christy gazed at his friend and former attorney, Lucias Hammaker. The lawyer was a tall man with a lanky, confident stride; his once-flaxen hair had taken on a silvery cast, and he still wore it long, although not to its former shoulder length. Even with the few yards left to close, Christy could smell Hammaker's cologne—spicy, tropical, and expensive. The lawyer was dressed in a tailored suit, and his starched white shirt served as an impeccable background for his perfectly knotted, wine-colored tie sporting tumbling golden leaves arranged in uneven rows. His skin was still clear but appeared dry and was stretched tightly across his cheekbones, as if to smooth the subtle wrinkles spiraling from the outside corners of his eyes. Hammaker's gaze contained the same mix of empathy and inquiry that it held when Christy had first met him some twenty years ago.

Christy's eye dropped to Hammaker's hand with four fingers as he took it in greeting. The fifth fingertip, Hammaker's right forefinger, was absent, and the remnant—a half-inch long stub—bobbed erratically against Deric's own hand. He had heard of men cutting off a finger or a toe to avoid the Vietnam draft, but Hammaker was the only such person he had encountered. The act wasn't one of a typical avoider. When Hammaker had performed his rash deed, there were so many other ways for an educated man to avoid the draft: go to college, diet severely, bribe the draft board, discover a trick knee, run to Canada, or go to jail. Even if he were dead set on maiming himself, Hammaker could have severed a good deal less flesh and perhaps no bone; a less drastic gesture would have surely served the purpose. But Hammaker, an intelligent man who was right-handed, had consciously dismembered the better part of his most functional digit and had once explained to Deric that he did so to remind himself of the permanence and solemnity of his choice. Although he did not understand him—not then, not now—Christy had long distinguished his lawyer from the rank-and-file avoiders, and he harbored a bewildering respect for the man of strange and lofty ideals.

Hammaker extended his arm, ushering Christy toward a park bench. "It was a bit of a shock to hear from you."

"I bet." Christy smiled stiffly and sat beside the lawyer.

"It's been, what, two years?"

"About that."

"I thought perhaps—"

"I was dead?"

"That you had somehow escaped your predicament. Are they still using you?"

Christy nodded sullenly. Hammaker's gaze shifted along the walkway, and he seemed suddenly embarrassed by the overtness of his anxiety and brought his eyes back to Christy. "I've been doing mergers and acquisitions for the last fifteen years, Deric," he said, his tone apologetic. "What I mean to say is that this is way out of my league. I'm not the same attorney, not the same man, that I once was. But I know some excellent criminal defense attorneys." Hammaker looked into Christy's surviving eye, which lay narrow and still.

"There's nothing a lawyer could do for me. Not the normal way. But I have some cash saved. Not the kind that you put in a bank—"

"You don't need to pay me, for God's sake."

"Money's not for you. I want to leave it to my nephew."

Hammaker rubbed his wrinkled forehead with his fingertips. "What do you mean *leave* it? Christ, Deric, what's going on?"

"I want to make a will. Last will and testament. Between just you and me. You can do that, can't you?"

With his eyes closed, Hammaker blew a stream of air through pursed lips and massaged his temples.

Christy extended a thick brown envelope. "The boy's name is Bran. Brandon Christy. The paper and money are in here."

After hesitating a few seconds, Hammaker accepted the envelope, slipping it into his pocket in an undisguised effort to conceal it quickly. He studied Christy. "It's a small matter, I'll keep it safe. But the reason why you'd need an informal will concerns me." Hammaker stared pensively, allowing the silence to gather for a moment. "I've been doing some thinking. Perhaps there are some people I could reach out to. Discretely. I don't want to raise false hopes, but there's the possibility of negotiating an expungement of your criminal record. It's been a long time since you, well, you disappeared, and so much has changed."

Christy remembered his efforts with Sage in which he had falsely spoken of having secured a lawyer to pursue expungement. "Expungement," he said, toying with the word as a child would with a stick. "You mean wipe it away?"

"There are different forms of expungement, but yes, it essentially means that."

"These people you know, they can wipe away the past?"

Hammaker rubbed the stump of his right forefinger in his left palm in a manner that seemed unconscious, as if it throbbed with an undercurrent of phantom pain. "No," he whispered in a tone of uncompromised surrender. "They can't touch the past."

"That's what I thought." Christy stared at the towering white obelisk rising from out of elegant pink cherry blossoms, almost transparent in the golden sunbeams, and he considered the spirit of irony with which he had selected the meeting place. It was here, under the auspices of Lincoln and beneath towering homages to America, that two decades ago his journey through the shadows of life took an ugly turn. In the lens of a past that was incapable of expungement, it was all before him again—the smells; the banners displaying inflammatory anti-war slogans; the thousand-fold voices burning with rage; and the three pounds of marijuana strapped around his waist, riding uneasily on his hips, up under his coat.

＊＊＊＊＊＊＊＊＊＊

"Ho... ho... ho... Ho Chi Minh Is Going To Win!"

A throng of protesters chanted anti-war slogans. Christy could feel the soft cloth of the eyepatch he had worn in 1972, before he had been fitted for a glass eye.

"Hey man," said a remembered voice. "You lose that eye in Vietnam?"

"What if I did?"

"Serves you right."

Christy quickened his pace; he had no interest in debating the morality of his participation in the War with screeching college kids in the after-throes of puberty who hadn't the slightest idea what they were protesting, or who had never been maimed or shot or watched a friend die or killed an enemy soldier in hand-to-hand combat. He walked briskly along the fringe of a mob of agitators woven between the thick marble pillars of the Lincoln Memorial, covering the steep steps and swarming like a colony of multi-colored ants. Banners and signs bobbed among them like buoys on a stormy sea. Uniformed policemen fortified a rope line that formed a fragile barrier between the throng and Lincoln's stone image.

Christy pulled the collar of his faded olive-drab Marine jacket to his ears—in Vietnam he had developed a revulsion for harsh noises. He was of average height, but his lean, athletic build made his presence formidable enough. Most striking was the black eye-patch that shrouded his left eye and the jagged scar notched deep into his temple, peeking from beneath the patch as if carved there to carry away tears.

"Hey you," a high-pitched voice said. "Carry a sign."

Christy turned to face a wild-haired young man dressed in faded bell-bottom jeans, a tie-dyed undershirt, and a thin denim jacket. He was pulling a red wagon brimming with handled signs. The facial features of Ho Chi Minh—the Vietnamese communist revolutionary leader—were painted on several of the placards.

"Uncle Ho has been dead for three years," Christy said.

The protester thrust a sign to Christy's chest. "In body only," he said. "The chant refers to his cause. The man was the spiritual leader of a movement. He's a symbol, and in that way he lives on. Come on, carry a sign."

Christy stood frozen.

"What, you don't like that one? Here, how about 'Give Peace a Chance?' No? Here's 'Bring All the GIs Home Now.' Or 'Not One More Dead.' If you're religious, I also got 'Thou Shalt Not Kill.' Come on, do something for your country."

Christy pushed the sign away. "Go to hell."

"What's the matter with you? Don't you care that we're led by patriarchal madmen who send our brothers off to be killed for selfish purposes? Or that we're bombing the hell out of a beautiful, ancient culture of gentle people?" The man paused to study Christy's ragged attire. "Hey, you a vet?"

Christy glared one-eyed.

"It's okay, man. You can help us. Couple of vets even organized this thing. They turned dead set against the War after seeing their brothers murdered and murdering. Hearing them helps you really understand. Come on, I'll introduce you."

"I got nothing to say. I'm meeting someone. That's all."

For two years, Christy had nothing to say to anyone about the War. A member of the Ninth Marine Regiment of the 3rd Marine Division, he had initially been stationed at Camp Carroll, situated a few miles south of the Demilitarized Zone. From there, he was sent on long-range reconnaissance patrols to gather tactical information about the movement of enemy units and supplies along the Ho Chi Minh Trail. In early 1968, just after the first skirmishes of the Tet Offensive, his unit was assigned to fortify Khe Sanh, where for months Christy crouched war-worn behind sandbag revetments as the Viet Cong pummeled the besieged Marines with mortars and artillery.

A month before he was scheduled to be rotated back to the United States, a mortar round exploded twenty feet off his left side, gobbling up his left eye and sucking the hearing from his left ear. After stateside operations performed by four military surgeons with skills of a quality he didn't like to consider, finally Christy decided he looked almost human again.

For a while, Christy had tilted his head back and forth in hopes of seeing colors and hearing sounds that he remembered with vague fondness, of perceiving the world in the way he did before the War. But it was all in vain, and he concluded that the world had been reborn while he was in Vietnam, and he abandoned the attempts. The new world was cast in impalpable grays and dismal blacks, and over it hung an intangible pall only penetrated by abrasive babble. It was a world neither capable of generating delight nor deserving of appreciation.

The drugs followed soon after he reached this conclusion. Christy wasn't certain of his motivation for selling them—he had been dead set against the use of them before the War. But principle seemed to matter little these hazy and confused days. He needed the money, and he did impose some limits by only dealing in marijuana, none of the hard stuff. And the game was exhilarating, the feeling of playing hardball against the cops and outslicking them. It triggered some feeling he couldn't quite identify, having the ephemeral quality of a dream.

The easiest way to sell the stuff was to the draft-dodging college kids. Christy hated the avoiders passionately, not for bypassing a War from which any sentient person would shrink, but for the manner in which they had escaped it, the way they evaded all of the suffering reserved for the downtrodden. Most had been born into a different world, a world of opportunity and privilege, and they knew it and exploited it to their advantage with abandon. It was with a tremendous amount of satisfaction that Christy had watched the avoiders' deferments dry up as the new lottery draft injected a degree of arbitrariness into the selection system that mirrored the favor of their birthrights. Now, the anger in their eyes was edged with the shadow of fear. Give them their drugs, Christy thought, to quell their fear, to fuel their counterculture, and to assuage their guilt.

"Hey, Eyepatch," a voice called from Christy's left side. Christy turned quickly, positioning himself to afford his one good eye its maximum field of view.

"Easy, man," the voice said. "You'll give yourself a heart attack." The voice emanated from a youthful face sheathed in a red bandana and set over a blue striped shirt. The attire signaled Christy that this was the man he had been sent to meet.

"Got a light, Bandana?" Christy said, mouthing a prearranged greeting.

"Lighter's in the bag." Bandana stretched his arm toward Christy, with the strap of a canvas carrying bag hooked around his forefinger.

Christy scanned the immediate area cautiously. He was too close to the crowd, the chants were too loud, and the mood was changing, becoming ugly—One, Two, Three, Four, We Don't Want The Fucking War! Amidst the tumult, three men jogged toward Bandana's position from his right rear. Christy watched them in his peripheral vision. Bandana's attention seemed securely focused on Christy.

"Maybe we should have a chit-chat first," Christy shouted over the rising noise. "Over there, by those trees." Christy dipped his chin in the direction of a manicured clump of shrubs on the north side of the reflecting pool. Bandana stood motionless, watching Christy move.

"Hey, watch out!" Bandana cried. The three jogging men had overtaken Bandana. Each carried a metal bucket, red paint spilling over the sides. The first bumped Bandana square in the chest with a broad shoulder. The bucket caught his chin as he fell, splashing blotches of red onto his torso. Bandana sat spread-legged, shaking his head in disbelief. He brushed his shirt and stared at his reddened hands.

The bucket bearers charged toward the monument. The demonstrators swarmed over the rope barrier, forming a human wedge between the protesters and a dozen police officers. On the floor of the monument, each man pitched the bucket's contents onto the statue of Abraham Lincoln. The splashing liquid covered the stone form in red from the neck down. Droplets speckled Lincoln's somber face, like falling tears of blood.

An enraged park policeman tore through the crowd. He smashed a billy club on the head of a bucket bearer. Christy thought that he heard the repulsive crack through the cacophony—it was the kind of sound his one good ear would not miss. Blood and red paint commingled, and the gruesome mixture slithered down the granite steps.

"You selling or what?" Bandana had approached Christy from his left side again, and he clapped his hand on Christy's left shoulder. "Come on, let's get it done."

Christy studied Bandana slowly, processing details. He was muscular, not a skinny runt like most of Christy's college-age customers; although his face was youthful, his gaze contained a street sense uncommon among students. And Bandana's attention was too firmly held on Christy, while the distracting pandemonium raged about them. No, he was no college-kid.

"Get your hand off me, man," said Christy. "I just asked for a light."

"Yeah? Maybe we should see what's under that jacket." Bandana retracted his hand, stepped back a pace, and smiled broadly. He dropped the canvas bag to his feet and pulled a snub-nosed revolver from under his jacket. "Hit the deck, 'cause you're under arr... Oh no, not again!"

Bandana recoiled, trying to avoid the path of the two escaping bucket bearers. This time, the second hit him broadside, pitching his body headlong into a clump of protesters.

Christy ducked into the crowd. He stayed low, keeping solid on his feet, bumping hard against the frenzied agitators below the waist to clear a path through the chaos. But, after a moment, he needed to find a way out quickly. Beneath the multitude of shoulders, a murky brown and gray underworld churned fiercely, surrealistically. Christy's throat burned, and his temples throbbed incessantly. His cheeks felt as if they were caving into his nasal cavity. The torsos were too close, pushing too tight. A giant rope net seemed to be dragging them nearer.

Then came the feeling of weightlessness. Christy knew what was next—the monstrous image of the net had visited him before. A putrid liquid would spill over him, into his mouth and nose and ears.And the ghostly rope would pull the people, no, they all were corpses, into the air and tighter and tighter against him. With all the force he could muster, Christy clawed against the broken bodies, straining to break free from the net. His fingertips shredded against the lines . . .

The rueful mud world collapsed around Christy as the nightmarish vision sucked hastily into the recesses of his mind. He had exited the throng by toppling into the reflecting pool, where he stood knee-deep in water, staring down stupefied at the stark reflection of his troubled visage. Then, instantaneously, he was clear-headed, feeling as if the flow of oxygen had been restored to his brain. His senses tingled with the sensation of danger. The state of mind was recognizable—it was like being in the midst of a blazing firefight.

Christy sensed Bandana approaching from his left rear; he could almost smell him. He stepped up onto the concrete walkway and broke into a sprint, turning his head over his right shoulder. He caught sight of Bandana and another pseudo-protestor dashing in his direction.

Shit, Christy thought, should have ditched the drugs. He ran wildly, shards of shrapnel burning inside him as if they still carried explosive heat. Christy didn't see the two uniformed policemen crashing into his side from his left front. He didn't hear the thirty-eight pistol crack against the left side of his head. And he didn't feel the cold handcuffs snapping shut around his slack wrists.

●—●-●————●-●"●-●-●————●-●●

During the year of confinement in which he awaited trial, the image of the rope net plagued Christy. It was at times insidious, at times vivid, and always insistent. He was aware that his incarceration aggravated the magnitude and frequency of the occurrences, and he longed for his freedom, not so much for its own sake but more so to dull the throbbing of the visitations.

A week after his conviction, Christy stood in a D.C. courtroom wrapped in a set of shackles, facing sentencing for his offenses.

"I've reviewed the presentence report," said Judge Thurmond Bailey. He dabbed his hawk nose with his finger and slid his hand over his elongated forehead and across the waxy gray hair matted to both sides of his shiny scalp. "I tell you now, I've got problems here. Serious problems."

Lucias Hammaker heavily laid nine moist fingertips atop the shiny surface of the dark cherry-wood counsel table, the remnant of his right forefinger undulating alongside his thumb. He drew his gaze down from the forty-foot ceiling to embrace Bailey's narrow-eyed stare.

"If I may, Your Honor," he said, "I'd like to begin with—"

His vision now centered upon Christy, Bailey ignored the resolute attorney. "Shall we begin with your service record, Mister Christy? Have you been provided an opportunity to review your record?"

"Uh-huh," Christy said.

Hammaker nudged his client. "Yes, Your Honor," he whispered.

Christy didn't acknowledge his attorney. Instead, he gazed lazily at the austere trappings of the courtroom: the cavernous realm of the chamber; the somber, gray-suited prosecutor; the elevated carved wooden bench that swallowed the forefront of the room; the black-robed ruler perched thereon; and the portraits of grim-faced lawmen who presumably preceded him. These symbols that held power over others meant little to a veteran of abandonment and anguish. Even the revolver holstered at the bailiff's side did not provoke Christy's regard, for he had confronted weapons of a hundredfold its destructive power.

"Are you familiar with your Separation Program Number?" Bailey said.

Christy refocused his attention. "I'm not sure."

"They are colloquially called SPINs."

"Yes sir." Christy's words lacked any color of expression. "They're codes the Army gave us to make our good paper into bad."

"Yes, they are numbers assigned to you on your discharge papers, and they reveal information about your conduct. Are you familiar with the number assigned to you?"

"No. They told everyone but us what the numbers meant. All I know is every time I went to get a job, I'd look over the desk at a frowning guy holding a copy of my papers. I went to the bank to get a loan, same thing. They even told some guys' wives what those numbers meant so they could pack their bags and leave before the guys got home. But they never told us."

Bailey winced. He opened a yellowed file folder and set a pair of narrow reading glasses on the precipice of his nose. "Well then, let's be frank. Your Separation Program Number is Forty-Six Alpha. According to the materials provided by the Marine Corps, these numbers designate qualities of 'unsuitability, apathy, defective attitudes and inability to expend effort constructively.'" Bailey's face evinced a cruel satisfaction as the words tumbled off his tongue. He allowed the folder to slide closed and toyed lazily with his wooden gavel.

Christy's lips were set in a tight forced smile. "At least they didn't say I wet the bed."

Bailey leaned back in his leather chair and stretched his fingers into a steeple. "Do you agree with the assessment of your superior officers?"

Hammaker stood erect and his neck twitched. He straightened his soaked collar with the one forefinger he had and ventured another attempt at lawyering. "What my client means to say—"

Bailey swept his hand before his face like a millionaire waiving off a dish unequal to his discriminating taste. "I'm having a chat with your client, Counselor. You'll have your opportunity. Mister Christy?"

Christy stood quietly, appearing as if he had not heard Bailey's invitation, or as if he simply had nothing to say. Then he spoke. "Sir, I was called a lot of things in Vietnam. Newbie at first and then Boonierat and Grunt. Most of my friends called me Esquire because I used to say I wanted to be a lawyer, just like Lucias. At times I guess the officers said some of the things you read. What can I say? Things were tense between the officers and the enlisted, no question. But I like to think that in times that really mattered . . ." Christy halted in mid-stammer, his thread lost.

Bailey cleared his throat. "Aside from a few blemishes, generally your service record is distinguished. Two Bronze Stars, a Silver Star, a Purple Heart, etcetera, etcetera. But my task isn't to evaluate your performance as a combat soldier. Today, I must consider your suitability to function in our community given your offenses. And I see the troubling suggestion from your superiors that you display a number of negative qualities."

"Your Honor, if I may," said Hammaker, expelling his words forcefully. "SPIN codes are prejudicial comments made by men of little moral courage. Rather than filing formal charges that could be defended in the open, they made their insidious remarks covertly, encrypting them and putting them on a man's permanent record, never explaining them properly and never confronting those affected by their charges. My client never had an opportunity to vindicate himself fairly before he was labeled."

"Well now I'm giving him the opportunity to explain, Attorney Hammaker, if you will just shut up. What do you say for yourself, Deric Christy?" Bailey leaned forward, his eyes squashed in the same narrow slit pattern as the glasses dangling beneath them. Christy stood silently, his hands clasped behind his back, his shoulders set in mid-shrug.

Bailey let his eyes fall to the presentence report. "Man of few words indeed. Well, I see you had no criminal record prior to your Vietnam service. But this indicates that six months into your service, you were cited for illicit drug use."

"Your Honor, I really must object at this point," Hammaker said. "Mister Christy did not testify at trial—"

"That's enough," said Bailey.

"—preserving his Fifth Amendment right—"

"I said enough."

"—against self-incrimination. That right remains in place even at this juncture as to—"

Bailey extended his graveled fist, leveling his arm like a pointer. "Bailiff, kindly remove Attorney Hammaker from the courtroom."

The bailiff lurched upright from his perch beside the judge, swinging his head as if trying to discern whether the judge might have summoned someone else. When his comprehension settled, he adjusted his wrinkled uniform and came around the defense table. He took Hammaker by the elbow.

"Your Honor, this isn't necessary," Hammaker pleaded. "I'll ... I'll behave."

"Stand your ground, Bailiff, in case we need you. Well then. All eyes on you, Mister Christy."

The advancement of the bailiff transformed Christy's mood. He wasn't accustomed to this strange form of combat limited to harsh words—he was balled up and full of adrenalin, ready for a physical fight. "If you're asking me if I used drugs in Vietnam, I'd have to say I did. We all did. Most of us did at one time or another anyway. Some guys, especially the Rebs, excuse me, the Southerners, they drank the juice. Gin and Coke, gin and rum, gin and just about anything. Rest of everybody else smoked."

"Marijuana?" Bailey asked.

"Mostly marijuana. Some harder stuff. Everybody got bombed at night, one way or another. Things got so tense that you had to find some way to cope."

Hammaker touched his chin to his chest as if poised in silent prayer. He could contain himself no longer. "Please, Judge, for God's sake. I didn't go. You must let me do something here today."

Bailey's stiff expression relaxed almost imperceptibly, although it did not soften. "Proceed with your statement, Attorney Hammaker. You have exactly two minutes." Bailey swiveled his chair toward a clock on the side wall, seeming to count the ticks of the second hand.

Hammaker wiped his brow and breathed deeply. "Thank you, Your Honor. Your comments at trial make it clear you were displeased with our defense strategy. You should know the design was mine and that Deric resisted at every juncture. As you know, I attempted at trial to establish that Deric suffers from a form of shell shock—that his war experience has had such a profound impact upon his life that, at least at times, he is virtually incapable of distinguishing right from wrong. I know the jury didn't accept our contentions as sufficient to negate criminal intent. But, Your Honor, I respectfully submit the evidence we presented should constitute a mitigating circumstance in sentencing." Hammaker crumpled the yellow pages of his prepared notes.

"You heard the witnesses. This man has been through hell. In Vietnam, Deric discovered levels of emotion he had never before experienced. Pure boredom. Sheer terror. Unfathomable exhilaration. But he never really understood the degree of these emotions. He probably never accepted them or how they made him feel. On his return home, there was only guilt and confusion, amplified by a lack of acceptance, indeed ostracism. From us at home, there was no grand homecoming to act as a catharsis as in other, more popular wars. There was only hatred and ignorance."

Bailey removed his eyes from the clock and seized Christy with them once again. "So you all got bombed, did you?"

Christy's muscles contracted so tightly that his neck appeared to be constructed from thick cable wire. "Sure. Like to know why? No, you don't wanna know. That's the real problem here, isn't it? Nobody really wants to know. You're just a—"

"Get out, Deric," Hammaker said, pushing Christy toward the door. "Just go into the hall and cool down. I'll get you in a couple of minutes."

Bailey leaned over the bench, his face a merciless slab of granite. He pointed a bony finger at Christy. "That won't be necessary. Our discourse is over. Next time Mister Christy leaves this room, he'll be in full custody, bound for the Department of Corrections at Lorton." Bailey shifted his eyes to the bailiff in a silent command and then back to Christy.

"You gentlemen attempted to make legal history in this case. Had the jury been more gullible, I believe you might have succeeded. I'm quite certain if you had, the floodgates would've opened to a slew of defense cases just like yours. Happily, the jury followed my instructions and reached the sensible result. So perhaps we've nipped this in the bud.

"I observed the testimony presented at trial carefully, your psychiatrist, your counselors, your hometown witnesses, and your 'buddies' from Vietnam. Sadly we missed your firsthand account. I tried to give you a chance today to state your case, but your attorney seems to find that unwise. Pity.

"I've thought a great deal about the 'shell-shocked' image your attorney sought to portray. Some of the testimony was quite poignant but, as it related to the law, it all was irrelevant, immaterial, and downright foolish. It appears to me that Vietnam was a cesspool of opportunity for moral degradation that presented each man with a choice of taking a hard stance or taking full opportunity. It's quite clear you chose the latter course, the drugs being your paramount downfall. Perhaps it's simply a sad commentary on young men today that so many compromise their principles.

"And these 'flashbacks' your lawyer alluded to... Mister Christy, yours was a crime of intent— you were not in some delusional state when you were purveying contraband on the streets of Washington." Bailey paused.

"It was the determination of the jury and it is my determination that you have no flashbacks," he continued. "At the time when you perpetrated violations of the criminal code, you had full *mens rea*, wrongful intent, the guilty mind. The circus you frolicked before this court only served to convince me that you are wholly without remorse. Accordingly, I sentence you to a term of five years at Lorton, where you shall have abundant opportunity to reflect on your errant ways. Court adjourned." Bailey spun in his chair and hustled through his chamber door, as if fearing a reprisal from Christy.

The silent prosecutor rose slowly, stuffed his papers into his briefcase and nodded to Hammaker. He departed with a light step, shaking his head in disbelief. Perhaps he was wondering to himself whether another facet of legal history had just been made, since he had obtained the maximum sentence without uttering a single word.

Hammaker stood with his mouth agape, with his shoulders slumped, and utterly speechless. Christy rubbed his own forehead, pinching a piece of shrapnel that floated freely beneath the skin. He gazed around the courtroom and momentarily locked eyes with the handful of green-clad veterans sitting frozen in the back of the courtroom. Their faces showed little sign of life; they appeared like wax likenesses of their former selves. Finally Christy reached behind Hammaker and lightly slapped him on the back. "It's okay, man. Take it easy. I was guilty as charged."

"You were railroaded," Hammaker said. "The judge committed a thousand forms of error we can appeal. He heaped prejudice on the jury—"

"You're not listening, Lucias. I'm guilty."

"And so are we all, Deric, and that's the shame of it. From where I stand, you're a brave and honorable man who's been horribly injured and is just a little confused. And I should know. I interviewed the witnesses, I prepared the case. I know the story you wouldn't let me tell the jury. Your innocence was betrayed. In every sense of the word, you are guiltless. It's just that I couldn't prove it."

Christy managed the wry smile of a condemned man. "Jail can't be all that bad," he said, although knowing that the worst was true. "Least they didn't send me back to Vietnam."

Hammaker rested his imperfect hand on Christy's shoulder. "We never should have sent you in the first place, my friend. Not in the first place."

<hr />

With Hammaker's soft touch on his forearm, Christy took his leave from the past, turning on the park bench to the aging and troubled face of his attorney and friend.

"I often wish I could clean up the past too, Deric," Hammaker said. "But I usually find myself relegated to finding ways to move on in spite of it."

Through the fabric of Hammaker's breast pocket, Christy lightly patted the envelope he had given to him. "That's what I'm trying to do. With the will, and for Bran. I'm looking to the future."

"Someone else's future. What about your own?"

Christy's only response was to stare off in the direction of the Vietnam Memorial, the shiny black granite containing the etched names of tens of thousands of Americans, whose own futures had been sealed long ago. Even his blind eye seemed to suggest his thoughts: What about theirs? What about their futures? Christy felt a sense of longing, for what he was not certain, but he could not subdue a nagging sense that his own future, like those of his comrades, was carved in stone on the face of some long, bleak wall with sharply defined boundaries. He nodded at Hammaker and stood.

"So that's it, Deric? You'll just walk away again for another two years? Don't do it, please. Let me try for you. These people I know, they truly have power. And I can reach them quickly. I can get answers fast. Just tell me where I can find you."

Christy smiled. It wasn't his habit to leave calling cards with anyone, particularly with those very few who he counted as his friends. But Hammaker's passion impressed him, just as it had so many years ago when the compassionate attorney had defended Christy in a court of law, free of charge. Even if he himself were beyond help, Christy sensed that Hammaker needed to reach out to him, and in the way beggars may sometimes become priests, he resolved in that instant to minister to his former lawyer.

"Parkside Motel," Christy said, only so loud as to be understood. "On Route One, Northeast. I'll probably be there a week. After that, well, who knows?"

Chapter fourteen

After returning from West Point, Ashford attempted to absorb himself in his work as a draftsman, but he could not quell his anticipation for the upcoming training at AP Hill or his perpetual concern about how he would approach the remediation of Nick Trent. Two days before the scheduled departure for camp, he was summoned to the flight facility for an impromptu meeting with command staff.

Ashford sat uncomfortably in a gray metal chair in a small office, in which four other seats were occupied by commissioned officers. Crawford entered the room, appearing somber, and he leaned against the wall. Behind a steel desk sat a gray-haired colonel, his back ramrod straight, his face set in what appeared to be a permanent scowl. The etched planes of his features were tapered with military preciseness, and his eyes were aggressive and seemed to push forward with his words. A silver eagle lay atop each of his shoulders, and the tag sewn onto his camouflage uniform displayed his surname in large black letters: *Harker*.

"Gentlemen," said Colonel Harrison Harker. "This aviation battalion is facing an Inspector General evaluation. Of my five companies, this unit is the one I'm most concerned about. The leader of the inspection team is an old wartime commander of mine, General Tarsavage. The way I remember him, I'm guessing his focus will be on combat assault operations. I don't have to remind you of the importance of this inspection to this unit."

"And to your coveted star," Winston said, entering the room, apparently uninvited and unwelcome. He spoke softly into his hand, but his voice was audible to those nearby.

"You have something to add, Mister Winston?" said Harker.

"I said we've come very far, so very far," Winston said.

Harker stroked his bloodless lips. "This unit has improved. But there's a long way to go. Who's responsible for Warrant Officer Trent?"

"Sir," said a young man name-plated Lieutenant Dickson as he came to attention. "That would be our new platoon leader, Lieutenant Ashford."

Ashford glanced at Dickson and made a mental note.

"Ashford," said Harker, locking his gaze upon the young lieutenant. "Have you taken appropriate action to remedy Warrant Officer Trent's military dress?"

"Is Trent wearing a dress again?" Winston whispered.

"Say again, Mister," Harker said.

"Wasn't worth repeating," Winston said.

"Well, Lieutenant?" asked Harker. "We're waiting."

Ashford stammered. "I didn't know I was supposed—"

"Didn't know? What kind of an excuse—"

Crawford leaned forward, his fingers interlaced. "Sir, if I might explain. Lieutenant Ashford arrived for his first drill last month. We've only just taken him through the basic orientation, and he hasn't had a full briefing on his assignment."

"I'm not interested in excuses," Harker said. "I want results. Lieutenant Ashford, you're responsible for Trent. Last drill he was out of uniform in his white T-shirt and gym socks, and his Fu

Manchu is totally unsatisfactory. That man shows up on Friday in less than full military attire, I'll hold you personally responsible. Copy?"

"Yes, Sir."

"You can say Roger to acknowledge. I like to use aviation lingo in our little meetings. With the responsibilities of command, I don't get in as much flying as I would like to. I like to feel as if I'm at the controls, so to speak."

"Probably logs flight time from his desk," Winston muttered.

"We're still having difficulty receiving your transmissions, Mister Winston," Harker said.

"Must be a problem with the avionics," Winston replied.

Harker raised his torso from his seat. His hands were balled in fists, and his elbows rode heavily on the desk. "Has anyone counseled you on your weight condition, Winston?"

"I started getting into shape," Winston said. "But the undertaker says 'what the hell are you doing? Are you trying to put me out of business?'"

"All right, all right." Harker waved Winston away. "We all know our jobs. Let's do them and do them well. I'll be satisfied when we get a full-combat ready rating from the inspection team."

Crawford straightened. "Sir, full-combat ready is a little unrealistic given our outdated equipment and—"

"In order to assure maximization of our resources," Harker said, "I've assigned Captain Zuckerman as acting Company Commander until I decide on a permanent replacement."

Crawford put his hand to his head. "I heard that was under consideration, but with all due respect, Sir, Captain Zuckerman is a staffer, ehr,... an administrator. He hasn't been in the field in years."

"Captain Zuckerman is an officer I trust to go by the book and obtain superior results. Over and out." The colonel rose to his feet, and the officers came to attention, the young officers abruptly, the older ones reluctantly.

·•—•——•••——•·

After the door closed, Winston spoke first. "Over and out? What a jackass! Kevin, all that guy cares about is his promotion. Screw Battalion. One minute we've got this staff puke in the classroom raving about communists, and the next instant he's our Company Commander. Not to mention this other moron pretending the office is his helicopter." Winston grabbed at an imaginary cyclic with both hands and mimicked radical control movements. "Pre-landing check please!"

"Enough," said Crawford. "I'll get the maintenance report from you in a minute, Gene. Right now let's finalize the plans for camp. Oh, I almost forgot. Lieutenant Ashford, the commissioned officers in this unit have extra-duty assignments in addition to regular platoon leader responsibilities. For now you'll be standing in for Lieutenant Witmore, who, well . . ." Having lost his thread, Crawford lifted a small black notebook from his pocket and leafed through yellowed pages. "Ah yes, the extra duties, you'll be taking over as mess officer and drug enforcement officer."

Winston laughed. "Congratulations, kid. That means you get to eat last and watch the guys piss in a bottle."

"Piss in a bottle?" Ashford said.

"We undergo annual urine screenings for illicit drugs," Crawford replied. "Each officer is required to fill a plastic cup. You'll supervise the festivities."

"Looks like you're Nick Trent's babysitter too," Dickson added.

"We'll talk about your specific responsibilities later," said Crawford, "but for now, you should know that drug interdiction is taking on an increasingly important role in our unit. It's not just urine screenings. The Defense Authorization Act of 1989 allows the use of the National Guard to aid federal and state law enforcement agencies in drug interdiction. Our unit will provide aviation support. It's a new area for us, and we're still learning the ropes. Supervising the program will be part of your job here."

"Yes, Sir," Ashford said unenthusiastically. Systematically, he was witnessing his visions of flight vaporizing. Mess hall, urine tests, babysitting, and what else, he thought.

Piss control officer. Shit.

Chapter fifteen

Courtroom Three of the Dauphin County Courthouse in center city Harrisburg was a dark-lit, old-style chamber with an elevated ceiling. A traditional railing separated the bench, tables, and jury box from the gallery, where cushionless wooden benches were arrayed to accommodate spectators. Rayful Bigelow sat listlessly behind a walnut table, awaiting the return of his public defender from the lavatory. The judge's tipstaff held a suspicious eye to him and a chubby finger on the doorbell-shaped alarm switch beneath his station. Hampered but not harried by chained wrists, Bigelow dealt imaginary poker hands to an invisible opponent. He counseled the air to always play a bluff first, no matter how bad the cards dealt.

A man dressed in casual street attire aggressively pushed through the railing gate, and a silver badge was dangling from a lanyard draped over his neck. He seemed pleased to find Bigelow alone. In his scrapes with the law, Bigelow had encountered the man before—his name was Stuart Zackaeus. He was a CAN cop, a member of Harrisburg's Community Attack on Narcotics, a squad of drug enforcement officers that employed assertive methods in its efforts to stanch the flow of product through the city's increasingly prolific drug market.

"Morning, Scrounger," said Zackaeus. He had coal black hair and eyes to match, and when he spoke, his cheeks lifted and his forehead creased. "How's the food in the tank?"

"My cooking's better," Bigelow said.

"So I hear. Care to tell me about the menu?"

"Specials are eggs Benedict and tuna casserole."

"What about Rocket Pack?" Zackaeus said, his voice dripping with derision.

"Song by Elton John, isn't it?"

Zackaeus smiled wanly. "That's Rocket Man, you idiot. But, so you're a funny man. Well, I just went through your jacket, and it's even funnier. It's longer than my credit card bill, and this distribution rap is your third big one. Know what they have to say about three strikes nowadays, Scrounger? Hell, I think the judge could knock you out of the park."

Bigelow listened intently as Zackaeus played his hand. He knew it was a good one, and he wished he could improve his own, but the cards lay face down on the table. All that remained was for him to stare blankly into his opponent's self-assured eyes and ante up. "I might have something. Something big, like the French connection. I'm not a player, see? Just happen to know someone who knows someone—"

"Where have I heard this crap before?" Zackaeus pointed a finger at the hollow of Bigelow's chest as if aiming a spear. "You wanna see what's behind door number one? You give me Cruise and his infernal Rocket Pack. That's the only deal in town. Otherwise it's door number three. Three strikes, get it?"

Bigelow recognized the edge in his own voice, and he knew that Zackaeus heard it too. "You're living in the old days. I don't deal with Cruise no more. No more street drugs for me. Learned my lesson. But this other thing, lemme tell you—"

"Keep dreaming, Scrounger. You're the smallest-time low-life I even take time to think about. That quarter-ki the locals found at your place doesn't even belong to you, I'd bet. My guess is you skimmed it off of Cruise. He'll be mighty upset when he gets wind."

"I got no business with Cruise."

"Maybe he'll have some with you. I hear he doesn't like losing his stashes. Feel safe in the tank, Scrounge?"

"I take care of myself."

"Don't be so sure. Have you heard that Jorge Munzo got himself arrested last night in Dauphin County?"

Bigelow's eyes widened with dread. "Munzo?"

"Yeah. Drunk and disorderly. Now I have no idea why one of Cruise's enforcers might be punching out parking meters across from City Hall, do you? Funny thing too, he didn't make bail, seeing as how the judge set it really low."

"Parking meters?" Bigelow echoed.

"Think someone wants you to have company in the tank? Will Munzo notice when I come see you every day?"

"Cruise will know you're full of shit." A mist of spittle trailed Bigelow's words. "You'd haul him in, in a second, if you had him by the balls."

"Maybe I will. I might bring him down to share your cell too."

Bigelow shrugged purposefully, putting on his bravest affect. "Suit yourself, the more the merrier."

Zackaeus smiled and retreated down the narrow corridor between the gallery benches. In the doorway he passed a thin, well-tanned man with a carefully clipped mustache, who was dressed in a brown suit and a paisley tie. The mustached man engaged Zackaeus with his eyes. "I hope you're not questioning my client out of my presence."

"Merely shootin' the breeze, Counselor." Zackaeus let the door swing closed behind him.

The lawyer gestured to Bigelow. "What did he ask?"

"Just what's for lunch," said Bigelow, returning to his imaginary deck.

• ▬ •▬━━━━•▬••▬•━━━━•▬•

A few minutes passed. A balding man, the prosecutor, entered from the hallway, and he was attired more smartly than Bigelow's attorney. A black-robed judge, young for his position, appeared through a wooden door behind the bench. Bigelow popped to his feet, his chains clattering. "Not guilty, Judge," he said.

The judge sighed, rubbed his eye with his forefinger, and shuffled papers on the bench. "Two counts of possession, two of distribution. Since your client took it upon himself to enter his plea, why don't we ask the Commonwealth for its views on bail?"

"We're asking for the maximum, Your Honor," the prosecutor said. "I intended to offer the testimony of a CAN officer, but unfortunately he doesn't seem to be present."

Bigelow smiled his Scrounger's grin. The CAN cop was gone. This might work out after all ...

The double doors to the courtroom unfolded inward, and the Scrounger's smile melted into nothing. "The Commonwealth is ready to proceed, Your Honor," said the prosecutor. "I'd like to present Officer Stuart Zackaeus."

Zackaeus stepped into the witness box, and the judge asked him if he intended to tell the truth. Bigelow was awed by Zackaeus's altar-boy gaze as he took the oath. He could learn a great deal about lying from cops, he thought, although unfortunately on this occasion Zackaeus wouldn't need to resort to falsehood.

The prosecutor touched his lapels. "Please tell us your duty assignment, Officer Zackaeus."

"Field officer in the city's CAN unit."

"Are you aware of the defendant's activities in Harrisburg's Hill Manor low-income housing area?"

"Very familiar." Zackaeus spread his arms wide. "Judge, we have evidence that this here defendant is involved in the sale of a designer drug being touted as some sort of crack and heroin derivative."

"Can you describe the defendant's involvement?"

"Word on the street is that the Scrounger... the defendant is playing himself as the chemist, a cooker in street lingo."

"What do you mean 'playing himself'?"

"Bigelow isn't smart enough to tie his own shoelaces let alone invent a designer drug. So he isn't really the chemist. But he's getting raw materials, cocaine hydrochloride and heroin powder, from a street-level dealer called Cruise. He shows up later with Rocket Pack, claiming to have cooked it up from the coke and smack."

"How do you know the defendant isn't manufacturing Rocket Pack from those raw materials?"

"We've got samples of Rocket Pack. Chemical analysis shows only modest amounts of cocaine and heroin."

"So what's the defendant doing?"

"We think he's playing the margin."

"The margin?"

"He buys the synthetic Rocket Pack for less than what he can get for the cocaine and heroin powder."

"What exactly is in Rocket Pack?" the prosecutor asked.

"Mostly Meth. That's methamphetamine, commonly called speed on the street. It has similar effects to cocaine, but they're longer-lived and the crash afterwards is usually more severe. There are also traces of fentanyl."

"Fentanyl?" the judge said.

"See, the rock he's pandering is primarily ice, which is a smokable form of methamphetamine. It normally has a crystalline appearance, but whoever's making this stuff found a way to crust it over with a grayish powder to make it look more like crack. And in the crust there are traces of fentanyl."

"Can you tell us more about fentanyl?" the prosecutor asked.

Zackaeus held his palms inches apart, intensely peering between the open space. "A synthetic opiate more powerful than heroin. Few years back it was sold as Tango and Cash in New York. I was working the Big Apple then, and I saw it kill dozens of people. All said and done, it killed hundreds. And now it's on the streets of Harrisburg."

"What evidence do you have that this drug is so dangerous?"

"I got here a picture." Zackaeus rummaged in his inside coat pocket, retrieved a photograph, and laid it reverently on the bench before the judge. "This here is Marisa Gazis. Rocket Pack killed her last Wednesday."

Bigelow was on his feet. "Not true," he whined. "Nobody would be stupid enough to smoke stuff like that if it'd kill them."

Zackaeus shifted his weight onto his thighs as if preparing to pounce. "Judge, an OD only increases the hype, and he knows it."

The prosecutor took the reins. "Under the circumstances, Judge, the Commonwealth is asking that bail be denied. Our concern is not only for the People but also for the defendant's safety. His charade cannot last long. His product is new and the market is hungry, but the people he's dealing with will wise up soon. When they do, his life will be in peril. At a minimum, the

Commonwealth asks bail be set at no less than two hundred fifty thousand dollars."

The judge rubbed his chin. "The Court accepts the Commonwealth's alternative recommendation. Bail is set at two hundred fifty thousand. Trial's on the next criminal calendar."

After the judge retired to his chambers, Zackaeus stepped down from the witness box and planted his stout frame solidly in front of Bigelow. "I did pretty good, eh?"

Bigelow gulped.

"See, I don't care what happens to you, maggot, but what happened in New York won't happen here. No more Rocket Pack goes out on my streets, even if I have to let out word that gets you wasted in the tank."

"About the other thing I was talking about. Remember? Like the French Connection?"

Zackaeus patted Bigelow on the back, a hard aggressive swat, and he turned his back. "Cruise is the only deal in town, Scrounger," he said, walking away. "Unless you got two hundred fifty big ones."

Bigelow's eyes drooped.

Zackaeus glanced over his shoulder. "I was guessing you'd come up a little short. So sit tight. See what happens. Dauphin County Jail's a nice place to visit, but I sure wouldn't wish to die there."

Bigelow sat on the table, deflated. There was always an angle to play, a game to run. But this cop was smart, and he knew his game too well. Zackaeus wanted his ace card up front, but a good player always holds back. A good player always plays his bluff first.

Wednesday afternoon, Washington.

Don Sage stood opposite Harry Crim in the drawing room of the White House aide's Georgetown townhouse. Crim was a tall man in his fifties, whose snow-white hair seemed to reflect the yellow from his button-down oxford shirt. Sage wore a gray blazer and a narrow black tie over a starched white shirt. He wished to look prim and proper for his meeting with the professor. It was his Joe Friday look. Just the facts, bitch, he thought.

"Can we talk about the ground rules now, Harry?" Sage asked, leveling his eyes to Crim's own.

Crim shook off Sage's scrutiny, lifted a china pot, and poured a steaming cup of tea. He held it out to Sage.

"Not for me, Harry," Sage said. "I get the feeling you're stalling."

"I merely think it would be appropriate to begin our substantive discussions when our guest arrives."

Sage flopped incongruously into a delicate Victorian chair and rested his chin on his hand. "It's been a real lousy weekend, Harry. Gimme a break, huh? I got a couple things in mind for the professor, but there will be some areas out of bounds. Critical operations—"

Crim unfolded a newspaper. "Tragedy everywhere these days. Would you look at this? Multiple murder up on 25th Street last week—the Saturday Night Family Massacre, people are calling it. Five-year-old girl and her parents brutally gunned down in their home. No witnesses. Looks like it was drug-related. My God, finally a family finds a way to stay together and then this. The President sorely wishes we could put an end to such atrocities."

"Me too, Harry. I wish someone could have stopped that one too. Now about the ground rules—"

Sage was interrupted by firm rapping. Closest to the foyer, he opened the door to face an attractive black woman, probably in her mid-forties. Not black. African American, he thought. Have to be politically correct nowadays. Everyone being so goddamn uptight.

The woman's medium-length hair was pulled naturally away from her face, and only down-like curls touched her forehead. Her skin was unadorned by makeup or jewelry. It was her eyes that engaged him though, sharp and quick and fearless. Even more, there was an urgency behind them. "Ruth Scarbrough to see Harry Crim," the woman said.

Sage studied her face for a few seconds longer. In his peripheral vision, he saw the rounded stomach protruding from under her knit blouse. He wasn't expecting her to be black. Or pregnant.

"This way please," he said with all the politeness he could muster.

"Ruth!" Crim said, stepping into the foyer with extended arms. "How have you been?"

"To tell you the truth, I've had better flights. And forty-five may be just a bit old for this baby thing." Scarbrough cradled her enlarged stomach in her hands.

"With three months to go, it looks to me like you're none the worse for wear." Crim ushered Scarbrough into the drawing room.

"How is the President?" Scarbrough asked.

"Getting along amazingly given the upheaval in Congress," said Crim. "He still seems to thrive on all of the activity."

Sage cleared his throat.

"My apologies," Crim said, nodding to Sage. "Professor Ruth Scarbrough, Agent Donald Sage from the DEA."

Sage peered down at his hand as Scarbrough took it, and he regarded the force with which she squeezed. Neither spoke in greeting. Sage felt a shared tension that wasn't intentional but was nonetheless inevitable. He flashed a smile meant to be engaging and regretted it immediately, knowing it rang as false as it felt.

Strange how a decade of undercover work had never taught him to smile disarmingly. "Why don't you tell me exactly what you want to accomplish, Professor, and I'll see how we can help you."

"Personally, what I want is unimportant," Scarbrough said, rather coldly. "I'm acting at the request of the President. The President wishes me, as acting chairperson of his new Special Committee on Drug Enforcement Strategy, to observe active DEA operations and report my observations."

"Would you like to tell me just what the President's looking for?" Sage asked.

"The President is interested in the effectiveness of current drug enforcement strategies and advice on alternative strategies."

"Alternative strategies? For example?"

"I'd think with your fourteen years' service, you'd know very well the tools you have at your disposal." Scarbrough smiled for the first time.

Sage studied the professor's set jaw. She knows my years on the job, he thought. Woman's done some homework. No wonder she hates me already.

Crim intervened. "Now, Ruth, days before you arrived, you were causing ripples in Washington. You're right, the President wants your committee to study enforcement policy and provide your assessment. But we need to tread lightly with entanglements in field work. Shall we do Agent Sage the courtesy of listening to his proposal?"

"Good Lord, forgive my poor manners," Scarbrough said. "By all means Agent Sage."

Sage was back on center stage. Throw the pitch, see how it goes. "I thought awhile about this. Maybe the best place to start is with the experts. I can set you up for interviews with specialists in any drug. Caine. King Kong pills. Smack. Joyweed, sopors, rocket fuel, crack, speedball. You name it."

"The DEA is that specialized?"

"Not the Agency. I'm planning to send you on to Marion or Lewisburg. The Big Houses. Federal penitentiaries. The real experts are in there. Wanna talk to Drug Lords? Got lots of Latins. Or smugglers or wholesalers or brokers? We got kingpins and gangs and rippers. Maybe a cook? You can even pick a brand. Black Magic, Kojak, The Beast. Or you want to get the inside on life on the streets? Plenty of knuckleheads and hopheads and clockers. Name your poison."

"That's not what we're looking for at all," Scarbrough said. "No, our initial focus is on field operations."

First line of defense down; Sage fully expected that. He rummaged in his briefcase for a legal pad. "Well, we got a couple things of pretty high priority I'm reluctant to open to a civilian. But under the circumstances, guess I got no choice. Right now in Durham, North Carolina we're working with the Coast Guard on Operation Seaside Sweep. We have reason to believe the Croatan National Forest is being used as a port for incoming cocaine traffic."

"So far up the East Coast?"

"Last few years, we put the squeeze on ocean traffic cruising up the Cocaine Highway from the Caribbean into southern coastline. Some smugglers think it's safer landing further north. We've dedicated major resources, including a radar surveillance balloon and a thirty-five foot catamaran with a nine hundred horsepower engine."

"Very impressive." Scarbrough stifled a yawn. "And you use these kinds of resources all along the southern border?"

"And more."

"And how much of the drug traffic, in volume, would you estimate you interdict?"

Sage swallowed hard. Statistics had just crossed his desk estimating the figure at less than eight percent. "A significant percentage."

"Significant? You win one, the bad guys win forty, I would venture. No shame, Agent Sage. God himself would have difficulty sealing off a three thousand-mile-wide southern border. Nevertheless, I assume you have written estimates, and I'd like to see them. But as far as this Seaside Sweep, in my condition I can't tolerate the ocean."

"Yeah. I didn't know you were . . ." Sage ruffled through the pages of his pad. "Well in Denver we're conducting Operation Eagle's Nest. We're watching a group of pilots we think are distributing cocaine interstate. We're using a Navy E2C surveillance plane—"

"My interest lies on the East Coast."

"Wish I'd known that. Only one thing fits the bill then. In Central Pennsylvania, we're helping local law enforcement search for a large-scale marijuana farm and processing operation we're calling Operation Nature Grow. We're coordinating with the FBI and dedicating resources from our Harrisburg and Scranton offices. We've also requested aviation assets from the National Guard. Fortunately the area is a routine training area for the Guard, so we don't think the increased aviation will draw notice. Good chance to see a large-scale interagency effort."

"North Carolina? Denver? Central Pennsylvania? Did you consider Bolivia?"

Sage felt small beads of sweat forming in the cracks in his forehead. At least she didn't say Peru, he thought. "One could get killed in Bolivia, ma'am."

"One can get killed right here in Washington too, Agent Sage, or don't you read the papers?"

Sage's eyes narrowed under furrowed brows. She had her finger on a sore spot, and all he could do was hope she wouldn't twist.

"I'd prefer to start with something more urban in nature," Scarbrough continued. "In fact, I have an operation in mind right here in northeast Washington."

Sage gazed at Crim who shrugged inquisitively. "We're on top of a few situations in the Metro area."

"One in particular," Scarbrough said.

"You'll have to help me along."

"Operation Soldier Man ring a bell?"

Sage felt as if he had been punched. He caught his jaw dropping but prevented his eyes from widening more than a fraction of an inch. "Operation what?"

"Nice try."

"Assuming there were an Operation, what did you say, soldier person, what do you think it's all about?"

"An informant deep in the heart of an international cocaine and heroin trafficking operation dealing in real weight."

"And how would you know about this alleged informant?"

"That's not important. What is important is the President's desire to develop new strategies for addressing the drug problem. Soldier Man is where I want to start."

"Harry, help me out here," Sage said, holding his palms forward. "What are you spoon-feeding the professor, Harry?"

"This is all news to me," Crim said. "Ruth, you'll have to slow down. Sounds like you may be treading in dangerous waters."

"I was promised full cooperation," Scarbrough said.

"Don?" Crim said uneasily.

"Hey, I'm cooperating here. Just I got nothing on this soldier boy thing."

"Soldier Man," Scarbrough said.

"Whatever. I'm trying to show you a very important operation in Pennsylvania. Local intelligence says it's big. We think it's somewhere along the Appalachian Trail between Harrisburg and Allentown."

Scarbrough leaned forward and sighed. "How have you narrowed that down?"

A hint of interest. Or was it? Sage understood now he was dealing with a viper. The professor had taken everything he was willing to give and then went in for the kill.

Sage crossed the room and sat on the couch beside Scarbrough. He slid several black-and-white photographs from a manila folder and extended one to Scarbrough. The picture showed a man wearing a knit ski-mask. He stood in a dirty T-shirt beside a bushy plant six feet in height, holding clusters of leaves and buds in cupped hands extended to the camera. The pose was discernibly a haughty one.

"Where did you get this?" Scarbrough asked.

"High Times Magazine."

"You're a subscriber?"

"We review the publication regularly for this type of thing."

"Looks to me like this is on an incline," Scarbrough said. "A mountain or perhaps a hill. Evergreens in the background, general ground cover. Could be anywhere on the East Coast."

The professor seemed interested, Sage thought; perhaps she was softening. "Look closer. Through the treetops on the right."

"I don't see anything."

"Nothing? Look here, closely." Sage pointed to a small, faded blur visible behind the tree branches.

"So?" Scarbrough said. "What is it?"

"A UH-1H." Sage was taking some comfort in his new teaching role.

"You speak in riddles, Agent Sage. We're not going to get along."

"A UH-1H Huey helicopter. Pennsylvania Army National Guard helicopter to be precise." Sage slipped two more pictures across the table to Scarbrough, enlargements of the blur. The image of a helicopter was clear in the first enlargement; the second contained a closer image revealing dark lines over a white blotch. "The seal identifies the helicopter."

"How does this narrow the location?"

"The chopper is flying low level. There are only a few military operations areas in Pennsylvania where low-level flying is permitted. Northern Training Area at Fort Indiantown Gap, a training area at the Michaux State Forest west of Carlisle, and one in Pittsburgh. Given the terrain, we've ruled out Pittsburgh for now."

"The DEA deeply cares about some backwoods pothead sprouting home grown?"

"Ma'am, I'm not sure what your agenda . . ." Sage felt himself half-rising and quickly brought himself under control. "It's part of our job to give advice to local agencies in dealing with this kind of thing. I brought some satellite photos to show how we can zero in on these fields."

Scarbrough no longer seemed to be listening. "Have you got any information that distribution is interstate?" she said. She didn't wait for a response. "I didn't think so. You'll have to do better."

"Well, ma'am, unfortunately there isn't a whole hell of a lot more I can do. You wanted to see what I do for a living, and I'm trying to show you."

Crim put his hand on Scarbrough's and patted, drawing a spiteful stare. "I've only so much leeway here, Ruth. I suggest you, I mean we, start where Agent Sage suggests. Quite candidly, I'm inclined to trust his judgment. I've seen reports that suggest that recently marijuana displaced corn as the Nation's number one cash crop. So I wouldn't belittle the operation. If this situation turns out to be unsatisfactory, perhaps we can get you involved in another. In fact, this will probably get you through the pregnancy without exposure to... the more unseemly elements we have here in Washington."

Scarbrough sat with her arms folded across her lap and impertinence in her posture, but she seemed to be considering Crim's last remark. "Let's do some straight talking. I wasn't asked to come to this job with an objective point of view. I'm expecting to find a misplacement of priorities and a misallocation of resources in our national drug enforcement policy. And it looks like you're going to prove my case for me right off the bat. You're sending federal agents and dedicating major aviation assets to look for some burn-outs from the sixties, who are dropping cannabis seeds in the woods. This is ludicrous."

Sage sat tight-lipped. "It's an important operation."

"It's a crock," Scarbrough said with matching terseness. "You're making my job very easy."

"We're done here," Sage said.

Crim intervened. "Look folks. Why don't we give Ruth time to consider your proposals? How long before you intend to get started?"

"I have committee meetings for the next two weeks."

"Two weeks." Crim glanced at his watch calendar. "Not much time. And Agent Sage probably needs time to arrange for your participation in whichever location you decide. Why don't I arrange a conference call for, say next Friday? By then we may all have some better idea where we're going. Any objections?"

Silence.

"It's settled then," Crim said. "Tea anyone?"

"No." Scarbrough wheeled to level smoldering eyes at Sage. "I don't want to be sent to the boondocks, Agent Sage, and I won't be placated. I want to observe the DEA's conduct of Operation Soldier Man here in Washington. Harry, I'll expect you to get me an audience with the Chief of Staff before Thursday afternoon."

"Hey yeah, Harry," Sage said, "and for God's sake don't forget to reschedule my golf game with the President. I gave you what I got, lady. I tried to roll out the red carpet as best as I could, in my own way. You should understand though, I'm understandably reluctant to bring a civilian, a pregnant civilian, into an ongoing operation."

"You can try to minimize, distract, and obfuscate," Scarbrough said, "and I can ride you like a jockey, or we can work together, in which case I can blend into the woodwork."

Crim chuckled.

"Something funny?" Scarbrough said.

"Sorry, Ruth, but in present condition you don't fit the bill of a jockey. And you certainly aren't going to do much blending."

Sage squeezed his clenched fist. "You'll excuse me, I gotta use the phone."

"By all means," said Crim. "Use the bedroom upstairs for privacy."

•—•—•————•—•••—•————•—•

Sage climbed the spiral steps. In the bedroom, he closed the door, flopped on the bed, and punched number pads on the phone.

"Ramírez," a voice answered.

"Yeah, Gerry. Just finishing up my meeting."

"How'd it go?"

"Uh, like clockwork."

"Gotta hand it to you, Sage."

"Any word on my gun?"

211

"We looked everywhere. Somebody's got to have picked it up. Office of Chief Counsel says we're to cooperate with the locals in the investigation of the Massacre but agreed we shouldn't go public with our involvement. Deputy Director said you should wait another week and then report your weapon missing."

"And take a chance no one shoots up the White House with it in the meantime. Damn."

"I feel better about it, Don. The locals have confirmed it was the machine pistol that hit the girl."

"I told you that."

"And everything's cleared through the Agency. Long as everything's clean in our statements."

"It was a clean shoot, Gerry." Sage paused. "Two more things. Call Harrisburg for me, will you? Tell them we may have to go with Operation Nature Grow. We'll need some aviation standing by. Better make this thing look good."

"Sure, Don. Something wrong?"

"Nah. Nothing."

"Real pushover, huh?"

"Don't worry. I can handle her. Second, who besides you and me knows anything about Soldier Man?"

"Standard chain of command."

"I want to know of any contacts with the professor, her name is Ruth Scarbrough, or any member of her committee or anyone who has anything to do with that damn committee."

"We got a leak?"

"Just check." Sage dropped the phone in its cradle and hesitated as long as he thought was practical before heading down the stairs.

Ruth Scarbrough left the meeting feeling exhausted. She had so much to do in Washington, and obviously Sage would do everything in his power to obstruct her. As she drove through the narrow streets of Georgetown, she focused on what she would need to do to bring about a change in the way the Nation looks at drug enforcement. Since the incident at the University, she had made this into her campaign.

In 1984, the University of California at Los Angeles seemed an oasis from the violence in the surrounding city. On the campus, Scarbrough had raised her son Preston, while she taught classes. Preston grew tall and strong, like his father but less fickle. At sixteen he was broad through the chest, like a Greek sculpture, yet he was slim and flexible at the waist, and his curly black hair was cropped closely around his rugged young face. He was truly beautiful. Beautiful and safe.

But Preston was a boy, still subject to the whims of children. Drugs were a mainstay at the University, and Scarbrough's choice was not to intrude too much into that part of Preston's life for fear he might reject her guidance altogether. She mentored him whenever possible, but she avoided overt intrusion. He would make the right choices on his own. He was becoming that kind of man.

One choice, however, had been wrong. Preston involved himself with a group of gang members from East Los Angeles. He began coming home late. Coming home stoned. Bringing those awful boys to the University campus. By necessity Scarbrough changed her parenting strategy. She coaxed Preston, begged him, to extricate himself from the perilous clique, but in the end she knew he would have to recognize on his own where his priorities should lie. Where they must lie. Finally, Preston began to come around. He refused their calls. He walked the other way.

Then, before her eyes, they gunned him down on her front lawn. As a nurse in Vietnam, she had seen the remains of stout men blown to bits, but she would not have thought it possible of her boy, the boy sculpted of stone. Yet the ballet would play over and over in her head, in slow motion. Preston, walking in his tank top and shorts and with a book bag slung over his shoulder. The loud engine noise, a black sedan rounding the corner, fast, very fast. Preston turning. A look of recognition, a look of horror.

Then the stone boy, the safe boy, the beautiful boy, was torn to pieces. There must have been ear-shattering explosions and heart-wrenching screams. There would have been laughter from those monsters. But in her remembrances, Scarbrough couldn't hear the sounds; she guessed she shut them out to defend her sanity. The pictures remained though, Preston's shoulder imploding, his disembowelment, the crumpling of his frame, her kneeling over his wrecked body, cradling it, looking into shock-filled eyes, and her jaw straining to scream for help. Although there was no sound.

Months after Preston died, when she felt strong enough, Scarbrough returned to the University. She shifted her teaching emphasis from battered women to drug-related violence. Her efforts culminated in her controversial book: *The Accounting: A Vision for the Future of Drug Policy.*

As time passed, she scrutinized her graduate students for the right one, a tall one, a smart one, with good muscles and an even disposition. It was years before she found him, but when she did, she wasted no time in seducing him, getting him to plant his seed in her. She had to restore hope. A boy would give her hope again.

Scarbrough parked on Pennsylvania Avenue in front of the massive Willard Hotel. Extravagant and exclusive, the white marble high-rise housed a number of executive office suites and a few boutique law firms. She stepped from the elevator and paused before the shiny gold placard of Hunsler and Hammaker, P.C.

Lucias Hammaker greeted her at the lobby door and ushered her into his office. Scarbrough noticed that the hollowness in his cheeks starkly contrasted with the paunchiness around his beltline.

"A little weekend work, Lucias?" Scarbrough said.

Hammaker laughed. "Saturday, Sunday, midnight, whatever it takes to stay on top. I've got a corporate merger closing Monday, and it's taking me all weekend to straighten out the documents. Hell of a racket I've gotten into."

"Slaving for the corporate masters," Scarbrough said with a reserved smile. "Whoever would've thought?"

"I suppose so. But business has turned to pleasure with your arrival."

"Always the consummate gentleman."

"Can I offer you a drink? Nonalcoholic of course."

"That would be wonderful."

Hammaker stood over a cherrywood wet bar and dropped several cubes of ice in two tumbler glasses. He poured water into the first and vodka into the second. "So you've been selected to head up a committee under the Crime Bill?"

"I'm very excited."

"Indeed." Hammaker walked to the window overlooking Pennsylvania Avenue. "Working for a government administration seems a bit out of character for you."

"Oh? That's the pot calling the kettle black."

Hammaker stroked the sheen of his silk pinstripe suit. "Touché. Remember May of seventy when we stormed the White House lawn?"

"How could I forget. That bastard Nixon was ruthlessly bombing innocents in Cambodia and Laos."

Hammaker stood somber-faced. "I did some legal work on behalf of the former President recently."

"You what?"

"Things have changed, Ruth. I've mellowed. I still carry my scars, don't get me wrong. Not the least of which is my finger. But in some ways I've moved past them."

Scarbrough scanned the office. She saw green fabric wallpaper and upturned gold wall lamps fanning muted light across the ceiling. Lush leather chairs trimmed in chrome stood sentry to an immense desk. "Yes, I see."

"Well, how can I help your committee?"

"You can do something very valuable."

"I'm flattered."

"I'm glad. You see the challenge we've accepted is to find alternative national strategies for combating the drug endemic. But before I can credibly propose the right solutions, I've got to find a way to tear into the current system at its roots."

"Shouldn't be too hard. Courts and prisons are flooded with drug offenders. Our cities are like purgatory. Governments at all levels have shattered budgets over the mess. You should be able to assemble a wealth of statistical support."

"Lies, damn lies, and statistics. No, I don't need more numbers. I need something tangible. You see, in packaging the War on Drugs, the Reagan Administration ran an incredibly effective media campaign. They exchanged social and medical images of a drug plague and disease for the military image of a war. And they managed to twist our perspective, so every failure seems to vindicate our coercive efforts and justify escalation. Yet, at best, conventional drug enforcement efforts have had a limited short-term effect. At worst, they've contributed to the decimation of families and communities and created a legion of alienated youth with no stake in society whatsoever."

Hammaker rose to pour himself another drink. "As usual you're out on a limb, Ruth. Progressive approaches to dealing with the drug problem have had little popular support."

"As proven by the paucity of an audience for my book. But the truth remains obvious. Drug use, like gang violence, is only one of many symptoms of deeper social problems we're unable or unwilling to face. We let our children grow up in blighted, crime-infested cities wrought with social and economic havoc, feeling their lives are cheap and disposable. Then we scratch our heads for a reason why we have a problem with drugs and violence."

"So to attack the problem you propose attacking the roots?"

"Yes. Abandon the hateful and misguided War on Drugs. Stop the alienation of American youth. Find new ways to foster self-esteem and self-realization for them. Help them discover something to lose, some stake in our society."

"At some level I agree with you. But I've seen the destructiveness of the street gangs even here in Washington."

"Oh, I don't pretend we can save them all. There are indeed bags of wasted flesh marauding our streets. I've seen them too." Scarbrough paused, breathing deeply, fighting to prevent the image of Preston's murderers from surfacing into her consciousness. "But some can be helped. I don't deny the difficulty of trying to replace a lifestyle replete with the thrill of risk-taking with the drudgeries of entry-level employment, even if we had jobs to offer. But it's no excuse for not trying, for not looking to the future."

Hammaker sat glassy-eyed. "I'm not saying I disagree. It seems to me you've developed your platform eloquently. And you already have your vehicle for bringing these views before Congress. You have your committee."

"Yes, but as I said, before my theories will be taken seriously, I have to deal with the conventional system. To discredit it in a novel and specific way. Then I believe there will be an opening for a new direction."

"I don't understand where I fit in."

"The drug problem will never be solved by moral indignation, coercion, and fear. You see, in our zeal for results, I believe we've abandoned our morality. That's what I want to show. That the frontline soldiers in the War on Drugs have become nothing but immoral bullies."

"I still don't understand what you want me to do."

"Remember several years ago when we met in San Francisco? You were out there for a business meeting."

"Sure. We had dinner at the Waldorf."

"Your treat. You may not remember because you had too much wine, but you were spouting off about how horrible you thought the DEA was."

"I don't deny it."

"You mentioned a case in point. An undercover operation involving government blackmail."

"Ruth, I—"

"Soldier Man, you called it."

"Oh my God."

"Yes, it was Soldier Man. Total raw abuse of governmental power is how you described it. I want to know everything there is to know about Operation Soldier Man."

"Ruth, I should never have spoken—"

"Ah, but you did. And now you must tell me the rest."

"But I exaggerated it."

"Then tell me the truth."

"I can't. There's the... First there's the attorney-client privilege."

"You're his lawyer?"

"Yes. No. Well I was. Long ago. Not that I was able to do any good. My first major disaster, actually." Hammaker quickly contained his wistfulness. "I can't tell you anything."

"I've already put the DEA on notice of my interest in the case."

"You did what? Good Lord, Ruth, you have no idea what you've done."

"This may be just what I need to embarrass them, to shake them up, and to make my point."

Hammaker returned to the bar, his gait ponderous. He stood with his back to Scarbrough, his palms resting on the smooth surface. Then he turned to face her again. "Whatever I told you, I said in strictest confidence. It was meant as an example, a generality, an abstraction, not a case study. For heaven's sake I didn't intend for you to use him as a weapon."

"I can get a subpoena," Scarbrough said quietly. "Believe me, I have power in this."

"You wouldn't. Even if you did, it would do you no good. Take a look at my finger, Ruth." Hammaker held up his stub. "I did this to myself as an act of conscience. Don't expect me to bend now under bullying."

"You didn't have so much to protect then, did you?" Scarbrough swept her arm to the office trappings. Suddenly the anger in her eyes twisted into an expression of pain. She bent at the waist grimacing.

"What is it?" Hammaker grasped her elbows from behind.

"Braxton Hicks contractions," Scarbrough said through heavy breaths. "They'll subside in a minute." She looked down at her swollen ankles and felt the blood pounding in her temples.

"You seeing a doctor?"

Scarbrough straightened, and her face cleared. "I call in to my ob-gyn in California." The relief in her face faded to anguish. "Sorry, Lucias. I didn't mean what I said. It's just this is so very important. I want to interview him."

"Please, Ruth. You're not listening to me. I have a moral responsibility to the man. He comes to me as a friend."

"So they're still using him. I saw that in Sage's eyes. And you're still in touch with him."

"What's happened to you?"

Scarbrough allowed her eyes to plead. "I need this."

"Even if it means our friendship?"

"You don't mean that."

"Don't I?" Hammaker turned away again, this time to the window.

Scarbrough lowered her eyes to her abdomen, stretched by the growth of life inside. It was the child's future she was trying to preserve, she told herself. For him, she would do whatever was necessary. "Give it some thought, Lucias. For now, that's all I ask."

• ● • —————— • ● •• ● • —————— • ● •

Later that evening, Lucias Hammaker sat in his office, tapping lightly on his computer. Almost finished with the merger documents, he paused to gaze at the stump of his finger. How much easier it would be to have that finger now. He could hit the *y* and *h* on the keyboard with ease, and he could grip a golf club. There would be no phantom pain. What had he gained by taking it? He could have obtained a deferment otherwise, on the basis of his legitimate conscientious objection or with his family's money. What did it really matter now?

Hammaker stood before a full length mirror. He was surprised by his bulk, and he recalled the sharp, almost emaciated look of his youth. The lines of his Polo golf shirt and tweed pants made him look like an inflated model from a Brooks Brothers catalog, more mannequin than man. His professional specialty made him feel that way too, dealing in matters of corporate governance and leveraged buy-outs, counseling the rich and powerful.

Ruth, God bless her and God damn her, had pulled him from his morose tower, if only for an instant. There was one gritty obligation he had now that could not be accomplished over cocktails in the safety of a smoke-filled, private bar. He would have to find Deric and warn him of the danger. He would offer the option of meeting with Ruth but would strongly advise against it. Her agenda was too aggressive and her approach, too brazen.

•••——••••••——••

The elegance of downtown Washington melted into a blur of despondency as Hammaker guided his Mercedes into the sinister tenements of Northeast Washington. Hammaker thought about how Washington, D.C. was the most powerful city in the world, yet the ultra-rich and the most desolate poor coexist in feigned ignorance of the others' presence.

Hammaker parked thirty feet from Christy's room at the Parkside Motel. He locked the car and knocked on the door at the motel, but there was no answer. He pushed on the door, and it opened into darkness.

"Them's some nice rags, pops," a voice said.

Hammaker turned and set out for his car at a fast pace. He was restrained by the thick arms of two muscular black men in their twenties. One waved a knife.

"Out for a night stroll, huh?" said the one with the blade. "Who you looking for, pops?"

Hammaker tried to think quickly on his feet. "Just a hooker."

"Oh some trim? Way up here in the jungle? Rich man like you? Shit, you can get laid in the Mayflower Hotel."

"I must've stopped at the wrong Parkside Motel."

"Stopped at the wrong pad aright, muthah."

"Easy man," the unarmed man said. "Yeah. Rest easy. We won't beast on you for no good reason."

"Thank you."

"No. We got a real good reason. That right Clinch? You came up here to visit with Deric."

"Deric?" Hammaker said.

The unarmed man laughed. "Yeah, Deric. Know where he is?"

"Where who is?"

"Oh yeah," said the man with the blade. "Play it that way. Take a look at this. Guy's missing a finger. He all out of balance. Only one way to make that situation right. We need to even him up."

"Tell Deric that Rodney and Llamar Drexler miss him," the unarmed man said. "We'll give you something to remember the message."

The men pushed Hammaker into the motel room and onto the bed. They pummeled his face. Hammaker writhed with the sharp blows. When he had taken his own finger, he had not uttered a sound; he had squashed his suffering for something nobler.

God, how soft he had become. As the switchblade cut through the bone of his left forefinger, Hammaker let out a long, loud scream.

PART III
SUMMER CAMP

Chapter sixteen

Friday evening marked the commencement of annual training at Fort Indiantown Gap. The low cloud ceiling was chalky gray, a fine mist hung suspended in the air, and the weather report promised little improvement.

Ashford arrived early. The hallway of the flight facility was a blur of olive green, as warrant officers and enlisted personnel hurried between the administration building and the hangar, greeting each other, readying equipment, and attending to pre-mission planning. In the flight planning room, pilots studied multicolored charts and maps that decorated the walls. The commissioned officers congregated over angled tables, topped with clear plexiglass, with more maps and papers beneath. Captain Jerome Zuckerman bent over a table, tracing his index finger along the route from Fort Indiantown Gap to AP Hill, Virginia, while Crawford stood at his elbow. Ashford approached from behind, unnoticed.

"Jerome, what chalk are you flying?" asked Crawford, his tone serious and not subordinate.

"Lead." Zuckerman seemed to be irritated by the lack of an honorific in Crawford's address, although the men were of equal rank.

"Who are you flying with?"

"My new first platoon leader, Lieutenant Dickson of course. We'll be leading the first flight of five, and I've assigned Lieutenant Ashford to lead second platoon's five Hueys. His pilot in command will be Mister Trent."

Ashford felt a surge running through his senses. He needed more time to sort out what he had learned about Trent and develop a strategy for dealing with him. He had decided to approach the matter gingerly, perhaps in a friendly conference, and if possible over a drink. He wasn't ready to be paired with Trent in the helicopter.

Crawford bent his neck forward. He closed his eyes and ran his forefinger and thumb over his eyelids, and when he lifted his face, he wore a strained jackal's grin. "You check the weather, Jerome? Low cloud ceiling, poor visibility. Marginal VFR if that, and we're being pushed to get to the Hill tonight. Everyone's worked at least a half-day at their full-time jobs, and some have already traveled many hours. They're all beat. Not the best conditions for a night flight into the soup."

"The Colonel says we're going." Zuckerman's manner seemed to convey the decision was beyond questioning.

"Colonel Harker's following the ground convoy to Fort AP Hill in his minivan," Crawford said. "He's not the air mission commander of this flight. He's not responsible for exactly thirty-three lives. You are. The decision is yours alone."

Zuckerman's shoulders swayed like a teetering scale and then pulled level and stiffened, as if settling under the weight of his responsibility. Crawford stepped closer, lowering his voice in a conciliatory manner. "If you've really made a decision to go tonight, why don't you assign two experienced pilots to lead each flight?"

Zuckerman's muted response was overshadowed by Trent's entrance. Although Ashford had not thought it possible, Trent's appearance had deteriorated since the weekend drill. He wore a green fluorescent T-shirt and blue visor sunglasses, and the shadow upon his jaw suggested that he hadn't shaved for a day or more. Slung over his shoulder, he carried a distinctly unmilitary flight bag, adorned by dozens of multi-colored patches.

Trent paused before the battered chalkboard where crew assignments were posted. He jerked his thumb toward the scrawled identification number of the lead aircraft. "All right, who's the joker?"

"What's the matter?" Ashford whispered to Crawford.

Absorbed in his thoughts, Crawford ignored him. A soft voice spoke into Ashford's ear, and he smelled the sweet aroma of fine perfume. He turned to face Jesse Morrow.

"Somebody's played a prank with crew assignments," said Morrow. "They replaced your name with Colonel Harker's. That pairs Trent in the lead Huey of second platoon with Harker. But Harker won't fly with Trent. Or Trent won't fly with Harker. Only a few guys know what the deal is for sure and they aren't talking. But everyone knows not to assign them to the same helicopter."

"I found out some about their problem this week," Ashford replied. Of course the colonel didn't wish to fly with Trent knowing what he knew, he thought. It was a wonder the colonel permitted Trent to fly at all.

Trent dropped his flight gear with a clatter. He lifted a dusty eraser and patted it over Harker's name, concluding with a flourish of chalk dust. "That's better," he said, stepping back and eyeing the remainder of the crew assignments. He pointed to the pairing of Zuckerman and Dickson in the lead helicopter of first platoon. "Hey, Gene, one good shot would take out the whole officer corp."

"Sounds like a damn good idea to me," Winston said.

Trent probed his fingers into his breast pocket, plucked out a silver-sheathed bullet, and held the glistening object to the light. "I was saving this for camp," he said, turning his gaze through the window to the thickening layer of clouds. "But if we're planning on flying in this, I might just as well blow my brains out now and get it over with."

Ashford turned to speak with Morrow, but she had disappeared. Crawford's attention refocused on Zuckerman. His hands were set high on his hips, and his cheeks resembled puffed red globes. "Jerome, putting an inexperienced copilot in the lead helicopter flies in the face of everything we've been teaching."

Zuckerman looked at Ashford. "Lieutenant, I have a very important mission for you. My personal gear is on the flight deck by the Skycranes. Please see that it's properly loaded into my helicopter."

Ashford had plenty else to do to put his own gear in order, but he knew his proper and only response. "Yes, Sir. Which aircraft is yours?"

Zuckerman seized the opportunity to affect a command presence. His shoulders billowed in condescension, and he took a dramatic half-step backwards. "The big green one."

Ashford smiled awkwardly. "I'll check the blackboard," he said, retreating into the hallway.

● — ● ● ●● — ● ● — — ● ●

Ashford moved outside among the darkening shapes of the Hueys. At the far end of the hardstand crouched Company F's three modern Sikorsky UH-60 Blackhawks. Staring at the sleek twin-engine helicopters, Ashford felt a wave of frustration, but he resolved to concentrate on the task at hand. He had little trouble finding Zuckerman's gear. Bright-colored coolers, duffel bags, and foot lockers were stacked in a pile as large as an industrial trash dumpster. Ashford stared at the heap despairingly. He sighed and hefted a duffel bag onto his shoulder.

"Hey, Zimbabwe." Reggie Spencer emerged from behind a Huey, his thick chest shaking with his chuckle. "It'll take you until Thanksgiving that way."

Ashford greeted Spencer, stifling his breath to mask exertion.

"You should learn to do things the easy way," said Spencer. "I'll get a line truck."

Ashford thanked him.

"You'd think he was moving his house," Spencer said. "You flying with Jay Zee?"

"Captain Zuckerman?"

Spencer nodded mirthfully.

"No. He just told me to load his gear."

"That's quite a stroke of luck for you, LT. The part that you're not flying with him. Though just being in the same sky with him ought to make you nervous. One thing for sure, his copilots never get sleepy."

Ashford grinned in bewilderment.

"Before I go flying with Jay Zee," Spencer continued, "I practice speed-reading my rosary." He raised his hand high in the air and made a long sweeping movement, whistling from a high to low pitch, simulating a crash. He lifted his eyes expectantly.

"I get it."

"Then you're pretty sharp for a lieutenant. Come on. Let's get this crap loaded."

Spencer cut a fast pace toward the open hangar, and Ashford followed eagerly. "Hey Reggie," Ashford said and then hesitated. "Okay if I call you that?"

"Call me what you want. You hold the rank."

"You really Catholic?"

"Naw, I was just joking around."

Ashford felt his body relaxing. "I noticed you're pretty close to Mister Trent."

Spencer's lips tightened. "I've known him for some time."

"I know this is a personal question, and you can wave me off if you don't want to answer, but how did you end up in the same unit after the War?" The force of Ashford's voice dwindled at the end of his sentence. It was only the second time he had raised the subject of the Vietnam War with a combat veteran.

"Oh that," Spencer said, his breath flowing freely again. "Nick found me. I was working at an aviation hangar at Philadelphia Northeast Airport back in eighty-two. He was passing through on a weekend drill and recruited me into the Guard."

"You two were with Colonel Harker in Vietnam?"

"That's right, Harker transferred from the North Carolina Guard four years back to take the Battalion Commander job here. Nick almost quit on the spot."

"Why here?"

"A command position opened up. At the colonel's level, you go where the jobs are that you need to punch your ticket. Only thing is, no one has punched Harker's ticket, and four years in the same slot is a long time. Word is he's desperately counting on the results of this camp to put him over the top for a general's star."

"I don't mean to pry, but I've heard Colonel Harker and Mister Trent don't get along. I don't want to have the same problems with Mister Trent."

"You don't have to worry about that. Nick's problems with Harker go back a long way."

The logical next question was on the tip of Ashford's tongue—what happened between them? But Ashford sensed that he had exceeded his immediate quota of questions about the past and would gain no more willing responses. Hedging, Ashford said, "You think there's anything I can do to—"

"You want my advice, LT. I can't tell you how to deal with the warrant officers, because they're their own can of worms. As for the crew chiefs, you wanna know how to lead us? Well, you can't really be one of us. Hell, you're a college boy. But ask for some advice on your preflight technique. When you can, give us a hand buttoning down the helicopter. Don't walk away right after you shut the helicopter down like some of the pilots do. Get to know what we do. I'll follow a man who takes an interest like that, even if he wears a butter bar and is a little wet behind the ears."

"A little?"

Spencer laughed. "So you do have a sense of humor."

"What will you be doing at AP Hill?"

"You think I'm crazy? I'm not going to the Hill. My crew and I are staying behind to do phase maintenance on one of the birds. Every hundred and fifty hours we have to tear the things apart and put them back together again. We're setting up a cantonment area over the other side of Peters Mountain."

Ashford remembered the allusion to the Phase Bird from the final briefing during the weekend drill. "Why are they leaving you behind?"

"Last year at the Hill, we had to make so many runs back to the Gap for equipment and parts that they decided to leave the Phase Bird here this year. Besides, the colonel wants us out of his way so he can dazzle the evaluators with his fabulous air assault operations."

Spencer halted beside a faded Huey and patted the machine. "This is the Phase Bird here. She saved my life once, a long time ago. But that's another story. Maybe I'll tell you about it sometime if you get me drunk enough. Anyway, right after we do the Phase Maintenance, she's off to Corpus Christy, Texas."

"What will they do there?"

"Phase maintenance."

"A different phase?"

"No."

"Then why are we doing it first?"

"Don't ask me the big questions, LT. That's for you college boys."

"Is she coming back here after Corpus Christy?"

"No, I told you that. They're sending her to the Huey boneyard in Arizona."

"So we're performing duplicative phase maintenance on a helicopter so she can be retired?"

"Now you got it."

"No, I don't."

"To think I was starting to wonder about you."

Ashford regarded the big sergeant. He flew with Trent on every mission his last three weeks in Vietnam. If Trent were responsible for the Massacre at Ba Long, that would put Spencer behind one of the M-60s that slaughtered innocent civilians. But that just didn't fit. Spencer wasn't like Trent. He was quick with a jab or a cut, but with him the banter seemed to be just that—there was no malice behind it. Spencer seemed to have reconciled his War experiences and, indeed appeared to credit Trent for his ability to do so.

Any assuredness that Ashford possessed in his suspicions about what happened at Ba Long was beginning to fade.

• • • — • • • • • — • • •

After they loaded Zuckerman's gear, Ashford spent the balance of the early evening in the supply room checking out field gear and in the classroom listening to seemingly endless speeches about air-assault techniques. He studied the flight route and performed his own pre-mission planning in the planning room, where he was in deep thought when Crawford approached him.

"Remember your extra duties, Mark?" Crawford said nonchalantly.

"Sure. Mess officer and drug enforcement."

"I'll introduce you to your mess sergeant when we get to AP Hill. It's time to start performing your latter responsibility now. We'll begin sending the men into the latrine for urine screenings in groups of four. Sergeant Spencer is familiar with procedures for marking and storing individual bottles and preserving the chain of custody. Because we're short on time, the best way you can help is by monitoring."

"I have to watch them piss?" Ashford's voice rose up the musical scale.

"Somebody has to. As you can imagine, there are all sorts of ways of cheating on the test. The Army requires the presence of a monitor to discourage such shenanigans."

Ashford strained to conjure an excuse, but there was none to be found. "Yes, Sir," he said finally.

<hr />

In the latrine, Spencer had arranged a wooden table against the wall facing away from the urinals. He sat behind the table on a metal chair, his left ankle resting on his right knee. A cardboard box sat before him, containing dozens of small plastic cups. The room was brightly lit and contained the redolent scent of antiseptic and mildew. "Hey, LT," Spencer said. "Cap'n tell you your job?"

"I get to watch," Ashford said glumly.

"Don't get too serious about it. Just stand over there by the sinks. And I hope your skin isn't too thin. Or should I say your *foreskin*?"

The first quartet to arrive consisted of Crawford, Trent, Winston, and Dickson. Ashford tried to make his participation appear to be meaningful without staring directly at the men leaning into the urinals.

A voice called from a stall. "Hey, LT, can you come in here and wipe my ass?"

Ashford resolved to make the best of the situation. "Not until you kiss mine," he said in his best attempt at locker-room humor.

"You're a real *whiz* for a newbie," said Crawford, handing Ashford his filled cup. "*Ur-ine* my heart, kid."

Trent extended his cup toward Ashford with the lid off. He feigned a misstep, allowing the liquid to lap forward to the rim of the container. Ashford leapt backwards, his arms raised, palms flat out. Trent swept his arm forward in a scooping motion, containing the sloshing liquid before a drop spilled.

"What's the matter, LT? You look a little *pissed* off." Trent's eyes were hard in their refusal to share the joke, and he allowed a sneer to play across his lips, more insulting than epithets.

"Very funny," Ashford said, grimacing. As usual, Trent's prank was the most reckless; there didn't seem to be a moment when he released the pressure.

Winston followed. He handed Ashford his cup and asked him if Trent were circumcised, saying that he had always wanted to know.

Dickson stood close against the white ceramic long after the other pilots left. His head bobbed to the ceiling and then to the floor. He bounced at the knees, apparently trying to start the flow of urine. Ashford knew that in the Army, it was a mark of distinction to urinate on command, just as it was a badge of shame to try and fail. Ashford offered to open a faucet, trying to make the offer sound nonchalant, and he twisted a spigot head. Dickson said he would only be a minute, and his face turned crimson.

Ashford told him to take his time and that he had to get some things from his locker. He said he trusted Dickson, who nodded with an air of unfettered gratitude.

Spencer knowingly glanced at Ashford as the lieutenant passed by his table and out of the lavatory. When Ashford returned, Dickson was gone. Spencer held a filled cup up to the light. "Too bad you don't have a mean bone in your body, kid. You'd sure fit in better here."

Ashford smiled. "Who knows? Maybe I made a friend. I could sure use a few more."

After the last members of Company B finished in the latrine, Ashford and Spencer sealed the filled plastic cups in the cardboard box, and both men signed the official register. "Pretty rigorous procedure," Ashford said.

"They're concerned about tampering," Spencer said. "The process requires a strict chain of custody. If we let this box out of our sight, it has to be locked up."

"What will you do with it?"

"Soon as I get a chance, I'll stick it in the mailbox. From there, it'll go directly to the laboratory for testing. Battalion should get the results in a couple days."

"Anyone ever turn up positive?"

"Couple of enlisted a few years ago. No pilots I know of. Thank God they don't test for booze. They'd have to ground the whole unit."

━●━━━●●●●━━━●●

At eight-fifteen, Ashford returned to the classroom for the preflight briefing. Outside, darkness seemed to swirl in currents. The classroom was dimly illuminated by red bulbs so the pilots' eyes could adjust to the oncoming darkness, and the mood in the room seemed to match the lighting.

Ashford nodded at Trent and sat down beside him. Trent responded with purposeful disregard.

Suddenly, blaring white fluorescence flashed overhead and solidified. Eyes flooded with light, dilating painfully, and heads turned. In the rear of the classroom stood Captain Jerome Zuckerman with his finger touching the light switch and his mouth pulled into a sheepish curve. "Whoops," Zuckerman said. He moved his hand to dim the white lights.

A voice spoke loudly. "Leave it on now. Our night vision's already shot."

Zuckerman obeyed without question. He took the podium, appearing less confident than in his previous oration, although he did nothing to suggest that his instructions were open to discussion.

"Ah-hem," said Zuckerman. "Colonel Harker has directed that we proceed to AP Hill this evening to set up as much of our camp as possible tonight. Then we can get right into our pre-evaluation preparations tomorrow. I've posted crew assignments and the flight route in the planning room. Pre-mission planning should already be done. We'll depart in two flights of five, first platoon first and then second platoon. Takeoff times will be fifteen minutes apart for adequate separation. Any questions?"

"What if somebody inadvertently loses visual contact with the flight or the ground?" a voice said.

"What?" Zuckerman seemed to be stalling for time to formulate a response.

"Instrument Flight Rules," said Crawford. "Are you going to brief IFR break-up procedures?"

"Ehr, they'll be per the standard operating procedure of course."

"Would you mind refreshing our memories on the SOP?"

"Well, . . ." said Zuckerman with insecurity leaking from his voice. "Lieutenant Dickson will brief that aspect of the mission. Lieutenant?"

Dickson popped to his feet and spoke with staccato articulation. "IFR break-up procedures are designed to safely separate each helicopter from a flight in the event pilots inadvertently lose ground references. Upon losing visual contact, each helicopter will immediately level its wings, initiate a climb, and begin a turn, depending on the position in the flight. Chalk One holds its course; Chalk Two turns thirty degrees right off course; Chalk Three, thirty degrees left; Chalk Four, sixty degrees right; and Chalk Five, sixty degrees left." Dickson's face set in a self-satisfied smile.

Trent peered over propped boots. "Aren't you forgetting the most important part?"

"What's that?"

"Don't fly into a cloud."

Dickson remonstrated. "Mister Trent, I don't think it's appropriate—"

"Nick has a good point," Crawford said. "If you're still able to maintain visual flight rules when the rest of the flight pulls pitch, stay VFR and continue to clear your own aircraft. Don't follow the rest of the flight into the muck. There'll be one less blind helicopter for air traffic control to contend with."

⸻

After the briefing, the pilots of first platoon shuffled to their helicopters, while second platoon gathered informally in the flight planning room. Ashford listened to the informal conversation for a few moments, and then he walked outside to relax.

On the flight deck, rich colors were vanishing into grays, and objects were melting into shapelessness and gloom. A swelling clamor rose from multiple turbine engines and flapping rotors. A hand touched Ashford's shoulder, and he turned to face Kevin Crawford.

"Little nervous?" Crawford said. He was nearly shouting to be heard over the cacophony.

"Night flying wasn't my strong suit in flight school."

"Tonight you'll combine inexperience with marginal VFR and an unfamiliar flight route through a heavily trafficked Terminal Control Area at Dulles International."

"What can I do?"

"After first platoon departs, you could stand your men down."

"How can I do that?"

"You're wearing the bars."

"When the colonel and Captain Zuckerman say we're going?"

"Nobody said this job was going to be easy. I'd love to tell you that you could have a year to sit back and watch before you have to make any decisions. But that's not the way the Army works. The people with the least experience are often put in charge. Subordinates sometimes follow along behind like blind sheep."

"Is that what happens here?"

"Sometimes. Sometimes not on purpose. Often it happens out of frustration. There will be times when everything seems normal and no one's saying a thing, but things will be really screwed up. And it may take an act of will and courage to restore order and logic."

"Why don't you stop it?"

"I've tried everything short of mutiny," said Crawford. "I'm not the air mission commander of my flight. When that idiot Zuckerman says fly, I have to get in my helicopter and fly. But you are the AMC of your flight. When we're gone, you're in charge here."

Ashford exhaled slowly and leaned against the brick side of the administration building. "When I signed up for the Guard, I had a choice between the warrant and commissioned officer tracks. Nobody explained the difference, and I said either would be okay. Whichever got me to flight school first, because all I really wanted to do was fly. I put in the paperwork for both, and you can see which came back first." Ashford nodded at a cloth bar woven to his uniform at the shoulder.

"So here you are." Crawford's expression yielded only a trace of sympathy.

"What I'm trying to say is, I'm not very good at the leadership end of this right now."

"Then you may never be."

"If I believed that, I wouldn't still be here."

Crawford extended his arms toward the runway, bent his elbows, and cracked his knuckles. He gestured toward the five Hueys of first platoon lifting from their pads, four hovering toward the runway, and the last toward the administration building. "Check your watch when we take off," Crawford said, heading toward the approaching helicopter. "If you're going, your lift-off time will be in fifteen minutes."

The last Huey landed on a pad close to the flight facility. Crawford bent at the waist and hurried into the swirling air.

"Captain Crawford," Ashford called. "Kevin. What's it like flying with Mister Trent?"

Crawford looked over his shoulder, and from his profile Ashford discerned that his expression remained resolute. "He's good," the captain said. He resumed his course, and the motorized wind swallowed his voice, so that Ashford could barely discern his final words. As he watched the formation of five Hueys lift from the runway, Ashford decided that Crawford had said, "He'll have to be."

Chapter seventeen

Ruth Scarbrough spent the past two weeks in committee meetings that were invigorating to her. As members of her committee, she had handpicked a group of intellectuals attuned to her theories, and a receptive audience was a rarity for her. They discussed her view of the mistaken focus of the Drug War on punitive measures, the failure of outreach programs to touch the downtrodden, and the utter lack of job training and opportunities in the inner cities. They debated the best ways to bring these views before the public, although Scarbrough withheld her own master plan.

Between meetings, Scarbrough spent her time researching Operation Soldier Man. Hammaker had inadvertently revealed several important clues to the confidential informant's identity. First, he had said that Soldier Man was a client. Also he was an important client; at least to Lucias—the sentiment with which he spoke of Soldier Man was apparent. Second, she knew that Hammaker had lost Soldier Man's case early in his career, perhaps in the first third of it.

At first she thought about discretely interviewing members of Hammaker's law firm. But she concluded that word would get back to him too fast, so she decided to start where Hammaker had begun—at the courthouse. It was ironic, she thought, that in her attempt to alter the future course of the Drug War, she had begun by reaching deep into the past, a past steeped in conflict over a different but equally troubling War.

The massive gray stone building housing the D.C. Superior Court was a contemporary granite structure with a sloped entranceway resembling a funnel. Although the building was new, she sought out the institutional recollection within. Scarbrough began her inquiries with the older guards and staff, working her way into the chambers of several judges. Her maternal appearance lent her a non-threatening aura, and she had no trouble loosening her subjects' tongues with her accounts of the follies of a late pregnancy. But no one seemed to know of Hammaker.

In the late afternoon, she spoke to an elderly female judge in the criminal division. The judge remembered Hammaker from his younger days. She recalled a trial in the late nineteen sixties in which he defended a War protestor for pounding a sledge hammer against the Washington Monument.

Scarbrough telephoned the protestor, but his relatives told her that he had died in an automobile accident in 1985.

She returned to the judge's chambers. The woman knew nothing else about Hammaker but introduced Scarbrough to an elderly man who spent his retirement years watching criminal trials. He was formerly a bailiff for the Honorable Thurmond Bailey. Scarbrough found him in the back of a working courtroom. He was wrinkled and jowly, and tangled wires protruded from two hearing aids lodged in his blossomed ears. In a whisper he introduced himself as Edward. He said he would be glad to talk but didn't wish to go into the hallway, as he was following an ongoing murder trial and couldn't miss an instant.

Edward's responses were unfocused and distracted, and at first he didn't remember Hammaker. Then Scarbrough described the long-haired maverick. With the color of the details, Edward finally turned to meet her eyes and smiled with an exclamation. "Ah yes! The last one. Judge Bailey had a stroke and died shortly after that hippie lawyer tried a case before him."

"You remember the case?" Scarbrough contained her own excitement.

"The defendant was a Vietnam veteran, as I remember." Edward recalled how he was a black man, with an eyepatch, who was caught selling contraband on the Mall; he wistfully described how Bailey had nearly had him forcibly remove the hippie lawyer from the courtroom.

"Do you remember his name?"

"I wouldn't recall. Such a long time ago. Judge died around nineteen seventy. Seventy, or seventy-two."

At the Library of Congress, Scarbrough flipped through microfiche files containing past issues of *The Washington Post*. After a few hours she learned that the Honorable Thurmond S. Bailey died on May 15, 1972.

It was a spring trial in 1972.

The next day, Scarbrough arranged to meet with the court administrator. He was an accommodating bookworm who gladly granted her access to the court's closed files in Fairfax, Virginia. It was there that she found the transcripts from Judge Bailey's final trial and the record of the conviction of Deric Christy. It had to be him—Soldier Man.

Scarbrough checked the phone book for Christy but found no listing. She laughed inwardly. That would have been too easy, she thought. No, she would have to confront Hammaker again.

Scarbrough was surprised to find Hammaker wasn't in his office at mid-day, and she drove to his Virginia residence. Hammaker lived on a four-acre estate in Arlington, Virginia. The house was a gray-white stone designed of curved lines sweeping to a pinnacle. Solar panels protruded from rough-edged cedar shingles lining the multi-tiered roof, and whitewashed trelliswork supported creeping walls of ivy.

Hammaker answered Scarbrough's knock at the door. A deep black bruise surrounded his left eye, his left arm hung limp in a sling, and a bandage surrounded the protruding shortened forefinger. He stood broadside in the doorway and seemed to be deliberately blocking Scarbrough's entrance. She accepted the rebuff and halted on the steps. "What happened?"

"I was mugged," Hammaker said flatly.

"When?"

"Last Sunday."

"After I left?" Scarbrough stammered. "Are you all right?"

"Quite all right, Ruth. But you didn't come here to talk about me, did you?"

"Please, Lucias. It was a mistake to approach you the way I did. I see that now. I'm only trying to find a way to show people the truth about what's happening on our streets."

Hammaker's sullen expression remained impenetrable. "I went to see him."

"Soldier Man?" Scarbrough said, careful not to reveal her newfound knowledge. "What did he say?"

"Nothing. He's gone. For good from the looks of it."

"What?"

"All I can tell you is his place was empty."

"Were you hurt when you went there?"

Hammaker's embittered expression gave sufficient response.

"I'm so sorry," Scarbrough said.

"No need to be sorry for me, Ruth. Just end it here. The DEA probably moved him because of your involvement. Most likely he's in California by now. You'd probably stand a better chance finding him by going home."

Scarbrough allowed the look of sympathy to linger on her face, with a downcast chin, slightly raised eyebrows, and an open mouth. But her eyes sharpened in focus, like a predatory beast in waiting. "Where did this happen, Lucias?"

"Oh no, Ruth. No you don't. It's time for you to leave."

Hammaker closed the door, clicked the deadbolt, and turned inside. In his two-story, sky-lit library, he threw himself slanted across a brown leather couch, wincing as his injured elbow contacted the surface. His right arm hung over a polished mahogany table, and with the stub of his long-gone forefinger he touched a parcel that he had received in the mail. Inside, sheathed in a plastic bag, lay Don Sage's lost pistol together with a handwritten note from the sender, Soldier Man, who depicted the handgun as his insurance.

"Please keep this safe and quiet," Deric Christy had written, "As if my life depended on it."

Scarbrough sat in her rental car and stared at Hammaker's mansion, reflecting. Where had Lucias been, she wondered. From the looks of him, at the hospital—that would be her starting point. She drove back into the city, down the long stretch of brick row houses lining Massachusetts Avenue and ending at

Washington General Hospital, the most likely location for an emergency call.

Washington General was an old-fashioned brick structure that, with its multiple incongruous additions over the years, had grown into an unwieldy monolith. The emergency room was chaotic. Dozens of people were crowded in a small reception room, waiting their turn to rest on one of the few plastic benches lining the walls. Nurses roamed the room, performing some curious form of triage on the injured, barking questions, and scratching flurried notes on battered clipboards. Gurneys soared in the hallways, surrounded by white-clad attendants. Scarbrough attempted to question nurses and doctors and ambulance drivers, but most shunned her, rushing past with their charges in tow.

After an hour, she stumbled on a paramedic in repose. He was a thin young man, unshaven, with the sad face of an artist's self-portrait. He seemed not more than twenty-five. He sat upon a black box that presumably contained some form of rescue gear, with his head resting in his hands and his long black bangs hanging despairingly over them. "Can we speak?" asked Scarbrough.

"Not in the mood." The paramedic lifted his head only slightly. The circles lining his red eyes seemed to darken in the direct light.

"You all right?"

"Just brought in another DOA, you know, dead on arrival. Sixteen goddamn bullets in him. Sixteen. When I started, when we'd bring 'em in, they'd have a knife or gunshot wound. Nowadays they average four or five. Now this new benchmark. Sixteen. There just seems to be no end."

"Believe me, I know the feeling. I was a nurse in Vietnam."

"It's getting that bad, isn't it?"

"It's not the same, but it's bad."

"What will we do?"

Scarbrough resisted the urge to preach her crusade. "I don't know," she said gently. "Look, I was wondering if you know anything about a white man who lost a finger last week."

"That's just another example. Cruel freaking bastards can't even be human. Sure, I remember. They lopped the thing off almost to the knuckle. The guy was in shock pretty bad. Couldn't even speak. Funniest thing though, he was already missing a finger on his other hand. And guess which one he was holding on to?"

"The old wound," Scarbrough whispered. "Where," she said, compelling her voice to remain calm, "where did you pick him up?"

"Parkside Motel on Route One in Northeast Washington."

<hr/>

Scarbrough wasted no time setting out for the motel. Following her street map, she located the neighborhood quickly, but she had trouble finding the motel. On 25th Street, she began a right-hand turn, but she caught sight of strands of yellow police tape decorating the outside of a row house like grim party streamers. The house appeared gloomy and vacant.

Scarbrough remembered something she had seen in the papers. She pulled to the curb and draped her newspaper over her stomach. She flipped to the city pages and read about the continuing investigation of the Saturday Night Family Massacre, a drug-related killing that occurred several weeks earlier, at the 25th Street address. She sat for another moment staring at the house, suppressing her own dark memories. She reflected on coincidence and the fact that she didn't believe in it.

Scarbrough found the Parkside in her next attempt. The proprietor's makeshift office was combined with his living quarters in a large one-room unit. He was a wrinkled man with deep-set eyes. His cheeks and chin were covered with sparse clumps of whiskers, and he peered intently over thick glasses. Even at a distance he smelled of whisky.

Scarbrough introduced herself and asked if there had been a mugging on the motel premises. The old man asked who wanted to know, and she held out a twenty-dollar bill and said that she was only a curious pedestrian. The man wheezed and sputtered out a series of derogatory phrases. He lurched to the door, snatching the bill from Scarbrough's hand as he passed; when she hesitated, he asked if she were coming or not.

Scarbrough followed midway down the motel façade to a rental room. Inside the furnishings were worn, but the bed was neatly made and the room appeared as if it had been cleaned. "Can you tell me who rented the room?" Scarbrough asked as she looked in the closet.

"Johnson I think it was. Howard Johnson."

Scarbrough blinked. "Can you describe him?"

"Well... he was black."

"Was he tall or short, with a round or thin face, or a light frame or stocky?"

"Not any of those." The old man squinted at Scarbrough. "No sir."

"Anything else?"

"Maid didn't have much fuss with him. Real neat. Not a boozer or a pipehead, nothing like that."

"He leave anything behind?"

"Just like you see. Packed up clean as a whistle."

"Is there a phone in here?"

"Nope. No phones."

For ten minutes, Scarbrough combed the unit for some clue to Soldier Man's destination. She found nothing. The proprietor tired of waiting; he repeated that he knew nothing more and started toward his office.

Slowly, Scarbrough gathered her things. She closed the door behind her, hesitating before she allowed it to lock in hopes some unheralded inspiration might strike. Then she let the bolt click, realizing she had reached a dead end. Either the DEA had moved Soldier Man or he had run from the Agency, but one thing seemed certain—he wouldn't be back. She had come so far and was so close. A tear welled in her eye. She stepped off the curb to her car.

"Now who gonna pay his damn phone bill?" the old man said indignantly.

Scarbrough's eyes spread wide. "*His* phone bill? I thought there were no phones in the rooms."

"No phones in the room; that's what I said. But I got couple collect calls for him at the office. He always kicked in to pay plus a little extra, so I took 'em. 'Sides, lady who called said it was an emergency."

"I see." Scarbrough smoothed her stomach with her hands to contain her anxiety. "I can help you with those bills, sir. May I see them please?"

Minutes later, after surrendering another twenty-dollar bill, Scarbrough had the phone bills in her trembling hands. She quickly located a pay phone and dialed the number listed as the caller's for the collect calls.

"Hershey Medical Center," a velvety voice answered, the voice of a professional.

"Hershey?" Scarbrough said. "Is that Hershey, Pennsylvania?"

"Yes. May I help you?"

•●•――――•●●●•――――•●●•

"He's what?" Sage said, leaping to his feet. His knees knocked against his desk and his chair smacked the wall behind.

"Soldier Man's gone," said Ramírez, his tone matter of fact. "Everything's cleaned out."

"I want his room combed. Check on his friends and relatives and acquaintances. Put somebody at the bus station and the airports. Beef up surveillance on the Drexlers' at Hamilton Place. Get the locals involved if you have to. I need to know where he is, and I want to know now." Sage's thoughts drifted to the ice pick possibility. He contemplated the wasted years, the squandered effort; he felt the acid churning his stomach. "Better check any John Does at the hospitals and morgue too."

If he was alive, Christy could be difficult to find if he wanted to be. He had been on the run too long, and he knew the life too well.

"Agent Sage, line two for you," a voice called from the outer office.

Sage flailed in exasperation. "Who is it?"

"White House."

Sage lifted the receiver and punched an illuminated button as if squashing a bug. "Sage here."

"Good afternoon, Agent Sage," said the melodic voice of Harry Crim. "I have Professor Scarbrough on the line. As I suspected, a little time was all we needed to mend our fences. Ruth has agreed that Operation Nature Grow would be the appropriate jumping off place for her observations."

"You wanna go to Pennsylvania?" Sage's voice brimmed with incredulity.

Scarbrough's tone was pleasant and accommodating, almost eager. "I thought over your options. Pennsylvania looks best."

"You sure?"

"Of course. I'm so looking forward to seeing your helicopters in action."

"You want aviation?"

"Lots of it. Plenty of wonderful planes and helicopters. Can you get a jet too? Won't it be grand?"

Sage's jaw dropped and then lifted slowly to support a cagey smile. At least he could maneuver the professor out of the way for the time being, he thought. "Yeah, I s'pose it will be... what did you say, groovy? Take me a couple of days to set everything up."

"Then I'll meet you there."

"Oh, I won't be going. But check in with me tomorrow. I'll have the name of a liaison agent in our Harrisburg office." Sage placed the phone in its cradle and peered at Ramírez thoughtfully.

"Forgot all about the professor," he told Ramírez. "Call Harrisburg and tell them to get busy on Operation Nature Grow. Then call the Adjutant General at Fort Indiantown Gap. Tell him I need two helicopters for about a week, starting next week."

"That all?"

"No, that's not all. Find Soldier Man. That's all."

Chapter eighteen

Blackness lay like a cloak over the flight deck at Fort Indiantown Gap. Mark Ashford crouched in an enlivened Huey, gazing over the red-lit instrument panel at dozens of shapeless black mounds that he knew were parked helicopters. An eerie glow resonated from the cloud ceiling, a reflection of the ground lights groping through the mist like lost souls rising. A tongue of fire streaked from the tailpipe of a nearby Huey as the helicopter's engine roared to life, the smell of kerosene wafted through open windows, and voices spoke in hushed tones on the internal flight frequency, answering the radio check in sequential order.

Ashford turned to the cargo area. A young crew chief sat amidst piles of Army gear lashed to the seats. He leaned forward from his waist, extended his forearms between his knees and interlocked his hands as if he were praying. Suddenly Ashford also felt a sense of reality that had been blurred in the lighted, fan-cooled comfort of the flight facility. Despite Trent's qualifications as a pilot, his brooding presence in the cockpit only magnified the disquieting aura.

One by one, from their various berths on the flight deck, second platoon's five Hueys lifted to a three foot-hover. They appeared as phantoms, drifting and bobbing in the wind, running lights splashing red and green currents onto tides of vaporous fog.

The Hueys assembled on the runway one behind the other. Ashford angled the lead Huey to watch the flight form. "Pre-take-off check good," Ashford said quietly, trying not to disturb the crew's concentration. "You ready?"

"Looks a little cloudy to me," Trent said, a devil-may-care look playing across his features.

Ashford suppressed the tremor in his voice. "What do you mean?"

"Clouds. Big white fluffy things."

"You think we should . . ." Ashford's eyes focused upon Trent's expression, a muted sneer.

"You're the AMC."

For Ashford, the moment was one of personal decision and indecision. He knew Trent would be no help. He could take comfort in the fact that the edict to depart for AP Hill had been issued from a higher authority, but he found distress in what he knew was the undeniable truth—he should make his own decision. Even after Crawford's coaching, however, the fact of his authority didn't seem quite real to him. He was, after all, a mere second lieutenant, fresh from flight school.

Trent radioed the tower for takeoff clearance, and Ashford fumbled with the flight controls to reposition the Huey in the direction of takeoff. The Huey bobbled in a shaky float. Trent broke the tense silence in the cockpit. "Nice and easy, think like you're squeezing—"

"I know, my girlfriend's tit," Ashford said petulantly. From the corner of his eye, he saw Trent was surprised by his directness.

"I guess precision flying isn't one of your strong points," Trent said.

"Learning curve was a little steep for night flight. But don't worry about me. I'll hold up my end."

Trent's forehead creased, and the red instrument lights reflected in his intractable eyes. He dipped his chin as if goading Ashford to show him and then flicked his wrist in a gesture of impatience. The Huey shuddered as Ashford coaxed it into flight. The indistinct runway lights slipped away beneath him, and the elusive shapes of dormant Hueys below melted into the darkness. Ashford took it on faith that the four other Hueys of second platoon followed. Given the choice, he wasn't certain he would.

Aloft in the vast gulf of blackness, Ashford held the collective steady until the altimeter reached a thousand feet and the rotor blades nearly brushed the cloud cover. Ashford thought that he could see for about a mile, though his only visual references were clouds merging into darkness, and he knew that such fusion could create deadly illusions.

They cut a straight path through the cool night air, skimming in the void between the featureless earth and the swamp-like clouds. The moon and stars were somewhere above, but their radiance could not be seen to give comfort. In populated areas below, haloed ground lights amplified the outlines of clouds intermingling in intricate patterns, bending and swirling and reaching down from the soup. At one point, drops of rain pelted the helicopter, sluicing in streams down the windscreen and dissolving the little that could be seen beyond into a single homogenous blur. Some faint external light source projected silvery translucent shadows onto Trent's face, and he appeared as a pale, grim spirit.

Ashford reminded himself of his love of flying and that it was his dream. But at present, he wished for nothing more than to have his feet firmly on the ground. He glanced at Trent often for reassurance, but the warrant seemed detached as always. Trent lit a cigarette although Army regulations forbade it. When Ashford smelled the smoke and turned, he caught Trent's gaze resting upon him. "You're a brave man," Trent said.

"Come again?"

"Your seat belt."

Ashford lowered his eyes. He saw that he had forgotten to buckle the straps that should be cradling his shoulders and looped around his waist. He suddenly felt naked and afraid, not of sudden disaster, but of his own ineptitude.

"I have the controls," said Trent.

Ashford scrambled to arrange the harness. Over the engine noise he heard an indistinct chortle from the crew chief. His damp T-shirt clung to his shoulder blades.

Trent offered the controls. "Ready now?"

Ashford seized them with possessiveness. Outside, he recognized the ground lights of Hanover, Pennsylvania, a landmark almost halfway to Washington, D.C. A few miles past the town, Ashford began a shallow descent to remain beneath multiple layers of scud. He repeatedly glanced at Trent, who continued to blink feverishly into the boiling muck.

"*Lead, this is Dash Two,*" the radio crackled, one of the pilots in formation behind. "*How's your visibility up there?*"

"*Half a mile and dropping,*" Trent said.

"*Guys remember the IFR breakup procedures from the briefing, right?*"

"*Like I said, nobody fly into a cloud,*" Trent said.

Trent flipped the radio dials. Voices overlapped in Ashford's earphones.

"Who are you trying to raise?" Ashford said.

"We're getting pretty close to the Dulles Terminal Control Area. First platoon should be talking to Dulles Approach by now."

"We can call them on their internal frequency on FM."

"Let them call us. That moron Zuckerman probably has them out over the Atlantic."

They were nearing a midsize private airport at Gaithersburg, Maryland, about ten miles north of Washington. Ashford banked to circumnavigate a cloud layer. As the Huey canted, clouds seemed to envelop the windscreen. Desperation rose in Ashford's throat, as if it were a liquid filling his body. He shifted the cyclic in a circle, like stirring broth. He pulled in power.

The nose of the Huey tipped into a tuck. They fell forward into a dive.

"That particular maneuver is called a death spiral," Trent said calmly, gazing with his master pilot's stare. "Want me to take it?"

Ashford gaped into the windscreen. He found no visual references and couldn't judge the attitude of the Huey. Was he straight-and-level? Turning or diving?

"If you don't want to fly into the ground," Trent instructed, "quit staring into the murk and use your instruments."

Ashford's eyes grasped the globular artificial horizon in the center of the instrument panel; he quickly discerned that the Huey was in a right turn and diving. He pulled left rear on the cyclic and was relieved to see the artificial wings level. Through the chin bubble, he spotted smattered ground lights.

The Huey stabilized, and Ashford relaxed. He focused on several ground references and then gazed up at the clouds. The vapor seemed to darken suddenly, eclipsed by the outline of a black shape. Ashford saw a dim, throbbing red glow.

Suddenly, Trent lurched forward and grabbed at the controls. "I got it!" he shouted, staring at the same anomaly.

Ashford felt Trent bottom the collective and guide the cyclic sharply onto its side. Ashford tensed on the controls.

"Get your goddamn hands off the controls!" Trent cast a wilting leer that was both territorial and frightening, though it didn't seem directed at Ashford but into some other dimension of time or space. As Ashford dropped his hands away, the world seemed to slide onto its side; it felt as if the floor dropped away and they were plunging headlong into a bottomless mass of blackness. The black shadow that Ashford had watched emerge from behind the cloud and consume the windscreen was the outline of an approaching Huey, its anti-collision light flashing warning red.

"*Aircraft at twelve o'clock!*" Trent transmitted, his voice a restrained fury. "*Got 'em, Gene?*"

"*Shit,*" came Winston's response. "*There are more than one.*"

Out the side window, Ashford glimpsed the nose of a second helicopter thrust through a scud cloud; the first Huey crossed behind their flight path. Then he saw another.

The second Huey passed above them close enough for its skids to sweep across the upraised tips of their rotor blades; Ashford's muscles contracted involuntarily as he braced for a collision that, by grace, did not occur. The second Huey disappeared up into the clouds as if it were sucked into quicksand, and a third passed behind them, dangerously close.

Trent keyed his microphone. "*Dulles Approach, Guard Six Eight—*"

The panicked voice of another pilot cut out his transmission and another voice chattered overtop.

"*Goddammit, you're cutting me out.*" Trent paused and listened, and when there was silence, he transmitted, "*Dulles, somewhere between two and nine UH-1 helicopters just went inadvertent IFR ten miles northwest of the Terminal Control Area, twelve hundred feet and climbing. Request instructions.*"

"*UH-1, this is Dulles Approach. Are you declaring an emergency at this time?*"

Trent turned his taught, red-lit face to Ashford and sat there staring like some demon from hell. "You're the AMC," he said.

Ashford felt his rump tighten. "What happens if I declare an emergency?"

"Let's just say everyone from here to Missouri will be investigating every dump you take for the next five years."

Ashford swallowed hard.

"Well?" Trent's voice was devoid of sympathy. Ashford tried to speak, but the words seemed to cling to his tongue.

Trent clicked the mike button. "*Dulles, have you got any jet traffic IFR in the vicinity?*"

"*Negative.*"

"*Then it's not an emergency.*"

"*Aircraft declaring inadvertent IFR,*" the controller said. "*I need tail numbers of all helicopters that are inadvertent IFR at this time.*"

"*Not me,*" said Trent. "*I'm not IFR, and I'm outside your Terminal Control Area.*"

Sheepish voices reported in sequence. Four Hueys had ascended into the clouds, two from each platoon. The first to climb reported breaking out into the clear above the clouds at four thousand feet. The controller gave the pilots compass headings and instructed them to climb through four thousand feet and report upon regaining visual cues.

Trent released Ashford from his gaze. "Well, you found first platoon." He turned down the volume on the VHF radio and flipped up the toggle switch on the FM radio to transmit on second platoon's internal flight frequency. "*Second platoon, who's with me?*"

"*I'm up,*" a voice said. It was Winston. Another reported; they were a flight of three.

"*Other two idiots pulled pitch into a cloud,*" Trent said.

"*From where I sat, it didn't look like they had much choice, Nick,*" said Winston. "*That was damn close.*"

"*I'll take us down beneath the Terminal Control Area on the outer fringe so we don't have to go back up with Dulles,*" Trent said. "*We'll land on the south side of Washington at Fort Belvoir and refuel. Maybe we'll stay the night if our air mission commander grows a brain.*"

"*Zuckerman's on first platoon frequency telling everyone to go into Dulles,*" Winston said.

"*Does it look like I give a shit?*" said Trent.

"*I got no idea what you look like, Nick, but my copilot looks like somebody just tried to yank a piano wire through his asshole, and it didn't budge.*"

With surgical assurance, Trent held the controls for the remainder of the flight; he handled the radios and referred to his own map on his kneeboard. When Ashford tried to assist with navigation, his efforts were met with wordless rebuff. The silence gathered and dominated and wounded.

<hr />

The landing at Belvoir was smooth, and the pilots quickly quieted the Hueys. Remembering Spencer's advice, Ashford made a point to help the crew chief to secure the aircraft.

Then the pilots watched the two prodigal helicopters from second platoon appear, gliding down from the clouds, landing one by one on instrument approaches monitored by air traffic controllers. When all of the pilots were assembled, they congregated inside the operations center, a wood-paneled room with telephones and maps and weather information posted on bulletin boards.

Ashford called the flight service station for a weather update on the route to AP Hill, and the forecaster reported that the conditions were no better than they had encountered en route. Without consulting anyone, Ashford placed a call to Fort AP Hill and asked a clerk at Post Headquarters to relay a message to Captain Crawford. Second platoon was laying over for the night.

Crawford had given Ashford an Army credit card to be used for fuel. He called several nearby motels and located one that would accept the card to pay for accommodations. The aircrews borrowed a courtesy van, and the weary crewmembers drove to the motel.

After settling into his room, Ashford went to the motel lounge, where most of the crewmembers were perched on barstools. Ashford tried to listen to the conversations, but insecurity blocked his focus, and questioning thoughts flashed through his head. As he walked the length of the bar to an empty stool, pilots suppressed smirks and scowls, and others avoided meeting his eyes, but Jesse Morrow rose from her seat and pulled a stool alongside his.

"Pretty near miss," Morrow said, waving her glass in the air in a mock toast.

Ashford ordered a double vodka. He gazed balefully at his reflection in the glass as if trying to define the character of the person he saw. The image seemed blurred and fragmentary.

"Don't look so gloomy, LT." Morrow reached out to him with expressiveness in her eyes. "It wasn't your fault. Trent called Radley with first platoon after they landed at Dulles. Radley said that Zuckerman got them lost out to the east almost immediately after takeoff. They were talking to Baltimore Approach trying to find the way back on route. The time they spent wandering ate up their fifteen-minute lead time. And I won't kid you, Winston wasn't trying to give you a compliment, but he said if you hadn't

261

put us into that steep descent, first platoon would have collided with us for sure. That's the problem with scud running; everyone's flying at the same altitude."

"Trent called it a death spiral," Ashford said.

"The descent? Nonsense."

"I panicked, I—"

"Want some advice? Keep that kind of second guessing to yourself. Better yet, don't do it at all. There isn't a single one of these guys who hasn't had a dozen near misses in his career. They'll ride you about it for a while, sure. But don't let them get under your skin, and don't beat yourself up."

"Captain Crawford tried to tell me back at the Gap that we should wait until morning to depart. Mister Trent just kept saying, 'you're the AMC.' I'm not sure I can face them."

"So you made an error in judgment. They'll respect you as long as you learn from it. You were smart enough not to push us the rest of the way down to the Hill from here tonight."

"Who would have?"

"Radley said first platoon is gearing up right now to take off from Dulles. Some of the guys are ready to shoot Zuckerman."

The vodka blazing in his chest, Ashford leaned toward Morrow and spoke in a hushed tone. "Anyone ever have any problems with Mister Trent that you know of?"

Morrow licked the alcohol from her lower lip. "He pisses off commissioned officers pretty regularly."

"There was this moment when he took the controls from me. It was like he was wild or possessed; he wouldn't be denied for an instant. It wasn't just him reacting to the situation."

Morrow's features contracted into an inquisitive stare. "I'm sure he was just scared shitless. We all were."

"There was something else." Ashford lowered his tone another degree. "It was like he wasn't really in the here and now. As if he were re-experiencing something from the past."

"I think my life flashed in front of my eyes too."

"No, I mean,... I think he may be dangerous."

"We're all dangerous, LT. We're Army aviators."

Seated three stools down the bar, Winston leaned forward over the polished wood. "Hey, LT," he said, "wanna give us some pointers on that death spiral technique?"

Ashford blushed and smiled at Morrow. "It's been a long night," he said.

He breathed in Morrow's return smile and graceful nod, grateful that she still seemed to accept him despite all that had happened. He heard his voice, soft and distant, say good night. He was careful not to hold Morrow's eyes for too long, although he wished he could hold them longer, and his mind held them anyway. He withdrew to his room, shut the door, and settled in for the night.

Chapter nineteen

Late Friday evening, Ruth Scarbrough arrived in Middletown, Pennsylvania in a rented compact sedan. On the two-lane highway, she passed an abandoned military depot, a small-time used car dealership, outmoded gas pumps, and a convenience store bathed in anemic neon incandescence. The town was the site of the Pennsylvania State University's Harrisburg campus, but from the main thoroughfare, it lacked the dynamic feel of a college town.

Downtown Middletown, however, remained the home of Bart Turczynski, a man with whom Scarbrough had strongly connected in Vietnam, not on a sensual plane but on an emotional one nonetheless. In Vietnam, Turczynski was a member of an infantry company that, for four months, drew the coveted assignment of protecting the medical facility at China Beach. They met in the aftermath of a heavy influx of casualties; it was a time when Scarbrough was at her wits' end to cope with the despair that saturated her daily existence. Turczynski recognized her turmoil and shared his philosophical insights, his love of poetry, and his own distaste for the War. With his help, Scarbrough found new ways of coping with the meaninglessness that had overwhelmed her.

When Turczynski returned home, he made it his occupation and preoccupation to counsel and assist other veterans, and soon he founded Middletown's Vet Center. He wrote to Scarbrough often at first, sometimes raving about the progress he was making with a group, other times mourning the loss of a veteran to alcohol or prison or a bullet. The letters dwindled over the years, but he still sent a Christmas card annually, and with every contact he renewed his standing offer to open his home in Middletown whenever Ruth might wish to visit. Two decades since she had last seen him, she had finally found an ideal time to accept the invitation.

The counselor was, of course, only part of the lure for her visit—Middletown was a twenty-minute drive from Hershey Medical Center.

Scarbrough allowed her mind to drift from the small-town landscape back to Washington. Although she relished the camaraderie of her committee, her meetings had been steeped in rhetoric, generalities, and good intentions, but in the end, they were unsatisfying. She longed for manifest action, tangible forward progress in her quest for a rapid victory in the War on Drugs.

As Scarbrough drove, she practiced aloud an address she intended to make to Congress after she exposed the shocking scandal of Soldier Man. She would begin with what was obvious to her: Christy was a Vietnam veteran who, for nearly all his adult life, was exploited by the federal government. He was a fugitive, of course, but that was only a symptom of his dysfunction, a malady created by an immoral War and perpetuated by a collective, albeit unstated, decision to condemn soldiers for the folly of their government. The role the government should have played in his post-War life was to nurture him back to stability and to help him correct his post-War confusion, not to manipulate his weaknesses. One of the many tragedies of the Vietnam War, she would say, is that we blamed these noble men for losing an immensely unpopular War, rather than gently lifting the onus from them when they had already shouldered more than their fair share of the load.

Then she would use the saga of Soldier Man as a bridge to apply the lessons of the Vietnam War to the War on Drugs. Christy's story was indeed the perfect link—after shouldering the burden of the old War, he carried forward a new onus his government chose to inflict upon him—fighting in the trenches of a new and, in her opinion, equally immoral conflict. She would characterize his manipulation as a metaphor for the all-time low the Government had reached in its interactions with its citizens, all in the name of winning the Drug War. The seizure of their property without due process of law. The incarceration of children and young adults whose crimes were little more than subscribing to the mores of their deteriorating communities. The shattering of lives in the wake of an unwinnable War fought by unprincipled means.

The potential variations of the speech were endless. Soldier Man was indeed the ideal vehicle for her campaign.

●━•━━━━•━••━•━━━•━●•

Scarbrough turned from the highway onto Turczynski's street. The thoroughfare behind her, a charming town blossomed before her eyes. The street was lined with great gnarled oaks and sprinkled with sprawling Colonials with sweeping porches and unusual Victorian structures, houses crafted of steep peaks and sharp angles. Turczynski's home was a mid-sized brownstone with violet trim and stylish narrow shudders.

When the thick oak door swung aside, their smiles were spontaneous and wide. Before a word was exchanged, it seemed as if the passing of decades had merely strengthened the bond of their friendship. Bart Turczynski was a man of slender build, and the loose fit of his open-collar sports shirt made him appear hollow at the breastbone. Curly gray hair circled his round, kindly features, and wide-set eyes seemed to anchor his face to a soul of compassion. The countenance appeared well-suited to the unassuming counselor.

"My God, Ruth," Turczynski said, "you're—"

"Big."

"Not at all." Turczynski backpedaled into the house and swept his hands in a welcoming gesture. "Beautiful is what I was about to say."

"Nice recovery. You're as rotten a liar as ever, but thank you."

Scarbrough followed Turczynski into a wide living space containing overstuffed furniture arranged on a rough-textured wooden floor around four sides of a braided area rug. Her eyes were drawn past the conventional decor to a brick fireplace angled in the corner of the room. The fireplace boasted a thick oak mantel with graduated tiers bearing a host of Vietnam memorabilia, carefully arranged in the manner of a sanctuary. A miniature bronze statue dominated the center, a replica of the three-soldier statue at the base of the Vietnam Memorial in Washington; the unpolished brown metal was molded into faces frozen with hard experience but seeping traces of suppressed anguish and grief. Framed black-and-white photographs were arranged on lower decks, containing images reflecting a youthful Turczynski ringed by young men dressed in combat fatigues; the expressions the men wore seemed a meld of vigorous hopefulness and grim awareness. On the wall opposite the fireplace was a framed print of a gray-bearded businessman in his forties, leaning with anguish against the black granite face of the Vietnam Memorial, straining to touch the visible spirits of his fallen comrades as they drifted behind the sheen of the polished stone.

A strong outdoor scent floated in the room, like a combination of hay and mint. Scarbrough recognized the aroma immediately, and her eyes roved until she found it. Balanced on the rim of an ashtray cut from the brass base of an artillery shell, dry weeds peeked from the tip of a thin-rolled paper squeezed in a metal clip.

"I see you're still at it," Scarbrough said with thinly veiled disgust. She flopped onto the sofa.

Turczynski sat in an overstuffed recliner and plucked the joint from the ashtray. He examined it as an entomologist would a specimen of a rare insect. "Don't be so judgmental. It has its therapeutic value. You'd be surprised the barriers it's helped me overcome with vets in counseling over the years." Turczynski extended his arm, his fingers pinching the joint. "I don't suppose—"

Scarbrough lifted her hand. "Those days are long gone for me. Isn't it about time you grew up too?"

Turczynski retracted his own hand. "Your telephone call, it brought back so many memories."

"China Beach. Seems so long ago."

"For me, it's still like yesterday."

"I like to think I've found ways to move on."

"Ah, so do I. That's exactly what I've been working toward for twenty years with so many vets. But you can never wipe away the past. If you're lucky, you can merely find ways of reconciling it."

"You missed your calling, Bart. You should have been a priest."

"I think I found my calling, thank you." Turczynski's tone was still light, but it had taken on overtones of forthrightness. "So you're in town on business."

"Yes, but I really can't discuss the details."

"You'd pique my curiosity if you said it had anything to do with Vietnam."

"You'd probably say everything I do has something to do with Vietnam."

Turczynski chuckled. "It remains part of your life."

"Ironic. You spend your professional hours trying to help people move on and your spare time trying to get your friends to look back."

"An obsession indeed." Turczynski struck a match, lit the marijuana cigarette, and sucked fiercely, squinting at Scarbrough through the smoke. "I still believe we have an obligation to remember the lessons of Vietnam lest we repeat our mistakes. I'm teaching a night class on the War at our local Penn State campus. Thursday evening we're having a panel discussion among veterans."

"Sounds very interesting."

"I haven't got a nurse lined up."

"You're not thinking—"

"You'd be perfect."

"Oh, Bart, I simply don't have the time."

"Whoever does? We have to make time. These are good kids. They're interested in the past, and you can give them a unique perspective. What do you say?"

"I'd have to think about it."

"Do you have some difficulty speaking publicly about the War?"

"You know better than that. What would you like to hear? About sucking chest wounds? Neuro cases, men with their brains blown to jelly, who we laid aside in a secluded room so others didn't have to watch them die? The New York marathoner whose leg was blown off? Or should I speak of stripped illusions, lost faith, and utter meaninglessness?"

"I'd like to hear about your son," Turczynski said softly through a pot-induced haze.

Scarbrough's face went slack.

"Sorry." Turczynski snuffed out the joint as if it were at fault for his remark. "I didn't mean to open old wounds. It's the counselor in me, you see."

"Of course," Scarbrough said haltingly. "I do have difficulty speaking of Preston." She cleared her throat, preparing to change the subject, straining to prevent the horrible details of Preston's murder from rising into her consciousness. As she parted her lips to speak, her mouth suddenly went dry. She felt light-headed. She leaned forward involuntarily, lowering her head between her knees.

Turczynski rose quickly. He assumed a supportive posture beside her, resting his left hand across her back and his right hand on her knee. He asked if she were all right.

"I've been having Braxton Hicks contractions." Scarbrough righted herself. "And I tire easily. In fact, I may need some help with the legwork on my project. Nothing really intriguing, but it might call for a private investigator. Know anyone in the area?"

Turczynski seemed reassured by Scarbrough's recovery and returned to his seat. "I know a few. Are you going to be secretive about what you need done?"

"Just a bit of surveillance work."

"Well, Maize Anderson does missing persons work. She's a grandmother, but she has an incredible knack for locating people. Her two sons are Harrisburg policemen and moonlight for her. They might take on the job. Who are you staking out?"

"Not who, what. Nothing dark and dangerous. Just a big, bright, harmless hospital."

Turczynski lifted his eyebrows. "Come on, Ruth. Will you really keep me in the dark as to why you're here?"

Scarbrough brought her eyes squarely to Turczynski's. "I've come to end the War on Drugs," she said.

Turczynski's jaw tightened and the silence grew. A sustained laugh sluggishly commenced in his diaphragm and gurgled up through his lips. He ground the joint into the ashtray as if for good measure.

"Have it your way, Ruth. The pleasure of your company is more than compensation for your secrets. I won't ask any more questions."

Brandon Christy hurried through two sets of sliding glass doors flanking the main entrance at Hershey Medical Center. He'd worn his new jeans and his best shirt, and he walked with a step that had lightened considerably since his last visit. On the telephone, he had spoken with the doctor about his mother's recovery, and the prospects were much better than had been expected. If her improvement continued, extensive skin grafting might be avoided. The hospital staff had relocated Peg Christy from the intensive care ward into a private room on the third floor; while the quarters were expensive, the special accommodation was necessary, because the risk of infection remained.

Bran saw her from the hallway, lying on the sterile hospital bed with the steel side-guards raised, thick gauze bandages arranged neatly over her naked form. He shuddered at the ooze-soaked bandages, and he considered the deep wounds that lay beneath—new ones that could be seen with the eye, and the old ones that lay within.

As Bran entered the room, from beneath the bandages Peg Christy blossomed, gazing at him in the way she always did, with hope, with trust, and with unremitting faith. When he was with her, he wanted nothing but to live up to her aspirations.

She greeted him as if she had not seen him in years, and he asked how she felt. She said she was fine and that he was not to worry. Then she asked if he'd seen Bigelow.

"No, Ma."

"He's still in jail?" Peg turned her cheek against her pillow.

Brandon nodded.

"I don't want you to see him. I feel awful about taking you to live with him. He said he would change. I thought he would change. As soon as I'm well, we're leaving him for good."

Bran felt as if a weight had been lifted from his midsection— he had longed to hear those words of release for nearly half a decade. The Scrounger was like a sticky blob that had attached itself to their lives; for the first time, he felt the parasite's adhesion weakening.

"Does he have you into any of his dirty business?" Peg asked.

Bran quickly said no so the lie wouldn't seem so brazen, and he averted his gaze to his own shuffling feet. He wanted to tell his mother he had been to the Garden twice by himself since the Scrounger was jailed, how afraid those trips made him, and how the Scrounger had put him into contact with Cruise, one of the badest actors in Harrisburg. But he held his tongue. His mother needed to concentrate on healing. His job was to comfort and protect. And help pay the bills.

Peg Christy peered at Bran with suspicious concern, as if trying to survey into his soul. "He'll try to get you to help him. I know Rayful. Don't go near him. Understand?"

Bran nodded silently, striving to contain the number of false-hoods passing through his lips; he was due to visit the Scrounger at the Dauphin County Jail on Saturday morning.

A monitor beeped and ejected a narrow sheaf of paper. Bran gazed at the implements of medical technology that thicketed the room: blinking lights, tangled cords, and a silver metal tray with shiny medical instruments protruding over its rim. "How much does it all cost?"

"What? Oh the hospital? Not your worry."

As Brandon swiveled his head toward his mother, in his peripheral vision he saw a black man standing just outside the doorframe, so that only a narrow sliver of his body could be seen. The man appeared to be watching them. When Bran turned square to the door, the figure disappeared.

Bran listened to his mother tell him about God, and how He was taking care of her, and how He looked after Brandon too. She spoke about a bright future for him. She talked until a nurse brought a paper cup filled with capsules and asked Bran to leave, and he kissed his mother good night.

⋅—⋅———⋅⋅⋅⋅⋅———⋅—⋅

In the parking lot Brandon unbuttoned his shirt and allowed the breeze to seep under his arms and around his waist; it felt cooling against his damp skin. He spotted his car. Nearby, silhouetted in shadows, a man stood beside a thick clump of shrubbery just beyond the beam of a streetlight.

Bran approached cautiously. With closeness, details of the man's form and face became almost discernible; Bran was certain it was the same man he saw outside his mother's hospital room. The man had a lean but sturdy frame, carried in a way that suggested he meant no harm. But there was a reticence in his manner, an apparent desire to approach but a contradictory unwillingness to act, as if, in a halting sort of way, he was struggling to settle on his own purpose. And there was something vaguely familiar about him.

"Who are you, man?" Brandon said into the shadows.

The form slouched and slipped away from the puddle of light in a way that seemed instinctive, like a nocturnal beast gliding to the comfort of blackness.

Bran got into his car and started the engine. He stared into the beam of his headlights until he was satisfied that the man was gone, and then he drove forward, unable to shake away his unease until he accelerated onto the highway.

Deric Christy stood on the fringe of the hospital parking lot in the shadow of an immense pine tree long after Bran drove away.

He was proud. His nephew had grown strong and kind, caring for his mother in the gentle, loving way that Christy had observed inside the hospital. More than anything, Christy wanted to speak to the boy. But when he tried, the vision of the rope net descended upon him, afflicting him just as it did twenty years ago, the day he was seized by the lawmen in Washington. It wound its infernal coils around his throat and pulled the grisly dead men close against him, and his only escape was to retreat into contained solitude.

Whatta Deal lay just outside Harrisburg on the far end of a mature commercial strip. It was a dilapidated, wood-paneled shack with an attached barn-like garage surrounded by a thicket of aged vehicles in varying stages of disintegration. Brandon Christy lifted the center garage door that let out a screech and clatter. He backed a dusty Toyota pickup to the bay entrance. He heaved a heavy burlap bag of bone meal up onto the bed of the truck, food for the Scrounger's Garden.

Footfalls sounded behind him. Bran's stomach quivered. He expected to confront the man who he had seen in the hospital lot, but Mike Daniels stepped around the front fender of the pickup.

"Need a hand, son?" the Life Lion pilot said, a hint of kindness written into his otherwise stony features.

"I got it," Bran said.

"I stopped to see if everything was okay."

"Doctor says Ma will be okay."

"It'll take some time for her to mend. I meant you though."

Bran paused. The silence grew around him, contradicting his words when he finally said that he was all right.

"Where are you staying?" Mike Daniels said.

"Here."

Daniels peered over Bran's shoulder; his eyes came to rest on a crumpled sleeping bag draped over a sagging canvas cot in the rear of the garage.

"What's it like?" Bran said spontaneously. "Flying I mean."

Daniels appeared thoughtful, as if what he was about to say were very important. "There's a feeling of freedom in it that defies description. But you carry a tremendous amount of responsibility."

"What do you mean?"

"You have lives in your hands. I fly people who are badly injured. Some are dying. I have to make sure they get to the hospital quickly and safely. Other pilots carry passengers commercially and are responsible for their safe passage through the air. Military pilots carry weapons that they must make sure, if used, are used properly. Even pleasure pilots have to consider the lives of others in the skies and on the ground."

"I'd like to fly again someday."

"Was the Life Lion ride your first?"

Bran nodded. "Were you in Vietnam?"

Daniels dipped his chin in a shallow nod, as if startled by the sudden change in subject and indicating the new subject was a sensitive one.

"My uncle was in Vietnam too," Bran said.

"What did he do?"

"Just a soldier I guess."

"I always admired the infantrymen in Vietnam. Us pilots took plenty of chances and sometimes scared ourselves almost to death, but at night we came back to our bunks and mess halls. The infantry was out in a dangerous jungle no-man's land all night long for weeks on end."

"I haven't seen my uncle in a long time. Ma says there are some things from the War he couldn't figure out."

"That's true with a lot of veterans. For some reason, something they carry pulls them away from their family and friends just when they need each other most."

"That happen to you?"

Daniels stiffened. "Not so much after Vietnam. But back in the States,... I let someone talk me into doing something I shouldn't have. Something stupid. I shouldn't have followed along, I should've stopped it. But I didn't. And the consequences... Some good men died."

Bran stammered.

"I lost my wife and friends after it happened," Daniels said. "I guess I drove them away. And I quit a job that I loved in the National Guard. My whole life changed... What I'm trying to say is sometimes you get caught up in things. If you could just take a step back, just be an observer of yourself, if only for a moment, maybe you could think things over differently and they might come out better." Daniels paused, his eyes leaking earnestness. "That's why I came here. I heard a little of what your mother's boyfriend said at the hospital, and it seemed to me maybe you're caught up in something too."

Bran took a step backwards. "What did you hear?"

"Enough."

Bran turned away, as if Daniels's statement were a thing that could be evaded. "I'm just taking care of business. Helping pay the bills. You know how much it costs? To be in the hospital?"

"Are you worried about that?"

"I have responsibilities too. Just like you."

"Would you like me to find out how your mother's care will be paid for?"

"Rayful says we have to pay it all."

"That's not necessarily true. I'll do some checking for you. It's something you shouldn't have to worry about. At your age, you're supposed to be thinking about going on a date and getting in trouble for drinking a beer."

"I don't like beer."

"You don't like drugs either, do you?"

"How'd you know that?"

"Something about you. I'll stop back in a couple of days maybe with some answers for you. You still have—"

"I have your card."

"—my card." Daniels paused, as if mulling something over. "I brought something I wanted to give you. It's something I used in Vietnam."

He pulled from his pocket a square contraption twice the size of a pack of cigarettes. A swaying rubber antenna protruded from the top of the device. "It's a survival radio," he said. "Just an old thing, a souvenir I kept around."

Bran started to reach for the device and then retracted his hand, unsure. "Does it work?"

Daniels tipped his head in a *who-knows* gesture, as if minimizing the importance of the gift. "It should. It's old, but I always keep the battery in it fresh. It transmits on a frequency we call 'guard' that pilots monitor in case of an emergency. Now, if there were an actual emergency, someone could get word to me fast by asking a pilot to contact me through Life Lion."

Bran studied Daniels as he stood there with his hand extended like a lifeline. He reached out and took the radio, wondering what trouble the pilot foresaw in store for him. Long after Daniels said good night and left, Brandon sat on the front seat of the pickup and cycled the radio's on/off switch, imagining he was making a call for someone to fly him away.

• — • • — — — • — • • • — • — • — • •

In Washington, D.C., Don Sage stood in the filtered light of a soot-covered streetlamp. He leaned on the hood of his parked sedan and examined the leaved pages of a building plan. He and Ramírez were surrounded by unmarked police cars and a dozen of D.C.'s finest in plain clothes.

Sage waved a lit cigarette; the glowing tip sketched a circle on the air. "Yes sir, we'll have some fun tonight, Gerry. I intend to turn over the crib of every known ripper in Northeast D.C."

Ramírez stomped his feet in frustration. "We're the DEA, Don. We're supposed to be fighting the Drug War at the highest levels. This is rinky dink. This kind of crap doesn't get us anywhere. You know that. We crack down on one group on this nickel-and-dime stuff, another pops up somewhere else. This is a cover-up, pure and simple."

"It's an official multi-faceted operation. Two birds with one stone. We're targeting known rippers, guys who rip off drug dealers. They're bad actors, Gerry. They'd bludgeon their grandmothers for a nickel."

"And what's the public supposed to think?"

"That's the beauty. The media will report we're tracking down the perps from the Saturday Night Family Massacre. Like I said, two birds." Sage slipped a thick bulletproof vest over his head. He buttoned his nylon jacket over the vest and fastened a Velcro flap over the white DEA emblem silkscreened on a rear panel. "Why you so down, Gerry?"

In the pale light of the streetlamp, Ramírez appeared drained. "I just keep seeing that little girl," Ramírez said huskily. He lifted his eyes to the light as if envisioning her soul in the glow.

"You didn't shoot her. It was the bad guy. Try to remember that."

"But if we hadn't been there?"

"If we weren't here, the Drexlers would rule the streets, or any one of a thousand like them. How many more precious little kids do you think would get shot up in the crossfire?"

"What about your gun?"

Sage halted and turned; a scowl lay vulnerably across his face. He recovered quickly, flashing a silver-toothed smile. "It'll work out. You know, I'm an optimist."

Sage leapt forward and pounded on the hood of his sedan. Murmuring voices halted, and eyes fixed inquisitively upon him. He suddenly felt alive, here, in his element, not parrying with bookworms in the drawing room of some Georgetown townhouse but on the gritty, plagued streets of a drug-ridden city.

"Listen up," Sage said. "Unit One from Headquarters Division is with me and Gerry here. We have the Twenty-Fifth Street apartments. We'll take down the door, rest of you follow. Expect anywhere from three to eight perps, armed and dangerous. They're rippers so they know the game, but they won't think turnabout is fair play, so be careful. Rest of you get your briefings from your individual team leaders. Any questions?"

Minutes later, Sage's group slipped onto the ground floor of a tenement building. Inside, a naked bulb swung from its electric wire, illuminating a rickety staircase. As Sage climbed the stairs, he flicked the bulb with his fingertip, the filament snapped, and the light perished into darkness. Pointing a flashlight, Sages slid his shoulder along the rough-textured wall, stepping over a three-wheel scooter. He scanned numbers hung on broken doorframes until he located apartment 26A. "This is the place," he whispered, drawing his pistol, a substitute nine-millimeter. Stepping to the far side of the door, he lifted his foot.

"Wait a minute," Ramírez said. The paleness of his face was visible even in the unlit hallway. Sweat pooled under his eyes.

Sage planted his foot back on the floor. "More pissing and moaning?" he hissed. He squinted at Ramírez's face, leveled his tone, and asked if Ramírez were up to the task.

"I'll be fine. Just watch out for kids."

Sage rolled his eyes and cocked his knee. He drove his foot into the door just below the handle. The doorframe splintered and cracked, and Sage put his shoulder to the fragmented wood. He burst into the room. "Federal Agent!" he shouted, twisting to blade his body and extending his pistol.

The room was a flurry of movement. A cluster of young men scattered. They sprinted and crawled and flew into doorways. They leapt out windows onto the fire escape, grasping at objects that there was no time to identify.

Burly police officers hurtled into the room. They pounced on the rippers, throttling them with clubs and pistol butts, shouting obscenities and Miranda warnings in the same heaving breaths.

A silver street-gun flashed close to Sage. Ramírez dove for it, thrusting the barrel away. It erupted, hurtling its load into the pixel-sketched face of a television talk-show host. Shattering glass fragments sprayed the room.

Sage leapt onto the shooter's back, grabbing a forearm and twisting it until he heard a ligament snap. He pressed his pistol hard against a convulsing spine. He whispered into the writhing man's ear, until he surrendered to the futility.

In only a few minutes, the rippers were subdued. Those still in the room were roughly seated on the floor in a group facing a wall; the ones who had made it outside were being loaded into police cars. Sage lifted a grocery bag from the couch and dumped its contents onto a coffee table. Dozens of tiny plastic bags spilled across the smooth surface, each containing a cluster of salt-like rocks of crack cocaine.

"Hubba, hubba," Sage said, almost singing, his silver tooth glistening. "Yes sir. You have got to be an optimist these days, Gerry. Can't you see everything will work out just fine?"

Chapter twenty

The five Hueys of second platoon arrived at Fort AP Hill at ten-thirty Saturday morning. Although Trent was caustic, the night's sleep seemed to have erased from his memory the events of the previous night. He let Ashford handle the controls for the bulk of the flight.

AP Hill appeared from a thousand feet as a flat, forested diamond dissected by a naked strip utilized as a parachute jumping area. The barren segment was bounded by a multi-fingered lake marked on the map as a Wildlife Preserve. Once on post, Ashford started a descent. From a hundred feet, Trent spotted first platoon's helicopters nestled against the tree-lined border of the triangular-shaped strip that was Company B's fieldsite. Ashford circled into the wind, and the blades clapped loudly against the sky. He guided the Huey down a shallow approach, grounding the skids at the far edge of the field to allow plenty of space for the helicopters behind him. Trent rolled the throttle to flight idle, and Ashford dropped from the cockpit. Crawford and Zuckerman waited just inside the tree line. Crawford motioned.

Turbulent air swept Ashford's hair, the dust was gritty in his mouth, and he fought to keep his eyes from tearing. When he reached his superiors, Ashford saw Crawford's forehead was wrinkled in worry. Crawford told Ashford that Colonel Harker wanted to see him immediately. Zuckerman stood silently with a cross-eyed stare that was difficult to interpret but that Ashford decided masked diffidence. Ashford said he would go face the music; he put on his best bravado and set off for the Battalion operations tent, and Crawford followed. They picked their way along an eroded dirt trail; the ruts were the gouged stamps of wheeled and tracked combat vehicles, the lumbering dinosaurs of AP Hill.

Ashford managed a deflated grin. "Don't say I told you so."

Crawford checked his watch. "If you'd followed my advice, you'd have left Indiantown Gap this morning. You'd be arriving in just about another hour."

Ashford laughed. "That's true. And I'd still be facing the colonel."

"Only he'd have another hour to stew. Harker will give a whole different line, but for what it's worth, my opinion is that your error in judgment last night was in leaving Indiantown Gap in the pea soup. You did the best you could after that, and you were right to lay over at Belvoir. I talked extensively with several of the pilots about what happened. It wasn't your fault, but you'll probably take quite a bit of the heat. Our illustrious new Company Commander's not much of a stand-up guy."

"Maybe next time I'll be smart enough to listen to you."

"I'm used to talking to myself." Crawford lifted his jaw.

"I know I shouldn't whine about this, but will I ever get a chance at camp to just be Peter Pilot? To do some flying without all the leadership baggage?"

"If it were up to me you would. Traditionally we haven't been co-located with Battalion at camp, and I've had more say. This year, because of the evaluation, Battalion is sitting right on top of us, and the colonel is micromanaging our operations. Unfortunately he'll likely direct what you do and don't do for the next two weeks."

The trail bent around a huge oak tree. On the leeward side of the curve, ponderous trucks lined the roadside, and a cluster of tents were staged among the low branches beyond. Crawford pointed to a large tent draped in mesh camouflage, the site of Battalion Operations.

Reluctantly, Ashford pushed the tent flap aside and squinted as his eyes adjusted to the cave-like atmosphere. The air was dank and unbearable, as if he had entered a chamber in a medieval castle. After a few seconds, Ashford discerned the colonel's rectangular frame. He stood with his back to Ashford, leaning over a sweat-soaked man seated at a table-mounted radio microphone, and Lieutenant Dickson sat before a map board at the radioman's side.

"Sir, Lieutenant Ashford reporting."

Harker ignored the greeting. "What do you mean I can't talk to Post Headquarters yet, Sergeant?" he said to the radioman. "I want that landline operational by zero-ten-hundred. Copy?"

"Copy, Sir."

"Can't anyone do a goddamn thing around here without my having to read them the manual?"

"Sir, I uh—" Ashford closed his mouth when Crawford tapped him on the elbow, and he felt relief with the veteran having accompanied him into the lion's den. Another minute passed before Harker turned; when he did, he stood for another minute, hands anchored on hips, glaring. Finally he nodded at Crawford, thanked him for stopping by, and said he was dismissed. Crawford remonstrated, but Harker's expression remained persistent, and the captain shrugged furtively to Ashford, winked, and was gone.

"Ashford, lieutenant type," Harker said. "I heard strange rumors about Company B second platoon."

"Rumors, Sir?"

"Rumor has it second platoon bivouacked at a motel in Northern Virginia last night on a government credit card, when my orders were to fly directly to AP Hill."

Ashford swallowed. "It's not a rumor, Sir."

"What are you saying?" Harker's demeanor was not yet threatening, but there was that promise.

"The weather last night—"

"I'm not interested in the weather. First platoon arrived safely. Therefore, the weather was satisfactory. Are you confirming the rumor that second platoon didn't follow my directive?"

"Yes, Sir."

"Yes they did, or yes they did not?"

"Did not."

Harker blinked. "I see." He paced for an instant and then turned to Dickson. "Lieutenant Dickson, who was the air mission commander for Company B second platoon last night?"

Dickson's voice was quiet like a whisper; he seemed to take no pleasure in Ashford's discomfort as he once had. "Lieutenant Ashford, Sir."

Harker returned his attention to Ashford. "Your name just keeps popping up. Tell me, it was Trent, wasn't it? He talked you into disobeying my orders, didn't he? He's dangerous, you know."

Ashford would have liked nothing more than to lay the blame on Trent. He also felt a desire to explore the colonel's assessment of Trent's menace but resisted the temptation. "No Sir, the decision was mine."

"Yours?" Harker allowed his penetrating eyes to widen aggressively. "So you made a mistake?"

"I did." Ashford knew Harker's perception of his mistake was different than his own, but he saw no reason to provoke the colonel and said nothing to clarify his response.

"I admire a man who can admit his mistake. Perhaps I can use you. How would you like to work for me this summer camp?"

"Sir?"

"How would you like to work for me?"

Ashford slid his upper teeth over his lower lip. "I'm not sure I can."

Harker let his shoulders slump and then cupped his chin in his right palm. "Your enthusiasm is outstanding, Lieutenant."

"I meant, I'm not sure how much extra I can handle on top of my platoon leader and extra duty assignments. And I'd like to get some flying in." Ashford regretted his final sentence as the words passed through his lips.

"Hear that, Dickson? The lieutenant wants to fly. Well, so do I, Lieutenant. It may surprise you, but I enjoy flying too. You think I like being cooped up here for all my waking hours? How many flying hours do you think I've logged at summer camps over the past ten years? Bet I haven't averaged five hours a camp. Know why? Because I have command responsibilities. When you took your commission, flying became secondary, copy?"

"Yes, Sir."

"Say I copy to acknowledge. All right. I want you to supervise the Nuclear, Biological, and Chemical training for the next several days in addition to your other responsibilities. NBC's an area your unit doesn't practice, and it's sure to be among the evaluators' priorities. I want the men to don their protective gear three times a day."

Ashford silently bit his lip. He knew the men hated the bulky NBC protective suits and masks—the equipment was particularly uncomfortable and potentially dangerous in the summertime. But the colonel's invitation left him little choice. Ashford thanked him for the additional responsibility and was dismissed.

"Oh, Ashford," Harker said just before the tent flap fell flat.

"Sir?"

"I also want you to report to me any information that may be counterproductive to this evaluation. That includes any and all deviations from acceptable military standards. Copy?"

"I copy." With the use of radio phraseology, Ashford finally thought he saw Harker's expression soften, as if he had struck some common chord, although it wasn't a chord he cared to strike often.

Outside, Crawford sat on a stump chewing on a candy bar from an Army meal packet. He rose and joined Ashford on the path. "What did he tell you?"

"Just that I'll get to have fun and make lots of friends at camp. I have to conduct NBC drills three times daily."

Crawford winced. "He say anything about the near miss?"

Ashford squinted quizzically. "Nothing."

Crawford bent to retrieve a long straight stick and halted for a moment, trimming the rough bark with a pocketknife. "Perhaps he figures he should let a sleeping dog lie. What else did he say?"

"He doesn't like Mister Trent."

* ◆ • ─────── • ◆ •• ◆ • ─────── • ◆ •

They returned to Company B's fieldsite. Ashford picked a shady spot for his canvas tent and began assembling it. Around the perimeter of the campsite, men shoveled earth from foxholes and built defensive positions of logs and dirt. Ashford noticed a group of older pilots, Trent and Winston included, walking discretely from camp, over a rise, and deep into the woods. He followed to the crest of the hill.

In the basin, behind a thicket of mountain laurel, stood a blue-and-yellow-striped civilian tent. An extravagant awning swept forward from the entrance, topping a bulky screened-in porch. Inside the netting, Trent sat on a lawn chair, his foot propped on an open cooler. He appeared to be dealing cards to the others who were there with him. Winston cradled a cardboard box, a case of beer.

Ashford stood in repose on the rise. He was responsible for these men and had been warned to report anything that did not conform to military standards. As for the tent, there was little room for interpretation.

A hand touched his elbow, Jesse Morrow's hand. "I see you found the boy scouts," she said.

"These guys will get me fired," said Ashford.

Winston's voice drifted from the hollow. "And we were hoping to get you shot."

"We're forbidden from having beer in the field," Ashford said.

"This isn't the field," came Winston's response. "This is the forest."

"Not everyone will give you a hard time at camp," Morrow said. "I heard one of your extra duties is mess officer. Come on. Let me introduce you to someone."

❧

Ashford and Morrow returned to the official Company B fieldsite. They ducked under a rope connecting two medium-sized tents separated by a trailer draped in camouflage netting. Young enlisted men stripped to their T-shirts and pants stood outside the tent. In a flurry of activity they bent over boiling pots, chopped vegetables, scrubbed potatoes, and mixed drinks in large jugs.

"Why if it ain't our favorite warrant officer," a voice said, addressing Morrow. He was a slim black man with narrow features. His body seemed so thin, as if he didn't have any muscle; veins popped through his taut skin. He was clad in white, and a triangular paper hat covered his bristled hair. On his collar were the black stripes of a sergeant first class. His name tag displayed a single word: *Shoopie*.

Morrow smiled at Shoopie and asked him how he was doing.

"Bein' all we can be, right boys?" said Shoopie, his grin exposing crooked teeth.

"Lieutenant Ashford," Morrow said, "meet your mess sergeant."

Shoopie grabbed Ashford's hand and pumped from his elbow. "Know the way to a man's heart, LT?"

Ashford laughed. "Don't tell me, through his stomach."

"No, Suh. Pardon me ma'am, but I must start the LT out with the absolute truth. Way to a man's heart is through his willy. See if it weren't for my mess section, all the young soldiers would spend all night thinking about their girlfriends and masturbating. That's where we come in, right boys? Our job is to load the food up with saltpeter. Know what that does to a man's willy?"

"No."

"Just say he won't be winning no longevity contests. No suh."

"These are some of the best guys in the unit," Morrow said. "They work their asses off and do a great job. They rise at three a.m. to start breakfast and aren't finished with final clean-up until nine at night. Best part about it, they run themselves. There's virtually nothing to do except take credit for their excellent performance."

"You were kidding about the saltpeter, weren't you?" Ashford said.

"Hell no," Shoopie replied. "Army's been putting shit in the food for years."

Chapter twenty-one

Ruth Scarbrough arrived early Saturday morning at Hershey Medical Center. She spoke first with Peg Christy's day nurses, a diverse group with a collective disinterest in conversation. A chatty candy striper, ill-versed in policy matters, told Scarbrough that Peg Christy's only visitors were her son Brandon and the police. The young woman also mentioned that the pilot who brought the boy in seemed to have taken an interest in him.

On the ground floor, Scarbrough found Mike Daniels in the emergency room corridor. The pilot stood over a gurney, and he was speaking gently to a young girl who peered hopefully into his eyes. The girl's face was blood-spattered, a foam brace encircled her neck, and her arm was wrapped in thick gauze. Scarbrough watched Daniels patiently. He appeared in a way stoic, but there was a calming evenness in his manner, and his strong presence seemed to put the girl at ease. After a few moments, a nurse wheeled the child into a treatment room.

Scarbrough mussed her hair. She perched a battered pair of reading glasses on the bridge of her nose and approached Daniels. "Sir, might I have a word with you?"

Daniels turned, his face unmoved and unmoving. "Depends. You with a newspaper?"

"Heavens no. Social services. I was assigned Brandon Christy's case. I'm doing some checking on him since his mother—"

"I brought them in."

"I see. Do you know where the boy is living?"

"At a used car dealership. In the garage."

"Goodness. Does he have any assistance? What I mean to say, is there an adult?"

"Ms. Christy's boyfriend is in jail. From what I can tell, he belongs there."

"He's a criminal?" Scarbrough said, honestly taken aback.

"I saw a baggie of cocaine the police confiscated from his rinky-dink laboratory."

Scarbrough managed to hold her eyebrows level, and she pulled a notepad from her shoulderbag. "Terrible influence indeed. Allow me to take a few notes."

"You with the county or the state?"

"County. Has the boy had any visitors? Perhaps an aunt or uncle?"

"I wouldn't know about that. But I do think the kid is in some trouble. The boyfriend gave some instructions I overheard."

Daniels asked if his answers might get Bran in trouble. Scarbrough clucked, feigning mild offense. "We act exclusively in the child's best interest."

"Yeah. Sounded to me like the kid is to take care of the boyfriend's drug deals, while he's in jail."

"How interesting. I mean how horrible. What kind of deals?"

"I only caught the tail end of the conversation, but I think the kid is tending the boyfriend's marijuana plants. I didn't think that was so bad, but then the boyfriend mentioned some bad actor from Harrisburg."

Scarbrough scribbled furiously. She asked several more questions, but Daniels seemed to know little else. She thanked him and left the hospital.

※———※

Scarborough returned to Turczynski's house. In the bedroom, she transcribed her notes of her conversation with Daniels onto her laptop computer. The final line she typed in bold letters: *Is the boy the key to Soldier Man?*

Scarbrough stretched out on the bed and felt the baby twist off her spine. Things were moving fast, she thought, very fast. Her ankles throbbed, and she felt mildly nauseated. She needed more time to rest, to mind the baby's health. Her task would require assistance. She examined a card Turczynski had given her and lifted the phone.

"Anderson Investigations," a voice answered.

※———※

Rayful Bigelow skulked at the edge of the open yard in the center of the Dauphin County jail, a bright orange jump suit crumpled around his sickly frame. Coils of razor-edged wire topped the walls on four sides. In the yard, men bounced basketballs and lifted wheels of iron. Bigelow preferred solitude; he was, after all, an entrepreneur, not an athlete or socialite.

A tall man of Latin-American descent approached. His face was featureless, apart from multiple scars forming a hash mark on his cheek, and his scalp was shaved at the sides and cut close across the top. His hands rested loosely in his pockets. Bigelow nervously wiped his palm across both cheeks. Zackaeus had been right—Jorge Munzo was here. The thought of why Munzo would allow himself to be arrested on a two-bit charge sent chills up Bigelow's spine; there was no doubt he was on a mission.

"S-up, Jorge," Bigelow said without taking his eyes from Munzo's fists, hands with a reputation for wielding implements of death.

"Scrounger." Munzo's tongue protruded slightly between his teeth.

Bigelow scanned the yard. Munzo wouldn't kill him in the open, he told himself, knowing full well Munzo would kill without restraint where and when he pleased.

"You been skimming 'caine off the Cruise." The statement was flat and simple, not one seeking a response, only a truth to be acknowledged and accepted like a prison sentence. Munzo moved in close and brushed his elbow against Bigelow's stomach.

Bigelow remonstrated. "No, I—"

"Yes, you did, and your bullshit don't pay the bills in here. We'll deal with that later. Right now you got to tell me how you'll make things right."

Bigelow's thoughts spun. Apparently Cruise still believed Rocket Pack was synthesized from his own cocaine and heroin and that Bigelow merely skimmed a small measure of the ingredients from the top. That crime warranted a beating but might not merit the death sentence that Bigelow knew would follow if Cruise discerned the truth. "I need some time," said Bigelow.

"Got no time. You was to cook up a new batch of Rocket Pack for Cruise. Now, he got no cooker and he got no Rocket. All he got is your ass in a sling. Was up to me, I'd do you right now, 'cause I don't like the accommodations."

"All right," Bigelow stammered. "Okay. I got an option. My man. I got my man, he does most of the cooking anyway. He's young, but we've been through the drill a dozen times. I'll send him by Cruise's digs. Get word to Cruise to give my man another two kilos of coke and half a ki of smack. Cruise'll have his Rocket Pack in no time."

Munzo hovered over Bigelow. "I hope you're pulling your old bullshit, Scrounger. I hope."

"No bullshit. I'll send him straight away."

The Scrounger was running low on options. It was time to play an ace.

Chapter twenty-two

For the next three days, Ashford didn't fly. The bulk of his time was devoted to drilling Company B on NBC procedures and operations. The training was dangerous, because the men were required to don the protective gear—heavy rubber suits and gas masks—and in the summer heat and humidity, the risk of heat injury was serious. Monitoring the training was a difficult, time-consuming task. Ashford devised an acclimatization schedule based on guidelines contained in Army regulations and Fort AP Hill's operating procedures. He divided Company B into four groups to alleviate the monitoring burden and began the training in fifteen-minute increments, three times a day, working toward a goal of a single forty-minute period in the suits by the end of two weeks.

Supervising the training did not improve Ashford's popularity among the pilots or enlisted men. He struggled to conceal his disillusionment, but his hope of accumulating flying experience at summer camp was waning like the dying embers of an unfed fire. Each day, the pilots held briefings, collected their gear, boarded the helicopters, and disappeared into the skies. Ashford was left with the enlisted personnel and the few officers who remained behind. Later, the pilots landed in formation and slapped each other on their backs and congratulated themselves on good approaches and tight formations, seeming intoxicated with the vigor of accomplishment. Inside, Ashford brooded.

On Tuesday morning, Lieutenant Dickson approached Ashford in the Company B operations tent. He volunteered to conduct the afternoon NBC drills to liberate Ashford to join a flying mission. Perhaps the gesture was a response to the small kindness Ashford had shown Dickson in the lavatory back at Indiantown Gap. Whatever the reason, Dickson presented an opportunity Ashford could not resist. He explained the training procedures and gave Dickson his acclimatization schedules. He coached Dickson on techniques of close monitoring, emphasizing the safety measures he had implemented.

• • — • • • — • •

The flight was exhilarating. Ashford flew in the lead Huey with an experienced and kind warrant officer. For the first time he felt like both a pilot and an air mission commander. They met their time schedule perfectly and were heartily congratulated by the commander of the infantry unit they were supporting. The mission was not only a success, it was a triumph.

They landed at the Company B fieldsite in the sweltering heat of the late afternoon sun. Ashford's rump ached. He should have been bone-tired, but he was filled with energy and self-satisfaction. As the rotor blades wound to a stop, Ashford heard a rustling sound. From the tree line emerged an unrecognizable figure swathed in heavy green rubber-like material. The man appeared like a grotesque creature from a science fiction film, although he lacked the forceful manner of a monster—his step was ponderous and his frame teetered.

Ashford dropped quickly from the cockpit and hurried to meet the man clad in a protective suit. Through a fogged plastic face shield, he recognized Shoopie's features, drawn with exhaustion. "Suh, you have to do something," came the muffled voice through the filtering apparatus. "LT Dickson got the whole unit in rubber monkey suits. We been in them over an hour."

"What?" Ashford envisioned Dickson posed in a bombastic stance, lording over the drill. "Get out of that thing, Shoopie."

Shoopie raised both hands ravenously, scooping the rubber mask from his head. His forehead and ears were gouged deeply with marks from the elastic straps, and his curly hair was matted to his forehead. "Thank you, Suh," Shoopie gasped. "Can I call the all clear?"

"Get some water and sit down in the shade. I'll call the all clear."

Shoopie shed the top of the suit and struggled to disengage the rubber pants. "I'm done being all I can be, LT. Can I go home now?"

Ashford sprinted around the perimeter of the campsite. He lingered over foxholes and defensive positions. He shouted toward the interior of the camp. "All clear! All clear! Get out of the suits."

Some of the men had already removed the gear on their own initiative, but others dutifully awaited the signal. Masks and coats flew from foxholes, followed by pants and boots. Shouts of relief and exuberance echoed in the woods, although some voices were lowered in anger. Ashford shouted to the last defensive position. When he reached it, he saw it was empty. He turned away and bumped headlong into an aged, steely-eyed man in a pressed battle-dress uniform.

The man had a great tanned forehead that sloped like a wedge into his Prussian-style crew cut. His elevated cheekbones appeared to support the silver-rimmed glasses perched on his hawk nose. His mouth was pinched, he moved his bloodless lips with the crispness of a withered aristocrat, and his manner exuding an unqualified expectation of deference. "What are you doing, Lieutenant?" the man said. He wore two stars on his collar, the markings of a major general. Two younger men flanked him, presumably his aides.

"Sounding the all clear, Sir," said Ashford.

"That hole is empty, son."

"Yes, Sir, it is."

"Do you always talk to empty foxholes?"

"No, Sir."

"Well where on earth is your field gear? Your helmet and firearm. And your mission protective equipment?"

Ashford glanced at his flight suit. In his haste, he had forgotten to strap on his field gear; it remained dangling over his seat in the helicopter. He shrugged unabashedly and spoke with an even voice. "I just returned from a mission. Now if you'll excuse me, I have to finish calling the all clear."

"And why is that?"

"My men have been in full protective gear for over an hour. Army regulations call for gradual acclimatization, half-hour increments maximum until—"

"Do you know who I am, son?"

Ashford shook his head.

The general tilted his ear toward the screaming-eagle patch on his shoulder. "General Tarsavage, 101st Airborne Division. I've come to administer an IG Inspection on this unit. This particular drill is being conducted per my specific direction."

Ashford looked straight into the general's highborn eyes. "I'm still calling the all clear," he said, speaking through a lump forming in his throat. As his lips moved, he imagined the remnants of his chances for a flying camp floating from his grasp like a balloon caught in an updraft.

• • • • • • • • •

Less than twenty minutes passed before the word came from Battalion Headquarters summoning Ashford to the Battalion operations tent. This time he borrowed a jeep. As he drove, he considered stomping on the gas pedal and flinging the vehicle into a tree. Perhaps he could claim he had had a heat stroke; maybe he should have a medic hook a bottle of saline solution to a vein for theatrical effect.

When he arrived at the operations tent, Ashford threw the tent flap back as gallantly as he could manage. Colonel Harker stood like a bulwark against some unseen disaster, shouting commands into the flurry of activity unfolding about him. Sweaty men pointed to a topographical map and talked frantically into radio microphones; others gathered in clusters and spoke in hushed tones.

Ashford slipped over to Dickson's station, where the lieutenant was hunched over a radio. Ashford dropped his hand onto Dickson's shoulder with force greater than needed to gain his attention.

"Huh?" Dickson stammered, spinning.

"What happened with the NBC training?"

"I'm sorry, Mark." Dickson's expression was genuinely troubled. "I got called back to handle this mess. Colonel Harker's orders were to let the men train until I finished here."

Ashford let his frown linger. "Well, what the hell's going on?"

"Couple things. First, we got the results from the urine screening."

"And?"

"A Company B soldier tested positive for marijuana."

Ashford clenched his teeth. He supposed it would be his job to confront the man. "What else?"

"General Tarsavage made his entrance this afternoon."

"I know." Ashford grinned nervously. "I already met him."

"We heard. But that's not what all this is about. See, at fourteen-thirty, when the general arrived, he piloted a Huey low level directly over the Fort AP Hill Wildlife Preserve. That's an area highly off limits to military air traffic. Apparently he buzzed a Washington congressman who was on the ground currying favor with a local, high-powered birdwatcher. They want the pilot of the Huey grounded and a public apology from the Army. Colonel Harker's trying right now to diffuse the situation."

Harker's barking suddenly ceased. He turned to face the lieutenants. "Ah yes, Ashford, lieutenant-type. I understand that you've introduced yourself to our evaluation team."

"I ran into them." Ashford held his hands tightly fisted along his sides. "I was calling all clear on an NBC drill."

"General Tarsavage said you were running around the camp like some unhinged madman. What the hell did you think you were doing?"

"I made a judgment call."

"Who gave you the authority—"

"You did, Sir. You put me in charge of the NBC training."

"You insolent idiot."

"Sir, it's not just the drills. When conditions are oppressive, like today, the men should dress appropriately. We should let them strip to their T-shirts and pants and give them frequent breaks from the sun."

Harker's features suddenly narrowed and his neck twitched. "You'd let the men loiter around out of uniform in the middle of an IG inspection?"

"This is a health and safety concern. I'm sure the evaluators will understand."

"Let me tell you something," Harker said, his eyes flaming. "The evaluators are from the 101st Airborne Division. They eat rusty nails for breakfast and live lizards for lunch."

"I did some research, Sir. Battalion is required to monitor the wet bulb and provide reports to subordinate field units. We haven't had any. And the men need to become heat acclimated before we step up training. Army regulations and Post SOP require—"

"Don't quote me chapter and verse, you little prick. I don't give a damn what Post SOP requires."

"Sir, the beauty is that it's part of the game—the regulations require graduated training, limiting the amount of time the men spend in protective gear according to their acclimatization. The evaluators have to accept that."

"Now you're telling me my job. Right in front of my staff, I have a lieutenant who intends to challenge me."

The radio operator slid headphones over his ears and turned away. "Clear the tent," said Harker, his voice resounding as if in a steel chamber. All other voices ceased as Harker repeated his command, and it was obeyed instantly. When he and Ashford were alone, Harker said, "Were you in Vietnam, Lieutenant?"

"Sir?"

"Were you in Vietnam?" Harker spoke with indignity, sharp and raw. His eyes swarmed and interrogated.

"No, Sir."

"No. You were not in Vietnam. I, on the other hand, was in Vietnam. Many of these men were in Vietnam. You think we had your precious Post SOP?"

"Probably not, but—"

"No we did not. We survived in a foreign country in the middle of a damn war without your Army regulation or Post SOP. Now how is it you think these same men won't survive a little training exercise in AP Hill, Virginia?"

"It's a matter of acclimatization, Sir. Many of them are older and out of shape—"

The redness in Harker's face darkened to a deep crimson. "You're grounded for the remainder of this camp. From this moment on, if you fly, it'll be as a crew chief. Is that understood?"

"Yes, Sir."

"Next item on the agenda. As drug interdiction officer for Company B, you're to relieve Ronald Shoupenheimer of his duties. You'll arrange for his immediate transport to Indiantown Gap to meet with a review board and for out processing."

"Ronald Shoupenheimer?"

"They call him Shoopie. Whatever kind of name that is. His urinalysis was positive for THC, and I want him gone."

The change of subject had thrown Ashford off balance. He collected his thoughts. "Sir, I know this man. He heads up our mess section. He's not in a flying position, so the possibility he may have used drugs is less critical. He's been with the unit a long time, and he's an outstanding performer. I recommend a letter of reprimand and counseling—"

Harker shook his head. "Immediate transport. Furthermore, as penance for your insubordination, you'll sign this flight log indicating you were the pilot of Army helicopter zero-zero-niner-six-four this afternoon."

Ashford scanned the log. The helicopter Harker said had arrived at the Battalion fieldsite at fourteen-thirty—it was the aircraft General Tarsavage had flown over the Wildlife Preserve. Ashford stood dumbfounded. He had been selected to take the blame for the general's blunder. "I can't sign that," he said.

"There's nothing for you to do or not do," Harker responded, his voice harsh and arbitrary. He penciled Ashford's name into the log with a perfunctory flourish. "I'll handle the official end of it. You're simply grounded and aren't to speak with anybody about the reason. Copy?"

In disbelief Ashford stared at the colonel's severe mouth as it delivered its decree, worse than a prison sentence. He tried to protest, but the words caught in his throat. "But—"

"Loud and clear."

"What?"

"Loud and clear."

"I understand."

"Loud and clear."

"I said I understood."

Ashford stepped out of the tent, and the ninety-five-degree air felt cool against his boiling forehead.

❧

Ashford found Morrow reclining on a mesh hammock. Her body swung gently in the breeze, her eyes were closed, and the foam pads of earphones covered all but the round tops of her exquisite ears. She looked lovely and content, almost angelic in her repose. Lacking words, and reluctant to disturb her, Ashford turned to leave.

Morrow suddenly sat up, her legs folded casually in a triangle. "Hey, LT, what's up?"

"I thought you were sleeping."

"Just listening to Harry Chapin."

"Kind of old stuff, isn't it?"

"It's got universal appeal. Before there was Farm Aid and Comic Relief, there was Harry. He played benefit after benefit on his own. I saw him in my hometown just before he died."

"Sorry to disturb you, but I was hoping for some advice."

"Ask away."

"Battalion just got back the results of the urine screening."

"Somebody came back dirty?"

Ashford nodded. "Shoopie."

Morrow flopped backwards, flinging her forearm onto her forehead. "You tell him?"

"I came to see you first."

"Let me guess. Harker wants to ship him out."

"I tried my best—"

"Please let me tell him."

"I didn't come to ask that."

"I know, but I want to do it. It'll be easier coming from me."

Ashford considered for a moment. "Should I wait somewhere?"

"You should come along. It's just that I should break it to him. We're friends, you know."

They walked across the soft forest floor and ducked under the ropes into the mess area. Shoopie stood over a huge steel pot brimming with boiling water. Clad in a heavy apron and rubber gloves, he was scrubbing a soiled tray and singing poorly. "Yo, LT," Shoopie said. "Heard you got into some hot water, no pun intended. I deeply appreciate what you done for my men."

"Is there somewhere we can talk?" said Morrow.

"Anything for you, pretty lady. Come into my humble adobe."

Shoopie shed the gloves and ushered the officers into a circular canvas tent with room for several cots. Cooking implements of all kinds lay cluttered on the ground floor: silver pots and elongated utensils, rectangular immersion pans, cookie cutters, and pie plates. The sergeant moved among them as if he were intimate with each piece. He tied open the flaps at the far end of the tent to allow a cooling wind to buffet them. Shoopie bounced with a light dance step, still moving to his internal music. "Have a seat where you can find one," he said. He asked if they wanted some bug juice and, before either pilot could answer, he poured two cups.

"Why don't you sit down too, Shoopie," Morrow said.

Morrow and Shoopie sat on opposite sides of a cot like bookends, and Ashford nestled on his haunches beside a portable refrigerator. "We have some bad news for you, Shoopie," said Morrow. "Your urine tested positive for marijuana."

Shoopie lifted the back of his hand to his forehead and began to quiver. "Oh, that thing."

"You shouldn't say anything," Morrow advised. "A legal officer will talk to you back at the Gap. Thing is, they want to send you back now."

"Who want to send me?"

"The colonel. He's concerned about his evaluation."

"What about my men?"

"They'll be fine. The LT and I will look after them with special care. You have to be concerned about your own rights."

Shoopie blinked abashedly. "I screwed up, didn't I?"

"Guess you did, Shoopie."

"LT, what chance do you think I got?"

Ashford glanced at Morrow; she nodded encouragingly.

"I'm not an expert," Ashford said, "but I learned a little in officer training. They'll convene a board of review, and you'll have a lawyer if you want one. There's such a thing as a false positive, but the test results are rarely questioned. If you're lucky, they'll let you stay in the Guard and reassign you to an infantry company."

"And if not?"

Ashford cast his eyes on the ground. "Dishonorable discharge."

Shoopie's elbow jerked involuntarily, contacting a fork; the utensil lifted airborne and landed on an immersion pan with a clatter. "Oh man, I smoked that jay at my brother's wedding two months ago. Stuff is only supposed to stay in your system thirty days."

"Don't say anything else, Shoopie," Morrow said. "The LT and I could be questioned."

"Oh, it don't make no nevermind now. Could you just leave me alone awhile? I gotta get together. Mean my things, I mean."

———

An hour later, Shoopie sat alone on a bench-seat in the cargo area of a running Huey. Ashford and Morrow stood in the churning wind, watching the anguished face of the mess sergeant as the helicopter lifted from the ground, bound for a place where they could be of no help to him. The fabric seat strap looped around Shoopie's waist was positioned to protect him, but it seemed to imprison him too. Separated from his work, he seemed wholly deflated, as if he had no esteem or dignity or future. A solitary tear rolled down Morrow's cheek. Ashford wanted to wipe it away and comfort her with his touch, but he said and did nothing.

The helicopter disappeared in the distance.

———

For the next few days, Ashford flew in the rear of Captain Crawford's helicopter, serving as his crew chief. He watched the captain handle the reins of command and how the pilots responded to his authority. They rode him and bucked him to a degree, but there was cooperation there, an accordance that seemed born of respect and shared experience.

On the third day of Ashford's grounding, Crawford led a flight of three Hueys into a tight field. Ashford jumped to the ground to strap in boarding troops. The rotors churned, and the noise of the engines was deafening. Soldiers ran in every direction.

A young infantryman seemed confused. He bent under the weight of his fieldpack and started for Crawford's helicopter. Then he seemed to change his mind. He moved toward another Huey and then came toward Ashford again. He seemed oblivious to the deadly spinning tail rotor directly in his return path.

Ashford shouted a warning but realized he couldn't be heard in the cacophony. His toes bit hard into the dirt. He leapt and dove. He hit the straggler in the midsection, tackling him to the ground.

The inertia cast the soldier's helmet into the tail rotor's spinning blades. The metal-on-metal contact sounded like grinding gears. The blades chucked the steel pot into the air.

Crawford shut down the Huey on the spot. Winston was summoned. When he arrived, he shook his jowly face and pronounced that the tail rotor would have to be replaced.

"Congratulations, LT," he said to Ashford. "You broke your first helicopter."

When Ashford returned to the Company B fieldsite, he was greeted with jokes and catcalls, but the tone of the comments had lightened. If there were not a degree of respect in the voices, there was at least an absence of impertinence that was in its own way comforting.

Ashford went to bed early. He lay in his tent with his flashlight, leafing through aerodynamics and weather manuals. His head ached from the day's worries. He began to doze.

A rustling sound awakened Ashford from his half-sleep, and he lifted the tent flap. Suddenly, darkness overcame him. Instinctively, he touched his face. He felt the rough texture of a burlap sack covering his head. Strong hands grabbed his arms and lifted his body.

In another moment, the canvas bag was removed. He was seated in the bed of a moving half-ton truck. A dozen warrant officers sat around him, most stifling smiles. Trent was perched on the tailgate; Winston was there too, and Morrow. "What are you doing?" asked Ashford in bewilderment.

"Sitting on your pants," said Winston. He lifted his backside and retrieved a wrinkled flight suit he was using as a cushion.

Ashford looked at his body. He was naked but for his undershorts. He grabbed the uniform and pulled it to his chest, casting a sheepish look at Morrow.

"It's okay, LT," she said. "I won't look."

"Not much to look at," Winston said.

"Actually I saw a nice bulge," said Morrow.

"So you did look. Shame, shame."

Ashford felt more comfortable once his flight suit was zipped tightly to his neck. "What's going on?"

"We're headed into Bowling Green for a little drink," Winston said. "Thought you might like to join us."

"Bowling Green?"

"Closest town with a decent tavern. We decided you deserve a drink."

Ashford felt jittery since it was impermissible to leave the fieldsite, and alcohol was off limits until camp's end. But something inside him craved acceptance from the older men, and this was the first window of opportunity they had allowed him to break through the walls of their clan. He bit his tongue.

They arrived at the bar and ordered beer after beer. The place was noisy and the air, smoky. Glasses clinked, voices exchanged anecdotes, and barmaids hurried after tips. The warrant officers christened Ashford an honorary crew chief. They ridiculed him for his inability to please Harker, though they seemed most fond of the incapacity.

"How come you don't kiss ass like Dickson?" asked Winston.

"Guess I'm too dumb." Ashford hoisted his drink.

"You're sure not like Dickson. Boy knows the cock size of every captain and above in centimeters."

"I don't think he's that bad."

"What do you think of Harker?"

Ashford appeared pensive. "I should probably just hold my tongue."

"He's an asshole," said Trent, staring at the far wall. "In Vietnam, there was a time when he'd get loaded and goose the waitresses. Let it all hang loose. Then he decided to stick his nose straight up Tarsavage's ass."

"You were in Vietnam together?" Ashford asked. He knew the answer but was searching for some doorway into Trent's past.

"Funny how the Army's such a small world," Trent said dryly, staring vacantly across the dance floor. Ashford saw in the lines of Trent's face that the conversation was over; if Ashford had created an opening, Trent had slammed it closed.

Winston hammered his mug on the bar. "Time to decommission the lieutenant. Warrants, we must determine the proper rite of un-passage."

"Let's strip him naked, stand him up on the bar, and make him sing Danny Boy," Trent said.

Winston shouted at the bartender for a beer and slid it across the bar to Ashford. "Chug that."

"Huh?"

"Chug it."

Ashford shrugged. He opened his mouth, and he turned the glass upside-down.

"Very nice," Morrow said, joining the proceedings.

"I hereby decommission you," Winston said.

"Pretty heavy honor," said Morrow. "In fact, I've never heard of it happening to a commissioned officer before."

"A decommissioned officer," Winston corrected.

The warrant officers laughed about Ashford's grounding and talked rowdily about sports, women, booze, and flying. They told stories about Vietnam, some of them lighthearted tales of thwarting authority, others of the ruminations were more serious, although Ashford sensed each man held within him some story he would tell no one.

Winston was in the middle of a story of a bout with venereal disease. "Most wonderful feeling in my life," he said, "was when I could piss again and it didn't hurt. Some guys say the first time they had sex is best, but this was better. Soon as I got well, I bought a case of latex condoms. Put one on every protrusion of my body every time I even thought about having sex."

Ashford laughed at Winston's animated presentation. He turned to the sunken dance floor. On the far side a stereo blared; the bass throbbed, and the music enveloped him with its pulse. Random and strange video images covered a large screen and splashed colors onto the enervated dancers, creating roving pockets of shadow among the strobes. The pilots were scattered about the room. Some stood at the bar; others leaned against a rail overlooking the dance floor.

In the sea of movement, a stillness gradually unfolded. Trent stood paralyzed at the rail, one boot on the floor, one hooked on the banister.

Ashford followed the line of Trent's gaze to the giant video screen. The screen flashed images from the War in Vietnam: fire-fights, soldiers dragging limp broken bodies, bloodied bandages, and choppers flashing through the trees. The once-vibrant colors flashing from strobe lights melded into a steady dull green. The stereo blared chanted lyrics about the youth of the soldiers in Vietnam.

One by one, the veterans at the bar turned to the screen. Their bodies appeared to rise without internal direction, as if lifted by invisible strings. They seemed transfixed in the same complete and monstrous stillness, as if an unseen Medusa were turning each to stone. The surreal radiance lit their motionless faces, diverse in features but the same in indecipherable expressionless-ness, as if the green glow contained a solvent that washed away emotion, leaving behind only mute and empty suffering.

As the chant neared its conclusion, a glittering ball dropped from the ceiling and a beam of light projected spinning patterns and fragments onto the floor. The light appeared as if it were fil-tered through a giant, uncontrolled fan. And in the vortex stood Nick Trent. The scene reminded Ashford of Olofson's story about Trent's unbalanced fan in Vietnam. Ashford guessed from Trent's expression that he remembered too.

Several videos played before any of the veterans spoke. Soon they were laughing again, spilling beer, and slapping each other. But their interactions contained a hint of desperation, suggesting the disturbing visions lingered in their minds.

When the mood seemed to have lightened, Ashford attempt-ed to corral the warrants, lifting his voice above the barroom noise. "We have a seven-thirty mission tomorrow."

"So?" Winston said.

"Army regulations," said Ashford. "Twelve hours bottle to throttle."

Trent poked at Winston's stomach. "I thought you decommissioned him. What's he doing quoting Mickey Mouse regulations?"

"Must be a conditioned reflex," Winston said.

"That's enough guys," said Ashford. He was suddenly conscious of his boyish face, lacking any ornament of command. "I had a good time, but it's time to wrap up. Let's go get some sleep."

"I'll get plenty of sleep when I'm dead," Trent said.

Morrow took Ashford lightly by the arm. "Take a walk?"

"Still thinking about that bulge?" said Winston.

Morrow wrinkled her nose. "Jealous, old-timer?"

"You bet."

Outside, the air was free from smoke and the moon was high on its night course. Morrow breathed listlessly. She flattened her hands on her lower back and stretched. "Give them another twenty minutes, LT. They'll run out of gas. They're old."

"Sure," said Ashford. He squatted on the cement curb under a blinking red beer advertisement, and Morrow sat cross-legged beside him. "It's hard to know what to do with these guys."

"They are a breed apart."

"It scares me sometimes. Especially Trent. The places he's been, the things he knows."

"Don't be intimidated. They're a lot like children sometimes."

"It's more than that," Ashford said. He told the story of his arrival at Indiantown Gap and his near-mishap with the line truck that Trent had witnessed mutely. He spoke of his visit to

Major Olofson and what he had learned about the Massacre at Ba Long. He shared his suspicion that Trent might be responsible.

Morrow exhaled. "I can't believe Nick Trent could be responsible for a massacre."

"I really thought he was. Everything he did convinced me he had some major axe to grind, and there was the possibility that he's a sociopath. It made perfect sense that Ba Long was the answer. And I'm not yet convinced he's not responsible."

"But?"

"But according to Major Olofson, Colonel Harker stood as his principal accuser."

"And?"

"And Harker's a liar." Ashford continued to tell Morrow the details of General Tarsavage's botched arrival at AP Hill and his own selection as a stand-in for Tarsavage, to shoulder the blame for overflying the Wildlife Preserve.

"So you think Colonel Harker may have falsely accused Nick too?" Morrow asked.

"It's possible."

"Then it's just as possible Colonel Harker's responsible for the Massacre at Ba Long?"

"I hadn't thought of that. But I suppose it is."

"Why are you so interested in this?"

"I'm not sure exactly. It started because I wanted to find out about Trent. Now it seems that it's like a cloud that hangs over this unit."

"Nick does have pretty deep-seated problems with authority."

"Tell me about it."

"You've taken it about as far as you can without going to the horse's mouth."

"There's one more thing I can do. I learned that Sergeant Spencer flew every mission with Trent their last three weeks in Vietnam."

"You want to ask Reggie?"

"He's been a lot more approachable than Trent. That's something I wanted to thank you for too." Ashford's tone softened to a sensual whisper. "For being so, uhm, approachable."

Ashford looked at Morrow in the white moonlight, unadorned but beautiful. He felt as if he should avert his eyes, but he held hers as if in invitation. The silence lasted a long moment, until Morrow turned and combed her fingers quickly through her soft hair. In the diffuse light, her eyes took on a silvery cast and gleamed over her darkened cheekbones. Underneath, the shadow of her mouth was maddeningly round and full.

Suddenly, Morrow said, "You know I lost my husband?"

"Yes, I heard. I'm sorry."

"He was everything to me. My whole world. When he left me, I had nothing. No career, no personality. No nothing. I was an Army wife and had only the Army. And I was afraid, so afraid of losing anyone else. So I decided I had to conquer my fear, and flying was the way I found to do it."

"You're a very good pilot. Everyone says so."

"But I still haven't overcome the fear. I can be friendly with the guys but can't get too close. You see, I'm afraid... scared of losing him again."

Ashford blinked his eyes. He had an almost uncontrollable urge to gather Morrow in his arms and kiss her, and he knew his impulse was apparent. But he also understood that she wasn't speaking of a fear of the other pilots getting close; she was talking about him. She was pushing him away, indirectly and gently.

Against the ache to touch, he felt an impotence like he had never felt before; he could do nothing and say nothing. The only thing he could think of to say, once again, was that he was sorry for her loss. But the truth was he wasn't sorry that she was there, or that she was unattached, or that he felt for her. He was only sorry he couldn't hold her in that moment, and that the ghost of a dead helicopter pilot stood between them, banishing him from the comfort of her soft touch as long as he pursued his own life-long dream.

Chapter
twenty-three

Late Saturday morning, Brandon Christy arrived at Dauphin County Jail. It was an ominous institution, the facade a collage of pale yellow brick and darkened glass. Bran passed through a doorway-style metal detector and glass doors, and a uniformed guard waived a hand-held metal detector over his chest and stamped his hand. As Bran negotiated each security device, he felt as if he were plunging deeper and deeper into an inky cave. He could think of no good reason to continue but couldn't terminate the descent, and the sensation escalated into a headlong free-falling spiral. In the center of the maelstrom was the Scrounger, somewhere deep in the bowels of the prison.

When Bran reached the visiting area, he found it was not steeped in shadows as he had imagined; it was lathered in fluorescence and decorated in light pastel colors, presumably an attempt to soothe the more beastly inhabitants. Bigelow was seated at one of several tables. Dressed in a baggy surgical outfit, Bran imagined a doctor after a long shift in a city-hospital emergency ward. No, Bran thought, the Scrounger could never pass for a healer.

He seated himself opposite Bigelow who inched forward and spoke in a hushed tone. His face was animated by troubled twitches. "Where the hell have you been, kid? I been in here for weeks."

Bran's response was precise and unapologetic. "Tending after Ma."

Bigelow laced his fingers behind his head and reclined in a calculating manner. "How is your Ma?"

Bran hesitated. Bigelow hadn't asked about his Garden first, although Brandon was sure the order of his questions was a matter of strategy rather than concern. Bran repeated the doctor's optimistic report.

"Good. But she's been there a long time. Weeks of doctors and nurses and treatments. It'll cost plenty. Been thinking about that? How we'll pay?"

Bran said nothing.

"You been up to the Garden?" It hadn't taken the Scrounger long to maneuver to his true concern.

"Everything's fine."

"When's the last time?"

"Three days ago."

"Go again soon. It'll help pay the bills."

"I'll go tonight."

Bigelow nodded incessantly. There was more trouble coming—Brandon could feel it.

"There's something else you have to head off for me," Bigelow said. "Some real business."

So many times the story, Bran thought. If only his mother had jettisoned this miscreant from their lives long ago, instead of trying to mold him.

"Let me tell you something." Bigelow put on a haughty air. "When I was young, I ran fast and lived high. I was something to see. Hard to describe, but it was like I was standing on top of the world."

Bran strained to avoid attaching mental imagery to this illusion.

"Then I got busted. Lucky for me, it was nickel-and-dime. They dropped the distribution charge, but I spent some time on the inside, and after that I made a fundamental decision."

"Shouldn't mess with drugs?"

"Shouldn't get caught. See, kid, drugs is one hell of a game. There's a market out there with a need—people want to get twisted. You've got to face it sometime; life sucks and folks need relief. When I sell Rocket Pack, I sell relief. Nothing wrong with that. Hell, everyone sells something. Only difference is where you come from and what you're good at. Is it any better to sell booze to drunks? Or Marlboros to cigarette junkies who spit up chunks of their lungs? Or blocks of video junkie wasteland to kids who blow out their minds in front of the screen?

"Rocket Pack is my angle. I got no televangelist ministry, and I can't soar like Michael Jordan. I got no face like the pretty boys in the movies. Rocket Pack's my shot, and it's got to fly."

Bran leaned away as Bigelow hovered closer, his Scrounger finger wiggling in a *come-here* gesture. "Now I screwed up. I got caught, this time pretty good. Take me some time to figure a way out. While I do, I need someone to keep me in my game. You do this one chore for me."

"Chore?"

"You gotta make Rocket Pack."

Bran's chair screeched with his physical reaction. Bigelow straightened and pivoted his head so quickly it appeared to rotate in a circle. When he placated himself, he leaned in again. He explained that he didn't really make Rocket Pack and that the drug was synthesized by a man called Iron Flannigan, a member of the Monoliths, a motorcycle gang based in Mount Cobb in the Pocono Mountains in northeastern Pennsylvania. The town was sufficiently isolated from law enforcement and convenient to the New York drug market. Bigelow explained that he tendered to Flannigan the cocaine and heroin that Cruise provided under the pretense that they were the raw materials, and Flannigan gave him Rocket Pack, already packaged for distribution, as well as a bonus of ten thousand dollars.

"Rocket Pack's been selling like wildfire in the Burg," Bigelow said. "That's the beauty of the game. Everyone's happy. Cruise thinks I'm some kind of genius. Calls me his cooker. I even used to skim a little coke off the top, before I gave it to Flannigan. But that gets tricky, so I'm not asking that."

"What are you asking?" Bran said hoarsely.

"Pick up the dope from Cruise, give it over to Flannigan, get the ten grand and the rock, and give the rock to Cruise. Put the money aside for the hospital bills. Simple."

Bran exhaled in a gust. "Who am I to say is making the stuff?"

"You are. Give Cruise some mumbo jumbo about acids and bases, solvents and superheating. Tell him we throw in some meth with the coke and smack. Just make it sound like you know what's up."

Bran's lips moved in protest, but words were slow to follow. "Rayful, this is too much."

"Come on, kid. Live the life; feel the thrill. Play the game. If that's not enough, do it for your Ma. I swear, this'll get us by the bills. Tuesday next week, you show up at the five block of Hill Manor. Knock on any door. Ask for Cruise. He'll be expecting you."

Brandon's attention was distracted by two men seated at an adjacent table, who had paused their conversation. One was dressed in inmate garb. The other wore a brown T-shirt and jeans and appeared to be an ordinary visitor. The men resumed their interchange. Paranoia, Bran thought. And it would only worsen on the Scrounger's get-stupid-fast program.

"Just this once, Bran," the Scrounger said, never having ceased his diatribe. "Help me out. For your Ma's sake. I'll be out soon."

"What if I get caught?"

The Scrounger straightened into a professorial posture—this seemed to be his area of expertise. "Nothing will happen. Odds are tremendously in your favor. Hundreds of these types of deals go down every day. The cops only bust a tiny fraction. But something goes wrong, remember always hold back. Tell them stuff they already know, or make something up. Always keep an ace."

A few minutes later Brandon left the jail. He expected the gloomy sensations would subside, but as he emerged into the outside world, only murk remained in his vision. He felt like a broken fragment of some wayward asteroid, detached from its roots and spiraling wildly into an immense barren wasteland.

⁕ ⁕ ⁕

The guards ushered Bigelow to his cell a few minutes later. As the main door closed behind him, Harrisburg CAN Officer Stuart Zackaeus stepped into the visiting room through a side door, his silver badge jangling on its lanyard. He hunkered beside the two men seated near Bigelow's table, and they spoke for a long time.

⁕ ⁕ ⁕

Ruth Scarbrough met Maize Anderson in a small office in the walk-in basement of the Anderson home on Maple Street in Middletown. The walnut-paneled walls were dotted with bright pictures of children's faces. Some were tagged with notes announcing that a child was missing; others were surrounded by colorful balloons and flowers and bore the label: *Found!*

Anderson was a gray-haired woman of indeterminate age. The crow's feet about her eyes echoed thousands of smiles, perhaps a reflection of her joy in finding so many lost children. An intelligence in Anderson's features rivaled the sharpness in Scarbrough's eyes—a wise, calculating owl to Scarbrough's brash and relentless bird of prey. She liked the old woman from the start.

"I'd like you to help me find a man," Scarbrough said, after introducing herself.

Anderson's smile invited candor. "Any man?"

"I'm not in the market generally." Scarbrough patted her enlarged stomach.

"I see. Might I ask why you need to locate this man?"

"We were in Vietnam together. I treated him at China Beach. It's a sensitive subject for both of us, and he must be approached carefully."

Anderson studied Scarbrough, the wizened eyes drawn back in questioning lines. There was an openness behind those lenses, yet there was a measure of disbelief too, probably born of hard experience. Scarbrough could not be displeased; she had laid no foundation for trust. The best she could hope for was for oversight.

"Who would I be looking for?" asked Anderson.

"He's a black man in his mid-forties. I don't know exactly what he looks like now, but I have a picture from long ago." Scarbrough produced a photocopy of Deric Christy's picture that she had retrieved from the D.C. court archives, trimmed to omit the surrounding newsprint.

Anderson held the paper to the light. "Copied from newsprint, I see. May I see the article?"

"I threw it away years ago."

"But the copy is so fresh."

"I made a copy to bring. The original is in my scrapbook at home. I've come a long way to meet this man, Ms. Anderson. I hope you can help me."

Anderson touched a finger to her cheek. "Don't you mean find him?"

"What?"

"You said you came to meet him."

"Yes. After twenty-six years, I suppose it will be like meeting him again."

As the two women considered each other's reactions, an interior door opened. A tall, well-built man in his mid-thirties appeared in the doorway. Scarbrough immediately recognized the Anderson eyes.

"Hi, Ma," he said. He leaned over Maize and kissed her forehead.

"Manny, we have a new client. She seems a bit closed-mouthed about the work she wants us to do. What do you think?"

"Missing person?" asked Manny.

"Not exactly missing," said Scarbrough.

"Any idea where we would begin?" Maize asked.

Scarbrough smiled. "Have you ever been to Hershey Medical Center?"

Chapter twenty-four

At six-thirty on Friday morning, Captain Crawford sat hunched over a table in the Company B operations tent. He wiped the sleep from his eyes, sipped steaming coffee, and reviewed the daily mission requests. A radio set buzzed, and the operator lifted a headset in one hand and a pencil in the other. He said three affirmatives, jotted some notes, and then said over and out. He handed Crawford the paper.

"Just in from Battalion Operations," the operator said. "Special mission request. The DEA is coordinating a search-and-destroy mission called Operation Nature Grow targeting marijuana growers. They want two Hueys based from Indiantown Gap. Battalion specifically requested Lieutenant Ashford to lead the mission."

"Ashford?" Crawford said suspiciously. "We know any more?"

"Nothing."

Crawford examined the notes. "Do me a favor and cover for me here. I'm taking the jeep to Battalion."

A few moments later, Crawford pushed back the canvas flap to Battalion Operations. The Operations Officer swiveled in his chair. "Kevin Crawford. What are you doing up here with us desk jockeys?"

"We just got a mission request from you, and I need some clarification."

"We're in the dark too. Probably the usual cornfield drill."

"Not in the middle of an IG inspection. The request would've been rejected. And who up here is making crew assignments for unit level missions?"

"I am," said Colonel Harker, appearing silhouetted in the entranceway.

"Then quite frankly, Sir," said Crawford, "you're out of line. I'm concerned about the lieutenant's confidence. His flying is good, but he needs to develop command skills. Two weeks flying air assaults would give him a solid foundation. Sending him back to the Gap, you'd be putting him out on his own too early. It's a real mission. Could be some tricky flying and on-the-spot judgments to be made—"

"The real missions are down here, Kevin. This is where the difficulties lie. I need my best men to put on a good show for the evaluators. Plus, I checked Company B's extra duty roster, and Ashford's the goddamn drug interdiction officer. It's his extra duty."

"Not the best utilization—"

"Let the little prick do his job." Harker sighed. "Tell you what you can do, just to keep the lieutenant safe. Use Trent for the pilot in command. I'd like him far away from the general with his blasted white T-shirts and teeny-bopper sunglasses. And put that fat guy on the mission too. What's his name?"

"You mean Gene Winston. He's our maintenance officer, and he's indispensable here."

"He's a fat lout, and he'll make us look bad. When's the last time you put a tape measure around his gut? He should've been washed out years ago. Give them another copilot, oh yeah, send the woman. General Tarsavage never did cotton to women in green. That's it. Those are your crew assignments."

"Sir, I request Company B be permitted to make its own crew assignments."

"Denied. Now let's get ready for this inspection. Copy?"

"Will Lieutenant Ashford be upgraded to flying status?"

Harker rubbed his jaw. "All right, Kevin. I'll throw you that bone. The lieutenant can fly."

●━━●━━━━━●━●●━●━━━━━●━●

Ashford awoke.

Darkness filled the tent, interrupted by narrow needles of pale daylight filtering through pin-sized holes in the canvas. Ashford's mouth was dry and pithy. A tick had affixed itself to his forearm, and he pulled it off rashly, leaving a red bump. Straining to clear his head, Ashford reached for his alarm clock. Although he couldn't see the dial, he touched the alarm switch and realized he had forgotten to activate it.

The woods were quiet around him, very quiet. Ashford struggled into his flight suit and stepped into his boots. He didn't bother to lace them, and the leather sides flopped to the ground as he set his feet outside the tent. The sun beat down upon him from a quarter-way across the sky. He recalled the seven-thirty mission. Panic set in.

He ran to the landing area. The helicopters were gone.

Ashford stood at the edge of the empty field, his hands idly by his sides. A solitary helicopter crossed over the landing zone, its rotor blades clapping loudly against the sky as if laughing at him. He surmised the men inside were laughing too—Ashford was assigned to fly with Trent. Trent had not woken him, and there could be no question the failure was intentional.

Ashford fixated on the blur of the blades. He could feel the thrust that propelled them and caused the helicopter blithely to defy all laws of nature. The energy seemed to be draining from him correspondingly; he was red-eyed and pale, tired and hungover. The vibrant colors of the forest should have been soothing to him; the outdoor breeze should have been cooling. But they were not.

He couldn't seem to communicate with his superior, even when his concerns involved the safety of his men. He could not control an indomitable subordinate. He had been required to remove a man from his beloved job in the kitchen, on the strength of a single error. He had glimpsed love in Morrow's eyes, but Army regulations forbade fraternization between commissioned and warrant officers, and worse, Morrow's unhappy past distanced her soul from his own.

Ashford touched the lacy branches of a sapling. The limbs reached skyward but were stunted and the leaves they bore, half-starved, choked by the arms of great trees interlocking above. Ashford also felt smothered by the awe-inspiring and appalling qualities of the veterans in his command. The muscles in his stomach quivered, and a hollow feeling underneath radiated up his trunk and down into his legs. Ashford held the sapling in a vice grip, as if clinging to the edge of some precipice. Suddenly and unexpectedly the bark in his fingers split with a crack. Shards of green fiber sprung from the break.

He had never felt so alone in his life.

Chapter twenty-five

Late that night Deric Christy stole into his sister's hospital room. Visiting hours had long since passed. He didn't turn on the light and was grateful that Peg lay in a deep sleep. He sat quietly at her bedside and peered into her placid features.

Years had passed since Deric had last spoken his sister. He often thought about bridging the void he had opened between them. But he had refrained from acting on those intentions as the terrible vision of the rope net always seemed to lie in wait. The moment he attempted to act on thoughts of family or friendship or intimacy, the net would pull its coils hard against him and he would rail against it until it strangled him into submission, and he abandoned the vain hope that he could once again connect with the outside world. He was safest tucked deep inside, all alone, roaming the dark corners of his mind.

Peg Christy's soft voice drifted from her mouth. "Who is it? Who's there? Deric? Oh my God, is it you?"

Deric was sure his sister couldn't see him, but somehow she knew, and he answered her.

"I knew you'd come."

"I'm here."

"It hurts, Deric."

"I know." The images were welling, the net drawing closer. His grip tightened on the chair rail.

"Can you stay?"

"Not long."

Peg laid her cheek on her pillow. "My God. How did we drift so far apart? Seeing you again makes me remember when you were just becoming a man. You were so proud in your Marine uniform, standing at the airport, so tall and strong."

Deric swallowed and tensed the muscles in his chest and arms. It helped to bring his body into the fight, to send impulses into his sinews, to clench his fists until his joints ached, and to press his hands against his eyes. He said the airport was a long time ago.

"Seems like yesterday to me. It's the last good memory I have of you being who you were. Come closer, so I can see you."

Deric leaned forward. Tears glistened on Peg's cheek, sparkling in the light from the window.

"You haven't seen your nephew in so long."

"I saw him."

"Did you speak to him?"

Deric said he didn't.

"I know you have problems. But he needs a man. He needs you. Can't you take some time?"

"It's not the time."

"When then? Since Vietnam, you've been so distant. It's like you don't care."

The struggle was becoming unbearable. "I care," Christy said. It astounded him, but the words brought some relief.

"Then where have you been?"

"Mexico, for a while. I'm in some trouble."

"I thought that was over."

"Never seems to end."

"He needs you now, Deric, more than ever. I think he's in trouble too." She told him about Bigelow, how he manufactured drugs, cultivated marijuana plants, and kept dangerous liaisons in Harrisburg. Deric listened intently. But as he considered reaching out to help his sister and her son, the net and its gruesome contents descended, clambering over him with such force he stumbled to his feet to escape.

Standing, Christy's mind cleared. He seized the instant of lucidity and kissed his sister. The effort was painful, but his sister's touch felt soft and comforting, even healing. He said he needed to straighten some things out and that he'd return in a few days.

"Please, Deric. My son needs you now. Promise me you'll help."

The silence grew around Deric, until he coerced himself to speak. "I'll try," he said, slipping through the door. "I promise to try."

More than anything, it was a promise he wished he could fulfill.

•—•—————•—••—••—————•—•

In Washington, D.C., Ramírez burst into Sage's office. "Sage—"

"Would you look at this," Sage said, his eyes glued to a hardbound book. "It's the professor's book. *The Accounting*, or some bullshit like that. She wants to legalize drugs. Oh, not right away, she says. She'd do it insidiously, starting with addict maintenance programs and moving toward education and treatment for abusers. Away from hard time for users. Meantime she'd wash away every ounce of deterrence, every advancement we've made. Harm minimization, she calls it. What do you think, Gerry? Should we minimize the fucking harm?"

"Don, I'm trying to tell you—"

"Seems every yahoo with a master's degree has another touchy-feely theory that is supposed to bring everybody together in a multi-million-mile human chain to sing the Pepsi song."

"It's the Coca-Cola song."

"You on her side? Ask me, the War on Drugs has never been fought. Give us the manpower and the firepower and the say-so, and we'll win the goddamn thing. Harm maximization. That's the answer."

"He has a sister, Don."

"Who?"

"Soldier Man."

"So?"

"She's in the hospital. Burn victim. Happened several weeks ago in a trailer fire."

"So that's where he is." Sage rubbed his hands together like two sticks to start a fire. "Which hospital?"

"Hershey Medical Center."

"Hershey?" Sage jerked to his feet. "Hershey? That's in Pennsyl... The professor, she knows! The sanctimonious bitch, oh she... God damn her, she knows. Go get the car. Bring it around right now."

Ramírez circled the desk with his hands extended. "Easy, Don. Want some water?"

"No water, no time," Sage said, as he consciously checked his emotions. "Don't you see? She's miles ahead of us. Get the car. Have Iris start calling motels to find out where she's staying. And get somebody digging into her liberal-ass background. Gloves are coming off, Gerry. I want the low-down dirt on that whore now."

PART IV
THE MISSION

Chapter twenty-six

Resurrection.

Mark Ashford's spirit was rekindled by the news of his return to flying status. Mixed emotions assaulted him as Crawford briefed him on the mission. He reflected on forgoing the hot-and-heavy air assault training, but the vision of strapping in behind the controls of a helicopter far outweighed any wistfulness over leaving AP Hill far behind. Ashford knew there were few second chances in life. He would make the best of this one.

In concluding the briefing, Crawford produced two black-and-white photographs, one of a ski-masked man gloating over bundles of an illicit harvest and the other, an enlargement revealing a Huey flying low-level. Ashford studied the photos and stowed them on his clipboard.

By mid-morning it was time for Ashford to assemble his crew. He found Morrow in the mess area with Shoopie's men, her sleeves rolled above her elbows and her T-shirt damp from steam. Winston was in a makeshift latrine; they waited ten minutes until he disembarked. Trent lay on a cot in the screened-in porch of the civilian tent, flipping through his third paperback novel of summer camp. His flight suit was tied off at the waist, and he wore a faded green T-shirt imprinted with the words: *Participant—Southeast Asia War Games—Second Place.* Trent stared at the group with a faraway look in his eyes.

"Another admin mission back to the Gap," Winston told Trent. "How come you always end up on the gravy train?"

Trent shrugged. "A little luck, some hard work, and lots of ass-kissing. What's the mission?"

"Looking for unusual foliage, of the illicit variety."

"Our secondary mission after combat assaults is drug interdiction," Ashford said. "This mission is to search for a clandestine marijuana field somewhere in the Appalachian Mountains."

"Our secondary mission is to find the stuff," said Winston. "Our tertiary mission is to land and smoke it."

"Anyone know about spotting marijuana plants from the air?" Ashford asked.

"We were briefed in D.C. Guard," Morrow said. "They sent a trooper from the Virginia State Police. He told us to watch for shades of green that are different than what we're used to seeing. Depending on the strain, the plants can show up as vibrant greens or as deeper shades. The leaves cluster like firebursts. From the air they look like fuzzy balls."

"What about security?"

"They grow the stuff in the crannies of the mountains to avoid detection, and no one is likely to be there," Winston said. "So there's not much to worry about from the air. You send in ground troops though, they have to beware of booby traps. Some of these growers are dead serious. They put out bear traps, use punji sticks—anything to discourage trespassers."

Ashford briefed the flight route. He begged Trent and Winston to lower the poles on the civilian tent and cover it with leaves to conceal it from the evaluators. To his astonishment, they acceded, and the pilots separated to gather their gear.

◆━━━◆◆◆◆◆━━━◆◆

The pilots reconvened on the makeshift airfield, where they met up with two crew chiefs. Ashford was performing a pre-flight inspection, when he spotted General Tarsavage in the tree line with two members of his evaluation team. As Tarsavage approached the pilots, Ashford saw Trent's eyes blazing with recognition. The general though, didn't acknowledge familiarity with the warrant.

"May I inquire about your mission?" said Tarsavage.

Winston was closest to the general. "We're headed back to the Gap. We have an administrative mission."

"Of what nature?"

"Ask LT Ashford," Trent said caustically. "He's the—"

"I'm the AMC," Ashford said, saluting. "Morning, Sir."

Tarsavage returned the salute stiffly. "Lieutenant, what's your mission?"

"We're attached to the DEA for an interdiction mission."

"Hmm. You men wait here." Tarsavage strode back to the tree line and conferred with his assistants and then returned to the group of pilots. "I'll be joining you," he said. "I have some admin duties back at Fort Indiantown Gap. And I'll evaluate your flight's procedures along the way. Isn't often we get to observe a unit on a real mission instead of these trumped-up air assaults."

Trent pursed his lips.

"Something on your mind, Mister . . ." Tarsavage squinted to read Trent's faded name tag. "Mister Trent?" he mouthed. His jaw slackened in mute recognition.

"Just that Colonel Harker was figuring you'd do back flips to see his air assaults," Trent said. "He know you're joining us?"

"Not yet. I've only just made up my mind."

Trent smiled malevolently. "Welcome aboard," he said, his voice particularly unwelcoming. He stroked the stubble on his chin.

As if on cue, Colonel Harker appeared in a jeep. He vaulted the side, double-timed to a position directly before the general, and heaved a rigid salute. Ashford had never seen Trent and Harker so close—each man's eyes appeared to be straining to avoid a clash from which neither would be prepared to walk away.

"Sir," Harker said to Tarsavage, "I was hoping to discuss the evaluation process with you prior to your conferring with my troops."

"That won't be necessary, Harrison. My men are fully capable of briefing you and conducting the entire review. I need to discuss base-closing matters with the Fort Indiantown Gap Command Branch, so I'm signing on board this mission back to the Gap. The trip will also give me a chance to observe an actual mission. I assume you're sending your best men . . ." Tarsavage eyed Morrow inquisitively. "Ehr, people."

The color drained from Harker's face. "If you really must go to the Gap, I can arrange much more comfortable travel accommodations."

"This will be fine. Now if you'll stand aside, I believe these aviators are ready to go."

Ashford navigated the first leg of the flight and handled the radios. He concentrated on his role as air mission commander, but he silently longed to take the controls. The group was quiet, although Tarsavage voiced an occasional question about unit procedures.

After a query Trent seemed to find particularly annoying, he switched the radio selector switch to the private channel between the pilots. "Be a lot nicer flight if the crew chief flipped open the Savage's seat belt, I put the bird in a sharp bank, and well, ass-holes away. Or we could land on a steep hill and let the Savage walk up into the rotor blades."

Ashford glanced back at the general to assure he wasn't listening. Tarsavage's expression remained vacant.

After a few moments, Tarsavage keyed his intercom. "Gentlemen, I'd like to take the low-level route through Washington."

Ashford replied, "I thought we weren't authorized—"

In his peripheral vision, Ashford caught Trent's hand darting to flip the voice box selector switch off intercom, so the remainder of his protestation was said only to himself. "Sounds like a plan," Trent said over the intercom. He winked at Ashford, not softly, as Mark reflected on how infractions seemed to serve as enticements for Trent.

From his flight bag, Trent retrieved a special map of the low-level route; Ashford studied the markings, memorizing the air control points and the required altitudes. The two Hueys would have to separate to even a greater interval than was Winston's custom, since aircraft security in Washington, D.C. was tight, and aircraft were forbidden from flying in formation.

The Hueys picked up the shiny path of the Potomac River at the southern point of Washington and swooped down to eighty feet above ground level. Out the right window, Ashford stared down the green corridor of the Mall. The Washington Monument held his gaze, magnificently straight and solid; its image mirrored perfectly in the angular reflecting pool. With its thick pillars, the Lincoln Memorial resembled an ancient Greek palace. The elegant half-moon profile of the Jefferson Memorial wound into view overtop a glimmering tidal basin, where equally distinguished trees kept silent vigil over the great chunk of rounded marble. The Capitol complex in the background gave dignified closure to the scene.

As they ascended from the river, Ashford caught sight of another side of the schizophrenic city. The Northwest section stretched before him, a puzzling grid work laid out in right angles illogically interrupted by sporadic circles and triangles. He saw broken rooftops laid over blighted row houses that seemed to lean upon each other for support, seedy storefronts with roughly drawn signs, and crumbling masses of discolored cinderblock. Idiosyncratic church spires rose strangely from the wreckage like arms lifted in supplication. Wires lay strewn randomly over the mess, and the narrow streets were choked by gridlocked vehicles. The nation's capital seemed to totter beneath him as if in the process of a prolonged disintegration.

•—•———•—••——••—————•—•—————•—•••

An hour later they landed at Indiantown Gap. On the approach, Ashford's eyes seized the three Blackhawks parked on the hardstand; he watched them until his aircraft reached a hover above the landing pad. Up close, the powerful, streamline helicopters seemed imposing, and Ashford recalled the exhilaration he had felt when flying them at Fort Rucker.

As Trent hovered toward an open parking space, Ashford discerned a pale, lean man clad in a black suit standing on the flight deck, his dark hair flopping mop-like in the rotor wash. Trent rolled the throttle to flight idle for cool-down, and the man approached, bent at the waist.

"Agent Don Sage, DEA," he shouted into the window. "I'm looking for Professor Ruth Scarbrough. She's supposed to be here."

"I have no idea what you're talking about," Trent said, still seated in the copilot seat.

"You the guys assigned to me?"

Trent nodded. "If you're the DEA, we're the guys."

"The briefing was to be at noon," said Sage. "She's supposed to be here. A black woman. Pregnant."

Trent arched and then relaxed his eyebrows in a surrogate shrug. "Didn't come with us."

Sage rapped his temple with his knuckles; he appeared thoughtful and furious at the same time. He spun and jogged toward the parking lot. Ashford cut the throttle.

"What about the mission?" Ashford called after Sage in the newborn quiet.

"What mission?" said Sage.

"The interdiction mission. The search for the marijuana field."

Sage waved Ashford off with both hands. "Screw the mission."

Ashford glanced at Trent, who also appeared perplexed. Then Trent laughed. "We're scrubbed," he said. "I look clean?"

"Want us to start the operation without you?" Ashford called after Sage.

"Whatever you want," replied Sage. "But if that... that woman shows up, you call me right away. Reach me through the DEA Harrisburg field office."

General Tarsavage stepped to the ground and started after Sage but was ignored, and the pilots watched the strange and impudent man disappear around the side of the hangar. Ashford flicked off the battery switch, rubbed his gloves through his fingers, and wondered why they had been brought all this way, if there were no mission.

Chapter
twenty-seven

Over the weekend, Maize Anderson's sons, Manny and Robert, kept vigil inside the main entrance at Hershey Medical Center. Their efforts could only loosely be called a stake-out; as a rule they loitered conspicuously in the lobby. To their knowledge there was no need to act surreptitiously, since nothing Scarbrough had told them suggested they were tracking a criminal or fugitive. The subject was an ordinary citizen, a man who should not hesitate to use the front door. By Wednesday, Manny grew weary of the lobby chairs. His policeman's instincts left him seated in his car, positioned with a panoramic view of all entrances. He sipped coffee and chewed cold french fries, occasionally stepping outside to stretch his legs.

The subject arrived early afternoon, entering through a side employees' door. The selection aroused Manny's suspicions, but he quickly dismissed them. The subject's demeanor was open and assured; he walked neither slowly nor quickly but like a man with a legitimate purpose, a man visiting an injured relative, and a man who inadvertently picked the wrong door. Manny placed a call to his client to report the observation.

●—●————●—●●—●—————●—●

Scarbrough was in her rented car the instant after Manny telephoned, speeding toward the hospital. She recalled that she should have been on her way to Indiantown Gap for the briefing on Operation Nature Grow, but she dismissed the thought without reservation.

Twenty minutes later she met Manny inside the hospital lobby. Her veins pulsed as Manny gave his report. As calmly as possible, Scarbrough instructed Manny to wait for her, and she started for the third floor.

As she moved toward the elevators, Scarbrough cast a swift glance over her shoulder. As she did, her heart fell. Through the streaked glass of the main doors, she saw a gray sedan parked impertinently on the outside waiting ramp. Two men stepped from the vehicle. Emerging from the driver's seat, Agent Donald Sage stridently barked orders to his Latin-American companion.

Settled on a vinyl bench, Manny grasped a newspaper and yawned. Scarbrough hurried back to him. "Uh, Manny. I need... Well, I could use a sort of diversion."

"What?"

"Those men." Scarbrough gestured toward the ramp. Sage was thirty yards from the door, still lecturing his companion. "You must distract them."

Manny sized the approaching men, their imposing dark suits, their healthy and lean figures, and the sunlight glistening from their sunglasses. "Look like cops to me."

Scarbrough feigned earnestness. "Oh no, certainly not police. They could be trouble of the worst kind. Please. I must have a few moments."

Manny rose slowly, studying Scarbrough's features. She scrambled to catch an elevator, hesitating long enough to see Manny slip through the entrance doors. She pressed her palm against an illuminated button. Her stomach heaved with anxiety; she was so close. Before Sage's intrusion, her plan was to spend an hour or more with Christy. Using Hammaker as her introduction, she would explain how she knew he had been manipulated, convincing him of her sincerity, cultivating his trust, and selling him on the hope that she could help him—that they could help each other. But she had no time for that now; she could never spirit him away to safety with Sage at her heels.

Her mind reeled, searching for an alternate plan, and the silver elevator doors opened. Deric Christy was there before her—she was sure it was him. No time for introductions.

Scarbrough lowered her face and stepped forward, fumbling in her pocketbook, all the while fixing Christy in her peripheral vision. Just as she was about to pass by him, she swerved and bumped into his shoulder. She furtively lifted the corner of her purse to spill the contents.

"Sorry," Christy said. He squatted to retrieve several scattered envelopes, halting in mid-crouch, as if concerned about her privacy.

"It's okay. Nothing here's terribly personal. Just put everything into the bag, please."

When they finished, Christy nodded and moved toward the doors.

Scarbrough squinted in her best inquisitive gaze. "Don't I know you?"

"I don't think so." Christy glanced blankly over his shoulder.

Scarbrough overtook him. From behind, she caught him by the left elbow. His muscles tensed against the unexpected contact. When Christy turned, his left eye appeared glassy and fixed, and it was another instant before Scarbrough recalled that it was artificial.

Christy put her in his good eye. "Easy, ma'am, I'm a little sensitive to—"

"I knew it. I treated you at China Beach in seventy-one."

"Sorry ma'am, seventy-one I... I wasn't in Vietnam."

"Nonsense. I spent the better years of my life treating vets. I know it when I see one."

Christy arched an eyebrow meaningfully. "I meant I wasn't there in seventy-one. I shipped home in sixty-eight."

"Perfect then. Nineteen sixty-eight. We don't have anyone from that period."

"Huh?"

"I'm guest-hosting an evening class at the Penn State campus in Middletown. The idea is to put together a diverse panel of Vietnam veterans to share their experiences with the students. I need someone who was there during Tet, and you'd be perfect."

"I've got to go."

Scarbrough grabbed Christy a second time; he seemed to anticipate her grasp and didn't react so edgily. "You can't leave yet," she said urgently. "Not until I have your promise."

"I can't."

"I haven't even told you when. Thursday evening. Seven-thirty sharp. And I won't take no for an answer."

"You don't understand. I can't."

"Can't talk about it? Lots of veterans have difficulty sharing their experience. Especially if it's been bottled up inside for such a long time. That's part of the reason for sharing it. You'll find it cathartic, actually. Yes, we absolutely must have you."

Christy scanned the hall, as if considering whether he was making a scene. He smiled mildly, not a forced smile, but there was something untrue in it nonetheless. There would be a lie on his lips. "Okay," he said. "Sure. I'll be there."

Scarbrough slipped a card into Christy's hand. "I've written down the building and room numbers. All you need to do now is swear on your word as a Marine you'll be there."

"What?" Christy's eyes narrowed with suspicion.

"We're counting on you, soldier. Swear on your word as a veteran."

"How did you know I was a Marine?"

Scarbrough had said too much, but she didn't miss a beat. "I told you I know vets. And there's no mistaking a Marine. Now swear."

Christy took another brief look around. "I swear on my word as . . ." His face gathered an air of solemnity as he continued. "I swear on my word as a veteran of the United States Marine Corps."

Scarbrough looked into his eyes. The unglazed eye was soft and honest, and she had no choice but to trust what she saw. "Very well. I'm so glad we met."

Scarbrough turned away, straining not to look back. She tried to imagine how to guide Soldier Man past Sage without arousing suspicion. But she could think of no credible artifice. No, she would have to leave him to his own devices with Sage; she would have to trust in his instincts developed over years on the run.

As the elevator doors closed, Scarbrough came face-to-face with her own reflected image staring doubtfully from behind the silver metal. Her eyes appeared scornful, almost as if the reflection were chastising her for something she had done or something she was about to do.

Sage fumed.

An annoying young punk confronted him in the hospital entranceway, trapping him between pairs of electric sliding doors as if in some glass menagerie. The interloper was demanding explanations he hadn't time or intention to give; the fool was obstructing an agent of the United States Government from the performance of his official duties. Sage reached into his breast pocket for his identification.

The younger man slipped a revolver from under his own armpit. "Ah-ah. Too big a bulge under that shoulder to be poking around in there."

Ramírez's left side was partially obscured behind Sage. He stepped to the right, revealing a drawn pistol.

"Everyone stay cool." The tip of Sage's tongue moistened his silver tooth.

"I'm cool," the younger man said. "Hand out of your jacket, nice and easy. And have your enforcer back there put down the forty-five."

"It's a nine millimeter, son," Sage replied. "And that should scare you."

"No question I'm scared, dad," the man said, apparently irritated by Sage's patronizing. "Fact is I can hardly hold this thing still. Hair trigger and all, I'm getting worried somebody might get hurt."

Sage nodded with uncharacteristic somberness. He retracted his hand from his pocket; his fingers straddled a leather identification holder. He extended his hand.

The man lowered his gun. He cursed and holstered the revolver. He retrieved his own badge.

"You're a cop?" Ramírez inquired.

The man nodded. "Harrisburg Police. I was—"

"But you're not on the job now?" A sneer slithered across Sage's features.

Manny Anderson lowered his head submissively. "Not at the moment."

"Then you won't be a cop for long." Sage snatched the badge from Manny's hand. "I'll drop this off downtown when I'm through talking to your superiors."

•—•————•—••—•:————•—•

Deric spotted Sage the instant after he left Scarbrough— the agent seemed locked in confrontation with another man who Christy didn't recognize. Unseen, he disappeared quickly down a first-floor corridor, before Sage and Ramírez started for the elevator.

•—•————•—••—•:————•—•

In the Toyota pickup, Brandon Christy rounded the corner of Paxton Street in downtown Harrisburg. He turned onto an avenue lined with long, flat-roofed apartment buildings of crumbling red brick. The units of Hill Manor had shutterless windows and nondescript doors; the place had the look of an institution. Paint peeled from the aged wood trim in flakes the size of dinner plates, and rust-bucket jalopies decayed in odd juxtaposition with a shiny BMW and a new Acura parked curbside. Bran scanned white numbers painted on building corners, until he located the building number five. His skin felt cold and oily, and he strained to contain his anxiety. Bran reminded himself of his purpose—he needed money to pay for his mother's medical treatment. Painfully, he recalled the hundreds of fights between his mother and the Scrounger over money; from their example, dollars seemed the source of all adults' efforts and frustrations.

Bran threaded his way through toppled, plastic-wheeled contraptions, wagons, and tricycles. He selected a door in the center of the building and rapped—the Scrounger had said any door would do. A short black man answered. He offered a gruff response to Bran's introduction and then disappeared as quickly as Bran had uttered Cruise's name.

Suddenly and menacingly Cruise appeared. His body was well-muscled, and he was attired in a gold two-piece suit, the neckline of which resembled a cleric's collar. His almost shaven hair was arranged with a faint slice part. His face was at once wise and cruel, with his eyes set in savvy slits that seemed accustomed to the ways of the predator. "What you want?" Cruise hissed.

"Rayful Bigelow sent me."

"Speak up, little man. I better hear you when you talk to me."

"Rayful sent me," Bran repeated loudly. His voice cracked.

"He said you was young, but I didn't expect no baby."

Bran felt naked.

"Scrounger said you done this dozens of times," said Cruise.

Bran's voice simulated confidence. "I've done it before."

"Yeah, uh-huh." Cruise spoke with an air of disbelief. "Well, what you waiting for? Come on in. Take a walk. Up to you. Live fast, die young, and leave a good-looking corpse. That's what I always say."

Bran reluctantly followed Cruise's path into the apartment's musty chamber. The interior was cluttered with furniture a thrift store would eschew. Large free-standing stereo speakers were aimed at half-open windows serving as the only interruption to the bare and blotched walls. The decor seemed selected to emphasize the abundant shadows.

Cruise halted at the far wall. With his foot, he slid aside a cabinet, revealing a hole in the wall, and he ducked through the opening into the adjacent apartment. Bran realized why the

Scrounger had said any door would do—the apartments were interconnected.

They emerged in a kitchen. A man lay against open cupboards. He was very still and a piece of surgical tubing was tightly tied around his exposed bicep. A syringe stood free in his limp, pock-marked forearm, and a white string of saliva drooped from his lips. His face was frozen between an expression of ecstasy and one of intense pain. He was either very high or very dead.

Bran stepped over the junkie and followed Cruise into a back room. The window was covered with a battered quilt draped over a curtain rod. A round table was the solitary furnishing. On it were piled three plastic bags stuffed with white powder.

"Go to town, little maestro," said Cruise.

"Huh?"

"Whip me up some Rocket."

"I can't here." Bran contained his desperation. "It isn't like making plain crack. To make Rocket Pack you have to use a complicated chemical process. I need the Scroung... ehr, Rayful's laboratory."

"Yeah, uh-huh. You expect me to let your little ass walk out the front door with a couple g's of my drugs. I look stupid?"

Bran resisted the impulse to answer.

"Stand fast, little man," Cruise directed, and he disappeared.

While he waited, Bran reflected on his abhorrence for drugs. He pictured the blank-eyed man lying in the kitchen and pondered how Rocket Pack would feed his addiction and render him and thousands like him useless in their excesses. These bags of white powder, Bran thought, were much like the Scrounger—sick, cunning, infectious, and ultimately useless, yet they had the power to change the character of entire neighborhoods and more. Then Bran considered whether it really was the drugs that were changing the world. They were, after all, inert and lifeless. The substances did not insinuate themselves into bodies and homes and lives. It was people who used and abused them. And he was fast becoming an abuser.

Cruise reappeared with a boy at his elbow, perhaps a year younger than Bran. He had a round shaved head that seemed a poor imitation of Cruise's grooming. He bounced on the balls of his feet, and his face wore an expression that exuded absolute confidence or utter stupidity.

"This here's Zipper." Cruise pointed his thumb at the boy. "He's my man."

"What up?" Zipper said, extending an arm and retracting it in a bopping gesture as if nodding with his hand.

"Know why they call him Zipper?" Cruise asked.

Bran shook his head tentatively.

Cruise cocked his hand with his forefinger extended and his thumb raised like a pistol hammer. "Zip, zip, zip." He leveled his eyes to Brandon. "Till you get back here with my drugs, he goes where you go. Take one kilo of coke and a quarter-kilo of smack and get back here day after tomorrow. Got it?"

Bran tried to protest against Zipper's involvement, but Cruise swept his forearm and flat palm on the air horizontally, waving the subject closed. Bran glanced into Zipper's eyes; there he saw a child with an executioner's compulsion, one of those frightful zombies without fear or regret or restraint or compassion. The eyes were connected to a boy who had committed murder and had no idea.

Bran tucked the drugs into a knapsack and retraced his steps to the outside world. Zipper followed. Bran felt those bizarre eyes sweeping across his back, playful and homicidal. He tried to remember the Scrounger's advice, but it all seemed muddled and meaningless. The tautness of Brandon's body did not subside, until Zipper found a loose bolt in the passenger door of the pickup, which seemed to occupy his attention until they reached the highway.

Chapter twenty-eight

Wednesday morning.

The windscreen was an opaque sheet of white. A flat, dull light burned through the chalky murk. Ashford and Trent hunched in the cockpit, their faces lit red in the glow of the instrument panel. Ashford focused on the attitude indicator and cross-checked the radio magnetic compass; he made tiny corrections with the flight controls. Trent studied the instruments and charts to track their position.

"*Six-One-Niner,*" the radio crackled, "*Harrisburg Approach. Radar contact, six miles southeast of Ravine VOR.*"

"*Roger Harrisburg. Six-One-Niner. Descending through three thousand feet,*" Ashford said.

"*Roger Six-One-Niner. Exercise extreme caution. You're entering a parachute jumping area.*"

Suddenly the cockpit quaked violently. The shadowy outline of a human form swallowed the windscreen, thudding hard against the clouded glass. A voice released a blood-curdling scream.

Trent rolled his eyes and opened the cockpit door. He stepped out. The cockpit filled with a hydraulic buzz and began a steady descent.

Ashford stepped onto a metal platform beside the cockpit mock-up, the Huey simulator used to practice instrument flying technique. A warrant officer, clad in an Army summer uniform, sat on the nose of the mock-up, grinning widely.

"Very funny," said Trent.

"Time's up guys," the warrant officer said. "Pretty good flight. But you do have to watch out for those skydivers. They'll screw up your day every time."

Three other simulator platforms were positioned in the other corners of the two-story, open-bay room; each cockpit tipped and bucked independently. Ashford followed Trent down a steep ladder onto the floor of the control center. They nodded at a smiling technician seated at an illuminated console.

For the past two days, the flight crews waited vainly for instructions from the DEA. Ashford contacted Battalion at AP Hill and received unequivocal instructions to remain at Indiantown Gap until the DEA officially released them. They pitched tents on the north side of Peters Mountain where Reggie Spencer and his crew worked on the Phase Bird. During the day, Ashford planned flight and simulator training to keep the pilots occupied.

Ashford had also commenced an informal but coordinated search for the DEA's strategic objective. Day by day, the flight crews spent part of their training flying various flight routes, scanning the foliage for signs of an illicit crop.

In the flight planning room, Ashford found Spencer gazing out over the flight deck. "How's the Phase Bird coming?"

"Ahead of schedule. I gave the guys a couple hours off. Thought I'd come over and see what's going on."

"Very little." Ashford laid his cap on a chair and looked outside at a departing Blackhawk. "I called the DEA four times but can't get through to the agent in charge. Everybody's tired of sitting around. Believe it or not, I think they'd rather be back at AP Hill."

"Don't get carried away."

"I was just thinking maybe we could get this over with if we did a blanket search, some sort of crisscross pattern. Scouring the whole Northern Training Area in manageable segments."

Spencer aimed a finger at the topographical map. "Beats me why anyone in his right mind would plant dope in the middle of a military air traffic area."

"Doesn't make sense to me either." Ashford slid his fingers over the map's plexiglass cover, allowing his fingertips to linger over a red-circled No-Fly Area. "Wait a minute... Maybe it's not so idiotic after all. What if they planted the stuff where no one flies?"

Spencer's eyes darted among the red circles. "I see what you're driving at. A No-Fly Area would be a logical place. Civilian air traffic is restricted from overflight of the entire military operations area, and the military traffic has to go around the No-Fly. Nobody sees."

From his flight bag, Ashford pulled the black-and-white photographs Crawford gave him. "Look at this. The Huey in this picture is a klick or two away. Could've been skirting the edge of a No-Fly. How hard is it to get the designation?"

"Usually somebody just calls in and bitches about the noise," Spencer said. "The brass is sensitive to complaints. I don't think they even investigate. They just mark it off limits on the map."

Ashford scanned the map. "Seventeen No-Fly's in all."

"But most are populated areas. And this one's the ammo dump.˥

"That eliminates another and leaves these three."

"Two are relatively near LZs. But they're a pretty piece of ground to cover."

"And we can't do it from the air without violating Army regulations."

They considered options for reconnaissance of the two No-Fly Areas Ashford targeted but found no practical solution.

* * *

In the hallway, they passed two black soldiers. Ashford recognized them as the sergeants he had inadvertently offended at the NCO Club when, at Trent's instance, he mentioned Club Zimbabwe. Spencer said a few words of greeting, but both men appeared sullen upon seeing Ashford.

"Look guys," Spencer said, "you and the LT got off on the wrong foot. Believe it or not, he got suckered. Let us make it up to you."

"How you gonna do that?" said the tall sergeant.

"How about the LT here gets your enlisted people helicopter rides?"

"We're scheduled for air assaults with the Virginia Guard later this week."

Spencer cocked his head. "Where you two from?"

"Harrisburg."

"What high school you go to?"

"Midland High."

"How would you like to land one of our birds there to show the home boys?"

A flicker of interest snapped in the tall sergeant's eyes. "In Harrisburg? You'd do that?"

"Sure. The lieutenant can arrange it, right LT?"

Ashford brightened, taking Spencer's cue. "Maybe. Perhaps we could combine efforts. We'd like to do some land reconnaissance in the Northern Training Area. We might be able to integrate that into your training." Ashford showed the sergeants the two targeted No-Fly Areas on his tactical map. The tall sergeant repeated that his unit already had air assault missions scheduled.

"Do this for me," Ashford said, "and we'll fly you to Midland High, and you can show your friends what you do in your spare time. I know people in city government who can clear it."

The sergeants silently reached a consensus. "Yeah okay, LT," the tall one said. "We'll talk to our commander." The infantrymen disappeared into the break room.

"Pretty smooth, LT," Spencer said. "But what if it doesn't work?"

"Maybe they'll bust me to warrant officer and let me fly for a change." Ashford started to fold his map, but he paused and smoothed the crinkled paper against the wall, studying the No-Fly Areas so closely it appeared as if he were searching for miniature living foliage on the page.

Chapter twenty-nine

Locating the professor wasn't a simple task, even for DEA Agent Gerry Ramírez, whose experience in such matters was expansive. He had begun with the Hershey area, checking every motel, lodge, and bed-and-breakfast. When the search bore no fruit, he expanded its area. When he continued to come up empty, he concluded that Scarbrough must be using an assumed name. Sage was impatient and irascible, but he made the useful suggestion that Ramírez look for a friend or acquaintance.

Ramírez began telephoning members of Scarbrough's committee. His third call was to a retired sociologist who recalled Scarbrough's mention of a friend in the Middletown area. The sociologist didn't know the friend's name, but he recalled that the man was a counselor at the local Vet Center.

Sage and Ramírez arrived at Turczynski's house early Wednesday afternoon. They found a parking space several doors down and waited for forty minutes, watching. They observed children passing by, a plumber visiting Turczynski's neighbor, and an elderly woman sitting on a porch swing, her gray hair drifting in the gentle afternoon breeze. When the woman disappeared inside the house, Sage stepped to the sidewalk and moved gingerly up Turczynski's front steps. He knocked on the front door. No answer.

Sage returned to the sedan, drove one block south, and turned into an alleyway running behind the row of houses. He parked in a gravel lot several doors past Turczynski's residence.

The agents casually checked Turczynski's back door. A bathroom window yielded to Sage's prodding. Inside, Sage and Ramírez sniffed the air instinctively and locked eyes in mute recognition. The fresh afternoon air swept through open windows, but there was a residual odor, unmistakable to their trained nostrils. In less than a minute Sage located the source—an artillery-shell ashtray boasting a roach clip balanced on the edge.

"Party time," said Ramírez.

"I like this," Sage said, "I like this a lot."

Ramírez paused before the fireplace. He stared at Turczynski's Vietnam memorabilia as if trying to discern some clue to Turczynski's character.

Sage climbed the narrow stairs to the second floor. In the bedroom at the far end of the hall, he found three suitcases laid neatly open on a smartly made bed and rummaged through the contents. The professor was fairly conservative for a whacko, he thought, while ruffling Scarbrough's pastel maternity blouses.

Sage found nothing significant in the suitcases. He peeked under the bed, sifted through the closet, and then paused at the window. His foot kicked something, and he picked up a leather briefcase. Inside he found a laptop computer. Please don't let her use password protection, Sage thought, flicking the toggle switch to fire the machine. Ramírez joined him, as Sage flipped through Scarbrough's electronic files.

"Go find a five-and-dime and get a three-and-a-half-inch disk," Sage said. "Come back in if this window shade is open. If it's down, meet me at the car."

Ramírez left him. Sage quickly located Scarbrough's notes from the past few days. He read about the professor's impressions of her first encounter with him. Sage found the degree of obsession in her writings about him to be peculiar, like the absorption of a teacher with her worst problem student. He was relieved, however, to find nothing in the professor's notes that tied Operation Soldier Man to the Saturday Night Family Massacre.

The notes she was preparing for her fantasy speech to Congress surprised him most, as they best exemplified her gall. Her plan was to bring down a five-year DEA operation, the supervising agent, and ultimately the DEA, all as an attention-getter she believed would whip the public into a frenzy and create an audience for her hogwash theories. Still, he couldn't help but admire her investigative work—without the sophisticated resources available to federal law enforcement officers, she identified Soldier Man and tracked him across several states, surpassing even Sage's efforts.

Sage next found Scarbrough's notes of her meetings with Hammaker. He smiled as he read. So that was how she discovered Soldier Man, he thought. Her connection was with the lawyer. Finally, he reached Scarbrough's final entries. He read about the Scrounger and Brandon Christy. He lingered over her final words—*Is the boy the key to Soldier Man?*

●━●━━━━━●━●●━●━━━━━●━●

Maize Anderson was angry.

Manny had told her about his dangerous confrontation with the DEA agents at the hospital—he voiced his deep concern that

Sage would make good on his threat to report the incident to his superiors. The Department frowned on unauthorized moonlighting, and the incident jeopardized Manny's badge. Maize was a firm believer in forthrightness. She was anxious to confront Scarbrough as soon as possible, and so she had arrived at Turczynski's house in the late morning. She had found the place empty and decided to wait. An old friend owned a greystone across the street, and she waited there on the porch. Nothing is more inconspicuous, she thought, than an old woman on a porch swing.

When she saw the wiry man knock on Turczynski's front door, she immediately associated him with Manny's description of the jittery, silver-toothed DEA agent. Through slits between houses, she watched the gray sedan roll down the alley behind Turczynski's house. She heard the crunching gravel as the car glided to a stop, and she discerned an opportunity—a chance to salvage Manny's job. As stealthily as her sixty-year-old frame could manage, Maize climbed the wooden porch-stairs in front of Turczynski's house. She slid her hand across the top of the doorframe and retrieved Turczynski's spare key. Nothing in Middletown was sacred, she thought.

She opened the door and saw one of them, the Latin American, exiting the back. He hadn't seen her. She heard the car engine and was glad it would only be her and the boss.

Maize made no further efforts to conceal her footsteps; at this point, stealth could get her shot. When she came upon Sage in the bedroom, he was sitting on the bed, with his back to her, chuckling like a spoiled child. He heard her footfalls and said, "Gerry, I thought I sent you—"

Maize cleared her throat. Sage's spine straightened. He laid the laptop carefully on the bed beside him. When their eyes met, he appeared relieved. He was probably expecting Scarbrough, and instead he saw the little old lady from across the street. Just some old busybody, he must have been thinking.

"I, ehr… " Sage stammered. "I'm an old friend of Barney's—"

"It's Bart," Maize said.

Sage smirked. "Barney's my pet name for him."

"I don't think so. Know what I think?"

"I could probably guess."

"I think you're an agent of the federal government."

Sage's eyes hardened. "What makes you think that?"

"What's more, I think you're with the DEA."

"We know each other?"

"No."

"Okay, lady. Play whatever hand you got. This is already getting old."

"All right," Maize said. "I'm a private detective."

Sage suppressed a smile. "Really?"

"Really. I was hired by Ruth Scarbrough to find this man." Maize dropped Christy's photocopied picture on the bed.

"I see." Sage held his lips tight. "You find him?"

"My son did."

"Your son?"

"Sergeant Manny Anderson of the Harrisburg Police."

Sage smiled broadly, and the silver tooth darted and flashed, as if celebrating the fact that the old woman had played into his hands. "Good old Manny. How is he?"

"Worried about his job."

"Bet that could work itself out."

"Really?"

"I'd need something in return."

"My turn to guess?"

"You don't care much for your client, do you?"

"I feel a bit betrayed."

"Me too, Ms. Anderson, I presume?"

"That's right."

"Suppose you disremember this little incident," Sage said. "Then I can forget about what happened at the hospital. That what you came here to ask?"

Revulsion set upon Maize's features, directed not at Sage but inward at herself and her own decision and conduct. Never in her life had she betrayed a client's confidence; never before had she betrayed trust.

But sometimes a deal with the Devil, Maize thought, is better than no deal at all.

The information Stuart Zackaeus had obtained from the surveillance on the Scrounger in jail yielded gold. Zachaeus's two informants in the visiting room had overheard enough of the Scrounger's conversation with Brandon Christy to identify the chemist who fabricated Rocket Pack and his location at Bonanza Used Cars at Mount Cobb in the Pocono Mountains. Zackaeus notified the state police, who arranged for a search warrant. Working with the troopers, Zackaeus contacted the local police to coordinate the search. Although his presence was not required, Zackaeus started out for the Poconos.

He arrived in Mount Cobb in the late afternoon. The town was a quaint, sleepy village nestled at the foot of a looming mountain ridge. Bonanza Used Cars was located on the feeder road to the highway. The dealership was easy to find; a dozen police cars with rotating beacons atop surrounded the wooden shack, and uniformed troopers swarmed the attached, four-bay garage.

Zackaeus looped his lanyard around his neck and crossed under a stretch of yellow tape. He paused before three officers escorting a portly, middle-aged man in a muscle T-shirt from the garage. The unshaven man had a face that was determined and grim; his hands were cuffed behind his back.

"That Flannigan?" Zackaeus asked an officer trailing the fat man.

"Iron Flannigan," the officer said, shaking his head. "Used to be with the Monoliths motorcycle gang. We'd thought he had reformed. Became sort of a pillar of the community, believe it or not. Me, I never would have guessed." The officer lifted his hand. In it were five plastic bags stuffed with gray rocks.

"Rocket Pack, I presume," Zackaeus said.

"Doesn't look like cotton candy."

"I'll be needing one of those dandies."

"Not thinking of setting up shop?"

"Closing one down."

"Have to go through channels."

"Of course."

Zackaeus returned to his car. He lifted his carphone and pushed the speed-dial programmed for the Harrisburg CAN Unit Headquarters. "Sandy, I want you to get someone out to Whatta Deal on Route 22. Should be a kid coming and going. Name's Brandon Christy. Tell whoever you send to keep an eye on him till I get there."

"Anything else?"

"Yeah," Zackaeus said, watching a trooper lower Iron Flannigan into a cruiser. "Tell 'em not to spook the kid. He doesn't know it yet, but he's about to help me finally nail that prick Cruise. Help me nail him good."

Chapter thirty

"You agreed to what?" Winston shouted. "How the hell could you agree to land a helicopter in the middle of a Harrisburg slum? We'll be lucky to get out of there with our flight suits."

Ashford met Winston's eyes and answered the rhetorical question with a measured calmness that he knew would rankle the fat man. "Mister Winston, have I ever given you a direct order?"

"I guess you haven't."

"Here's my first. Shut up."

"I do the jokes." Winston crossed his flabby arms. "You clear this with the DEA?"

"The agent-in-charge left four days ago in a huff, and I haven't heard from him since. Anyway, Mister Trent and Jesse will stay behind just in case."

Winston rolled his eyes, as if tracking his excuses, slicing through the air as they escaped him. When his dramatics subsided, he said, "Well, hold on to your wallet."

"I've got a couple calls to make to clear the mission with the city," Ashford said. "I'd appreciate it if you two would get the helicopter prepped. You'll need to remove the weapons."

"Naw, leave them on. Show 'em some real firepower."

"I'm sure they've seen enough violence in Harrisburg. They don't need us encouraging it."

"The kids love guns."

"The guns stay here." Ashford was surprised at the deliberate tone of his own voice.

Two hours later, Winston and Ashford were in the cockpit of a Huey over the outskirts of Harrisburg. From the air, Harrisburg appeared as an attractive river city; the skyline boasted an assortment of structures, a majestic capital building, a sparkling hotel, lofty office towers, and a river drive speckled with elegant mansions. But like other northeastern cities, Harrisburg had its dark side too. As they banked to make their approach into the wind, they passed over an industrial strip, pock-marked warehouses, and rows of tenement houses with derelict gardens.

In the rear of the helicopter, Spencer sat beside the two infantry sergeants, who seemed charged with anticipation. One pointed to a weed-grown lot behind a faded-brick school building. Ashford set up his approach.

"What I wouldn't give to be in a Cobra gunship right now," Winston remarked.

"What?" Ashford said.

"One of the most deadly killing machines known to man. One Cobra could vertically envelop this whole area with the firepower of a battalion of grunts. Four thousand rounds a minute, forty millimeter canon firing grenades at machine gun speed and seventeen rounds of rockets, each of which could devastate this block. Just take out a neighborhood here and there, and we could end the damn Drug War pretty quickly."

Ashford stared at Winston, considering whether his words were heartfelt or bluster. He drew no firm conclusion.

As the Huey descended, the schoolyard flared into focus. The macadam was cracked like the surface of a dried lake, and worn, empty backboards stood lonely and useless, their rims long gone. A curtain of loose pellets rose as the skids touched ground, and suddenly a hoard of children appeared from nowhere to envelop the Huey.

Ashford barked instructions. He, Spencer, and the sergeants jumped to the ground. They formed a perimeter to hold the children at bay until Winston was able to shut down the engine.

As Winston worked, he flailed his arms at the children. When the blades finally stilled, Winston had no excuse remaining. He sagged helplessly over the inert controls, while the children swarmed the Huey like a colony of enraged ants.

The boys were dressed in popular attire: baseball caps turned backwards and brims cocked to the side and jeans and trousers worn low on the hips to expose colorful boxer shorts. Some reluctantly propelled forward, but most preened and strutted and grabbed without request or apology.

"Don't touch that, you urchin," Winston scolded, swatting at climbing wrists and roving fingers. "Hey you, leave that alone."

"Relax, Mister Winston," Ashford said. "There's a shady tree by the school. Why don't you take a break?"

"Just don't let 'em make off with the avionics." Winston surrendered the helicopter to the throng.

"You fly in Vietnam?" a child asked Ashford.

"I was too young. But Sergeant Spencer did."

The boy gazed admiringly at Spencer. "What was it like in Vietnam? Was it worse than here?"

Spencer mumbled some response that seemed like he meant to be comforting, but it was only vague and evasive.

"How do I get in the Army?" another boy asked.

Ashford deferred to Spencer again. A few moments later, he took Spencer aside. "Thanks for fielding the recruiting questions. I don't like to recommend the military as a career choice."

"Shit, LT, look around you. How many other choices do you see?"

Two older boys, in their mid-teens, strutted cockily through the brimming sea of younger bodies. They wore clothes with clean lines and unlaced high-top sneakers, the kind that cost a hundred dollars. One wore a black bandana tipped back from his forehead. Streamers of gold chains lined his neck and wrists.

"This your crew, huh?" said the boy with the chains, raising his hand to Ashford with thumb and small finger extended laterally, his brown eyes glinting. "Well, this my crew right here." He grabbed a young boy by the neck and rubbed a ringed knuckle on his head, while the boy squirmed in distress. "Everybody be trying to get with us 'cause they know all the bitches want our boys."

The tall infantry sergeant imposed his large frame imposingly. "Let the kid go," he said.

The boy with the chains cast a sharp glance at him, assessing his resolve and examining his authoritativeness. Then he dropped the boy and turned away, peering inside the helicopter cockpit. He grabbed the cyclic, hoisting himself toward the pilot seat. The cyclic gave way and lay on its side. The boy fell backwards, chains clattering. The tall sergeant caught him under the armpits, but the boy furiously shook loose.

A few giggles resonated in the crowd, muffled and nervous.

"Easy with the flight controls," the sergeant said. "This thing has to get us back."

"That's right, homes." The boy brushed his shoulders as if whisking away residue from the sergeant's touch. "Someone messes with your property, they need to be checked. That's just tightening up business, understand? This here chopper your property?"

"I'm responsible for bringing it here."

"Oh, I see. It don't belong to you. Then you got no right to be telling me what to do, understand? I pay my taxes."

"I doubt that."

"You dissin' me? Better watch your step. Our crew enforces when people ill on them. Huh. Shit. You're not the man. You just a boy."

"You got that wrong. I'm a man."

"You not flying the machine. Who you be?"

"You're clocking, aren't you?"

"What if I was the candy man? Would you tell my mammy? Or my old man? I got news for you, 'cause my old man's gone and my mammy's a crackhead, and she don't give a fuck."

The sergeant stood silent.

"Not clocking anyways." The boy gestured at Ashford and then pounded his own chest forcefully. "I'm just like him. He a lieutenant? Well I'm a lieutenant too."

"You're nothing like him," the sergeant said.

The boy fell silent for an instant. "How would you know?" he said finally, his tone almost defensive.

"I'm from here too, homie."

"You in the Army?"

"Part time."

"Shit. What they pay you?"

"Enough so I don't have to sell crack on the streets."

"I don't gotta sell no crack. Could do what you do. No sweat."

"Prove it."

"Now how'm I supposed to do that?"

"Go for a little ride?"

"Up in that egg-beating thing? Shit."

"You scared?"

"Scared? No way. Not me. Not the kid." The boy's eyes made a loop through the attentive audience of his peers, monitoring, assessing. "Ah, okay," he said, flopping into the rear of the Huey. "Home, James."

Ashford knew he had no authority to offer helicopter rides to civilians, but he sensed the importance of his challenge to the sergeant and didn't question it. He motioned to Winston, who rose cumbersomely from the ground, lifting his hand to stifle a yawn.

* * *

The pilots donned their helmets, the engine moaned to life, the rotors flapped out their singular cacophony, and Winston commenced an incessant series of complaints over the intercom. "Relax, Mister Winston," Ashford said. "You can fly low level over the mountains and make them puke."

Winston's eyes twinkled like little stars. "Yeah, I could do that. But we get caught, it's your ass. I'll say I was following orders."

That didn't work at Nuremberg, Ashford thought. "I haven't got much of an ass left to chew," he said, wearily.

As the helicopter climbed, the despair of the schoolyard lost power, and the blue sky seemed to wash them in its brilliance and clean away the residue of what was below. Ashford watched the boys when he had the opportunity. On the ground, their faces had been locked in a struggle to maintain the impenetrable front that was expected of them and which they seemed to have come to expect of themselves. But as the Huey lifted them from the ground and a panorama opened before them, they seemed to enter another world.

At first, terror seized the features of the boy with the chains, while other faces beamed with delight. The frightened aura quickly melted, and the boys shouted wildly and cooed and kicked their legs and slapped palms. They appeared as superheroes and astronauts and birds and captains of jetliners; they suddenly seemed to be anything they wanted and more.

The instant reminded Ashford of a similar scene he had witnessed at West Point. With their feet on the ground, the cadets were subject to rules and regulations as compelling as those of the street, yet those young men also found release in the air. Like the cadets, the terrible mores that held dominion over the boys melted away in the wide, free space and, in those precious few seconds, far away from people and attitudes and conditions that oppressed them. They were free to be boys again too.

Just boys.

Winston banked the Huey hard. Knuckles tightened on seatrails. The boys quickly realized that centrifugal force held them in their seats in the turn, and there was no danger of falling out. The boy with the chains dangled his feet recklessly over the floor edge, staring at the houses and fields below as if he were a magical prince walking on the air above them. "Hey, Bobby, look at me. I be flyin'!"

Winston dove low over the mountains, but the only sounds he was able to draw from his passengers were shouts of delight.

"Man, I got to me get one of these," the smaller boy said.

"Yeah, man," said the boy with the chains. "This is better than crack."

With that remark, reality overcame Ashford, and he told Winston they should head back.

•━•━━━•━••━•━━━•━•

When they landed, they were swarmed by children again and besieged by questions. Why don't you take off straight up in the air? Can you fly as fast as a jet? Does the chopper explode when you crash? But it wasn't long before the mouths of the older children tightened, their enthusiasm faded, and their cynicism resurfaced sharper and more desperate than before. Ashford could feel the dullness of their lives throbbing in their chests and overwhelming them again.

The boy with the chains and his companion seemed to melt back into the bleak landscape. When they finally departed, they made a scene, waiving off the helicopter ride as if it had been nothing at all.

Ashford wanted to remember them as he had seen them in the air, and he hoped in some slice of their lives, they would remember it too. He turned to the two sergeants, who were talking to several of their peers from the neighborhood. Ashford waited until they paused to address him. "Are we even?" Ashford asked, extending his hand.

The sergeant clasped it into his own. "We're okay, LT. So let's go do your recon mission."

Chapter thirty-one

The Scrounger's Garden had few positive attributes, but Brandon found repose in the long hike through the woods, because it gave him time to think. The physical labor was distracting as well, pulling his thoughts from flights of fancy to a reality known of straining muscles and tendons. The last thing he needed on the journey, however, was Zipper interrupting his peace and worse, learning of the Garden and its location. Bran sat on his cot in the dusky garage bay at Whatta Deal and fidgeted with the survival radio Daniels had given him and considered how to rid himself of Zipper for the afternoon.

"What dat?" said Zipper, flicking an ear at the radio. He sat cross-legged against burlap sacks of fertilizer; it seemed as if he had no sense of smell.

"Just a toy," Bran said, standing. "Look, I'm off to see my Ma at the hospital." He had no plans to visit his mother until the next day; the excuse was a pretense for his escape.

"I gotta go too." Zipper hopped to his feet.

"To the hospital? It's boring."

"Cruise says I go where you go."

"To the hospital? I was there yesterday. The cops had dogs sniffing for drugs. They patted me down too. You know, for guns."

"What they do that for?"

"Whole world's gone to pot I guess. Wait here and sit on the drugs. That's all Cruise cares about. I'll be back in a couple hours." Brandon jammed the survival radio into his jeans pocket and disappeared in the pickup before Zipper could protest.

Thirty minutes later, Brandon pulled off the paved road into a narrow dirt inlet running into the mountain forest. He drove fifty yards under tree boughs and coasted off the dirt trail. He opened the bed of the truck, hoisted a burlap sack, and started down a narrow footpath into the woods.

Thistles scratched his legs, spider webs broke over his face, and the forest thickened around him. But he took little notice. The image that snagged in his mind was the junkie in Cruise's kitchen, the poor wretch caught in the throes of some muddled craving. Bran could see the paleness of his face, the gauntness of his shadowy features, and the rigidity of his body frozen in mute and desperate ecstasy. The image reproduced itself a thousand times—it seemed as if he were peering through the multi-faceted eye-lens of a housefly. Suddenly there were thousands of junkies, maybe millions, doped-up zombies, succumbed to their own weaknesses and inadequacies thrust upon them too. Then his own form appeared in the picture a thousand times too, and he handed the cloned junkies fistfuls of syringes. The hoard hungrily devoured the gifts, plugging them into their spidery veins and swelling physically with the rush of the elixir. But something was wrong, and the little color there was to them drained from their faces, and their features contorted horribly; their bodies twisted and stiffened in a surrealistic inhuman way, until they transmuted into the fixed and brown boughs of the trees overhanging the pathway beaten into the woods.

A breeze drifted through the leaves, rustling them lightly, almost musically. The sun filtered through the canopy, decorating the ground with little beams and spots mixed in lacy patterns. The forest was full of the smell of moist earth and burst with new growth, but the grandeur of the old timbers still dominated. Bran wondered if he could return to these living woods to forget and be cleansed after he became the man in his vision, after he delivered a batch of Rocket Pack for distribution on the hungry streets.

A twig snapped. Bran glanced at his feet planted on soft moss. He looped in a circle, sweeping his eyes among the slatted tree trunks, but he saw nothing and tried to dismiss the concern that he might not be alone, and he resumed his journey. He was accustomed to following the Scrounger through these woods and needed to be careful not to lose his bearings. As he moved, he felt unsettled. He kept his ears pricked for sounds that didn't belong in the forest. Shadows seemed to follow his tentative tread.

Ten minutes later, Brandon left the visible path into uncharted woods until he reached a steep drop-off. He lay on the soft ground, sliding over the edge until his head and shoulders hung in the air over a thin waterfall. The smell of peat was thick. The gushing water was thicketed by brilliant green plants growing from terraced ledges slanting into a clear deep pool. Surrounding the pool were dozens more plants, their leaf clusters erupted like firebursts.

The gully was the Scrounger's Garden.

Bran slid to firm ground and pushed aside a shiny sweep of mountain laurel, uncovering a hidden pathway to the Garden. He dropped his burden on the slope and allowed it to slide thirty feet down onto a shelf at the base of the waterfall. He sat on his rump and followed, dragging his hands in the dirt to slow his descent. He pulled a trowel from the sack and began poking holes in the topsoil.

As he moved among the plants, another twig snapped, louder than before. Bran held his breath. He made out human footsteps on the forest floor, faint and subdued, as if in imitation of a stalking beast. Bran could not discern the proximity of the steps; he had no means to measure how long until they would be upon him.

Instinctively, he scrambled up the steep path. Pebbles slipped from under his footholds, clattering noisily and splashing into the pooled water. Bran struggled for traction but lost his balance. He fell on his belly, sliding feet first down the slope.

When he came to rest on the shelf, Bran lay still and kept his head to the ground. Several moments passed before he gathered the courage to lift his chin to peek at the ledges above.

The grillwork of branches overhead seemed like the lid of a cage. On both sides of the gully, floating over the precipice, peered green-camouflage-covered faces, capped by shell-like helmets. The faces were attached to the unseen, prone forms of soldiers whose bodies lay back over the cliff-edge, trapping Brandon stupidly below in the Scrounger's beloved Garden.

In the late afternoon, Ruth Scarbrough finished transcribing her notes of the day's happenings and descended the stairs. She poured a drink in the kitchen and joined Bart Turczynski in his living room. The counselor sat leather-bound in his chair, sucking on a marijuana cigarette and reading a hardbound book.

"Bart," Scarbrough said, "have you been in my room?"

"Not at all. Why do you ask?"

"No reason, I suppose." Scarbrough considered how her blouses might have become so sloppily arrayed in her suitcase. Dismissing her concerns, she waved her fingers over her nostrils. "I probably shouldn't even be breathing that stuff," she said, gesturing to indicate the baby in her womb.

"Like me to put it out?"

"Please."

Turczynski spit on his fingertips. He dabbed the end of the paper until it sizzled, carefully preserving the dried grass for another occasion. "Better?"

"When the air clears," Scarbrough said, still swinging her hand.

"Have you given any more thought to my class?"

"A great deal."

"You're coming then?"

"I wouldn't miss it. And I was hoping I could offer some input into the presentation."

Turczynski appeared nonplussed. "For the first half-hour, I planned to cover course materials. We've been discussing the Viet Cong, and I need to do some review. For the remainder of the session, I've planned an impromptu talk with the vets. I want you to relate as much of your experience as you feel comfortable. Say whatever comes to your mind. I've found many times there's a synergistic effect. One vet's sharing will encourage another and so on."

"Have you ever considered discussing the similarities between the War in Vietnam and other wars?"

Turczynski scratched his chin thoughtfully. "Well, we've two Persian Gulf vets in the class. I intend to draw on their experiences, but the War in Vietnam was so different."

"What about other wars?"

"I haven't focused on any connections. No."

"What about the War on Drugs?"

Turczynski leaned forward, lowering the footrest of his recliner. "As I said, Ruth, my intention is for us to share personal experiences. I don't want to do a lot of broad-based philosophizing. Besides, the connection you seek to draw is somewhat abstract."

"Is it? Don't all wars merit study and comparison? To see if we're repeating our mistakes. History is a great teacher. What if we're missing the point today in the Drug War, just as we did twenty years ago in Vietnam? What if now, just like then, we can't see the forest for the trees?" Scarbrough swirled the water in her glass as if it were a martini.

"Certainly you must admit both are political wars," she said.

"All wars are political, Ruth. But you're assuming the euphemism the government employs for the struggle against drug addiction actually equates to a war."

"Doesn't it?"

"Perhaps. Perhaps not."

"Don't you believe our decades-long entrenchment in both wars is similar?"

"I suppose. But the War in Vietnam was fought in a foreign land against people who were fighting for their country with xenophobic zeal. The drug scene is about money."

"True, you've found a dissimilarity. But perhaps people out there in the drug world also feel that they are in a country of their own, since the one that claims them doesn't seem to give a damn about them."

A faraway glaze set over Turczynski's eyes. He reached instinctively for his joint and then recalled his manners. "You're certifiable, my friend," he said.

"Come on, Bart. Don't sit there and suck sanctimoniously on your joint and pretend to be above the whole fray. You see the similarities, I know you do. Just as Vietnam became a metaphor for our once-divided society, the War on Drugs divides us today. Just as you could go home in the late sixties and early seventies and turn on the television and see our young boys blasted to bits in a rice paddy, now you can flick on the screen and see flashing images of destruction right here on our war-torn streets. It's become the new American nightmare."

Turczynski sighed. "I read your book some time ago," he said, "and if I may be frank?"

"Always."

"I thought you went too far. Particularly where you compared the Strategic Hamlets of Vietnam to the ghettos of today."

"Don't you see the analogy? The Strategic Hamlets were isolated villages where the Diem government warehoused peasants to isolate them both from the political influence of the Viet Cong and to prevent them from becoming a political influence of their own. The effort backfired, generating untoward anger that helped topple Diem and his cronies. Today, our ghettos are where we allow undereducated people to languish, jobless and without prospects. The lines of demarcation are social and economic rather than the physical moats and bamboo fences, but they're nonetheless as real. As long as we can put barriers around them, as long as they hurt mostly each other, we can live with that. It's only when what little influence they have reaches outside the ghettos that we become truly uncomfortable."

"Ruth, the Strategic Hamlet Program was an intentional, focused effort to stifle the will of the people. It was evil at heart. The ghettos are an unintended and tragic consequence of the way our society and its industries have grown away from the cities."

"I'm far from sure it's not intentional."

"What's made you such a fanatic?"

"We've got millions of people out there feeling they'd be better off if they hadn't been born. Their everyday lives are punishing.

Their daily quest for drugs is nothing more than their search for a meaningful life, and the methods we've chosen to attack and imprison them for their afflictions are nothing short of barbaric."

"Many would call that liberal rhetoric."

"I can prove it to you."

"How?"

"In your class."

Turczynski extended his arms in a frustrated stretch. "Oh God, Ruth," he said. "The class is about Vietnam, not the mess we've got out there today."

"I'll show you they're related."

Turczynski sighed again and surrendered to his urge to reignite the marijuana cigarette, although he stepped to the door to blow the smoke outside. "You might as well spring it on me in my weakened condition," he said.

"Have you covered Post-Traumatic Stress Disorder with your students yet?"

"That's next month's material."

"I brought some fascinating papers. They're a case study of a Washington, D.C. prosecution. I believe it to be the first criminal drug trial where the defendant relied on a PTSD defense based on a War experience in Vietnam. It'd be a perfect vehicle for presenting PTSD to your class."

"Ah. How did the trial fare?"

"Miserably."

"Need I have asked. All right, Ruth. I'll look over your materials. But I'll make you no promises."

◆━━◆◆◆◆━━◆◆

Over the past few days, Mike Daniels had spoken with several people in the hospital billing department. He learned about the various hospital, government, and charitable programs for reimbursement and forgiveness of hospital bills incurred by people without means to pay. He assembled pamphlets and handwritten notes in a folder, and on his afternoon off, he set out for Whatta Deal. Daniels harbored a burning desire to help Brandon, perhaps for philanthropic purposes, or maybe as much for his own atonement for failing to save another young man, the lieutenant he'd watched die fifteen years earlier.

Daniels pulled onto the lot at Whatta Deal. The place was still and lifeless, like a ghost town. He slowly approached the closed garage bays. A weather-beaten door was cracked open at the far side. He pushed the door. It creaked and groaned as it yielded.

Daniels stepped inside and spring-loaded hinges slammed the door behind him. In the closed quarters, the must and filth almost made him choke, and a pungent lime odor lingered. Daniels's eyes took a few moments to adjust to the gloom. A blur of anemic light sifted through a scum-covered window. In a moment, shadows and intimations jelled into junk cars and piles of burlap bags.

Daniels called Bran's name and waited. After three attempts, he was satisfied the place was empty. He turned to leave, but as he moved toward the door, among the half-dissolved shapes, his eye caught the shudder of a shadow's movement.

"Brandon," Daniels said to the shadows. "I know you've got trouble. I want to help. To get you away from these drug people. Come stay with me for a couple of days until—"

An explosion suddenly concussed in Daniels's eardrums; it seemed to rock the enclosure. Daniels felt pressure on his left arm. The heaviness escalated to shooting pain, running into his nerves and up his spine.

He slapped his bicep. He felt warm, sticky blood. His knees buckled, and he fell onto them.

From the shadows appeared a boy, smaller than Bran. He walked with a strange cocky be-bop. At the end of his extended arm, he held an automatic pistol that appeared far too large for his hand. His young features were shaded, but Daniels could see a strange and contradictory glee glowing in the darkened eyes; the emotion lacked calculated malevolence but was brutal and ruthless, nonetheless. Daniels held his arm and stared into the boy's eyes, and without a doubt he understood he was about to die. In the child's eyes, there was no interest in delaying or toying; although an unflinching murderer, he didn't seem a sadist. His sole concern seemed to be to position himself close enough to end it with a single shot and to have full view.

The boy moved within a few feet of Daniels. He smiled a stupid and joyful grin, as if he had hit a buzzer beater. He said zip, zip, and lifted the gun.

Daniels heard a crash. Light suddenly flooded the bay. A man's voice boomed and bounced in a surreal echo.

Daniels thought it was over, but the pain held him to the earth. He squinted and tumbled forward. As he fell, he saw the barrel of the boy's gun lift from its lock on his face to take aim at the door behind him.

But the boy never set up the shot. The adolescent chest imploded with a sudden blast. The tiny feet lifted from the ground. The lithe body levitated, gathering itself in the air, hovering, and then descending fast, impacting with a heavy thud. The boy lay in a still, dead heap.

Daniels snapped his head toward to the door, swung wide open. The light flooding the room was from the outside and not from some heavenly intervention. A man, standing in the doorway and gun smoking in his hand, blocked the light. He was a tall man, and when he stepped inside, Daniels caught the glint off a silver badge swinging from his neck on a lanyard. The cop knelt beside Daniels and lifted the torn edges of his sleeve. He eyed the wound and whistled. "Little sucker got you pretty good."

"I've seen worse," said Daniels stoically.

"Me too. Wanna tell me what the hell you're doing here?"

Daniels's head swam, and he fought off the onset of unconsciousness. "I came to help a kid in trouble."

"Good Samaritan, huh?"

"Something like that."

"Kid got a name?"

"Bran. Brandon Christy."

"Oh yeah," the cop said, nodding. "Don't worry. I'm taking care of that one personally."

"Who are you?" Daniels said, although his eyes went blank, and he lapsed into unconsciousness before CAN Officer Stuart Zackaeus was able to formally introduce himself.

Chapter thirty-two

Landing Zone Priscilla was an oval-shaped, grassy field cut between the forested foothills of Broad Mountain, just north of the second No-Fly Area Ashford had targeted for reconnaissance. Ashford, Trent, Morrow, and Winston waited in the meadow with two dormant Hueys, while the infantry soldiers of Delta Company performed their reconnaissance. Ashford crouched in a cockpit with his helmet perched atop his head to monitor radio reports. The sun simmered over elongated cloud reefs; the enclosed cockpit was like a greenhouse, and Ashford's flight suit was soaked with sweat. He longed for something to happen, anything, if only so they could fire the helicopters' engines and create a cooling breeze.

"How's it going?" Morrow said, tapping on Ashford's helmet.

Ashford started. "Okay, I guess. All three squads are on course, but they've all drawn blanks."

"Well, it was a nice try."

"Guess we should get ready to pick them up."

"I'll round up the guys."

"*Charlie Oscar One, this is Delta Five. Over,*" the radio broadcast.

Ashford lowered the earcups of the helmet. *"Delta Five, Charlie Oscar One. Go ahead."*

"We reached our objective," the voice said, full of excitement.

"Say again," Ashford said. His own emotions were flaring.

"I say again, we located our objective. And... Don't know how to say this, but we have got a prisoner. Request instructions."

"Oh my God . . ." Ashford quickly unkeyed the mike. He lifted his helmet and turned to Trent, who sat on the bench seat behind him, engrossed in reading. "Nick, uh, they found it."

Trent's eyes widened. "Well I'll be."

"They... they have a prisoner," Ashford stammered. "Any suggestions?"

Trent bit his lip as if trying to control a spasm of laughter. He stood, stretched, and sat again, returning to the pages of his book. "You're the AMC," he said.

Ashford chided himself for repeating past mistakes and resolved to make his own decision. He slid his helmet over his head again. *"Delta Five, Charlie Oscar,"* he said. *"Are you closer to the LZ or the pickup zone?"*

"About the same."

"Then transport the prisoner to the LZ location. I say again. Bring him in."

<hr>

Thirty minutes later, the two infantry sergeants Ashford had come to know stood before him. Between them was a sixteen-year-old boy clothed in shorts and a dirt-covered T-shirt.

Ashford asked the boy his name. The boy returned a blank stare, and Ashford wondered what the hell he was going to do with him.

Morrow suggested they contact the DEA before doing anything else. She volunteered Winston and herself to take their helicopter and climb high enough to contact Operations at Indiantown Gap, which could relay a message to the DEA and return instructions. Ashford agreed and gave the order.

From a thousand feet, Morrow transmitted the DEA's instructions. Ashford was to take the prisoner to Indiantown Gap and detain him at the flight facility until the DEA's agent-in-charge arrived. Winston's voice came softly and seriously on the radio, a tone that was unsettling, because Ashford had never heard it from the man before. Winston inquired whether the infantry soldiers had live ammunition. The response came back in the affirmative, and Winston relayed the order for Delta Company to set up an armed perimeter around the illegal crops until they were relieved.

The soldiers departed into the woods, and Winston and Morrow left for the flight facility. Only Ashford, Trent, their crew chief, and the boy remained.

Ashford guided the boy into the helicopter and helped him strap the belt around his waist. Then he started to assemble his own flight gear. Trent shoved his novel into his pocket and stepped in close to Ashford. "You really want my advice, LT?"

Ashford nodded rapidly, his frustration willfully apparent. "I've been asking for it since the day I arrived."

"Okay. Let the kid go."

Ashford dropped his flight bag in surprise. He lifted his face to meet Trent's. The warrant's squinted eyes contained intensity and certitude. "What?" Ashford asked.

"I said to let the kid go. Before this goes any further. Say he got away. Hell, you can say you left me to watch him, and I screwed it up. I don't care."

Trent turned to the boy and asked if he had a car somewhere. The boy nodded anxiously and said it was on Mountain Road.

Trent told Ashford they could drop him there. No one would be the wiser.

Ashford's jaw hung low. "Why?"

"You'll regret it if you don't."

"Care to elaborate?"

Trent just shrugged, and Ashford exhaled a puff of air, as if a heavy object impacted his diaphragm. "If I have to make a tough decision," he said, "I need advice and input that's supported by facts and logic. You have anything to support your recommendation?"

"Nope."

"Then why should I follow it?"

"Instinct."

"Instinct?"

"If you want to be a half-decent pilot, you'll have to learn to depend on your instincts."

Ashford climbed into the cockpit and stared at the instrument panel. The silence grew, until he said, "We've got our orders."

Trent walked around the Huey, touching his finger to his forehead as if massaging against a headache. He climbed into his seat and put his helmet on. Ashford asked if he was ready to go. "You're the AMC," Trent said.

The Huey lifted from the field. Ashford glanced to the rear repeatedly, checking on the boy. He didn't shout or coo as had the West Point cadets and the boys from Midland High; this boy didn't seem to notice the world opening before his eyes, turning, and sliding under his feet. He sat still and expressionless with an air of leaden silence. He appeared as a child who bore some invisible and crushing weight, something he had carried a long time and could not escape.

They landed at the flight facility. They hovered to the hard-stand, shut down the Huey, and escorted the boy into the administration building. In the hallway, waiting near the doorway, stood Colonel Harker and General Tarsavage.

"Sir," Ashford said, "we didn't expect you." He saluted, almost as an afterthought.

"I arrived from AP Hill this morning," Harker said. "The evaluation was nearly complete, and I thought it was time to check the progress of my little mission. We monitored your calls from Operations. I must say you followed my orders perfectly, Lieutenant. The general is very impressed with my little operation."

Ashford stifled a protest to the colonel's usurpation of credit for the successful mission.

"Is this the prisoner?" Tarsavage asked, gesturing.

"Yes," Ashford said.

"Just a boy." Tarsavage inspected the prize and stroked his own chin. "Could be problems. Harrison, we'd better get hold of Command Branch and make sure we're not overstepping our legal bounds by holding him."

The field grade officers disappeared, leaving a wake of solemnity. Ashford escorted the boy to the break room, where Reggie Spencer was seated at a table in a corner. Spencer nodded knowingly; news of the mission had spread rapidly. Ashford offered the boy a seat at the table.

"Can you just tell me your first name?" Ashford said.

The boy hesitated. Ashford reconsidered his request and repeated the admonition to the boy that he didn't have to say anything if he didn't want to.

"It's Brandon."

Ashford held Bran's gaze. "Can I get you anything, Brandon?"

"Maybe a drink."

"Coke okay?"

"Sure."

Ashford left for a few moments and returned with three sodas.

"I'm curious," Ashford said, distributing the drinks. "Off the record, you don't look like someone who would grow dope. And you're obviously not the guy in this picture." Ashford pulled the black-and-white photograph from his pocket.

Bran winced and said softly, "He calls it his Garden."

"And he makes you help him?"

Bran nodded.

"Guess I'd better not ask too much. Can I get you something else?"

"Nothing."

"We were just looking for the field," Ashford said, as if in apology. "Like a game. I didn't expect to find anybody there."

The local police arrived first, and the state police followed in severe gray-and-black uniforms. Two FBI agents attired in dark suits followed them with a woman from some undisclosed federal agency. Trent entered from the break room; he assessed the scene and, with his usual measure of sarcasm, asked if there was anyone from Interpol.

Sage arrived last and most importantly. He introduced himself and quickly dismissed all other law enforcement personnel from the room. He argued that their jurisdiction was confined to the illegal plants, explaining that he had no present interest in the foliage, but the boy was in his exclusive jurisdiction, because he was part of an active DEA operation. When Sage was satisfied he was the only Drug Warrior in the room, he centered his eyes on Bran. "Brandon Christy, I presume," he said.

Bran gazed at the agent guardedly.

"I know your uncle," Sage said, answering the silent question. "Come on, kid. We've got some talking to do." Sage took Bran under the armpit and started for the hallway.

"Sir," Ashford called after him. "I led the mission that brought Brandon here, and I feel responsible. Any way I can come along?"

Sage sneered and said no. He turned back to the hallway. Ashford asked where Sage was taking the boy, but the agent didn't acknowledge the query. Ashford touched the agent on the elbow from behind, and Sage suddenly and violently wheeled around. He threw flat palms out to his sides and glared at Ashford, as if he had been accosted by a derelict.

"What's going to happen to him?" Ashford said.

"Take some advice, kid," Sage said. "Keep your nose to your own grindstone and mind your own business and be very careful whose elbow you take hold of. Any more questions?"

Ashford stood dumbfounded as Sage and the boy disappeared out the door and into the parking lot. When Ashford composed himself, he turned to say something to Trent, perhaps to seek some small measure of reassurance or at least consolation, but the warrant officer only peered over his novel with an unsympathetic pout that said, more clearly than words:

I told you to let him go.

Chapter thirty-three

Inside the Educational Activities Building at the Middletown campus of the Pennsylvania State University, Ruth Scarbrough flicked nervous glances at her watch. Seven-thirty in the evening. Deric Christy was late.

A dozen students had shuffled past her. In the classroom, Turczynski leaned on a triangular podium arrayed on a platform. A cardboard mock-up of a wood-trim railing was arranged before a chair in the manner of a stage prop. On the podium, a red-hued wooden gavel rested. Two long tables were set before the podium, and two men were seated behind the table on the right, one in a chrome-plated wheelchair. The students were seated on twelve chairs lining the windows in two rows of six, and a second artificial railing surrounded them.

Under the circumstances, an adequate courtroom.

Turczynski was reviewing a pop quiz with the students. He appeared comfortable in his teaching role and seemed to have a rapport with the students based upon mutual fondness. Lifting his face, Turczynski's eyes met Scarbrough's. He motioned her forward. She padded noiselessly into the room and sat somberly at the nearest table.

"A counselor of mine was fond of saying there are as many Vietnams as there are veterans who fought there," Turczynski told the students. "Although this course is called 'The Vietnam Experience,' that is a misnomer, because the individual ordeal of each Vietnam veteran was decidedly unique. As you know, my approach on topical areas has been to sample the range of experience. But we'll experiment tonight by covering a narrower slice— one individual's experience—a case study, if you will.

"The broader focus of tonight's session is a syndrome experienced by a significant portion of combat veterans, recognized in modern professional literature as Post-Traumatic Stress Disorder, PTSD for short. PTSD has been used, successfully and unsuccessfully, as a defense in numerous criminal trials. Hence, tonight's classroom decor. Compliments of a recent student production." Turczynski paced before the jury box, sliding his fingers along the mock railing, mimicking the flounce of a seasoned trial attorney.

"Perhaps you've seen news stories about veterans who seemingly went berserk and injured a fellow bar patron or a seatmate on a bus. Cases like those, where the offense makes little sense, though disturbing, fit our traditional notions of insanity. There, the application of a PTSD defense in criminal court seems plausible. But much more troubling is the application of the PTSD defense to crimes we traditionally consider premeditated—trafficking in drugs, for instance.

"Tonight we'll recreate a little-known trial from 1972 orchestrated by a clever young lawyer who appears to have been the very first to mount a PTSD defense to charges of drug distribution based on the defendant's Vietnam War experience. Although the term PTSD was unknown at the time of trial, we'll take advantage of the information available today. Our witnesses have been prepared with the actual court record, but our ground rules allow them to supplement that record with current literature and their own experiences. Also, the real trial took two-and-a-half days. So obviously we'll shortcut the process. Some of the witness roles are composites.

"Let's set the stage. You've been selected for jury duty and seated for a trial, the Honorable Bart Turczynski presiding." Turczynski pulled a flowing black robe from behind the podium and mirthfully wrapped it over his shoulders.

"Order please," Turczynski said, rapping the gavel playfully. "Our prosecutor is our own David Vanasdalin, the real District Attorney for Dauphin County. He's also a decorated combat veteran."

Vanasdalin had sharp facial features, but most of the eyes in the room were drawn to his thighs. They were thick and muscular, but the shapes rounded into stubs. His pant legs lay neat and flat below them, draped over the seat of the wheelchair, ending in nothing.

Vanasdalin wore a plain gray suit, a pressed white shirt, and a wine-colored tie—his current combat attire as a prosecuting attorney. A fierceness beamed from his face, that spoke of untold battles not limited to the courtroom.

"Seated beside Mister Vanasdalin is Archie Boetcher," Turczynski said. "He's an assistant district attorney, but this evening he'll take the role of the prosecution's expert witness. At the defense table is Ruth Scarbrough, a professor of sociology from the University of California, a Vietnam veteran, and a dear personal friend. She'll play the roles of the defense attorney and the defense expert witness. We'll have to do a little imagining when she conducts her own direct examination. We also have Arnold Peterson, owner of a local contracting firm specializing in high-end woodwork, and a veteran of the siege at Khe

Sanh." Turczynski nodded at a huge black man seated in the back of the room.

"Anyone thinking of adding on a room or fitting out a den, give me a call," Peterson said, spreading a fan of business cards.

"Mister Peterson will play the part of a comrade in arms of our defendant," said Turczynski. "Which brings us to our defendant." Turczynski's eyes asked a silent question of Scarbrough. Her face returned blank melancholy.

"I suppose we should select a student," Turczynski said.

When Scarbrough took a last hopeful glance at the doorway, her eyes opened wide with amazement. There, circled by the doorframe, consuming the open space, stood Lucias Hammaker.

When she composed herself, Scarbrough begged indulgence from the class and hurried from the room, closing the door behind her.

• ⬦ • ———— • ⬦ •• ⬦ • ———— • ⬦ •

Scarbrough stared at Hammaker. His sling was gone, but his newly injured finger was still wrapped in thick gauze.

"How... ?" she stammered.

"A client contacted me last week," Hammaker said. "He told me he was invited to this class. A pregnant black woman, a Vietnam veteran, made him swear on his honor as a Marine he'd come."

"Is he here?"

"My turn to ask a few questions."

"It's... Oh, Lucias, I wanted to reach out to him somehow. You see, I want him to show the world what the DEA has done to him and how he's been manipulated. It'll make a difference, I know it. Tonight is to be the start. I can show him the world has changed since he faced a jury twenty years ago. There's a different generation with a deeper understanding of Vietnam and its impact."

"You want to use him just like they do."

"No, please, Lucias. I can bring tremendous political pressure to bear for his benefit. Let me show you the first step. You must come inside."

"What's your intention?"

"To show you an updated criminal trial in which the defendant employs a PTSD defense."

"A trial?"

"His trial."

"*His* trial?"

"No one knows he'll be playing himself. They'll think he's just another local veteran. But the trial will be based on his and your experience. I got the transcripts in Washington. The instructor and his guests are veterans who've studied the testimony. We'll present the case to the students, who'll deliberate and reach a real verdict."

"If I didn't know you, I'd say you were joking."

"Don't you see, Lucias? It's your chance to undo a grievous wrong."

"Absolutely and positively not."

"You've no idea what I've gone through to arrange this."

"I said no. I only came because Deric felt he needed to be here to live up to his word."

"He's here then?"

Hammaker lifted his eyebrows noncommittally.

"You're his attorney, not his guardian," said Scarbrough. "Isn't the final decision his?"

Deric Christy suddenly appeared, like an apparition, stepping from behind the cinder-block wall. He seemed older than at the hospital. The fluorescent glare appeared to magnify the blemishes on his face; the jagged scar notched in his temple seemed like it was a deep canyon. In his manner there was an aura of curiosity; he studied Scarbrough as a scientist would a glass beaker filled with an unknown and potentially dangerous solution.

Scarbrough approached with her palms open and her soul too. "I know I've got a lot of explaining to do and at this moment, I'm undeserving of your trust," she said. "But I need you to do this for me. And maybe it's something you need to do for yourself. Please, please, come with me. I swear on *my* word as a veteran, I won't betray you."

Christy gazed in silence. Scarbrough compared the dead-still glass eye with the live one in which emotions seemed to be coalescing; she saw their bewilderment, apprehension, and if she was not mistaken, hope.

Hammaker insinuated his body between the two veterans. "I strongly advise against it. Ruth is a personal friend, and I believe she has the best intentions. But I think her judgment is clouded by zeal. She could do you harm."

"Will I have to say anything?" Christy's voice sounded as if a thick liquid were rising in his throat.

"You didn't testify at your original trial," Scarbrough said. "There's no reason why you should tonight."

"I can't say anything."

Scarbrough heaved a long sigh. "God bless you," she said, pushing Christy toward the classroom, so he would have no time to change his mind. "I'll make you a believer, Lucias. Can't you see? The play's the thing!"

⁑

The trio reappeared before an audience that was growing anxious. Scarbrough seated Christy at the defense table as she would a prince. The veteran's eye scanned the room but revealed nothing.

"Thank you for your patience, class," Scarbrough said. "It is my honor to introduce another distinguished veteran, Mister, uhm... Johnson, playing the defendant."

A vanquished Hammaker treaded toward a seat in the back of the room.

"And we have Mister Hammaker," Scarbrough said, "a distinguished Washington attorney to play defense counsel."

Hammaker took a seat at the defense table without hesitation, almost greedily. He knew that Scarbrough had planned to defend Christy and thereby win his trust by demonstrating her impassioned belief in his cause. He would have protected Christy from the rear and whisked him to a quick exit if it had become necessary; from the counsel table he would be poised to act instantly.

But there was something more that was grounding his desire to participate. Scarbrough had awakened a hunger in him, the same craving that gnawed at his core in Judge Bailey's courtroom two decades ago. Deric's cause—right or wrong—was a real one, a human cause, not the mere preservation of wealth for the wealthy or the promotion of some dubious corporate venture. Scarborough had rekindled his love of a flesh-and-blood fight, the search for truth, and the yearning for vindication.

"Well then," said Turczynski. "Shall we begin? Ladies and gentlemen, you've been seated at the trial of Deric Christy, accused of selling three pounds of marijuana on the streets of D.C. The defendant was caught rather red-handed by undercover police officers and admits his offense, but the defense claims that he has a psychological syndrome that should excuse him from punishment. I'll dispense with any further legal mumbo-jumbo and ask the prosecutor to begin with an opening statement."

Vanasdalin wheeled himself to the open floor. His chair caught the corner of the counsel table; he made several choppy turns before he centered himself on the makeshift jury box. There, he paused in apparent self-reflection. "I'm here tonight playing a role," he began. "But my words are not those of an actor. They are from my heart. I'm here to ask you to decide that people must take responsibility for their conscious choices and actions, regardless of the horrifying circumstances of their past. You see, I truly believe, no matter what sympathy you may feel for Deric Christy, it's your duty to find him guilty of the offense charged.

"I am a Vietnam vet too. I saw as much horror in that War as the defendant did, and I've spent more time recovering from my physical wounds."

Hammaker bounded to his feet. "Your Honor, I must object," he said. "All due deference to Mister Vanasdalin, this case isn't about his own Vietnam experience. It's about my client's and how it's robbed him of the ability to distinguish right from wrong."

"Under the circumstances," said Turczynski, "why don't we allow Mister Vanasdalin some latitude?" His hushed tone imparted great concern for the passions of his guests.

"The objection stands," Hammaker said, seating himself.

Vanasdalin stared despondently, waiting for Turczynski and Hammaker to finish their dialogue. When they did, he rolled his chair back at an angle and flicked his eyes to Hammaker. Hammaker couldn't be sure, but he thought Vanasdalin winked and smiled furtively, the wry grin of a card shark.

Vanasdalin pivoted to the jury. "Attorney Hammaker is right that this case is about Deric Christy," he said. "But he's wrong when he says it's about what happened in Vietnam. This case is about what happened in Washington, D.C. when Deric Christy strapped three pounds of marijuana under his coat to conceal it, walked twenty blocks across town, and solicited an undercover officer to purchase the drugs. The rest is smoke and flash.

"The defense will tell you that Deric Christy isn't responsible for his crime, because he suffers from Post-Traumatic Stress Disorder. Please don't misunderstand me, there is a syndrome recognized in the medical community as PTSD. And although there's some disagreement over the numbers, many veterans suffer the effects.

"But it just can't be an excuse for a crime as volitional as dealing drugs. The defendant's conduct shows he knew very well he was breaking the law when he sold drugs on the city streets. The assertion of the PTSD defense in this case is an affront to me and all other law-abiding veterans who've got by on honest sweat and tears."

"Your Honor, please," Hammaker said.

"Yes, that may have perhaps been out of order, Dave," Turczynski said. "Finished?"

"One last word," Vanasdalin said, panning his eyes across the students' faces. "Maybe we'll have a wink or a chuckle tonight because of the artifice of this trial. I encourage you to relax, even to laugh if appropriate, to enjoy the session, and speak freely if you have any questions even though a real juror could not. We're here, after all, to learn something about each other. But at the end of the trial, I ask that you embrace your role as juror. I ask you to perform the role any citizen must and find this defendant guilty of his intentional crime, just as the jury did that convicted Deric Christy twenty years ago."

Vanasdalin rolled into position behind the table.

Hammaker approached the railing. Vanasdalin was good; he had an edge in his disability that evoked sympathy from the students, and he knew how to manipulate that advantage well. But Hammaker's mind only briefly reflected on Vanasdalin's tactics before it reeled off into the past, to April, 1972, when he approached a genuine jury railing. He clearly recalled the opening lines he delivered so many years ago. But this was a different jury and a different time; there would be different buttons to push. Different stops to pull.

"I come before you with as much passion as Mister Vanasdalin," he said, "because, as those who have reviewed the trial transcripts know, I'm not acting at all tonight. Therefore, although I'm appreciative of your audience, I'll probably have no winks or chuckles. You see, on April 2, 1972, in a Washington courtroom, I defended Deric Christy to a verdict."

Gasps came from among the students.

The remainder of Hammaker's opening was more akin to the one he delivered two decades ago than he would have liked. As he spoke, he wished there had been more time to prepare; he hadn't studied the recent scientific evidence related to PTSD. He would have to rely on Ruth to fill in the details.

He concluded his statement by reasoning with the students, carefully avoiding supplication, appealing to them only to keep their minds open to the possibility of diminished capacity.

When Hammaker finished, Vanasdalin called his assistant Archie Boetcher to the makeshift witness stand. In his early forties and balding, Boetcher was a quiet-mannered man with the deliberate manner of a technician. Vanasdalin artfully led Boetcher through a methodical explanation of the roots and symptoms of PTSD. Boetcher's approach was sterile and scientific; nevertheless Vanasdalin never missed the opportunity to express sympathy for Vietnam War survivors. His questions blended incisiveness and compassion, but when he focused upon personal responsibility and mental capacity, he remained relentless in his demand for full accountability.

"Will you explain to the jury the roots of PTSD?" said Vanasdalin.

Boetcher toyed with his horn-rimmed glasses. "After an unusually traumatic event," he said, "a psychological processing of the event must occur. The survivor must develop a personal understanding and reconciliation. He must integrate the event into his life and then move past it.

"When this process is interrupted or frustrated, for one reason or another, problems often develop. If enough problems are present, they may form the syndrome we call PTSD. The survivor may manifest profound sleep disturbance, flashbacks, nightmares, survivor guilt, depression, or explosiveness. There's often a repression of emotion, a numbness that others may think is coldness or calculated behavior."

"Does PTSD rob the survivor of the ability to distinguish right from wrong?"

"In certain circumstances, it might. If so, the behavior in question would be erratic and uncontrolled."

"Could it be violent?"

"Certainly."

"But wouldn't it be sneaky behavior?"

"No. If mental capacity were impaired, one would see no reason to sneak."

"So for example, one would see no reason to conceal drugs?"

"Objection," Hammaker said. "He's leading the witness."

"Attorney Hammaker's quite right," Vanasdalin said, his voice a measured beam of confidence. "One final question, Mister Boetcher. In your professional medical opinion, do you believe that for any reason Deric Christy lacked the ability to distinguish right from wrong?"

"Most certainly not," Boetcher said forcefully.

"Cross-examine," Vanasdalin said, retreating to counsel table.

Hammaker wasted no time formulating a question. "Isn't it true that at Deric Christy's original trial, you testified he had no mental affliction associated with his experience in Vietnam?"

"Objection," Vanasdalin said, bracing himself in his wheelchair as if unconsciously straining to rise on legs no longer there to support him. "This is our re-creation of Deric Christy's original trial, not a retrial. The ground rules are open and flexible and don't bind us to witnesses' former testimony."

Hammaker held his palms on his chest. "It seems Mister Vanasdalin would like us to consider Deric's real trial only when it suits his purpose. He made a direct reference to the seventy-two guilty verdict in his opening statement. But he doesn't care for the jury to hear his own witness concede that the evidence upon which the conviction was based is fundamentally flawed. Mister Vanasdalin cannot have his cake and eat it too."

"I think Mr. Hammaker's right," said Turczynski, looking like the conductor of a runaway train. "You can answer the question, Archie."

"Yes," Boetcher said into his shirtsleeve.

"Yes what, Mister Boetcher?" Hammaker said.

"I guess the guy testified that way in seventy-two."

"The prosecution's expert psychologist testified in 1972 that Deric Christy did not have any mental affliction whatsoever resulting from his experience in Vietnam? Is that what you're saying? You must speak up, Mister Boetcher, just as you did during your direct examination."

"Yes."

"Yet you'd be willing to concede today that Deric had PTSD?"

"Yes," Boetcher said, still grudging.

"No further questions," Hammaker said, waving off the witness.

Vanasdalin leaned back in his chair. "Your Honor," he said. "With the defense's admission of actual perpetration of the distribution offense, the prosecution rests. Before the defense case begins, I'd like to confirm Mister Boetcher's statement of the prosecution's position. Based on our review of the evidence, we offer to stipulate that the defendant had PTSD. With that concession, I believe we can dispense with the defendant's witnesses who shared his Vietnam experiences."

A clever strategy, Hammaker thought. In offering to be helpful, Vanasdalin would prevent him from putting on critical witnesses who could arouse the jurors' sympathies. Offer your opponent a carrot, but beat him over the head with the stick.

"The prosecution is to be commended for its graciousness," said Hammaker. "But we wish to put on all our witnesses."

"By all means," Turczynski said.

A very different judge than old Bailey, Hammaker thought. "Call Arnold Peterson," he said. "I take it he'll serve as a composite of Taylor, Jaworski, and Sanders from the original trial?"

Turczynski flipped through the pages of the transcript. "Correct."

"Do I have any of the hometown witnesses?"

"No, but you can make references to their testimony in your closing argument."

Vanasdalin moved as if preparing to object and then seemed to change his mind, settling back thoughtfully. Peterson lumbered forward, his presence incongruous with a classroom or a courtroom. He was a grizzled, thick-framed man with a severe mouth and a gaping slash cut between the rugged peaks and valleys of his face. The cardboard railing shuddered, seeming as if it might collapse under the weight of his immense hands.

Hammaker studied the witness. Part of the artistry in mounting a successful PTSD defense was to select witnesses who could finesse their references to the War is such a way as to arouse the jurors' sympathies without alienating them. From his appearance, Peterson did not look like a man up to that task.

"Mister Peterson, you are a combat veteran of the Vietnam War?" asked Hammaker.

"Yes sir."

"Can you tell the jury what you did there?"

"I ducked a lot."

Some of the students smiled nervously, and Hammaker smiled too. "Your Military Occupational Specialty?"

"Combat infantry soldier."

"Did you hear the testimony of the prosecution's expert witness?"

"I heard him. But I didn't understand a goddamn thing he said."

Hammaker looked at the students; perhaps they would warm to this witness. "I only understood part of it myself. Now, you spent time in the jungle with Deric Christy?"

"I'm supposed to be one of those guys I read about, so I'm supposed to say yes."

"And one of those guys was at Khe Sanh after Deric?"

"Sure was. Funny thing no one was at that trial who was at Khe Sanh with Esquire."

Peterson's use of Christy's nickname from Vietnam sent a jolt up Hammaker's spine. Then he recalled Christy's spoken reference to the nickname at the sentencing—Peterson must have picked it up from the transcript.

"Esquire was a nickname for Deric used by his friends?"

"Most of us called him that."

Was Peterson playing a role or testifying from personal experience? Hammaker sent a questioning glance at Christy, but the return gaze gave away nothing.

"Mister Peterson," Hammaker continued, "this may be a delicate task, but I'm going to ask you to keep your testimony as close to the written record as you can. Just tell us what Sanders and Jaworski saw and felt."

"Jaworski was an asshole. I'd choke on his words."

Vanasdalin spoke. "It's Mister Hammaker's fault if he didn't arrive early enough to coach his witnesses, Your Honor. He's got no business doing it now."

Turczynski made a gesture to get on with it. Hammaker knew he would have to use all of his skill to control his runaway witness.

"Let's talk first about the experiences in the field with Deric and not about Khe Sanh," he said.

Eagerly and earnestly, Peterson ignored Hammaker and spoke directly to the students. "Let me tell you a little about Vietnam first. Christ, most of you kids weren't even born then. I won't grind over the physical details of the War—you've seen the news flashes and heard sound bites. But what you have to understand is that those were real flesh and blood people at the other end of the camera lens. It was me. I was there."

Hammaker was softening to Peterson's approach. If a witness insists on running away, let him run, as long as he's heading in the right direction.

"What are your general impressions from Vietnam?" Hammaker asked.

"Rottenness. Everything I remember about the War is rotten. It all squishes around in my head, like the red mud I lived in, as if it soaked deep into my brain. The War was one huge atrocity."

"Can you tell us about your experience as an infantry soldier?"

"What do you want to hear about? Week-long forced marches through leech-infested jungles? Stretches of deathly boredom and then... Pop! Pop! Your buddy goes down just like that. You just knew there was a bullet with your name on it too.

411

"So we started doing things in ways we weren't used to. Learned to fight Charlie the way he fought us. In time, some of us did terrible things to the Vietnamese. Had competitions to see who could rack up the highest body count. The captain even took to putting a case of beer on the block."

"Body count is a euphemism for kills?"

"Yeah. I killed seventeen I know of. Those ones, I walked up to and kicked. Some of them, I don't even know for sure if they were the enemy. 'If it's dead, it's VC,' they used to say." Peterson lowered his head into his hands. "I said it too."

With Peterson somewhat subdued, Hammaker thought he could bring the focus back to Deric's ordeal. He quickly asked a question to control Peterson's rambling. "Please tell us about Deric's experience in the jungle."

"Why don't you ask him?"

"He's not here."

Peterson smiled at Christy. "Yeah, I saw from the papers Bart gave me that Esquire escaped from prison and was never seen again. Little doubt about it, he's dead. Just like a thousand other guys. Single car accident, barbiturates and gin, or a bullet through the head. Or maybe he's just dead inside because he bottled it all up for so long. Any way it happened, his name ought to be on the Wall, 'cause you ask me, he died in Vietnam just like the rest of them."

"No further questions," Hammaker said; he would get out now and cut his losses.

Vanasdalin remained at counsel table; his elbows set wide, his fingers tented. "Mister Peterson," he said. "Forget about Jaworski and Sanders. Were you personally at Khe Sanh with Deric Christy?"

"I'll take the Fifth Amendment on that one," Peterson said.

"You have no such right when answering a question that can in no way incriminate you."

"I don't care." Peterson sent a look that etched a line that could not be crossed.

Vanasdalin looked to Turczynski for help. "Judge?"

"Let's not take this too far, Dave," Turczynski said, beads of sweat running down his cheeks and collecting in the creases around his mouth. "Perhaps we should end this exercise here."

"I wouldn't miss the end of this for the world," Peterson said, stepping down.

The students chimed in. The consensus was to plunge forward. Hammaker gazed at Christy but received no sign.

"Call my expert psychologist, Ruth Scarbrough," Hammaker said.

The past forty minutes had been some of the most difficult of Scarbrough's life. She was accustomed to being in the thick of the fight, knocking heads with her adversaries until they pleaded for mercy. She had arranged this affair to unfold under her direction, but in an unexpected gesture of good faith, she surrendered her role and relegated herself to the sidelines to watch helplessly as events reeled forward out of her control.

But her patience had paid off. Her time had finally come.

She seated herself delicately on the witness chair and caressed her stomach. She had schooled herself on Vanasdalin's tactic of arousing the students' sympathies and thought she might engage in a bit of turnabout.

"Ruth, do you agree with the general principles Mister Boetcher spoke about concerning PTSD?" Hammaker began.

"Right up to his erroneous conclusion about Deric's mental capacity."

"You've interviewed Deric in the course of preparing for this trial?"

"I read the transcripts. Oh yes, in my role I interviewed him."

"And you learned certain facts about Deric and his experience that you relied upon in forming your opinion about his capacity?"

"I did."

"When Deric went to Vietnam, could he distinguish right from wrong?"

"Deric Christy was eighteen years old when he first set foot in Vietnam. Though his body and mind were still in a formative process, he was certainly aware of ordinary moral principles. But he underwent a reawakening in Vietnam. The experience showed him realities of life that few of us ever encounter."

"What happened in the first few weeks in Vietnam?"

"The Marines cast aside the mores Deric had been taught at home. He not only had the equipment and power to kill but the directive. Thou shalt not kill became thou shalt kill, and thou shalt kill a lot.

"Within a week of his arrival, he was surrounded by soul-shattering suffering and appalling devastation. He saw friends blown to bits before his eyes. He witnessed behavior in his comrades he had never seen in men before. A growing disregard for human life emerged around him. Life was becoming cheap."

"Could Deric at that point in time, several months into his Vietnam experience, distinguish right from wrong?"

"With the right kind of decompression, I think so."

"And as the War progressed?"

"It became worse. He became confounded by the debacle of a blurry guerilla war, almost surrealistic in character, where foe looks like friend and beaming children carry deadly explosives. Deric's government offered no clearly defined military objectives. By default, the War became one of attrition."

"What impact did the nature of the War have upon him?"

"Like other soldiers, Deric questioned the morality of the War and of the orders his superiors gave. But the concept of an immoral War could have little meaning in a battle-swept rice paddy. Deric was constantly forced to test the outer limits of combat—where it ends and where murder begins. He had to decide if he crossed that line, and regardless of the answer, he had to live with himself or become his own judge, jury, and executioner. He came face-to-face with the most depraved condition of the human spirit and looked upon the countenance of tangible evil. He witnessed acts of absolute barbarism."

"And Deric was badly wounded in Vietnam?"

"A mortar round racked his body. They sewed him back together the best they knew how."

"And his journey home?"

"Eighteen hours after he was discharged from the hospital, he arrived in San Francisco. He had no time to decompress. There, the skills that kept him alive in Vietnam were of no use; indeed they were frightening to others and to himself. He had been told to cast the commandments aside in Vietnam, but now they were back in full force and effect.

"There were those who found the fact he was a combatant grotesque. And there were those unable to separate the War from the warriors—many personally blamed him for losing an immensely unpopular war."

"What happened when he was discharged and later returned to Washington?" Hammaker asked.

"His job was filled by someone with a high lottery number, and his employer made sure there was no other job to give him.

The military coded his discharge papers, labeling him a trouble-maker. Unable to find a way back into society, Deric relived War memories over and over, though the emotional impact occurred on different planes. Sometimes the memories were completely detached from emotion. Sometimes the remembering was worse than the events. Everywhere he went, he carried the black and bitter war guilt with him."

"What happened with his family and friends?"

"Part of the syndrome is disaffection. Deric built invisible walls to shield himself from the possibility of emotional pain. In this way he unconsciously sacrificed the very means he had of getting better."

"All right," said Hammaker. "You and Mister Boetcher explained some of the symptoms of PTSD. Now let's talk about how it applies in this case."

"As I've explained, Deric had concentrated, horrendous experiences in Vietnam and no time for decompression when he returned to the States. When he came home, he was still, in effect, a soldier, not a civilian. His body and mind were accustomed to the huge charge of adrenalin that surged through his body in firefights. You see, there's a secret thrill to combat that's as addicting as any drug, and that rousing is perhaps the most revolting experience of all. But soldiers often unconsciously develop a craving for it."

"In other words, Deric became an action junkie?"

"Yes. In Vietnam, Deric vacillated between horrible, deathly boredom and the most intense and horrifying excitement he had felt in his life. When he returned home, without the proper decompression, the unconscious drives he developed as a soldier manifested themselves in his small-time drug trafficking. The cat-and-mouse game he played with the police satisfied his craving in a non-violent way his mind could accept."

"Did Deric have the capacity to distinguish right from wrong?"

"He could give lip service to societal mores, but his own values had been suppressed for so long, he lost the ability to understand his behavior was truly wrong."

"That's all I have," Hammaker said. "Cross-examine."

Scarbrough beamed inwardly as Vanasdalin adjusted his torso in his seat and rubbed the back of his neck, appearing frustrated and routed. She had done well, and she knew it. Where Boetcher was cold and technical, she had injected just the right quantum of emotion into her testimony. The students were whispering among themselves; she could tell they felt it too. She showed them not only that Deric Christy was a real person but that he was innocent too.

Vanasdalin was still rubbing his shoulders, and it was becoming apparent to Scarbrough that the delay was purposeful—he was seeing if she would sweat.

Finally he spoke. "Your testimony reveals your deep-seated compassion and you're certainly to be commended for that."

Scarbrough resisted the impulse to say thank you. In the courtroom, lawyers play on normal human impulses, and it would be best to restrain them.

"In point of fact, Professor Scarbrough," Vanasdalin said, "similar deep-seated convictions are eloquently expressed in your book, *The Accounting: A Vision for the Future of Drug Policy.*"

Scarbrough glared at Turczynski—he must have mentioned her name to Vanasdalin prior to the class, and the prosecutor had been diligent in his homework. Turczynski shifted uncomfortably in his seat.

"Your book draws a number of comparisons between the War on Drugs and the War in Vietnam." Vanasdalin said.

"Objection, Your Honor," Hammaker said. "Irrelevant."

Turczynski stared at Vanasdalin inquisitively. "It's okay for now, Mister Hammaker. Or how do I—"

"Just say overruled," Vanasdalin said.

"Yes. Thank you. Overruled."

"The comparisons, Professor Scarbrough?" Vanasdalin said. "Your book compares the War on Drugs with the War in Vietnam?"

"It does." Scarbrough's mind strained to decipher Vanasdalin's strategy.

"And it draws an analogy between the conditions in the ghettos and certain conditions in Vietnam?"

"Yes."

"In fact, on page 238, you artfully compare the Strategic Hamlets in Vietnam to modern American ghettos. I quote: 'In the ghettos, the economically disadvantaged are huddled into isolated War zones, blocked from opportunities to engage in meaningful work, isolated from awareness of their own collective political power. The phenomenon is much like Diem's failed efforts to isolate the Vietnam peasant population from the political influence of the Viet Cong by herding them into sealed villages.' Did you write that?"

"I did." Scarbrough struggled to sound confident.

"And your sense is that both Wars were unwinnable and that all participants in both Wars are subjected to inhuman stresses?"

"I believe I said—"

"The beauty of cross-examination, Professor Scarbrough, is that when you ask a direct question, you are entitled to a direct answer. A yes or no will do just fine."

Scarbrough scowled in frustration. "Yes, I said something like that."

"You also said that 'in many ways the bitter stalemate in Vietnam became a metaphor for our own bewildered society, dispirited by a government operating under a policy of minimum candor, relentlessly pursuing its own misguided value assessments. The Drug War has now culminated in the same bitter stalemate we saw in Vietnam. We will only continue to endure an insufferable waste of human resource in furtherance of similarly undefined principles.'"

"That's from my book," Scarbrough said. The students seemed to be gaping at her as if she were some sort of pariah.

"And you refer to the war-like conditions of the ghettos, in which the residents are subjected to, I quote, 'atrocities far beyond the normal range of human experience?'"

The snare was laid, the noose hung; Scarbrough could suddenly see exactly where Vanasdalin was leading, how he would spring the trap, and how she would be caught. But she could think of no response that would carry her to safety. They were her own words he was cramming down her throat.

"Did you say that, Professor?"

"I did," she said tersely.

"Now the terms you use in your book are very similar to those you quoted as the precursor for PTSD. Is it possible that ghetto residents, gang members for instance, have PTSD?"

Although there was no other answer but yes, Scarborough said, "It's possible."

"And gang members sell drugs?"

Scarbrough knew in effective cross-examination the questioner leads the witness down an inevitable path to a conclusion that cannot be avoided.

"Yes," she said finally.

"And gang members kill?"

She was fighting now to restrain Preston's image from surfacing in her consciousness.

Vanasdalin didn't need to wait for an answer. "And so the logical conclusion of your reasoning is that no gang member should be arrested or tried for selling drugs or for that matter, murder. Each has a complete and perfect defense."

"It's not that simple," Scarbrough said. She restated her original conclusion as to Christy's particular circumstances, thought her response was flat and unconvincing. With her virtual admission, Vanasdalin allowed her to simmer.

As Scarbrough stood to return to the serenity of the back of the room, a young student in the jury box raised a hand. "Ma'am, may I ask a question please?"

"Of course," Scarbrough said.

"What's the solution?"

"The solution?"

"How do we help them?"

"Help who, dear?"

"Help them all."

"I'm not certain," Scarbrough said humbly, trying to contain the warrior within herself. "As a first step, we might abandon our national rigidity and tolerance for human suffering. We might stop oppressing them and take some of the blame from their shoulders. It doesn't all belong to them, after all. Create support networks and engender an environment that nurtures them back to health. Find a way for them to achieve resolution and reconciliation. We should have done it long ago for our Vietnam veterans. We should do it now for our children of the Drug War."

"And what about those who have crossed the line you referred to?" the student asked. "The line of evil?"

The leering faces of the murdering demons who took Preston away tore into Scarbrough's consciousness and floated menacingly about the room.

"Some cannot be saved," Scarbrough said softly. "They exist as a sad legacy to our collective failure."

"Perhaps, but it's no excuse for not trying," the young woman said.

A tear fell onto Scarbrough's cheek, and she furtively swept it away. Maybe she had reached at least one.

Hammaker sat deflated.

Vanasdalin's cross-examination had been devastating. He had shown the students that floodgates would open with Christy's vindication, and the dregs of society would gleefully pass through behind. Even if the students' sympathies were with Deric, they would have to convict so order could be preserved.

But Hammaker wasn't willing to surrender yet. He had one chance, one witness who might save the day, a witness he hadn't dared to call to the stand so many years ago.

Hammaker spoke loudly and clearly, and his words brought shock to every face in the courtroom. "The defense calls Deric Christy."

The hard mold of Christy's face began to crack. He looked for an instant as if he might plead, but there seemed to be something inside him searching for a way to escape that had discerned this an opportunity. Christy stood with a quiet dignity, not of a soldier on parade but like a father who must comfort a son who has lost on a field of play. There was a sense of trepidation in his manner, overpowered by an air of inevitability.

The students responded physically to Christy's presence as he moved to the witness chair; they straightened in their seats.

"Is your name Johnson?" Hammaker asked.

"No."

"What is your name?"

"Deric Christy."

"You were the defendant in the trial in 1972?"

"Yes."

"Can you tell the jury why you did not testify at your trial in 1972?"

"I couldn't speak about the War then."

"Can you now?"

"I don't know."

"Try."

Christy's voice was barely audible. He spoke to the chair rail. "My saddest memories are of things that happened to civilians. They should've been kept off limits. But they weren't always."

"Can you tell the students of your most vivid memory?"

Christy was silent.

"Is it Khe Sanh?" Hammaker said, knowing the answer, but his voice was uncertain.

"Yes."

"Start with your arrival there."

Christy's words were still choked, but he seemed to be gaining a degree of momentum. "We came in from Camp Carroll in trucks at night. I remember the blackness and the dust and the sounds."

Hammaker knew he was leading his own witness but was confident Vanasdalin wouldn't have the heart to object. "Were you mortared and rocketed at Khe Sanh?"

"Every day."

"Conditions were bad?"

"Yes."

"People were dying, and the living were breaking?"

"Yes."

"And a helicopter crashed while it was landing with supplies?"

"Yes."

"And you went out into the open to help the pilots, didn't you?"

"Yes." Christy's responses were becoming steadier. Perhaps an open-ended question now.

"What happened then?" Hammaker asked.

"I was hit by a mortar round."

"Were you knocked unconscious?"

"No, but I couldn't move, I couldn't talk, and I could barely breath."

"Where did they put you?"

"They put me—"

"It's all right, Deric. If you can't—"

With unexpected urgency, the words gushed from Christy's mouth like water from an open faucet. "They thought I was dead. They put me with the dead. They ran out of body bags and were stacking us behind the sandbags. I was there with Zimmerman and Byers. I remember their eyes so clearly."

"Did you try to call out?"

"Desperately."

"And what happened to the dead?"

"We were airlifted out in a cargo net."

"And what do you see in your memories?"

"The rope net."

There it was. In a few words Deric had said what he hadn't been able to say for twenty years. The net that oppressed him was revealed, exposed for what it was, a repressed memory of a horrendous event.

Hammaker stood silently, hopefully. No matter what the outcome of this manufactured trial, it had brought Deric's past into the open; perhaps he could finally find a pathway to healing.

Peterson stood, his big hands trembling, tears streaming in the crevices of his face. "I'm so sorry, Esquire," he said, stepping forward. "I didn't know until it was too late."

"I know," said Christy gently.

"We took Khe Sanh," Peterson told the students. "We took it and we held it and we won there. We died there. Then they made us give it up. For nothing. That's all we meant to our government, our people. Nothing. To the day I die, I'm ashamed I fought in that damn War."

The room lay silent for a long time.

Finally Turczynski cleared his throat and looked pleadingly at Vanasdalin. "I don't think any more questions would be in order. Do you, Dave?"

Peterson gave Vanasdalin a look that would not permit him to say a word, and perhaps Vanasdalin had already made up his mind. "No questions."

* * *

Vanasdalin's closing statement was effective but anticlimactic. He emphasized personal responsibility and reminded the jury of Scarbrough's inconvenient comparisons between Vietnam veterans and gang members. "If we absolve one, we absolve them all," he concluded.

Hammaker began his closing somberly. He focused on Christy's experience at Khe Sanh, crafting images of half-naked rotting corpses stacked like cordwood; the smell, taste, and feel of death all around; a horribly wounded man, unable to distinguish himself from the dead, being loaded into a cargo net like some commodity, a carpet, or a log; the man hauled hundreds of feet into the sky with fallen comrades crushed against his body and his face; lifeless arms and legs batting against his own; fluid running into his nose and mouth; and those horrible ropes against which he clawed and clawed.

Hammaker glanced at Christy. He stared blank-faced in Scarbrough's direction but not really at her. He took a deep breath.

"When he arrives home," Hammaker said, "Deric tries hard to pretend he's the same man he was before the War, but he knows he is not. Still the net comes upon him in his waking hours and in his sleep. His only relief comes in inventing distractions capable of generating the exhilaration of a battle in Vietnam. And so, he came to challenge the police to catch him in the sale of marijuana.

"Did he know right and wrong when the net overtook him? Would you?"

Hammaker's voice lowered to a whisper. "Remember that in 1972, no one welcomed Deric Christy home," he said. "Welcome him home now."

Hammaker sat dignified beside Christy, proud to share the space. His hardened features seemed prepared to accept whatever judgment followed with the unshakable knowledge that his cause was just.

<hr />

While the students deliberated, Scarbrough went outside, hoping the cool night air would ease her swollen emotions. Christy and Vanasdalin followed. None spoke, but each seemed completely aware and utterly respectful of the others' presence. All three were so absorbed that none noticed the angular figure leaning against a parked gray sedan.

Flanked by Gerry Ramírez, Don Sage rested on the fender.

"Now there's a pretty picture," Sage said, wearing a cagey, self-satisfied grin. His steel-colored tooth shimmered in the light of the streetlamp.

Scarbrough flinched. Vanasdalin pivoted cautiously, assessing the newcomer. Peterson exited the doorway. He appeared to size up the situation and then lowered his head and began making his way to the far side the newcomers. "How . . .?" gasped Scarbrough.

"Got a look at your notes," Sage said. "You really should password protect."

"You—"

"You make a nice speech, Professor." Sage dangled an earplug and cord from his thumb. "But your little book does hang around your neck like an albatross."

Seriousness overtook Sage's face. He swept his hand at Christy. "Come on Mister Johnson. We got some catching up to do."

"You can't force him to go with you," Scarbrough said.

She suddenly felt dizzy and the quick, quirky movements that followed made her head spin. Sage took a step toward Christy. Vanasdalin wheeled into the agent's path and knocked his chair hard against the agent's knees. As Sage crumpled in pain, Peterson loomed behind Ramírez and took him by the shoulder.

Christy slipped away from the scuffle.

Scarbrough flattened her hands on a bicycle rack to steady herself. When she looked up, Sage was rubbing his knees. He straightened with a grimace and pointed at Peterson, who had one arm on Ramírez's shoulder and was reaching another in Sage's direction. "Just stay out of it, Godzilla," Sage said, waggling a finger. "Hey, Johnson, like to see your nephew?"

Nearly around the corner of the building, Christy halted and turned stiffly.

"I have him."

"How?" Christy breathed.

"Just like I have you. Lock, stock and barrel, body and soul."

Christy came back to squarely face the agent. Sage's tooth flashed menacingly. Christy held an open palm up to Peterson. "Easy, Arnie."

Peterson loosened his grip on Ramírez.

"Look here," said Vanasdalin. "You people haven't identified yourselves. We're witnesses to what amounts to assault and battery."

"That the way you would like to play it, Johnson?" Sage said.

Christy turned away. "It's all right, everyone. I'm among friends." He padded across the macadam and, with Sage's ushering, slid into the back seat of the sedan. Sage hurried around the other side, and Ramírez took the driver's seat.

Hammaker emerged from the door with Turczynski and the student who had questioned Scarbrough at his side. Both men's heads were low; Hammaker's hands hung loosely in his pants pockets.

"The verdict?" Christy said, rolling down the window.

"Guilty, I'm afraid," Turczynski said.

"Oh my God," Scarbrough said.

The young woman spoke. "We thought Mister Hammaker was a terrific lawyer, and his arguments were very powerful. But we just couldn't acquit Deric. Like Mister Vanasdalin said, if we did, we'd have to acquit every drug dealer who grew up on a hard city street."

An even-handed smile crept across Deric's face. He looked somewhat pleased, somewhat mortified, somewhat ambivalent, and somewhat alive.

Scarbrough's mind and body reeled. Nothing had changed. The world wasn't softer than in 1972; it was no more understanding, no saner. Everything was the same, abounding idiocy, crushing intolerance, cold rhetoric disguised as logic surmounting truth and compassion, and asinine justifications masking cruel oppression. Deric Christy would not be regarded as a symbol; he was merely another victim, pulverized by a society unwilling to make fundamental changes in its warped and decaying fabric.

Abruptly, Scarbrough bent forward as if she were hit by an invisible attacker, her shoulders arcing toward the ground. Liquid bled through her linen pants, between her legs.

"Oh my God," she sobbed, cradling her stomach as she crumpled. "Oh my God."

Chapter thirty-four

The air was heavy and the sky was dark when Ashford arrived at the NCO club. He spent the last hour on the phone in Operations trying, without success, to learn the whereabouts of the boy who called himself Brandon. Under the dispersant glow of an electric light bulb, Spencer threw darts with a group of enlisted men. Spencer asked Ashford to join them.

"Just imagine the bull's-eye is Harker's nose," said Trent. He hunched at the bar over a shot of clear alcohol: vodka or rum. Bathed in blue light, his jaw showed a good three days' growth.

"Hear anything about the kid?" Spencer said, joining the pilots.

"Nothing," said Ashford. "I'm not even sure where they have him. Nobody at the DEA seems to know anything."

"Not that they'll admit," Spencer said.

"I felt helpless when they took him. It was the same as with Shoopie. I wish there were something—"

"The kids know the risks. They get caught, they gotta pay the piper. They know how it is."

"But there was something about this kid. Like he's being corrupted."

"We've all been corrupted," said Trent, draining the shot. Trent glared over his shoulder at an oscillating fan on a stand in the corner of the room. The blades rattled in their cage, and the motor bounced lightly on its base.

In the next few seconds, Trent's shadow-swept face seemed as if it were passing through time, first barreling toward youth and then suddenly reversing direction and overshooting the present, hurling him somewhere past the dark reaches of oblivion. His features were reacting to an unexpected presence, a face from the long-ago past.

Major Paul Olofson stood before the pilots, clothed in dress greens, favoring his injured torso. He wore his coat open and the black tie loose around his neck, and his shirt was damp with sweat. Ashford gasped.

"Chief," Olofson said, nodding respectfully at Trent. "Oh, sorry, I heard you don't go by that tag anymore."

"What are you doing here?" Trent said.

"I'm not sure exactly. This little adventure started a couple weeks ago when a young lieutenant visited me. He asked me questions about the 162nd in Vietnam. He asked what happened at Ba Long. And he asked about you."

Trent's gaze penetrated Ashford but quickly released him as insignificant, and it was drawn back to Olofson.

"I've been limping around for twenty years, telling myself I'd forgotten it," Olofson said. "But I hadn't. His visit made that clear. So I started digging."

"Into what?" Trent said.

"The past."

Trent arched over his drink. His lower lip jutted forward in a pout; his fingers touched the tumbler but did not lift it. "What did you find?" Trent's voice carried the trace of a shudder, his tone invited no answer.

"About Ba Long, nothing. So I moved to the other end of the chain of events. Started looking into what happened at Wellspring and Stray Wolf. I never knew because I was all shot to hell."

"Paul, I'm not sure—"

"Remember before we departed from Vigilance Base Camp, in Harker's briefing, he never gave us the tactical report for Wellspring?"

"I remember." Trent's eyes flared.

"And he sent the VNAFs in first, remember that?"

Trent nodded.

"One of them was blown from the sky," Olofson said.

"Heat seeker," Trent whispered.

"And the other, who pulled us out after we crashed—"

"Didn't make it either."

"That's what I found. There's someone I want you to meet." Olofson stepped to his side. Behind him appeared a man with a rugged face anchoring a widow's peak, a rising shock of blood-red hair. A look of fervent reluctance lay over the man's features like a mask; he stooped in a cowering slouch. His name tag bore the inscription *Bender*, but Trent didn't look at it. The red hair was his focus, and the sight of it seemed to draw something from the dark corners of his soul—something old, something powerful, something dangerous.

"This is Master Sergeant Bender," Olofson said. "He was a medic with the 115th Medical Detachment on special assignment in Vietnam. I found him at Fort Eustis, Virginia."

"Stray Wolf," Trent said. "You were at Stray Wolf."

Bender's yellow eyes quivered in their sockets.

"You treated the VNAF." There was no question in Trent's intonation, only a statement to be acknowledged as bitter truth. "He was alive, wasn't he? When you left him. The VNAF. He was alive."

As Trent shifted position, the colored bar lights played red across his face. Suddenly he was the Devil, standing erect over the terrified master sergeant, face blazing with fiery demons, demanding its due and claiming retribution.

Bender nodded shamefully. A wisp of red hair fell over his forehead as he lowered it.

"And you dumped him out of the medevac bird?"

Bender cupped his head in his hands. "I was following orders," he said, his voice stale and toneless.

Trent's voice gathered wrath and potency. "Who gave the order?" Trent took Bender by the shoulder, turning him so he could not escape the penetrating eyebeams of his fierce interrogator.

"Captain Harker," Bender said, as Trent nodded knowingly.

"You never disobeyed an order?"

Bender's eyes rolled upwards. "Never in my twenty-five years, Chief."

With sudden violence, Trent's fist shot from his shoulder. Bender held his face still, as if welcoming a deserved oncoming blow. But Trent's fist swept wide of Bender's face, and he reeled with the force of his swing. His spin ended with his face to the circular fan, and without hesitation, he assaulted it brutally. He caught the round wire cage in his fingertips and flung it to the ground. The fan clattered, the blades continuing to spin wildly. Trent brought his hand down squarely on the motor, but the metal blades continued to turn.

Spencer leapt to his feet. He yanked the plug from its socket and went to Trent. He touched Trent's shoulder, and Trent straightened suddenly, as if released from the throes of an epileptic fit. He pointed a bloody finger at Bender.

"Don't call me Chief," Trent said with cold fury.

Ashford had also moved to restrain Trent, but he saw there was nothing left to restrain. As quickly as bitterness and rage consumed him, Trent suppressed them again; they lay dormant like embers inside a lump of coal, ready to flare against an unlucky wind. Trent stood formidably against the world, a camp unto himself, untouched and untouchable.

Something surfaced in Ashford too; Trent had revealed something to him, a thing Ashford had suspected but had never overtly seen. Hidden under layers of crust and sarcasm and put-on malevolence, Trent nursed an old and grievous wound, guarded by a moat of pure anger. And for the first time Ashford completely understood that Trent's wrath wasn't directed at him; it merely included him by virtue of the rank he held. To Trent, he was as insignificant as the dust on the bar lights. But for all Ashford's realizations, he also felt the danger increased, the ante upped; he had glimpsed a ray of madness in Trent's eyes. It was beyond anything he had ever seen before and seemed contained for the moment only by force of will. The stress of that repression was a fearful thing too, but most terrifying of all was the stealth and calculation in Trent's manner and in his eyes, divisiveness of a sort that told Ashford that this was far from over.

●—●-————-●-●●-●-●-————————●-●

Trent disappeared from the barroom. Olofson took Bender aside and consoled him over drinks. Ashford set a bottle of beer before Spencer and pulled a chair close and spoke in a somber tone.

"Do you know what happened at Ba Long?" Ashford said.

Spencer shook his head.

Ashford blew a long breath. "At one time I thought Trent was responsible. I thought it must have been an accident and that it was what's been eating at him."

Spencer gave a knowing and sad smile. "Nick Trent has his ghosts, but they're not the villagers of Ba Long. Remember I said if you got me drunk, I'd tell you the story about the Phase Bird?"

Ashford said he remembered.

"Well, I'm not drunk, but this might quiet your imagination. The last few weeks in Vietnam, things were nasty. Real downright ugly. All of us felt like we were soaked in the filthiest sludge you can imagine. Like we weighed a thousand pounds.

"I'm down on the ground, see. Marine infantry. My squad's caught in crossfire in a minefield. I see my best friend take a bullet in the head and then disappear in a cloud of dust. Four more of us buy it in that field before we get into the tree line. When we get there, we're confused, real confused. We're eighteen-year-olds remember, even younger than you are, and we had M-16s and M-60s, and we had just looked in death's eyes. There was no telling what we'd do next.

"We come on a little rice paddy village, probably not even on the map. Our lieutenant's dead, we got no direction, and we're ready for some retribution. We shoot at animals, buildings, and the sky. We're getting ourselves worked into a frenzy, pretty much knowing we're psyching ourselves to put some serious hurt on the villagers. We got them huddled in a ditch.

"Just when we're about to be swept away in a tide of madness, this chopper appears in the sky. It lands sideways right between us and the villagers. When the dust dies down, we look up and there's a gunner with his M-60 machine gun pointed right at us. Then out of the cockpit steps Nick Trent.

"He comes over and talks to us, real nice, like he knows what we've been through, where we're coming from. He says he can sympathize, but he won't let us hurt no one. He's firm on that. Very firm. He tells us about Lieutenant Rusty Calley, how screwed up he is because of what he did. He says there's some things aren't part of the War, some lines you can't cross and hold your head up after. He tells us about evil and that that's the land we're about to enter.

"Last of all, he says if we're dead set on razing the village, we'll have to shoot him and his crew first, because he won't stand to see women and children killed.

"Nick evacuated me along with some of the villagers we hurt. After that's when I flew with him last couple weeks in the Nam."

"Major Olofson told me about that part too," Ashford said.

Spencer grunted reservedly. "I meant to say you got some big balls tracking him down."

Ashford stammered. "The Phase Bird was the chopper Trent landed in the village?"

"Couple coats of paint, few hundred new parts, she's still the same bird. When I got back to the States after the War, I read about Lieutenant Rusty Calley and what happened at My Lai. A few times, I imagined myself back at that village, except Nick Trent never shows up, and I'm there smashing heads with my gun and shooting the stomachs out of children.

"But I can just put those thoughts out of my head, because for me it never happened that way, and in those moments I kiss the Phase Bird and get down on my knees and thank the God that lives for Nick Trent."

"Why's he so different?" Ashford whispered.

"Ain't none of us the same, LT," Spencer said. "There's none of us the same."

PART V
BA LONG

Chapter thirty-five

Chicken Licken was a modest diner tucked against the southeast corner of the Indiantown Gap military reservation. Despite its proximity to an interstate highway, most of the clientele were generally military personnel. Recently renovated, the dining room was bright and open, lined with wide-framed windows that permitted natural radiance to overpower the interior fluorescence.

Dozens of uniformed men sat in wide booths. Ashford, Trent, Spencer, and Olofson selected a table near the kitchen counter, and Harker and Tarsavage occupied a booth on the window side of the dining room.

A plump waitress in a pink uniform emerged from the kitchen and deposited steaming cups of coffee on the table. She wiped her hands on her lace apron, and she looked at Trent for a long moment, before she turned to go. Ashford recalled her face—she was one of the women with whom Trent had flirted at the NCO Club.

"Way things are going," said Ashford, "we'll probably have time to kill again this afternoon." With only a few days left of annual training, Harker had declared that their crew would stay at Indiantown Gap for the remainder rather than returning to AP Hill. "Any suggestions for something to do?"

"Haven't done slings yet," Trent said.

Ashford didn't need to feign surprise, but he exaggerated his gestures modestly for effect. "Mister Trent, are you actually making a constructive contribution?"

Trent's lips formed an amused smile. "I can be a bundle of surprises."

"Sling loads sound like a good idea. What can we haul?"

Trent said there were culverts in a field on the east end of the runway; great cement pipes, about eighteen hundred pounds each.

Ashford regarded the warrant officer. "Okay, slings it is."

Spencer leaned forward. "Anyone hear about Jay Zee?"

"Captain Zuckerman?" Ashford said.

"That's the guy. Harker's crew chief said that Jay Zee decided to supervise the NBC training after you left."

"Hope no one got hurt."

"Jay Zee was the first one. He was running around camp in full protective gear bloviating about Soviet chemical and biological weapons. Got himself so worked up he collapsed from heat exhaustion."

Trent rolled his eyes. Ashford asked if the captain were all right.

"They had him in the hospital a few days. Still pumping fluid into his system. And guess who they put in charge of Company B?"

"Don't keep us in suspense," said Trent.

"Lieutenant Dickson. My friend said he's been following LT Ashford's acclimatization schedules to a tee."

Ashford smiled. The waitress appeared again, this time balancing three plates heaped with breakfast entrees. As she passed the pilots' table, she giggled and winked. She deposited the plates before Harker and Tarsavage and returned for orders. Ashford detected more body language passing between Trent and the waitress, a swish, a dip, a nod; the movements seemed to be messages disguised in content but not for the fact of their exchange.

Ashford watched the waitress return to the kitchen. He felt a vague anxiety, as if he were the brunt of a joke beyond his comprehension. The waitress exchanged a few words with a gaunt black cook hunched over a grill, with his back to the customers. When the man turned, Ashford recognized Shoopie.

Ashford cast discrete glances at Harker and Tarsavage and then back at Shoopie. Ashford recalled how Shoopie had bragged about adding foreign ingredients to Army food. Harker bit down on a huge spoonful of home fries. Ashford imagined the colonel leaping to his feet, grasping his throat, and his face turning blue, the deadly consequence of ingesting some exotic poison. Instead, Harker's mouth turned upwards in a half-moon crescent, and he gouged deep into the potatoes.

Ashford glanced back at Shoopie; he had the feeling that Shoopie knew he was there but wouldn't acknowledge his presence. "You see Shoopie back there?" Ashford said.

"I talked to him last night," Spencer said. "They convened a board the instant he got back. Washed him out straight away. He's planning to head to Arkansas to live with his aunt. He said he'll work short-order until he saves enough money for the trip. He's taking it pretty hard."

"Guess the colonel doesn't know who's fixing his chow."

"Speaking of Harker," said Trent, "he told Operations he wants to get some flight time with our group this afternoon. He wants to take the Savage on a training mission."

Ashford looked at the colonel, almost wishing Shoopie had put poison in his breakfast. "Terrific," he said.

After they had eaten, Trent and Spencer excused themselves, leaving Ashford and Olofson to finish their coffee. Trent dropped a ten-dollar bill on the table, waiving off Spencer's objection. In the parking lot, Trent opened the passenger door of his pickup truck for Spencer. "Remember what we talked about, Reggie?"

"I remember."

"The Phase Bird in shape?"

"I need to make some adjustments, but it'll fly."

"What about your maintenance crew?"

"I gave them the whole day off."

"I know you have a problem with this Reggie, but it's something I have to do. The Phase Bird is the only helicopter on the reservation I can take up without anyone knowing."

"I know."

"You heard what Bender said—Harker murdered the VNAF pure and simple. And I think I know why now. I must've been too blind or stupid to put it together back then. It started at Vigilance Base Camp. Harker didn't brief tactical for Wellspring. Know why? Because it was hot."

"You're not suggesting—"

"Hear me out. I clearly remember how he told us to hang back on the approach, to let the VNAFs take the lead on the way in. Reggie, he was trying to eliminate the VNAFs."

"Why?"

"Because one or both of them knew something. Some dirty little secret Harker wanted buried with them." Trent recounted how the young Vietnamese pilot had told him Harker had promised the two VNAFs transportation out of Vietnam and how out-of-character that was for Harker. He said it only made sense if one or both of the VNAFs knew something Harker didn't want the world to know, and what if that something Harker was covering up was his own personal involvement in the Massacre at Ba Long? "It's burned in my gut for twenty years that I left that VNAF behind," Trent said. "I even remember his name, clear as day."

"Le Song," Spencer said faintly. "He saved my life too."

"You need to back out, tell me now."

Spencer's eyes focused on the intensity in Trent's face, the absolute and terrible resolution. How strange the once knowing and compassionate face had become, contorted under the strain of an insufferable burden. Deep lines marred the previously smooth cheeks of the brave and noble warrant officer, who twenty years ago insinuated a Huey between a band of unhinged warriors and a terrified flock of helpless Vietnamese villagers, saving those people from their deaths and rescuing Spencer from his own self-destruction. How close Spencer had come to the fate that had befallen Trent, the eternity of second-guessing and self-castigation. How different he would be too if he had only a villain to blame for his personal demise rather than a savior to thank for his deliverance.

"I'm with you," Spencer said. God, he thought. He really is crazy.

Chapter thirty-six

The electronic grating of sliding iron bars jolted Rayful Bigelow from his fitful sleep into a terrified stupor. Sweat burned under his clenched eyelids, and he swept his forearms across his face defensively. Visions of Jorge Munzo darted into his consciousness and then disappeared in a swirling haze, as if the monster lurked in the dark reaches of the cell, ready to emerge to plunge a cold steel shank deep into his shivering chest.

When Bigelow mustered the courage to pry open his eyelids, before him he saw two uniformed guards.

"What's the matter with you, Scrounger?" one said.

"Uh, nothing." Bigelow slid his feet off the mattress and pivoted with the momentum, apathetically permitting it to carry him to a slumped sitting position.

"Well get up, asshole," the other guard said. "You're out of here."

"Huh?"

"Your bail got lowered, and some gray suit showed up to pay."

"A lawyer?"

"How should I know?"

Bigelow lurched to his feet. He was finally being set free. But joy quickly surrendered to doubt; who, after all, was his benefactor? He knew no lawyers or anyone else with the cash to pay a bondsman except, of course, Cruise. Perhaps his moody business associate had finally come to appreciate his importance. The alternative was too frightening to consider.

The guards roughly ushered Bigelow down the rows of man-cages and through a series of double-locked gates. In the intake area, they closed a wooden door behind him. Bigelow found his crumpled street clothes set in a pile on a narrow bench. Another pile of clothes was stacked along the opposite wall, and the pile was more neatly folded for some other lucky stiff. Bigelow resisted the temptation to exchange shirts.

He finished dressing quickly and started for the door; he didn't wish to allow time for anyone to change their mind or for Zackaeus to get word of his departure. When Bigelow pulled the door open, he stood face-to-face with the creature of his nightmares.

"S'up, Scrounger," Jorge Munzo said. "Going somewhere?"

Bigelow's hands nervously tucked his shirttail into his trousers and made another trip around his waistline. "Getting out," he said, sputtering. "How about you?"

Munzo's murderous eyes glowed. "S'it look like?"

Bigelow didn't care to say. He moved past Munzo, down the long bright corridor, toward a freedom that was becoming increasingly uneasy. He stepped quickly but while shuffling his feet. He couldn't stop now; he was not often lucky enough to have a head start, and to squander it under the circumstances could be deadly.

"Scrounger," Munzo's voice taunted from a distance.

Bigelow froze, his heart thumping in his throat, his back still to Munzo. "Yes?" he croaked.

"See you on the outside."

Sage held a thick door open to the castle-like facility of the National Guard headquarters in downtown Harrisburg, where higher echelons had secretly lent the DEA space from which to direct Operation Nature Grow. He ushered Deric Christy inside, and they descended a stairway into the basement. They moved down a dark, damp corridor webbed with insulated pipes, and they entered a musty locker room.

Brandon Christy lay sleeping on a wood-framed cot. Agent Gerry Ramírez sat on a chair beside the boy, an open magazine propped on his thigh. He was positioned so a thin beam of light leaking around a pulled window shade illuminated the pages. The light also collected on Bran's cheek, lending an angelic quality to the boy's face.

Deric stood perfectly still in the doorway; he felt as if his blood were freezing solid in his veins and his sinews were transforming to iron. Although he had exposed the net, although he had come so far, although he was pressing with all his might to go further, and although he recalled his promise to his sister, he still seemed unable to transcend the distance between himself and the boy.

"We brought him here after he was picked up," Sage whispered. "No cops involved. We haven't entered him into the system yet."

"Will you?" Deric asked.

"That, my friend, depends on you."

Deric understood the rules for this game well; he had been an unwilling participant for many years. Between Sage's words was an invitation, bolstered by menace. This time the threat was not to Deric's own person but to someone more sacred. Christy knew the impassioned agent wouldn't rest until he had his Soldier Man back; until he controlled him again like some marionette swinging from a tangle of strings; and until Deric reentered the seamy world of the Drexlers, collected their dark secrets, and revealed them to the DEA.

From the safety of distance, Deric watched Bran's open mouth and his half-drawn breaths. The boy slept lightly, warily, in the way hard experience teaches one to sleep. The way he himself slept. Deric felt a gnawing urge to reach out to him, to be his uncle, his big brother, or perhaps even a father figure. He lacked the right qualifications, but if circumstances were different, he might have tried.

But circumstances were not different, and Deric sensed an unwholesome relief in that fact. He could see that the pathway Sage had paved for Bran's salvation would put him on his own trail back to darkness. But the gloom was at least familiar, lending it a degree of comfort.

"You'll really let him go?" said Christy.

"You have my word."

"No empty promises? Not like me?"

"His is a much less complicated case. Like I said, he's not in the system. Far as I'm concerned, it never happened. Come with me now, and he walks free."

Sage's answer was not wholly satisfying. Deric knew that to Sage, the difficulty of Bran's case or whether Bran had been processed by the criminal justice system, mattered little. If Sage wanted the boy, he would pursue him to the ends of the earth.

"How do I know?" Deric peered into the agent's intense eyes.

"It's not him I want. I only want you."

Deric nodded at Sage's bluntness. It was true. Sage had no reason to prosecute Bran or conscript him into a deplorable life of an informant. His zeal burned unfailingly in a single direction, a direction that pointed to Washington, D.C. and the sinister shadows of Hamilton Place.

"Can I have some time?"

"That I can't do, Deric. The Drexlers have already had too long to steam over your two-week absence from D.C. It'll take us a couple days to invent some kind of story to explain it and put corroboration in place. If there's any chance of pulling it off, it's now or never."

Deric looked at Brandon. "Can I talk to him?"

"If you want to."

After thinking about it for a moment, Deric said perhaps it would be better if he did not, and he turned to retrace his steps into the daylight. He was, after all, keeping his promise to his sister. In his own way.

* * *

As he pulled away from the headquarters building in his dusty gray sedan with his Soldier Man at his side, Sage nodded furtively to a man relaxing on a bench in a tree-shaded park across the street. The man wore a poplin sports coat. Under the lapel, barely visible, was a silver badge hanging on a lanyard.

When the sedan disappeared from sight, CAN Officer Stuart Zackaeus rose on cue and entered the headquarters building to conscript his newest and youngest informant.

Chapter thirty-seven

The afternoon sling load training mission didn't begin well for Ashford. He stood fireguard for Trent outside a Huey. The igniters clicked, the engine moaned, and the rotor blades began their laborious first turn, but they faltered, and the engine faded. Ashford approached the pilot door, and Trent reported a hot start, a condition that would ground the Huey for inspection and repairs.

"I'll get keys for a spare helicopter," Ashford said.

"No spare available today," said Trent. "I checked with Operations. Besides, I've got a splitting headache. Why don't you tag along with the colonel. Could be instructive." Trent's tone was infected with the usual derision.

Ashford glanced at the running Huey several parking pads to the east. It was a specialized helicopter fitted with high frequency radios to serve a command-and-control function. An unusual wire antenna ran the length of the tail boom, folding on itself like a suture.

Ashford's eyes picked out Harker's dour countenance peering inquisitively over the instrument panel. Tarsavage sat beside him beating his hands against an unfolded map in an effort to tame its folds. Trent remained in the lifeless Huey. He rubbed an eye between his finger and thumb.

Ashford collected his flight gear and boarded the cargo area of the command-and-control Huey. He plugged his mike cord into the intercom system and explained the delay and Trent's absence from the flight, bringing a self-satisfied grin to Harker's lips.

They were obtaining clearance to hover, when Reggie Spencer unexpectedly approached from the right front. He carried his flight gear and a large canvas sack stuffed with gear. Spencer paused beside the pilot's window, and Harker keyed his mike to allow Spencer's words to be carried into the intercom system.

"Headquarters requests Brenneman return immediately," Spencer said, tilting his head toward the crew chief. "Something about an evaluation of Company B's supply paperwork."

"Yes, yes," Harker said, arching his eyebrows at the general as if to say he were on top of such matters. "By all means. Hear that Sergeant?"

With a bewildered shrug, the disenfranchised crew chief gathered his gear, and Spencer offered to serve as crew chief in substitution.

Harker paused, his eyes lingering on the angled flashlight protruding from the pocket of Spencer's flight vest. "By all means," he said.

With impressive gestures, Harker brought the Huey to a less impressive hover. Following the Huey piloted by Winston and Morrow, he repositioned at a high hover to a grassy field on the east end of the runway. Among platoons of thick weeds, various items of impotent war junk had found their final resting place: the rusted-out hull of a truck, a disabled tank, and an aged artillery piece.

Several large cement culverts rested on a rise, great segments of pipe, about eight feet in length and three feet in circumference, large enough for a man to crawl through. The weight of each presented a substantial encumbrance for a Huey already burdened with a full load of fuel.

Harker set the skids aground beside a culvert. Spencer leapt to the earth. Expertly, he threaded the thick fabric straps of a sling through the center of the culvert and attached the sling's metal receptacle to the cargo hook beneath the Huey.

When he boarded the helicopter, Spencer rigged himself into a monkey harness, a collection of straps attached to a cord, like the tether for an astronaut. He attached the harness to the metal bulkhead. Then he lay on the floor and leaned over the edge. He was positioned on the opposite side of the bulkhead from Ashford, who could only see him by leaning toward the cockpit.

"Load's ready," said Spencer. "Is the cargo hook armed?"

Harker flicked a switch on the overhead console and a yellow bulb illuminated.

"Lieutenant," Harker said, "know when we disarm the hook?"

"The hook needs to be armed anytime we're below three hundred feet in case we have to jettison the load quickly," Ashford said. "Above three hundred feet we can disarm the hook so the load isn't jettisoned inadvertently."

"Roger," Harker said. "Pre-takeoff check?"

Tarsavage answered the check, and Harker raised the collective until the Huey drifted to a hover.

"Drift three feet back, and you'll be centered over the load," Spencer said, still spread on the floor.

Under Harker's control, the Huey swelled, until the sling beneath it pulled taut; Ashford could feel the Huey straining to hoist the load. Finally, the helicopter began an arduous climb, wobbling with the oscillation of its load.

"Winston up?" Harker asked.

"Up with a load," Spencer said.

"Roger. Let's head for the Northern Training Area."

———————————

After Ashford boarded the command-and-control Huey, Trent gathered his flight gear, closed up the grounded Huey, and headed to the parking lot. There, seated at the wheel of Trent's pickup, was Paul Olofson, awaiting the arrival of his teacher and coconspirator.

Silently they drove off the post, through the Gap, and deep into the forests that comprised the floor of the Northern Training Area. Trent pointed to a wooden signpost, and Olofson turned down a narrow dirt lane, weaving among the tall evergreens.

The lane ended in an open field. The Phase Bird was parked in the center of the meadow, the only unmonitored helicopter on the military reservation. Although it wasn't due to be restored to flying condition for another three days, at Trent's direction, Spencer had sent his crews into the barracks to sleep, and he had worked late into the night reassembling various parts, adjusting safeties and tensions, readying the machine for a clandestine flight. That morning, the master sergeant had put on the final touches.

Trent pulled a roll of duct tape from his flight bag. He stretched the tape over the identification numbers on both sides of the Phase Bird and on the nose. With a can of black spray paint and a stencil, he painted the numbers 69-00559 on the tail and nose.

They were the identification numbers of Harker's command-and-control Huey.

———————————

The command-and-control Huey cut through the gorge at Indiantown Gap. The Northern Training Area spread wide before it; the Huey containing Winston and Morrow could be seen in the turn, following at Winston's usual generous distance.

Spencer's voice resonated on the intercom. "Colonel you can fly with your finger on the hook release button while the hook is disabled," he said, "but remember that under three hundred feet, the cargo hook's armed. You need to keep that finger back. Mister Trent says it's best to practice that while you're at altitude."

"Yes, of course," Harker said. In a movement that appeared an involuntary response to Spencer's admonition, Harker's fingers unwrapped from around the lower handle of the cyclic control, the location of the cargo release button.

For an hour, they worked the slings out of Landing Zone Kim on the western edge of Broad Mountain. They set up an oval traffic pattern and practiced landings and takeoffs, dropping the rigging after landing and re-rigging the culvert and hoisting it into the pattern again. Each time they turned crosswind, Ashford observed Harker's keen interest in his house that was under construction at the base of the mountain; Ashford recalled his first flight with Crawford when he had seen the colonel hovering illegally near the house.

"Sir, fuel's getting pretty near reserve," Ashford said as they ascended into their seventh pattern.

"Chalk Two, this is Chalk One. Heading back to Indiantown Gap," Harker transmitted.

Then Harker keyed the intercom and said they would be taking a slight detour. As the Huey cleared the trees, Harker lowered the collective and allowed it to settle down the side of the mountain, closer and closer to the site of his new home. Beaming with pride, Harker described to Tarsavage the progress of the construction.

The radio clicked twice with static, although no one spoke.

Spencer said, "Colonel, watch that finger—"

The Huey lurched and then ballooned, relieved of a great burden.

"Lost the load," Spencer said.

"What?" Harker said.

"You jettisoned the load," Spencer repeated. "Must have bumped the hook release with your little finger."

Harker lifted his face to the illuminated yellow globe on the overhead console; the cargo hook was still armed. "I most certainly did not," he said, as if stating an absolute. He cleared his throat, forgetting to unkey the mike, and toyed with the cyclic, until he seemed satisfied the culvert was no longer beneath him. "Well, let's find it."

"It'd take days in these trees," Spencer said.

"Fuel's a little low to be monkeying with it now, Sir," said Ashford. Narrowing his eyes, Ashford leaned around the bulkhead and eyed Spencer inquisitively.

•—•—————•—••—•—————•—•

Landing Zone Custer lay on a low promontory at the end of Short Mountain. Less a landing zone than a fire break, the field contained blanched grass dotted with dark stumps and felled tree trunks set at odd angles, like scattered bones in a bone yard—good camouflage for a Huey. The field cut into the south side of the mountain and the trees were cleared from the fringe, permitting an unobstructed view of Broad Mountain's ridgeline and Landing Zone Kim. In Custer, Trent and Olofson sat patiently at the controls of the Phase Bird, keeping a vigil on the sling load training.

As the command-and-control chopper materialized from Landing Zone Kim, Trent watched it drop off the side of the mountain into the valley. He told Olofson that he knew Harker could not resist. His face was disdainfully blank as he listened to the two static reports on the FM radio, the signal from Spencer. Then a derisive smile swept across his face, a smile of power, the smile of an executioner.

Trent lifted the collective, climbing slowly from the cutout, and the sling beneath the Huey drew taut. Slowly, the culvert beneath them, which they had retrieved from a nearby abandoned construction site, cleared the treetops.

Trent dropped into the saddle between the mountain ridges. He skimmed along the base of Broad Mountain, banking with the curve of the contour. From this position of concealment, Trent watched the two other Hueys climbing and returning to Fort Indiantown Gap. Only one was burdened with a load, making it apparent that Spencer had done his job.

Trent dove off the mountainside, accelerating from sixty knots. He brought the culvert level with the ground, skimming ominously thirty feet above the earth. The Huey soared at Harker's house.

Level, aiming.

Trent pressed the cargo release button. A ton of rounded cement careened sideways in a free-falling, spinning slide. The mass struck the skeletal structure across the roof joists. Wood beams split and fell like bowling pins, and the house crumpled inward as if it were made of matchsticks.

On the road abutting the premises, a driver skidded to a stop, staring in astonishment at the dust rising out of the destruction. Trent pivoted the Huey on the mast. He hovered sideways toward the road, permitting the witness an unobstructed view of the phony tail number.

Olofson sat quietly throughout with a look of contentment upon his face. He was not only a silent witness but a willing accomplice.

Then Trent lifted the collective. The mission was complete. The time had come to return the Phase Bird to her berth in the woods, before anyone missed her.

After the command-and-control ship landed at Indiantown Gap, Harker didn't wait to squelch the engine. Without a word, he hopped from his seat and jogged into the flight facility. He moved like a man in a daze, as if he had been struck on the head. After a few seconds, Tarsavage followed.

As the rotor spun to a stop, Ashford turned to Spencer. "Reggie, what happened out there?" Ashford said.

"Like I said, Colonel dumped the load."

"No, he didn't. His hand wasn't on the release."

"You must be imagining things, LT." Spencer's tone seemed both pleading and apologetic.

"I'm not imagining anything. I watched him all the way, because you warned him. This is Trent, isn't it?"

Spencer met his stare with silence.

"Isn't it?" Ashford said. "You tripped the manual release, probably the one on the hook, with some kind of cord. And you did it for Trent, didn't you?"

Spencer lowered his head. "It was all my doing."

"Don't give me that. This has Trent's fingerprints all over it."

Spencer shook his head. "Nick took the morning off."

"Have it your way, Reggie. But I still think it's time I finally had a long talk with Mister Trent."

Chapter thirty-eight

In Harrisburg Hospital's newborn ward, Sage and Ramírez leaned against a glass barrier, watching an awkward-looking infant sheathed in a plastic box, her frail body decorated by snatches of adhesive tape and coils of clear tubing. A small tag on the incubator declared her name was Michelle Scarbrough. She was small and sickly. Until she opened her eyes, her only robust feature was the plentiful curly hair atop her tiny head. Then her eyes did open, and in those round, questioning orbs, Sage saw something burning, some inherited fire that quenched any doubt as to her survival.

They slipped past the nurses' station and located Scarbrough's room. She was awake but drifting. The sun held the left side of her face, magnifying the lines on her drawn features, highlighting the redness of her eyes. Sage arranged a bouquet of pastel-colored flowers on the bed stand, and Ramírez lingered at his heels.

"They didn't have any olive branches," Sage said, separating stems with his thumb.

"They're beautiful." Scarbrough fingered the flowers.

Their hands nearly touched, and then Sage retracted his with an unintended snap. "You're looking well. Doc said your daughter needs a little time in the hatchery."

"She's more beautiful than the flowers to me. As for myself, I've got wrinkles on the inside."

Sage paused, holding his breath and having exhausted his quota of small talk. "I know this may not be the right time, but time is something I haven't got. I need to speak candidly."

"Be my guest."

Sage's eyes skimmed the room in a professional manner. He extended his fingers and tapped Scarbrough's purse. "No tape recorder or anything?"

"I wasn't expecting you, or I might have been better prepared."

Sage offered a rapid flash of the false tooth. "No doubt of that. I uhm... set certain things in motion. Things that at the time seemed right, but... I have certain regrets. I want you to know I take no pleasure in this." There was a touch of irony in Sage's voice as he dropped a brown manila folder on the bed.

"What are you talking about?"

"Go on. Look. It's a police report. Your friend the counselor, what's his name, Turczynski. He was taken after your ambulance left Penn State."

Scarbrough thumbed rapidly through the pages. "Taken?"

"Seems he's a cannabis aficionado."

"You arrested him?" Scarbrough propped herself on her elbows, pushing her face toward Sage's.

"He was arrested. Local operation. Harrisburg's CAN unit handled it."

"The DEA arrested a small-town college professor and counselor for smoking a joint?"

"I told you, it was the locals. And it wasn't just a joint. We found enough in his house to classify as distribution weight."

"You searched his house?"

"Just hear me out. Hard part comes first. I have to tell you, I admire the way you played this. You've been a step ahead of me all the way. Way things were going, I had to deal myself some cards too."

"You think this is some game?" Scarbrough asked, her tone incredulous.

"I got Turczynski dead to rights. Under the drug forfeiture statutes, I can take his brownstone from him and his car and his doghouse to boot. I can do it right now. Just on the probable cause I've got in spades. No legal proceedings required."

"You said this is a local matter."

"I get involved when I have to. Point I'm trying to make is that the charges can be dropped. I never have to get involved."

"Bart would have no trouble retrieving his property in a court of law."

"Perhaps, but it'd take years. And what about his job? I can have him removed from the Vet Center and yanked from his job at the University."

"For smoking a joint?"

"We've got witnesses to say he's partied with vets at the Center. Not very smart. Then there are the criminal charges. With the weight we found in his house, I can send him away for a long vacation in a federal pen."

"Bastard."

"I told you. I take no pleasure in this."

"I don't believe that for a minute."

"I thought you'd say that. Thing is, I honestly came here to make peace."

"This is how you make peace?"

Sage rubbed his neck. "You got the drop on me and my Soldier Man, so I had to get the drop on you. I had to have a negotiating position."

"This is how you deal?"

"Uh-huh. I'll match your informant and raise you a counselor."

"Go screw."

Sage smiled with closed lips, holding the tooth in reserve. "Thought you'd say that too. You don't seem to mind if everyone around you gets torched, as long as you keep marching forward on your crusade like a tin soldier on overdrive."

"You're not making any sense."

"Manny Anderson would understand. Or that lawyer friend of yours, eight-finger Charlie who won't be playing the saxophone anymore. Oh yeah, I checked him out too. And I'm sure the counselor will get the message. As he's learning the hard way how not to take a shower in a federal penitentiary."

Scarbrough set her chin high. "It's all about change," she said. "That's what I represent and what you can't stand. You're painted into your little corner straining with all your might to protect what you have, the dirty little War that keeps you un-gainfully employed. The inertia you foster creates the suffering that accompanies positive change."

"What if that pain hits you square at home?" Sage dropped a second folder on the table.

Scarbrough flipped through the papers. Among them were several photographs, the first of a two-story whitewashed home with a bluish slate roof. Several other shots focused on the interior, particularly a corner of the hardwood floor. As she looked through the pictures, Scarbrough's eyes flamed, but her words came choked by horror.

"You had *my* house searched?"

"Locals had enough on Turczynski to search his house. And lo and behold, they found you were a guest there. It was enough to get a search warrant. They contacted LAPD and... you see the rest."

"You did this."

"If I'm ever asked again, I'll deny it. But like I said, I put things in motion. And more turned up than I ever expected. Dogs found a kilo of cocaine hydrochloride under the floorboards of your son's room."

"My God," Scarbrough gasped.

"Way I got it figured, that's what your son died for. Probably ripped off the local gang kids, and they came calling."

Scarbrough clutched at her ears. "Liar!" she shouted. "You planted drugs in my house!"

Sage wagged his head loosely. "I might have if I'd had to. But we both know the truth."

"Then you know I had no idea there were drugs in my house."

"Makes no difference to me."

"What are you saying?"

"I'm saying you have me, and I have you too, lady. Your personal property, your reputation, and your freedom. I can take it all. Then who'll take care of that little girl of yours?"

"You'll destroy me because of my son?"

Sage turned to the window and spread his hands in an exasperated gesture. "This isn't about your son," he said. "I don't get you, Professor. I can see you're from the school of hard knocks, just like me. You were brought up on the streets and went to Vietnam. What you've been through, you should be on my side. Save a child, shoot a drug dealer, doesn't that make sense to you anymore? You ask me, the War on Drugs hasn't been fought yet. Just give us the green light and get out of the way. We'll win the War."

"Grab 'em by the balls, and their hearts and minds will follow?"
Sage scratched his forehead. "Yeah, sort of like that."

"Bomb them back to the Stone Age?"

"Now you're talking."

"That's what they said in Vietnam. I thought that way once too, in Vietnam and on the streets of Los Angeles. But as both Wars dragged on, can't you see? You can't beat human misery out of people. When you oppress them, you only magnify it. People out there today are merely trying to cope with the meaninglessness of a society that holds out no hope for them."

Sage listened listlessly as Scarbrough spoke of new directions, of the children, and of her hopes for their futures. After a moment, he tuned out the substance of her words, and he only heard the passion and certitude that drove her. That was the part about her that fascinated him.

"What will it take?" Scarbrough said. "Self-immolations by people of conscience?"

Let 'em burn, Sage thought. What a bundle of misdirected talent she was. What a waste of precious human ambition and energy. How much this woman, this untamed spirit, could have accomplished with the right focus.

Growing impatient, Sage interrupted Scarbrough's monologue. "You just don't get it, do you? We're beyond a reason to be in the Drug War. We're in it. Look, Professor, Ruth. I'm trying to go easy here, but I have my own interests to protect. I didn't come after you, remember? You came gunning for me, so please don't lose sight of that. You invaded my world, and now maybe you see it for what it is. It's a hardball, everything-goes, free-for-all fight to death."

"You're nothing but a two-bit War criminal." Scarbrough bit her lip.

Ramírez stood at the far wall hanging his head, lolling it from side to side. "Let's get out of here, Don."

"What?" said Sage with astonishment.

"Leave her alone."

"Shut up, Gerry." Sage turned back to Scarbrough. "I'm offering you the chance to let this die. Just think about it. And I really do hope for the best for you and your daughter. It's all in your hands now. All you have to do is let go of my Soldier Man."

Scarbrough sat erect and watched Sage retreat toward the door. She felt a solitary tear rolling down her cheek, perhaps the last she had left. Still she wanted to recall it, to preserve her impenetrability, or at least the appearance. She wiped her cheek against her gown.

She knew she could defend herself in a court of law against any charges Sage could bring to bear; and perhaps she could reverse his efforts and use them to fuel her campaign with an element of martyrdom. But her crusade had already cost her infant daughter her health; the stress Scarbrough had placed on her body resulted in Michelle's severe malnutrition. And to defend herself against Sage's accusation, she would have to risk smearing the reputation of her other child, her lost boy, with the taint of a drug dealer— Preston's memory was the one sacrifice she was not willing to endure. Sage had cast the one stone she could not return.

But all was not yet lost. "Wait a minute," she called with restricted breath.

Sage caught the door with his heel and pushed it open slowly.

"Just you," Scarbrough said.

Sage shrugged at Ramírez and let the door close between them. He stood there looking gray and worn. The silver tooth was exposed, although it seemed lusterless and unthreatening.

"It's so wrong what you're doing," Scarbrough said.

"I told you—"

"I mean all of it. The whole ugly War."

"It's all I know how to do."

Scarbrough held her tongue. She wanted to tell him how violence begets violence; how he'd lost sight of the future and he was not the only one; how in our modern-day search for perfect virtual reality, we've lost touch with the human soul; how we only came to understand our mistakes in Vietnam ten years after it all was over; how much we could have done if only we'd seen the truth then; and how it was the same with the War on Drugs. An ocean of suffering could be drained if only we could just see the nose in front of our collective face.

But she knew her words would be wasted. Everything she had to say could be rephrased or characterized, refocused or ridiculed. Sage was a veteran at just that; he knew all the pat answers: how politically nothing could be done; how the road to hell is paved with good intentions; how people in the ghettos should be pulling themselves up by their own bootstraps; and how some do and why can't the rest of them, the millions that there are? No, there was no use beating her head against the giant collective brick wall. Those like Sage didn't understand logic or justice or virtue or compassion. They only understood power. Power was her final card.

"Since you've been so kind," Scarbrough said, "I have something for you too. Lucias, please come out now."

"I thought you said no tricks."

"I lied. Agent Donald Sage, meet Lucias Hammaker."

The bathroom door squealed as it swung into the room. Hammaker appeared from behind it. "I'm eight-finger Charlie," Hammaker said, extending his imperfect hand.

"I know who you are," said Sage, rebuffing the hand.

"Then you should also know I'm here representing Deric Christy."

"I believe I mentioned your War Crimes," Scarbrough said. "Show him the hard evidence Lucias."

Hammaker produced a Polaroid photograph. In the picture, a silver nine millimeter pistol lay on a velour cloth.

Sage looked as if he had swallowed a pint of dry gin on an empty stomach; his poker face was long gone. "What's this?" Sage asked halfheartedly.

"Why I believe it's your service weapon," Hammaker said. "It was found at the scene of what's being referred to as the Saturday Night Family Massacre."

"Seems we've come full circle, Agent Sage," Scarbrough said.

"There's a witness to go with the photograph," said Hammaker.

Sage stood, shrinking with the minutes, until he no longer appeared to be the imposing Drug Warrior Scarbrough had once seen, but only a tiny remnant of a man, struggling for his very existence.

Hammaker spoke harshly. "The deal is this. Full pardon for Deric, his nephew is left alone by your people. This pseudo evidence you cooked up against Ruth and her friend also disappears. Then, and only then, you get your gun back."

Sage straightened, and the tone of his voice echoed Hammaker's hardness. "I won't go for that. The so-called Saturday Night Family Massacre didn't go down the way you're playing it. All the shooting was done by the bad guys. We played it straight. Cleared everything through the Agency. We cooperated with the locals.

Got statements and evidence. I wasn't involved in the killing of innocents."

"Oh, you're involved," Scarbrough said. "Up to your ears. Even if you didn't pull the trigger, you and your damn War."

"And even if what you say were true," said Hammaker, "it's not the way the press will see it. It'll take years before rumor-laden versions of an official cover-up will dissipate."

"All right," Sage said. "Okay. So we get a little egg on our face. But not so much you get everything you want. You can have the boy, and I already agreed to deep-six the evidence against the professor and the counselor. But I've been after the Drexlers for five years, and I'm not quitting now. I want Christy for one more shot. Otherwise, we all air our dirty laundry."

Scarbrough and Hammaker exchanged glances.

"The decision will have to be Deric's," Hammaker said. "You'll have to give me access to him. And as his lawyer, I won't recommend it."

"Tell him it's the last run," Sage said with the desperate air of a salesman facing a slammed door. "Tell him we're going for broke. It's a full pardon, I guarantee it. I'll get it in writing this time. I've waited too long and worked too hard. I'm just not going away without finishing this."

Through the haze of her numbness, Scarbrough strained to lift her head in what was perhaps her last Quixotic gesture, a final spurt of rebellion, though she quickly seemed to forget her purpose. She sagged to her pillow and said nothing more. Even if Sage hadn't threatened the memory of her lost son, even if her daughter were not struggling for normalcy, she had lost her energy and motivation after the guilty verdict the students returned for Deric. She had been so sure it would be different, and she could not grasp the magnitude of her miscalculation. She drifted again, away from the thousand souls she heard crying to be lifted from misery; their faces disappeared into a rising mist. And she knew it was finally over, and she had lost.

But it no longer mattered. She was thinking only of her babies. Both of them.

$$\bullet\!\!-\!\!\bullet\!\!-\!\!\bullet\!\!-\!\!\bullet\!\!\cdot\!\!\bullet\!\!\cdot\!\!\bullet\!\!-\!\!\bullet\!\!-\!\!\bullet\!\!\cdot\!\!\bullet$$

Sage stepped from the hospital room into the hallway. He scanned the corridor for Ramírez. He checked the break room and asked at the nurses' station. A young woman told him his companion seemed upset and had taken the elevator several minutes earlier. Sage tried to blink the blurriness from his eyes, and he shuffled to the elevator, whistling vacantly. He pushed the call button. He shoved his hands in his pockets and stopped whistling.

And it dawned on him with an odd suddenness that Ramírez was gone for good, and he would be seeing to the fulfillment of Operation Soldier Man on his own.

Chapter thirty-nine

At Company B Headquarters, General Tarsavage sat behind a metal desk, tapping his fingers on the blotter. He occasionally looked into Harker's unsteady eyes, as the colonel stood with his rigid body centered before the desk and heels locked. He suppressed the urge to pace, ranting of deception and frame-up. More often, Tarsavage looked away, at file cabinets and empty desks and fluorescent bulbs and scattered field equipment.

"We were set up," said Harker, his hands squeezed in dampness. "No question in my military mind, Trent is behind this."

"A witness reported your tail number, Harrison. How do you fake that?"

"I tell you—"

"I checked with a number of people in Operations. It's a well-known fact that you've made a practice of hovering down over the valley in the vicinity of your house."

"My house. Damn it, General, this should be an internal matter. No one was hurt. No Army property destroyed. My house."

"It's an aviation incident. There's a civilian witness. Command branch got the call. There's no way to sweep it under the rug now.

There'll be phone calls and meetings. We've got to conduct a full incident investigation. There'll be photographs, urine samples, a report, and conclusions."

"The witness didn't see the high-frequency antenna on the tail boom—it wasn't the command-and-control ship."

"Small detail. Easily missed by the untrained eye."

"General. You were there. We lost the load over the trees."

Tarsavage adjusted a pile of papers, tapping the edge against the blotter. "Perhaps," he said. "But because of your stupidity, whatever the truth is, it looks awfully bad for you."

Harker pulled at his shirttail with a desperate fastidiousness. "I'll prove it was Trent." His voice cracked with melancholy. "I'll find the evidence."

"Better do it soon. Otherwise, we may have to resort to damage control."

Harker's throat went dry, and he swallowed hard but without relief. He understood only too well that Tarsavage's idea of damage control was to point a finger at someone else, and that this time he was the logical target. "General, you were there," he intoned.

"In the rear with my view obstructed."

"What?"

"You were flying with that young lieutenant of yours for your copilot. The one that keeps screwing up. What did you say his name was? Ashfield?"

"Oh no. You're not doing that this time."

"I suggest you hold your tongue, before you say something you'll regret." Tarsavage lifted a wafer of cracked paint from the ancient desk and held it to the light, examining it. "When's the last time you had these desks painted?"

"What?"

"Paint, Harrison. Paint. Sometimes you have to scrape off the old and start again." Tarsavage sighed as if his thoughts were far away.

"I put my career on the line for you," Harker said, but he withheld the rest of the words he longed to voice, having already said more than he dared. The past was cluttered with occasions in which he had acquiesced to the very sort of fabrication Tarsavage was suggesting. Only they had selected other scapegoats. Harker knew that his complicity in the past had supercharged his career advancement. But in the present, it prevented him from exposing the general for what he was—if Tarsavage resorted to his brand of damage control, Harker would remain utterly silent. Both men knew it.

"Comes to it, I'll see to it your discharge is neutral," Tarsavage said with conciliatory ease. "Take it on the chin with grace or, I warn you, this will get ugly."

Harker clenched his teeth and narrowed his eyes, boiling and festering. He made a sharp about-face and moved at route step into the night. Ironic, isn't it, he thought as the air swathed his forehead. He's the worst of us all and the only son of a bitch who'll walk away scot-free.

• • — • • • • — • • •

In the locker room of the flight facility, Ashford found Trent sitting alone before an open locker. The warrant officer's forearms rested on his knees, and his trunk was slanted down between his legs, as if he were resting in supplication. He wore the trousers of his two-piece flight suit, and a towel hung around his naked shoulders. Images from the past two weeks spun wildly in Ashford's mind. He could see himself throwing up barriers in the way of his own progress, like some alarmed cartoon character nailing boards across a window, only to discover his adversary standing unrestrained in the room behind him. It was time to confront that antagonist with a new approach. A direct approach.

"What happened at Ba Long?" Ashford said, his face cemented with savage determination. He heard his voice quiver, and he pushed from his diaphragm to maintain solidity.

Trent's damnable eyes grew wide, although he recovered quickly. He turned to the window, his refection appearing cadaverous. "People died," he said.

"Who was responsible?"

"We all are."

Ashford flung his kneeboard to the floor. "God, you must think I'm an idiot," he said, the words rushing from his mouth. "Since I got here, you've done nothing but fuck with me."

Trent's eyebrows drooped, and he sagged into a chair. Shadows collected under his eyes and in the hollows of his cheeks. "Twenty years ago, I might have recognized the potential in your flying and encouraged you."

"Why not now?"

"It's not in me anymore."

Ashford collected himself. "All right, let's not talk about Ba Long. Let's talk about the here and now. What happened in the Northern Training Area?"

Trent's face beamed rays of animosity. "Harker shit a big brick on his house."

Ashford squared up close to Trent's face. "Get up," he said, hovering there.

"Huh?"

"I said get up." Ashford thrust a clear plastic cup toward Trent, the kind used for urine samples. "Take this into the latrine and piss in it."

"What for?"

"I have to test everyone who was involved in the incident this afternoon. I already got samples from the colonel and the general and Reggie. Now I need to get yours."

"But I wasn't there."

"I'm not convinced of that." Ashford set his mouth defiantly.

Trent looked into Ashford's face, as if trying to peer behind his eyes to see how much the lieutenant knew, or how much he was guessing. Reluctantly, Trent walked into the latrine. Ashford dragged a wooden table into the room and put on it an unmarked, sealed plastic cup, already half filled with urine. Trent stood over the urinal, and Ashford heard the gushing flow gathering in the cup. Trent zipped his pants. He handed Ashford his filled cup.

Ashford compared the volume of liquid in the two filled cups he held in his hands. He took Trent's to the urinal. He dumped half, until the liquid was even with the sealed cup. Then he sealed Trent's cup so it appeared almost identical.

"What the hell are you doing?" Trent said.

Ashford sat at the table and fingered a cup. "This one's Colonel Harker's sample. Or is it this one?" Ashford shuffled the bottles in a circle. "Round and round and round we go, and where we stop, nobody knows." Ashford stilled his hands. "Have a preference?"

"His is the darker brew," Trent said, pointing.

"You certain?"

Between his thumb and forefinger, Ashford held a white label bearing Trent's name; he fastened the label to the cup containing the darker urine. His lips formed a forced, sinister smile.

"Done with your parlor tricks?" Trent said.

"I'm finished. And if I'm right, so are you."

Trent cocked an eyebrow. "What do you want?"

"The truth."

Trent turned to the tiled wall, leaning there. He appeared as if he were desperate to bury his face and mind in a paperback, to drift far away from the weight of his own present and past. "In Vietnam we called it fragging," he said. "Mine was the gentler, peacetime version."

"I don't care what you call it," Ashford said tersely. "You sent a man with drugs in his system up in a helicopter, didn't you?"

"How do you know that?"

"I'm still guessing, but I think the urinalysis will bear me out. I'm guessing from your friend the waitress who served Harker his breakfast this morning at Chicken Licken with a wink and a smile. And from the fact that it was Shoopie, with his own axe to grind, who fixed the colonel's dish. A sprinkling of marijuana resin in the hash browns, I'd guess."

"Wouldn't be a bad guess," said Trent, slyness surfacing amidst the gloom.

"Trashing Harker's house and blaming it on him just wasn't enough," Ashford said. "It was just round one, right? Probably not enough to end his career. But everyone gets tested for drug use after an aviation incident, even a minor one. So wouldn't it be just perfect, just the icing on the cake, for the colonel to turn up positive?"

"Not perfect, just the best I could do."

"How long do you have until retirement?"

"I can put in, in six months."

"Do it, Chief," Ashford said, lurching to his feet.

Trent tensed, but with a force of will, he turned to walk away.

"Hey," Ashford said. "This is finished. Hear me? It's over."

Ashford popped the lid from one of the plastic cups and poured the tainted liquid into the urinal.

"I hear you," said Trent.

"I misjudged you, you know. When I came here, I was ready to worship the ground you walked on."

"Your first mistake." Trent walked into the locker room appearing bleak and beaten, not from anything Ashford had said or done but because of that which lingered, from long, long ago.

———————

Thirty minutes later, Ashford sat over coffee in the break room. He breathed in the steam and tried to make sense of the past week. It all came back in a blur, the near miss enroute to AP Hill; the boys from Midland High; Brandon Christy and his apparent disappearance; and the enigma that was Trent. Although his thoughts seemed a clutter, in them Ashford discerned some blurry thread to which he had clung but which he couldn't name or subdue.

The hallway door clanged open, and Harker appeared sagging in the doorway. His eyes were bloodshot and hooded with dark circles. "Let's go, Lieutenant," he said, gesturing at Ashford.

"What?" Ashford said.

"I preflighted the helicopter. Get your flight gear."

"Where to?" Ashford squinted.

Harker paced viciously; his nostrils flared with each heavy breath. "Northern Training Area. I've got two pairs of night vision goggles. We're going to find the culvert we dropped in the trees. The light reflecting from the white cement should show up nicely in the goggles."

Trent entered from the locker room. The two older men regarded each other with quick, apprehensive eyes; an image flashed in Ashford's mind of two desperados circling each other with knives extended.

Harker was first to speak. "I know you did this to me." A slight hysterical quality was evident in his voice, and his eyes seemed disconnected from their targets. "I'm going to prove it."

Trent stared vacantly and assuredly. The curve of his lip seemed no curve at all; it lay flat and meaningless.

"It's about Vietnam, isn't it?" said Harker. "Olofson stirred this up, eh?"

"Not my problem your conscience isn't clear. That is, if you have one. You're right though. It is about Vietnam. It's about Vietnam, and Stray Wolf, and Wellspring, and Ba Long. They all go together, don't they?"

"I don't know what you're—"

"And it all begins and ends with Ba Long."

Harker leaned on a vending machine. "It wasn't me," he said hoarsely.

"Denial's rough on the soul."

"You fool, who was the most likely member of our unit to get lost over the jungle?"

Trent's lips moved laboriously, seeming to follow his thoughts. "The Savage," he said. "Never could read a map."

"And what do you think happened at Ba Long? What did you tell me after you reconned the scene?"

"Someone thought he was in a free-fire zone... Someone who couldn't read a map."

Harker nodded forcefully. "Now you see, don't you?"

"The Savage," Trent said with a gust of understanding.

Harker's visage glowed with animosity unmatched even by Trent's abundant quotient. "You've had me wrong all along, Nick. Now want to help clean up the mess you made?"

"What about the VNAFs?"

"VNAFs?"

"The one shot down at Wellspring, the other we left behind at Stray Wolf. You promised to bring them home."

Harker lifted his eyes in resignation. "Maybe one of them flew into Ba Long at the wrong time. What if he arrived just as a desperately lost commander opened fire in an area that he thought was a free-fire zone? What if his wingman tried to blackmail the commander afterwards? Don't you see now?"

Trent recalled that Le Song had told him that his wingman had arranged passage to America for the two Vietnamese pilots. But it was Harker, not Tarsavage, with whom he had been dealing. "What was the tactical report on Wellspring?" Trent said, the bitterness flowing anew.

"You don't understand—"

"What was the report?" Trent shouted.

"It was hot. Goddammit, it was hot. I told you to let the VNAFs go in first."

"You sent them in to die."

"I followed orders." Harker's eyes darted, but he spoke as if he had a complete defense; there was no shame to choke or thicken his words.

"You and the Savage planned to eliminate the VNAFs so there would be no witnesses to the Massacre at Ba Long."

Trent circled to Harker's rear. "It wasn't you at Ba Long. I see that now. It was worse than you. You had no stake in it. You could have reported him. Seen to justice for those people. But you saw a chance to profit, didn't you? Tidy up after the Savage and maybe have a promotion for your trouble."

Ashford remembered how Harker had shifted the blame to him for Tarsavage's illegal overflight of the Wildlife Preserve at AP Hill. The colonel's actions seemed a progression of an old pattern. Harker bent away from Trent, as if in repose from the onslaught. But Trent didn't falter.

"Then you ordered the medics to leave Le Song behind at Stray Wolf," he said.

"Le Song?" Harker said.

"The second VNAF, for Christ's sake. You killed him. You ought to know his name."

"It was twenty years ago. We all made mistakes over there. Let it go."

"I did," Trent said, canting his head in the direction of the Northern Training Area. "Up there today."

Harker wagged his finger in Trent's face. "That's why I'm going up there. Believe me, I'll find something, and when I do . . ." Harker's tone became more defensive than outraged. "I need a copilot."

"You won't find one here," said Ashford.

"Why you little runt," said Harker, billowing with rage. "I'll send you up the river."

"No disrespect intended, Sir. I checked the weather with flight service. Ceiling's below six hundred feet and visibility's under half a mile. I learned my lesson—I'm not letting any of my people up in that."

"You're as foolish as your has-been mentor," Harker said, indicating Trent. "You're already on the hook for overflying the Wildlife Preserve at AP Hill. And according to General Tarsavage, you were at the controls with me this afternoon when we lost the culvert. Yes, don't look so surprised. You think he'd allow himself to be implicated this time any more than the last time or the time before?" Harker's hand trembled as he extended a pair of night-vision goggles to Ashford. "Care to clear your name?"

"I'll go with you as soon as the weather clears," Ashford said.

Harker waved him off with his free hand and spun on his heel. "Have it your way, Lieutenant. I'll do this myself."

"I'll go," Trent said evenly, earnestly, but his eyes were unbalanced.

"What?" said Harker.

"You heard me. I'll even show you where it is. Would you like that? Come on, Harry. We haven't flown together in twenty years. Be like old times. You know, one blew east, one blew west."

Harker stared at Trent. Then his agitated eyes darted feverishly, and he wagged his finger again in rejection of Trent's offer. He disappeared down the hallway and into the night with his flight gear and his goggles and his justifications. He walked onto the flight deck alone, with the air of a man who was utterly lost but whose dignity was too great to allow him to ask the way.

Ashford climbed the stairs to Operations. He found Jesse Morrow behind the counter, looking curiously outside at an enervated Huey lifting from its parking pad. "Who the hell's that?" Morrow said.

Ashford said it was Colonel Harker and told her of the confrontation with Trent. Morrow said that the tower would surely refuse clearance given the poor weather. Ashford said he didn't think that would matter, and Morrow appeared to measure the tension in his voice. They watched the red-and-green navigation lights float into the mist like candles on a rising funeral pyre, until they dissolved into jagged streaks and faded into the blackness.

The silence grew between them. Morrow, who ordinarily seemed a well of inspiration, appeared sullen and gloomy, and Ashford tried to cheer her in what he considered a role reversal. He talked about Fort Rucker and his instructor pilots there and the missions he had flown. He spoke about everything he could conceive, short of what he really was considering. Her gentle eyes and intriguing mouth. The soft curve of her body.

A shrill whoop wrecked the stillness of the air. Their eyes interlocked and froze, and they shared a fearful gaze. The terrifying sound emanated from the radio, the warning cry of a helicopter's emergency beacon.

Chapter forty

On Saturday morning, Brandon Christy pulled the Toyota pickup curbside three blocks from Hill Manor. Zackaeus reclined on the bench seat beside him. With the manner of a coach rendering a pre-game pep talk, Zackaeus dictated instructions and handed Bran a clear bag stuffed with Rocket Pack.

Bran was to go inside Hill Manor, turn the contraband over to Cruise, and return to his pickup as quickly as possible. After he was safe, the policemen would descend and make their arrests. Zackaeus said it meant a lot to have Rocket Pack in Cruise's possession when he was arrested; he said it was the difference between a case constructed of fragmented testimony of fifty witnesses and a slam-dunk, dead-bang winner. Bran listened to most of Zackaeus's depictions, but he cared little about the cop's case against Cruise. He wasn't sure if he cared about anything any longer.

When he finally closed his mouth, Zackaeus winked and departed the pickup, sliding into the first of four beat-up sedans spaced unevenly along the street. Bran touched the survival radio under his seat and considered taking it, but he knew Cruise wouldn't understand it functioned only as a talisman. He tucked the Rocket Pack into his knapsack. A gloominess hung in the air and filled his lungs, and he palpably felt danger.

Bran drove into the Hill Manor complex, grateful that none of the unmarked cars followed closely enough to be seen. He parked outside building number five and knocked on the door he had previously entered; a different man answered and ushered Bran inside.

In a moment, Cruise appeared through a hole in the wall. "Where's my Zipper?"

"Waiting with the rest of your stuff. The cooking took more time than I thought, and I only half finished. I brought what I got done, because you told me to be back. I have to finish the rest tonight."

Cruise's eyes seemed to redden and glow. He stepped back through the hole in the wall, ushering Bran to follow him into the adjoining apartment.

Just as on Bran's previous visit, a junkie lay in his path on the kitchen floor. The poor wretch wore a sweatshirt with a hood pulled tightly over his head; a white arm extended at a right angle, wrist rigid and contorted, fingers splayed and curled like a claw. As he stepped over, Bran paused, remembering that the man he had seen before was black. And the beat-up sneakers on this man's feet seemed familiar.

"The street is a teacher," Cruise hissed, stepping from the shadows. "It teaches tears."

"Rayful," Bran whispered. He focused his lacquered eyes on the junkie, resisting the urge to stoop to verify what he already knew. The prostrate form was the lifeless body of the Scrounger.

"Man was a fool," said Cruise. "Didn't listen to his teacher. Tried to play me for a fool. Can't let anyone do that to you. Oh, you're gonna be tried, you will be tried."

Bran choked out some words. "I didn't—"

"Didn't what, little man? You told me you was a cooker. You a cooker?"

"No."

"No." Cruise snatched the knapsack from under Bran's arm. "Ain't no cooker and these ain't my drugs. How long you think you could rip me off?"

"I didn't—"

"Where's my Zipper?"

Bran couldn't speak.

"Now I want to be a right individual," said Cruise. "Think I'm into this killer-diller shit? No. Number one thing I do is sell drugs. It's quick, it's fast, and it's fun. But it's business too. And I got to lay down the law. Got to take control. See the game's got way outta shape, but that's the way things are. Got to hold my head up in the hood. Can't be used."

"Can I go now?" Bran said feebly.

Cruise shook his head in disgust. "No you cannot go. I'm trying to 'xplain why I have to break your tail. Look at you, little man. You got no attitude. Shit. This ain't no use. Come on, kid, it's time." Cruise pointed to the Scrounger's corpse. "This is relief," he said. "Peace man."

Brandon staggered. He had no signal to summon a rescue.

Cruise turned his head over his shoulder. "Jorge, git in here now."

As Munzo appeared in the doorway, Bran broke for the hallway. He rounded a corner into the rear of the apartment. He reached a sliding screen door tucked into a breezeway alcove. He flung himself headlong into the screen, like a wild colt flailing against a broken fence.

The screen shredded from its mooring, covering him. Holding him. He fought it, swatting, stomping, and swiping.

Suddenly, he was in the yard, free, sprinting for the pickup. He heard a popping sound behind him and a hissing noise by his ear. His head swam; he felt as if he were in a dream. A searing, stabbing pain in Bran's shoulder gave him a hard reminder of reality. The sting coursed down his arm and filled his fingers, but he told himself he couldn't afford to acknowledge that he'd been shot.

Bran looked over his throbbing shoulder. He saw no one. He turned forward. Four sedans screeched to a stop on the north side of the building. Uniformed police officers poured from the vehicles, running and kicking at doors.

Bran cast a final glance at the rectangular structure of Hill Manor number five. A gold suit flashed by a window at the far end of the building, fifty yards from the police assault. Cruise had travelled the entire length of the building through the interconnected apartments.

Bran staggered across the backyard and around the north corner of the building. He pulled his rubbery legs into the pickup and started driving, not certain where. Just getting away.

He drove two blocks. The adrenalin slowed, and the pain became agony; he knew he would have to get to a hospital quickly. He drove toward the highway in a daze, slowly realizing he was moving away from the hospitals. He braked to make a U-turn.

Another pickup truck spun around the corner behind him. It was neon-blue and jacked high on thick tires. Cruise's gold suit was behind the wheel; the hard features of Munzo were set over the passenger seat.

Bran stepped on the accelerator. He swung the pickup through traffic, shooting up a ramp onto the highway. The stilted truck followed. Bran heard the echo of tiny, precise explosions. The pickup lurched, a tire blown.

Brandon clutched the pitching wheel. Clarity was draining from his thoughts. He remembered Mike Daniels trying to help him, and he pictured Daniels's gift. He reached beneath the seat and retrieved the survival radio. He flicked the power switch and listened to the static report. Then he pressed a red button and began to speak, only hearing his own voice slurring words.

Chapter forty-one

From a hundred feet, Trent and Ashford spotted the command-and-control ship, such as it was, scattered in pieces amongst a wide stretch of boulders poured by some act of God into the ridgeline trough the pilots called Devil's Run. The wreckage appeared like a stationary shadow cast by some phantom chopper, hovering noiselessly somewhere over the ridgeline.

They landed on a flat. Winston, Morrow, Olofson, and Spencer exited the cargo space, while Ashford and Trent shut down the Huey and then joined them. They all walked slowly amidst the fragments, their throats constricted as if the enormity of what they saw would not permit the act of speech. Ashford knelt, touching his fingers to his temples. The place possessed the eerie solemnity of a graveyard projected into a dream. Humbly, Ashford marveled at the finality with which gravity had claimed the Huey.

Ashford reached reverently for an empty black boot, Harker's boot, its upper extending from between two rocks. It was laced tightly and tied in a perfect bow, yet there was nothing inside. The emptiness hovered there as a testament to the terrible force of the crash.

The pilots spoke in hushed voices, as if they were in a temple. Only the birds chattered with ordinariness. For an instant the whole world seemed to focus on Trent and Olofson, standing side-by-side, gazing blankly at the wreckage without jubilation or remorse, with no emotion at all, merely taking in the fact of the crash as if it were a thing demanded by the laws of nature. As if some balance had been restored.

•—•————•—•——•—•—————•—•

When they returned to the flight facility, Olofson slipped away for Harker's home in Hershey; he was determined to search the place for evidence of Tarsavage's involvement in the Massacre at Ba Long. It seemed he would do whatever was necessary to attain some sense of closure.

General Tarsavage gathered the pilots in the hangar and informed them that the entire fleet of Hueys was grounded pending an official determination of the cause of the crash. Trent said the cause was apparent: Harker had lost visual contact with the ground and had failed to transition to his instruments. Tarsavage only grimaced and repeated his admonition, intoning pure threat.

Trent and Ashford retreated to the flight planning room. They stared through room-length glass windows at the impotent fleet of Hueys, earthbound upon the Army's abrupt declaration. The machines suddenly appeared to Ashford as if they were not capable of flight, were never so capable, huge metal wingless shells that they were. They would be idle until the Army issued some enchanted proclamation to permit the rotor systems to work their magic again.

The phone rang. "Lieutenant, it's the tower," the desk sergeant reported.

Ashford took the receiver. The voice of the tower operator was touched with concern. "We're receiving a transmission on guard frequency asking for Life Lion," he said. "Sounds like some kid on a hand-held survival radio. Could be some kind of hoax, but I thought I heard gunfire in the background. Want to get up here?"

Ashford clattered up the metal stairs to the tower, emerging through a hatch in the control-room floor. Trent and Spencer followed. Windows surrounded them on four sides, yielding a panoramic bird's-eye view of the flight facility. Radio dials, microphones, and electronic gadgetry buttressed the windows. A round-faced man wearing a headset sat over a blinking console, and he nodded at Ashford and flicked a switch.

"*Say again, kid,*" the tower operator transmitted. "*What is your location?*"

A boy's voice floated from a tabletop speaker. "*Getting onto 81 North at the Harrisburg interchange,*" the voice said, immediately familiar to Ashford. Ashford had directed the capture of its owner and given him a Coke. Trent seemed to know too.

"*And repeat your situation,*" the tower operator said.

"*Headed east. Two guys following me in a truck. Trying to kill me. I'm bleeding like crazy, got a flat tire, and my truck's thumping like mad.*"

"It's no hoax," Ashford said, trying to contain his excitement. "I know that kid. Call the police."

The tower operator lifted the telephone receiver. Ashford turned to Trent.

"The Hueys are grounded, right?" he said.

"That's right," Trent said.

"But only the Hueys."

"So what?"

"So the Blackhawks can fly."

Trent inclined his head gravely and peered into Ashford's eyes, as if he were contemplating something he had not seen before. "You've been eyeing up the Blackhawks since you got here, haven't you?"

Ashford shrugged.

"Blackhawks don't belong to Company B," Trent said. "You'd be up to your neck in trouble if we took one out. Probably more than if we took a Huey."

"Trouble never seemed to bother you before. And we'll get there a hell of a lot faster at a 160 knots. The Company F trainers just pulled in with the Blackhawk sitting on the VIP pad, and the fuel handlers just finished gassing her up. What do you say?"

Trent smiled grimly and offered the nod of a coconspirator. "You up for this, Reggie?"

Spencer nodded eagerly. "I liked the kid too."

"Guess we skip the paperwork then," said Trent.

"Nick and I'll do a quick preflight," Ashford said. "Get the guns Reggie. We have any ammo?"

"Live ammo's locked up in the vault," Spencer said. "All we've got are blanks."

"Fitting," said Trent, heading for the stairs.

———————————————

Brandon tried to steady the lurching wheel with his trembling hands. The stilted truck was close behind. Two tractor trailers were ahead, riding abreast in both lanes of the highway.

Bran slowed. The truck pushed forward. Munzo's cold eyes leered over a glint on the machine pistol.

Bran threw the wheel hard right. The pickup skidded onto an inclined ramp, a rest stop exit. The stilted truck sailed by, swerving right but missing the exit, coming level back on the roadway.

Munzo cursed and waved the pistol rearward, spitting tiny flames in quick bursts.

Bran slowed in the elongated parking lot. He lost sight of the stilted truck behind a row of parked tractor trailers. His heartbeat throbbed in his arm and his muscles juddered involuntarily; he lowered his head to glimpse the torn flesh. When he lifted his face, the front grill of the stilted truck appeared high in the air, like the bow of an oncoming ship. Cruise had traveled the length of the rest area and wheeled around onto the exit ramp. The truck sped forward heedlessly, head-on.

Bran slammed his foot on the brake pedal. The rear wheels of the pickup spun in gravel, skidding, sliding out of control. The front end careened beneath the corner of a trailer, shattering the windshield, wrenching Bran's body, and crunching the steering wheel tight against Bran's chest. A waterfall of glass hit his face.

The pickup bounced, and the front end pulled free. The smashed vehicle shivered to a stop in the open parking lot.

Bran tried to move but was trapped by the bent wheel. He smelled the thick scent of gasoline. He peered out the window and saw the gas pooling at the rear of the pickup.

Cruise dropped from the stilted truck purposefully, approaching the wrecked pickup as if in slow motion. "The street is your teacher," he said, poking his head into the window and examining Bran's predicament. "And I am the street."

Cruise snatched a match from his shirt pocket. He struck it with a violent flourish, holding it like a torch to allow Bran full view of the death flame. Cruise stepped to the rear of the wrecked pickup. In mirror fragments Bran saw him drop the lit match into the pooled gasoline.

Cruise turned his back to Brandon's screams.

Chapter forty-two

The engines of the Blackhawk soared to life, wailing resonantly like the scream of some prehistoric beast warning of raw menace awaiting violent realization. Like the engines, Ashford was lit afire and his nerves sang. He struggled to collect his thoughts, but they raced randomly.

Ashford could see that Trent felt it too. There was energy and intensity in his eyes, overpowering the former glowering to which Ashford had become so accustomed. But in Trent the vitality was contained; he seemed to will it to course steadily through his body, measured and ready to be parsed out as circumstances required. His skill, once insolent, seemed a vast resource ready to be harnessed in fulfillment of their shared purpose.

Trent dialed the tower frequency into the UHF radio. "*Tower Guard Five-Five-Three,*" he said. "*Alpha Three West. Request present position takeoff to the west, emergency handling.*"

"*This is General Tarsavage,*" a corrosive voice answered regally. "*Clearance denied. Shut down the helicopter and proceed directly to the flight planning room now.*"

Trent gazed at Ashford, his look not fully sympathetic but at least a subtle reversal of his former sour glances and grimaces. Ashford expected to hear Trent say 'You're the AMC,' but if he thought it, Trent gave no voice to the sentiment. It was there between them, nonetheless; Ashford was the ranking officer in the aircraft—he *was* the air mission commander. He was responsible for the success or failure of the mission, the lives of the crew, and the security of the multi-million dollar machine.

"*Sir, we've got an emergency mission,*" Ashford transmitted.

"*Authorization denied,*" came the unhesitating reply. "*Are you deaf, Lieutenant?*"

Ashford faltered. He longed to act on a decision already made, but a hard truth he was learning about command is that a decision is never irreversible; the leader must always weigh each and every changed circumstance against the course he has chosen. Ashford recalled Crawford's guidance was to seek the advice of the warrants but that the final decision rests with the air mission commander.

"Nick..." Ashford said, struggling to formulate the question.

Trent stared into the windscreen as if it were a lens focused into the past; his expression was soulful, and his voice seemed for once a true reflection of his heart.

"I was in your situation once," he said. "Similar at least. I had to choose between orders and what I thought was right."

"What did you do?"

All at once the abundant energy seemed to drain from Trent as if suddenly leached from his body and caught in the gushing rotor wash. He appeared worn and miserable. "I followed orders."

Ashford studied the wrinkles on Trent's face. The marks of regret were layered like the rings on an ancient tree stump, each succeeding stratum seeming deeper and more profound than the previous. Ashford understood then that those lines were carved by the decision he so regretted.

Never before had Trent shared such a personal thing with Ashford. There was no bitterness left in those eyes, only an even-tempered hopefulness emerging from a long, long sleep.

"Make me a promise," Ashford said.

"What?"

"If the helicopter or crew is in danger, we'll pull out."

"It'll be your call," Trent said, evenly and without hesitation.

Ashford nodded, and the uncertainty that had claimed him for so long dissolved, completely and finally. He clicked the trigger mike. *"Aircraft in the vicinity of Muir Army Airfield,"* he said. *"Guard Five-Five-Three is a UH-60 making emergency present position takeoff from the hardstand, departing west."*

Ashford's words flowed over the radio waves without passion; all his energy was devoted to concentration. The throbbing power of the Blackhawk's dual engines seemed almost supernatural; the single-engine Huey was no match. With a touch of the controls the awesome thrust of the rotor dominating the wind, compelling the air to yield, impelling the tons of streamline metal straight up like a slow-burning rocket. When Ashford lowered the nose, the Blackhawk sailed greedily into flight, swooping first toward the ground and then, with another tug on the collective, swelling and rising.

Tarsavage's livid epithets clattered over the radio. *"Goddammit, Ashford, get back here now. You aren't on the ground in thirty seconds, I guaran-damn-tee your career is finished. You hear me?"*

Ashford held the cyclic true to its course. The commands of the general deserved no response; they contained no authority, personal or moral. They held only the faint dominion of rank, overpowered by what he knew was right.

"Trent, will you just sit there and let the boy finish his career before it's started?" Tarsavage whined.

"I'm just a warrant officer with an empty stupid pin head," Trent said, quoting Tarsavage's words of two decades before, long burned into the recesses of his consciousness. *"Only thing I do know is what happened at Ba Long. And we're gonna prove it."*

"You're both finished," came the hushed reply.

The earth glided beneath them as Ashford accelerated to 160 knots. At first trees and meadows and buildings merged into a steady blur; then with altitude, clarity overtook them. At its velocity limits, the Blackhawk jolted and knocked, giving the sensation of flattened tires on railroad spurs.

Ashford knew they were moving so fast that the helicopter was on the verge of a dangerous condition that could result in an uncontrolled roll. Trent seemed not to notice or care. The sweat collecting in Ashford's eyes sharpened his resolve.

"Don't fly the highway contour," said Trent. "You'll waste time. Just point the nose at Harrisburg. I have a feeling we'll find them."

"Instinct?" Ashford said, expecting and receiving no response. He aimed the cyclic at high-rise buildings set over the river.

"Everything okay in the back, Reg'?" Trent asked.

"Locked and loaded, Chief," came the reply, another echo from long ago.

"They'll know we don't have any bullets," Ashford said.

"Shit, LT," Spencer replied. "Where these guys come from, the guns are always loaded."

A plume of black smoke rose into sight in the vicinity of the highway, a mile to their forefront.

"Won't have to look too hard for the kid," Trent pointed. "Bring her down on the deck."

Ashford lowered the collective. Exhilaration coursed through him, the Blackhawk diving, the earth rushing to meet him, and only his instincts and skill to pull the machine from its plunge.

Ashford yearned to fly the approach. But he was the air mission commander and he had to decide what was best for the crew and mission. And this was no training mission; there was no margin for error. The gravity of the circumstances called for the skill of the superior pilot.

"You have it," Ashford said.

Trent said he had the controls, and he seized them without question or reservation. He flew with a precision too fluid to be described as mechanical; man and machine seemed merged. Jet fuel seemed to run through Trent's veins, his heart pumping it through his taut muscles and back into the fuel lines; hydraulic fluid seemed to filter through the synapses of his brain, from where it was redirected and swept back into the flight controls.

The Blackhawk sliced sideways, banking and diving. The ground rushed close, fences and branches and electric lines dangling and dancing around them in kaleidoscopic fashion. They skimmed over a plowed field north of the billowing smoke; only a shallow knoll remained between the helicopter and the objective.

Trent set up the approach masterfully to gain maximum surprise and to minimize the Blackhawk's exposure. With his eyes wide, Ashford leaned to the edge of his seat. They shot over the crest of the hill, with the nose low, the rotors screaming, and the engine wailing. Ashford felt the breath of danger.

Trent said, "Open up, Reg'."

Layered atop the shrill engine noise, the machine gun jack hammered, slashing into Ashford's nerves. A flat blacktop patch blossomed in the windscreen, the scene a chaos of contradictions. A man lay crumpled on the ground, his hands thrown over his head as if defending himself from a volley of imaginary bullets. One askew hand held a machine pistol, but the man didn't aim it; instead, he staggered to his feet and ran.

Another man, dressed in gold silk, sprinted for a truck on stilted wheels. Another truck, a burning pickup, belched the black clouds. Flickering edges of fire chased the smoke from the underside of the vehicle.

In a seamless maneuver, Trent accelerated and then decelerated, weaving the chopper sideways through a gauntlet of light posts, all the while banking to hold the retreating danger in his line of sight. Trent halted the Blackhawk in a powerful hover directly over the burning wreck. He pulled at the collective, turning the rotor wash into a torrent.

Smoke billowed around the helicopter, clouding the windscreen, and the choking smell of burning rubber filled the cockpit. Ashford glimpsed the wreckage through the chin bubble. The pickup smoldered, but the flames had been smothered, quenched by the intensity of the downwash.

"Learned that trick in the South Vietnamese school of warfare," Trent said.

He maneuvered sideways and down, like sculling a canoe, and the Blackhawk lit beside the wreckage. Ashford watched the stilted truck spin sideways and come to rest at fifty yards. It lingered there, like a maddened bull readying for a charge.

Taking advantage of the lull, Spencer jumped to the ground. He jogged around the wrecked pickup, trying to touch the door handle but retracting his hand quickly against the heat. He came back to the cockpit.

"He's alive but unconscious," Spencer shouted above the engine noise. "He's jammed in under the wheel. No way to get him out."

"Here they come," Trent said.

The stilted truck turned to face the Blackhawk squarely. Smoke poured from the tailpipe.

"Rig the pickup with the sling, Reggie," Trent said. "Do it quick. We'll have to haul it out."

As the loyal master sergeant rushed to gather his gear, Trent plucked his single silver bullet from his breast pocket. With his other hand, he reached into the holster in his flight vest to retrieve his revolver. "I was saving this bullet for camp," he said dryly, sliding the bullet into the chamber of the pistol. "You've got the controls."

"No," said Ashford. "You're not going anywhere. Reggie, strap in now. We're pulling pitch." Ashford grasped the collective, but Trent held it firmly in place.

"Sorry, LT," he said. "Not this time." Trent dropped to the ground.

Ashford held the controls, feeling helpless. He watched Trent gather the M-60 machine gun in his arms. In that instant, Ashford realized that he could not command him. He could never command him.

"Reggie, stop him!"

Spencer grabbed his monkey harness. He came up behind Trent. He threaded the harness through the shoulder straps of Trent's flight vest, tethering Trent to the Blackhawk. He clipped a D-ring on the strap to make a secure loop.

"What are you doing?" Trent shouted over his shoulder, the rotor wash whipping his hair, billowing his flight suit.

"Stay here," Spencer pleaded.

"Rig the pickup, Reggie. Now!"

Trent waived the giant machine gun, spitting fiery placebos from its muzzle. Spencer retrieved the sling and rushed to the pickup.

The stilted truck lurched forward. Trent swept the machine gun menacingly toward the windshield, but the truck rushed forward, as if its driver were playing a game of chicken. The gold-suited passenger leaned from the open window, pointing a machine pistol. Trent dropped the M-60. He aimed his revolver at the driver's head.

"No! Get back, get back!" Spencer ran at Trent's back, his hands flung forward.

"Go! Go!" Trent yelled, waving at Ashford.

As Trent aimed, a spray of bullets clattered across the Blackhawk's windscreen. Ashford ducked. He could see nothing, not Trent, not Spencer, not the truck. He only saw his instruments lurching and laughing at him. Suddenly Spencer's voice was on the intercom.

"Go, LT," he said. "Go."

Another volley of bullets pierced the glass.

The engine substituted as a surrogate for Ashford's heartbeat; his own heart had surely stopped. He remembered the death spiral enroute to AP Hill, when he lost visual references in the clouds. He recalled the solution that Trent showed him, to focus on the flight instruments.

Ashford fixed his eyes on the artificial horizon and pulled an armload of collective. He felt the straps tethered to Bran Christy's pickup truck pull taunt and knew the Blackhawk was at a high hover. Ponderously he sensed the pickup lift from the ground.

Finally, Ashford felt safe to allow his gaze to drift outside. Below, the stilted truck was smashed into the side of a tractor trailer. The driver's head was draped through the side window, a gap in his forehead marking the pathway of a single, well-aimed bullet. The gold-clad man wandered dazed in the parking lot, his silk suit glinting in the sunlight.

The Blackhawk gained altitude and airspeed. Ashford saw flashing red globes atop speeding police cars swarming in two channels of the highway.

Ashford turned. The copilot seat was horribly empty. He checked the rear. Only Spencer was there, appearing grim and ghastly, clutching desperately at a strap draped over the edge of the deck.

———————•—•

Suspended from Spencer's monkey harness, Trent dangled freely in a wide chasm of open space. He felt the strain of his weight gathered against the vest cradling his armpits. Coursing through the taut harness line, Trent could feel the panic in Spencer's desperate efforts to reel him in, and he felt for his friend, because he knew his own spirit could not be contained for long.

With a degree of wonderment, Trent poked his finger into the hole in his side. The pain struck him, but more intensely he felt the jaded cast clearing from his memories. Details he thought long since had been erased cascaded before his eyes and suddenly became vivid.

His recollections of Vietnam had for so long reached into the past only so far as the prolonged struggle with Harker for control of the helicopter over Stray Wolf; it was there that the best part of him seemed frozen for so many years. Finally he could see Wellspring again, twenty years ago, before he abandoned Le Song, before he abandoned his life. He saw himself sliding the silver bullet into his revolver, he recalled contemplating suicide, and for the first time in two decades, he tasted relief in the fact that he hadn't chosen that escape.

Peering further into the past, Trent envisioned himself clinging to Le Song's gunship, waving his revolver to defend Olofson against terrified infantrymen desperate to lighten the gunship's load. Trent watched his own grip loosening volitionally; he saw himself sweep away the anchors that held him; and he saw himself pull free so others could live.

Then another vision appeared, a Huey landing in the village where he met Spencer, and Trent watched himself thwart a massacre. He saw a young and virtuous warrant officer hauling wounded men from the midst of fierce battles.

He saw all he had forgotten.

Lastly, Trent closed his eyes and envisioned his little table fan from Vietnam. He realized that the fan was his life, knocked out of balance by the force of the War and, in his desperate attempts at repair, whittled away to nothing.

When Trent opened his draining eyes, he looked up at the belly of the Blackhawk, and his lips formed a bittersweet smile. Atop the helicopter the modern rotor blades sliced through the air in a tempestuous blur, like the blades of a giant and wondrous fan, smooth and sleek in its perfect timing, powerful and efficient in the way it directed the torrents. And at the heart of that new and perfect fan, fueling and directing it, was a young pilot so much like Trent in those memories of long ago, strong and full, at a time before the blades of Trent's fan were thrown out of kilter and before the ends were filed away to nothing. How fragile and beautiful the great blades seemed. What a magnificent thing if their synchrony could be preserved.

The Blackhawk leveled at a thousand feet, but Trent drifted up and up like a song. He was glad it was finished and that no more of life's inevitable backslides would follow to dim and tarnish the redemption of the moment. No more of those inescapable moments in life's jumble, those places where great men stumble and fools become great.

He blinked his eyes; he could no longer tell if his mind were clouded by drain of blood or cleared by the cure of absolution. Trent floated complacently in derangement or fulfillment, it mattered little which, and in the next moment some precious fragment of the world died with the knowledge of it Trent held.

Epilogue

In the hallway of the flight facility, the green plywood board loomed over Winston's deflated figure like a great guillotine poised to sever his body. His movements were sluggish and pained as he touched the rearranged white plastic numbers to confront the Board's terrible message: four days since the last Class A accident.

Outside, a misty sea of clouds floated far overhead, a cumulus sky that was, like the world, only perfect in its billions of imperfections. Winston was the last to join the formation; as he strapped into the Huey, four others hovered toward the runway. Winston landed in the trail position of a V-formation, spacing the Huey perfectly. It was the only day in his National Guard career in which he forewent his usual classification as a separate flight.

In flawless alignment, the Hueys ascended and then descended into a field a mile from the west end of the runway. On the shore of a glimmering lake touched gold by the sun, Ashford leaned against a tree, waiting. Pending consideration by a board of review, he wasn't permitted on the grounds of the flight facility, and the warrant officers had arranged for him to covertly join them for what he knew would be his final mission.

Ashford watched the Hueys land. He admired the complex and contradictory movements of the rotor heads and blades. He smelled the kerosene and felt the rushing wind twisting and swirling in the wake of the machines.

When the Hueys were earthbound, Ashford bent at the waist and jogged under the blurred blade-path of the second helicopter, his loose-fitting shirt fluttering like a flag. Jesse Morrow sat on the bench seat, and Ashford joined her there. Their eyes met but neither smiled. Her face seemed troubled but lovely in a way that made it difficult to look upon; she seemed to know and accept his unconfessed thoughts as she did the rays of morning sun.

The Hueys lifted again. The churning air was cooling on Ashford's skin. He still loved the feel of flying, the chasm of emptiness opening between the pilot and the earth, the magnificence of the panoramic view unfolding before him, the art involved in pilotage, and the sheer pleasure he found in it too. But his eyes were not so full of vigor and neither was his heart. He sensed the coldness of the machine's hull and its incessant vibrations, and he remembered the confinement and weight of a helmet. He breathed the helicopter's exhaust; it made his head ache, and he felt machine-like. He sensed all these things, once trivial, now suddenly real and momentous. The way the helicopter shattered the richness and tranquility of nature seemed for the first time tragic.

Through the Gap and five miles to the northeast, they approached a square patch on the side of a flawlessly green rolling courtyard, the velvet surface speckled with white dots. Beds of vibrant-colored flowers added an air of elegance, their beauty magnified by gleaming sunbeams.

Ashford spotted Olofson first, standing rigid on the periphery of the gravesite, in a plain, gray suit. His body exuded determination, which Ashford knew was unfailingly focused toward delivering accountability to Tarsavage for his perpetration of the Massacre at Ba Long. Olofson's discovery of several pages from Vigilance Base Camp's original flight logs, boxed in Harker's attic, had brought a final resolution within reach. The major had booked flights to interview the pilots, crew chiefs, and gunners whose names appeared on the logs. Ashford understood that it was only a matter of time before the truth about Ba Long would finally be told. The only open question was whether there would be more than a handful of people who would still care.

A glint marked Crawford's bald pate, one of a cluster of those ringed around an open grave. The captain held a brave posture, raising his hand to shield his upward-looking eyes from the sun in the manner of a dignified salute. A silver-haired woman clung to his bent arm, her black dress flowing in the breeze. Nick Trent's wife had refused military honors for her husband's funeral. She had insisted that it was Trent's express wish that he be buried the way he had once lived—as a free spirit. The only soldierly feature she would allow was the helicopters, a touch of irony she believed her husband would have appreciated.

Suddenly the world fell away from beneath Ashford.

The Huey broke from the formation into a steep dive. Ashford's trunk lifted from the seat as if his body had been sucked into a weightless void. His eyes rebelled against earthly focus and his thoughts scattered wildly into a tangle of fleeting and indecipherable impressions, scraps of conversation, and a torrential stream of formless images. A group of aspiring young West Point cadets on their first helicopter ride. The not-so-different boys from Midland High, caught in another set of life circumstances. Shoopie, unmercifully destroyed for a single error in judgment, while a bloody massacre went unredressed for twenty years. Brandon Christy, a badly injured boy lying beside his mother in a hospital burn unit. Nick Trent, a bitter warrant, rediscovering his heroism. And among the chaotic images, a pounding of lost and forsaken opportunity surfaced.

The chopper spiraled toward the treetops until it disappeared from the view of those on the ground; once hidden, the rotor blades caught the air, and the Huey seemed to float gently like a balloon. Ashford gazed high above at the remaining four Hueys riding the blue sky over the cemetery, the unfilled space between them serving a confession of the incompleteness of the unit and the grievousness of its loss. Peering up at the missing-man formation, Ashford felt through his own grief and disappointment a sudden and wild possessiveness for control of the Huey, an urge to fill space, to complete the unit.

Then he let go, completely and finally.

Morrow touched one hand to her open mouth and let her other hand fall along the muscles of Ashford's back; then she put her arm around him and kissed him on the cheek. Her lips were soft and wet. Her glistening eyes seemed to be made from light. Her touch contained invitation and promise and release—relief from her fears, from a once-inviolable bond to a husband lost to her long ago.

Ashford's heartbeat and breath flowed freely, undaunted by the baggage of doubts he once carried. Yet the price was profound, for it had cost him a dream.

But the quality of the lost vision seemed in a way childish and insignificant compared to the truth Ashford had found in its pursuit, a truth that persisted outside the stifling confines of the war machines he had yearned so fervently to master. He understood that such a discovery could only be made in the effort of reaching for an ideal and touching its zenith, even if the consequence was to see it dashed to pieces before his eyes.

It was a truth he had seen in Olofson and Spencer. In the end, he finally found it in Trent.

It was an axiom that couldn't be written on paper or dramatized in gestures. The best description Ashford knew came from the words that Nick Trent had uttered to Paul Olofson two decades ago in the mystical jungles of Vietnam. Not the exact words but the substance that underlay them and the rhythm and emphasis with which those who knew them spoke.

Trent had said it's all about judgment. Knowing when to go up, when to shoot, when to stand your ground. And when not to. How to live and how to die.

A monkey could do the rest.

●—●·————·—●··●●●·●·————●—●·

Parked curbside along Constitution Avenue, Don Sage sat alone at the wheel of his dust-covered gray sedan. Sweeping his eyes out over the Mall, his vision embraced a lone figure embedded in the reddening horizon above the Vietnam Memorial, standing straight and stiff, like a silent military bugler at full attention. Sage couldn't see the sloping walls of mirror-polished black granite, but he knew that Deric Christy stood on ground that to him was both familiar and hallowed.

The ground was familiar because it was the place where he had been shackled in handcuffs twenty years ago, marking his descent into the horrors of a new War to rival the terrors of the old one. The place was hallowed because etched in the embedded stone were the names of friends with whom he was now communing, seeking from them some affirmation for the arbitrary fact of his own survival.

When Christy climbed down from the green hill, they drove together into the heart of the nation's capital, not the nucleus of glitz and power but the heaving, sighing organ full of pain and sadness, engine of a land gone awry. Sage pulled to the curb at a meter on Route One, a block south of the mouth of Hamilton Place.

Wordlessly, Christy stepped onto the sidewalk and glided past the car as if he stood upon an invisible conveyor belt, moving him steadily and unfailingly forward to meet his destiny. His head turned slightly to Sage, but it was his blind eye that appeared, and his face gave no sign of recognition or acknowledgment.

Sage puffed fitfully on a cigarette and then flicked it out the window. He chuckled at the contradiction of his own addiction to nicotine. Just another man's drug, he thought. Perhaps we're all nothing more than absurd bundles of addictions, he with his cigarettes and vodka tranquilizers, as well as the crown jewel of his compulsions, the Drexlers, the obsession he transformed into a vocation, the addiction that propelled him to coerce a man he had come to admire back into the dark reaches of Hamilton Place.

Deric had been away too long, Sage thought, and the story they invented to explain his absence was flimsy, far from convincing, and only the best they could do. Sage lit another cigarette and exhaled a cloud of smoke and tried to console himself. Any way it ended, he would be a winner, or if not a winner, at least a survivor. If the Drexlers believed the cover story, Soldier Man would be back in business. If they disbelieved, there would no longer be a living witness to Sage's presence at the site of the Saturday Night Family Massacre.

But Sage could find no peace. He felt as if he was clawing at a disintegrating handhold on a cliff-face of sand. Like so many veterans felt of the Vietnam War, he was coming to despise the way the Drug War was being conducted and the way he himself was forced to act. And after his encounter with the professor, he sensed the magnitude of the dimensions of his actions in a way he had never felt before. Though Scarborough's actions were those of a zealot, her words carried some mark of truth; for in the same way the War in Vietnam could not be won for political and moral reasons, so too perhaps the War on Drugs would someday be lost. But the issues were far too complicated. And just as the phrase "immoral war" could have no meaning to a soldier in a rice paddy halfway across the world, it could bear no influence upon Sage in the trenches of the Drug War—to allow this would be paralyzing and deadly. As in Vietnam, the unflinching commitment to amorphous ideals belonged to the government, a commitment it once again seemed wholly incapable of reevaluating. Sage was merely a standard bearer marching in a crusade begun decades before, one that was no closer to cessation than the day it began. His resolve was and had to be limited to gaining territory one day at a time, even if it was to be lost the next day; to amassing a body count of arrests and convictions; and to his own personal survival of each skirmish on the myriad battlefields of the War on Drugs.

Sage straightened, knocking cold coffee onto the velour bench seat. His eyes steadied upon Deric standing frozen at the dark mouth of Hamilton Place, the blackness overhanging the dangerous street and looming as if poised to swallow him. Deric appeared to be contemplating something, perhaps in the narrow channel before him, or maybe something unseen but only felt.

Stiffly, Deric Christy extended both arms, as if coming to grips with an invisible presence. Momentarily his hands spread wide as if parting a curtain, and he took an odd stride—like a step through. Then he lifted his head high into a prideful soldier's farewell, a gesture that didn't seem intended for Sage but rather for phantoms he seemed to have finally let pass. In the next instant his shoulders went slack, and he evaporated into the gloom.

The War never ends.

Contents

Part II
Soldier man

Part III
Summer camp

Part IV
The mission

Part V
Ba Long

Made in the USA
Middletown, DE
05 July 2020

12054462R00307